FOLLANSBEE POND
secrets

— also by —
Barbara Delaney

Finding Griffin,
an Adirondack novel

Trails with Tales:
History Hikes through the Capital Region, Saratoga,
Berkshires, Catskills, and Hudson Valley

Adirondack Trails with Tales:
History Hikes through the Adirondack Park and the
Lake George, Lake Champlain & Mohawk Valley Regions

3-D Guide to the Empire State Plaza
and its Collection of Large Works of Art

Delaney has written a range of articles for magazines, and also does presentations on a variety of historical subjects for museums, libraries and historical societies.

FOLLANSBEE POND
secrets

Barbara Delaney

Follansbee Pond Secret
Copyright © 2018 by Barbara Delaney

This book is a work of fiction. Any references to historical events, real people, or real places are used fictitiously. Other names, characters, places, and events are products of the author's imagination, and any resemblance to actual events or places or persons, living or dead, is entirely coincidental.

All rights reserved. No part of this book may be used or reproduced in any form, electronic or mechanical, including photocopying, recording, or scanning into any information storage and retrieval system, without written permission from the author except in the case of brief quotation embodied in critical articles and reviews.

Painting on cover: 'The Philosophers Camp" by William Stillman 1858
Book design by Jessika Hazelton

Printed in the United States of America
The Troy Book Makers • Troy, New York • thetroybookmakers.com

To order additional copies of this title,
contact your favorite local bookstore
or visit www.shoptbmbooks.com

ISBN: 978-1-61468-455-8

*To Dan, Matt and Mike Canavan —
stalwart sons with deep roots
in the Adirondacks.*

INTRODUCTION:

Barbara Delaney's newest tale invites us to share in the moving story of a young woman living in a rugged mountain community at the edge of the Adirondack wilderness. Myrna Duffney's coming of age takes place in the twilight of America's sad experience with human slavery. This was an era especially perilous for African-Americans anywhere in the country. With the adoption of the 1850 Fugitive Slave Act, there was an open season on escaped slaves who were beyond the slave states. Bounty hunters could legally capture escaped blacks and forcibly return them to the enslavement of the South.

The isolated rural community of North Elba includes mountain people and small farmers living next to former slaves and refugees. Many freedmen and slaves came to the Adirondacks through the Underground Railroad, desperately seeking freedom. Some came with a final goal of escape to Canada. North Elba was a community that cherished independence, freedom and the opposition to slavery. No one hated bondage more than the fiery abolitionist John Brown and his family—living and mentoring in the celebrated settlement established by Garrit Smith in North Elba.

Myrna lives with her parents. She teaches the children in John Brown's school and, like all of her neighbors, labors constantly to survive in the harsh mountain climate. Yet the young woman's most cherished goal is to become a guide like her father. Since her earliest years, her attentive father has taught her the skills of hunting, fishing and recognizing the mysterious ways of the forest.

She is a proficient hunter and angler, and has already earned the admiration of other hunting guides, especially Alvah Woods, her guide friend.

Myrna, much to her mother's misgivings, earns her place as a guide on an important wilderness expedition for a nationally recognized party of Boston-based intellectuals. The party includes writer Ralph Waldo Emerson, scientist Louis Agassiz, painter William Stillman and seven other prominent liberal academics.

Before the venture begins, a tragedy interrupts, and soon the expedition confronts Myrna with the greatest challenges of her life; the need to rescue her closest friend, and the need to gain a better understanding of human nature. However, her total story is not to be shared with all those on the journey. Myrna's story is to remain the Follansbee Pond Secrets.

A scene painted on site by William Stillman, the group's artist, will soon become celebrated as "The Philosophers' Camp." More than a painting, the work will come to symbolize a model for progressive thought regarding nature, personal freedom, and philosophical discourse. But that ideal will soon be tarnished by the impending conflict and the final struggle over slavery.

The reality of mortal danger in the remoteness of the North Woods forces Myrna and her closest friend to travel to the safety of the city of Boston. Here Myrna reconnects with distant cousins and encounters a life much broader than the familiar rural life of the mountains. Still, the voice of an inner guide calls to her with the lure of the wilderness and the realization of a special love for the Adirondacks.

Barbara Delaney's story is an intriguing story within a story. Her details of the customs and tradition of the hardscrabble life style of the Adirondacks go well beyond just the tale of a bygone generation. The daily sewing, quilting, baking and household duties reveal a constant and intimate mentoring relationship between mother and daughter. And that is balanced by Myrna's exemplary skills as a woodswoman who harvests deer, small game, and casts a rod with the best of them. Her observations of her father through their endless treks into nature, establish a strong bond with him—and creates a role model that will endure through her lifetime and, for those who read her story.

    Jack McEneny,
        historian, author and former state assemblyman

- PROLOGUE -

1868 North Elba

Heroes died or disappeared, she knew that much.

Myrna watched the random flight of the bees in her garden—they seemed to favor the blue-rich dahlias. She missed the Brown family. John had been her hero, even before Harpers Ferry. And Mary, she was a hero for putting up with John's ways. Frederick Douglass and Harriet Tubman were awesome in their heroics, and most everyone in the North Country missed President Lincoln—a man of moral stature.

But the War was too bloody fresh to think about. She wasn't ready to face even her own actions in it. What she did occasionally consider were the years before the war, especially the now famous expedition in 1858 to Follansbee Pond—noted in newsprint as "the philosophers camp." She had had a strong part in leading that foray, now ten years past, into the wilderness surrounding the pond. Those distinguished Boston intellectuals that comprised the party had looked to her for tips on shooting and casting a rod. Myrna supposed that experience had given her the confidence to build her guiding business.

Of course, even at the time, she was aware of the fame of some of the men—Ralph Waldo Emerson, a celebrated writer and Louis Agassiz, a renowned scientist. She'd always remember James Lowell's thoughtful intelligence, too. All ten clients were Boston luminaries. Most were Transcendentalists and several were outspoken abolitionists. If it weren't for her established friendship with Bill Stillman, who initiated the excursion, she might have been overwhelmed by her charges. There were plenty of whispered secrets on that expedition. Some she still pondered, though the lens of time had softened her regrets.

Later, after John Brown was martyred at Harpers Ferry, Waldo Emerson, amongst others, spoke out in defense of Mr. Brown and his sons. Myrna would always be proud of her time with Waldo. Another bonafide hero by her accounting.

All in all, she was glad that she'd decided to call this part of the Adirondacks home. Turning her attention back to her garden and the nearby hives, she wondered what random events were in store for her future. But her reverie was broken as she squinted to see Alvah coming up the road in the distance...

FOLLANSBEE POND SECRETS
An Adirondack Saga

> Wise and polite, and if I drew
> Their several portraits, you would own
> Chaucer had no such worthy crew,
> Nor Boccace in Decameron
> —*Adirondac* R. Waldo Emerson

- CHAPTER 1 -
Stillman's Visit 1857

Like all good stories, this one begins, *one day*...It was a morning Myrna would always remember.

At sunrise a crimson glow lit the softly curdled clouds. Myrna stopped, entranced, in the doorway. Before she'd even finished a cup of coffee, the fullness of colors faded—the soft edges dissipated. She wished the image had lasted longer. Myrna quietly walked to the barn and mounted her horse, Star. Most of the children would already be in the classroom by the time she arrived at the Brown settlement, where she taught reading and arithmetic.

Myrna stayed at the Browns' later than she meant that afternoon—but she and Belle-Liz needed to grade the students' arithmetic lessons...and then they'd got to chatting. Now she'd have to ride her horse hard to make time before the rain descended. Already the wind was a gale.

There was a deep shush overhead before the sky blotted dark. Myrna glanced upward and dismounted: passenger pigeons. She took aim and fired several times. Four spiraled and hit the ground. It was not easy to make such accurate, delicate shots, she thought. She carefully laid the warm soft birds in her pack on top of cut grasses. She would hurry home now to avoid the certain storm.

Meanwhile, at the Duffney homestead, Sam Duffney stepped out on the porch looking west to the mountain. Were those gun shots? No matter. The sky had already turned from grey to clotted purple, thunder rang deep to the ear bones. Unless Bill Stillman was well on his way, he wouldn't be likely to come at all. A storm would break within the half-hour, Sam thought, closing the outside door. And then there was the matter of Myrna, too. But she was sensible about weather, and would likely hunker down at the Browns' until the worst had passed.

Once back inside, he stoked the fire in anticipation of a drop in temperature. Though still August, evenings turned chilly in the Adirondacks—winter was a challenge.

Sam first met Bill Stillman over a year ago. Bill had hired him to guide and carry the necessities when he took a notion to camp out for a number of days. It was a task Sam was happy to oblige. Later, after Stillman returned to his home in Boston, he continued to correspond about a major camping venture to Follansbee Pond in the Adirondacks that he was trying to muster. The idea was that Sam would guide an expedition for Bill and some of his Boston friends from Keeseville on Lake Champlain into the wild forest beyond the Saranac's to Follansbee Pond. The potential clients were an illustrious group of accomplished writers, scientists and academics, most of them famous beyond their Boston milieu.

Sam Duffney knew Stillman to be a fit, energetic fellow with a genuine love of the woods. He did not know about the fitness of the others. It would be a demanding trip from Boston to their final destination on Follansbee Pond. Hard to say, but Bill's enthusiasm might sway a bunch of Bostonians to travel as far as the Adirondacks. This time around, it seemed Bill was serious about spending a week scouting for next year's proposed encampment at Follansbee Pond.

William Stillman originally came to the Adirondacks to paint because he liked the mountain scenery. And he has continued to spend summers traipsing through the woods around Saranac Lake with his paints and easel strapped to his pack. He isn't the only one who fancies painting in the woods; there are other artists who travel to Keene Valley to do likewise.

The first time Sam met Bill Stillman he was not overly impressed with the man, thinking he was a bit of a fop and too fond of fancy words. That, and being annoyed when Stillman had showed him some paintings of forest scenes that he hoped to sell for a good price—making it clear his pictures were far beyond Sam's reach. Being a hunting guide, Sam was used to men from all walks of life, so he was quick to forgive the idiosyncrasies of others.

Late last summer, Stillman had stopped by the Duffney house several times in early evening. Sam figured he was either lonely or looking for a decent dinner, which his wife, Marion, was quick to offer. Gradually, after a number of visits, they had learned quite a bit about him, as he liked to 'converse'—his word. And Stillman was curious, too. He may have gone on about himself, but he also had a genuine interest in how the Duffneys came to settle in the mountains—why they'd picked this particular place; where they'd met; if they were planning to stay—and so on.

Stillman did some domestic and foreign traveling and told interesting stories of places he'd been and people he'd met. On the evenings Bill visited, Sam's wife, Marion, and daughter, Myrna, took to listening to him, too. They enjoyed hearing his anecdotes about exotic places.

Since the fire was now stoked and steady, Sam turned his attention to where Marion might be—the house seemed exceedingly quiet. When he saw she was in the side alcove reading a book, he let her be.

He had no sooner settled in the parlor by the fire with his feet up on an ottoman, when he heard clattering at the back door to the kitchen. The door slammed to the wall in the wind, and the wet chill of the rain reached to rustle the fire on the hearth. It was Myrna, of course.

"Come here and see what I've shot for dinner!" Sam obliged her. Myrna held up a freshly skinned clutch of passenger pigeons. "I caught the tail of a huge flock on my way home. There were so many, that for a moment I thought the storm had descended to capture me—such was the darkness and sound over my head. Their wings and cries made a terrific roar. The birds were so thick I could easily have shot a dozen! It seemed best to take only four today."

Marion came out from reading, her finger still holding the page place. "They'll make a tasty meal for tonight," she said. Then, frowning, she noted that Myrna was a muddy, wet, disheveled mess.

"For God's sakes! Myrna, please go wash-up and brush your hair before dinner—and put on a fresh dress. We're expecting Bill Stillman tonight, if the storm doesn't hamper his trip."

Myrna, for her part, felt angry at Marion's dressing down. She gave her an insolent stare, but held back her response. Stomping upstairs, she once again felt frustrated with her living situation.

Marion was habitually annoyed with Myrna's woodswoman ways. She caught Sam's eye and shook her head in weary exasperation. Her reading had been interrupted. There wouldn't be any point in continuing with the book now—she placed a proper marker at her page and set it down. Marion thought *The Deerslayer* by Cooper was a good story, so far— no point rushing through it, anyway. She pulled the small, blue, cushioned rocker next to Sam's chair by the fire and took his hand.

Sam didn't like getting between Marion and Myrna, but he sensed a need to smooth the friction between mother and daughter. He spoke hesitantly, "You know, Myrna looks very uncomfortable when you address her that way."

"What...I should let her walk around here like a backwoods tramp?"

"No...I'm just saying that when George was her age you weren't so quick to be critical."

Marion bristled. "That's not true, or fair! And furthermore, I'd thought when I had a daughter she'd grow up to be more of a lady, not some...well, warrior in the woods!" Marion drew a deep breath, chin quivering. Then after a calming pause said,

"No, you're right. She's doing fine. I hear she's a good teacher at the Brown settlement school. Mary Brown mentioned how pleased she and the North Elba tenants are with her in the classroom. I guess it's her wild, carefree side that bothers me. No, that's not it," she amended "...the practical side of me wants to see her fit in, not be an outcast—to be courted by a suitable fellow. Is that so much to ask?"

Sam looked perplexed. "Marion, all I was saying is we should remember Myrna has her own ideas. That's it—period."

After the brief squabble they were pleased to resume sitting companionably, watching the flames as the rain continued to fling its might rhythmically on the roof above.

Sam understood that Marion wished Myrna might marry a good prospect someday. The problem being that there weren't many suitable prospects, and Myrna wasn't interested in those available—she'd shown no interest at all. Sam thought of Myrna as an attractive woman, but Marion said he should be realistic. Truly, she looked a bit owlish with her close-set eyes and thin hawkish nose, but her blue eyes were direct and sharp. Also she had a quick smile and an abundance of brown curls—and then there were the distinctive Duffney cheekbones.

Marion says Myrna might be called handsome, but never pretty. Sam thinks that's harsh sounding. Well, true, she doesn't fuss over her appearance or dress like her mother. And in fairness, Marion's fine features and comely figure set her apart. Marion is undeniably pretty. But in her own way, Myrna's lithe slimness and chiseled features are attractive. Besides, at some point you've got to stop trying to steer someone else's boat. Myrna will find her own way—no matter.

Sam's reverie was interrupted. Feet stomped on the porch and there was a knock. Sam gingerly rose to open the door. Bill Stillman had arrived. Closing the door and standing on a rag rug, Stillman said he was lucky to catch a ride with Henry Thompson from the Deershead Inn in Elizabethtown to the Duffneys'. Bill was drenched by the rain, his dark hair dripping on the rug in the vestibule. He needed to towel dry and change.

"Should I store my baggage in the upstairs guest room?" he said.

Sam nodded. The so-called 'guest room' was their son George's old bedroom and a little plain to be elevated to a term denoting a special use. Nevertheless, it was suitable for accommodating a man and his luggage. Now that George was running the Duffney textile mill, and had settled across the lake in Vermont, he visited home maybe twice in a year.

After Bill came downstairs "freshened" they sat at table. Marion beamed at the dinner compliments. "We can thank Myrna for the main course," she said.

Following in the congenial mode, Myrna said, "I must say, passenger pigeons aren't much sport—but they are delicious. Marion is an excellent cook."

Though it was irregular, from an early age Myrna thought of her mother as 'Marion' and often addressed her as such. Myrna surmised that it might be that she had imitated her father's speech as a child—a thing the family had found amusing. Still, George, her brother, always referred to their mother as 'Ma'.

Bill nodded about the pigeons, asking about the bird particulars. He said he'd occasionally seen flocks around his home in Cambridge, but hadn't realized their superb culinary value. He also didn't practice much hunting in his home locale. Myrna nodded politely, she'd had occasion to observe Bill's unimpressive skills with a rifle. Truth be told, he wasn't much of a shot. Nevertheless, she'd noted that he was a competent woodsman, capable of setting a weatherworthy campsite. And he did cast a rod admirably.

They left the dinner table to sit in the parlor by the hearth. There were two blue cushioned rockers and a pair of maroon brocaded side chairs pulled to the fire's warmth. Unexpectedly, Bill rose from a rocker, excused himself, and headed back up the stairs. "Almost forgot something," he said, turning quickly in mid-step. There was an exchange of glances amongst the Duffneys.

"Wonder what he's up to," Sam mused. Myrna had no response, but was curious. Marion was involved with her needle work—she wasn't easily distracted by vague pronouncements.

Bill returned, and then set a pile of wrapped packages on the side table between him and Marion. "I was thinking of you all one day when I was in downtown Boston." He paused, "I do appreciate how thoughtful and generous you are…anyway, I hope you like these small gifts."

The altogether pleasant evening was abruptly taking a festive turn. Myrna studied the brown-papered package tied with dark green, grosgrain ribbon. Clearly, it was a book, but what book? Treating it like wrapped candy, she savored it longingly before opening it.

"Go on now," Bill teased. "Open it!"

Myrna laughed. Sam had already unpackaged a bottle of fine sipping brandy. Marion had opened her box containing spices and a variety of teas.

They watched as Myrna made a game of slowly unknotting the green ribbon—(almost playfully) smiling as she did so. Once the packet was unfettered and the paper loose, she dramatically closed her eyes and then, holding the book before her, looked at the cover. "Oh my!" she said, clearly pleased, "a brand new book—just published."

Stillman said, "I wasn't sure if you liked poetry or not, but I thought you might take to poems about nature. There's an especially good one called *Woodnotes*. The book is by my friend Waldo Emerson. In fact, he's one of the Boston men thinking of joining us on next year's camping trip."

Myrna, who was not easily impressed—being educated, even considered worldly by North Elba and Elizabethtown's standards—was for the moment speechless. Regrouping her thoughts, she said, "Well, I'll have to be sure to memorize a few poems by next summer then, since I might have a chance to meet him." She was so genuinely pleased with the book, she hugged it to her saying, "Thank you Bill, it is a wonderful gift!"

Meanwhile, Marion had managed to quietly go to the kitchen to brew a pot of tea, which she brought to the room on a tray, laden with cups and accoutrements—including small glasses for those who wished to sample the brandy. Sam stoked and banked the fire so they could settle in for a talk.

Sam asked Bill about a situation in Europe that he had alluded to earlier at the dinner table. Stillman had mentioned that he had had a perfectly horrid experience in Hungary a few years ago. And now saw it for the fiasco it was (perhaps after the snorts and guffaws of his Boston cronies).

Bill pursed his lips, slightly furrowing his brows, "Well, let me see, now," he said. Stillman was in his element. He knew how to spin out a good story to a receptive audience. "It's a story I've been hesitant to tell," he said, "and I'll admit it calls to question my judgment on some points. Anyway…this was a few years past, about 1851. You probably remember Louis Kossuth, the Hungarian patriot, and the ruckus over Hungary's independence from Austria?" The Duffneys had read news accounts of the former insurrection. They were fully engaged.

"Kossuth was a revolutionary spark, surely," Bill said, "I suppose after our government helped him avoid extradition from Turkey to Russia, it was inevitable that he come here to raise funds for another go at the Hungarian people's independence. And, as you recall, he did it with tremendous zeal. I think he didn't visit here in the Adirondacks, but he cut a wide, rhetorical swath across the northeastern coast down as far as Washington—gave several hundred speeches, I believe."

The Duffneys nodded in recollection of the news stories they'd read at the time. They had a good sense of the excitement here in America caused by revolutions for independence in Europe.

"I remember he spoke in Boston. I was visiting there at the time," Marion stated. "Though we didn't hear him, it was a keen topic of parlor conversation."

Stillman gave a polite lean forward, before proceeding. "Well, I was lucky to hear Kossuth speak on a number of occasions. He was a distinguished looking, dark-haired fellow with a beard—and not just a speaker, but an eloquent, fiery orator. Until this day, I've never heard his match. Needless to say, I was completely taken by the fervor of his rhetoric about Hungarian independence. I desperately wanted to be part of their revolution."

Stillman paused, "As an aside, I may have overly romanticized our own Revolution, having been born beyond it. I was twenty-three years of age when I heard Kossuth speak," he said, smiling at Myrna. "While he was in Washington, I got in the habit of stopping by his lodgings in the evenings to visit him. Once I'd convinced him (and, of course, my family) that I was sincere in my intent to assist in the Hungarian revolution, it was soon settled that I would follow him to London upon his return to Europe. My father was doubtful about this endeavor, but once my affairs were in order, I left for London with a letter of introduction to a Madam Schmitt—a German refugee sympathetic to liberal causes. That alone was an adventure for me! I was a young man with more zeal than good sense.

Anyway, every Sunday night her home was a jolly gathering place for an assemblage of refugees discussing European politics—all terribly exciting. Meanwhile, I was impatiently waiting to hear from Kossuth about further instructions.

Myrna was fascinated by Bill's worldly adventure. She marveled at the thought of traveling abroad. "Why did he leave you waiting?" she asked.

"At the time, I too wondered...much later, I came to realize that he was habitually tardy in these matters." Stillman shrugged. "In fact, finally, he did send a messenger to my rooms. Following that, I went to a late night, secret meeting place at Kossuth's quarters. We met several times, but negotiations dragged. I won't bore you with the planned escapades that didn't reach beyond the stage of discussion, except to say I felt thwarted in my desire for action. Still, I believed in the Hungarian peoples cause."

In the brief pause, Sam poured more drink all around. Even Marion and Myrna accepted a 'thimble' more. Sam chuckled and said, "You managed to get yourself in the thick of it."

Myrna added, "It sounds exciting and dangerous!" She could only imagine such an adventure.

"Oh, and this was just the start of it!" said Bill, taking a hearty swig. "You might think my enthusiasm would have waned at this point, but, no—I was dedicated. The schemes continued. I'll skip over my various failed tasks... and get to the really bizarre final mission I came to be charged with." Stillman smiled at his enthralled companions.

"When I think about it, I wonder that I got caught up in this last escapade. All I can say is that Kossuth made it seem an act of urgent necessity. He said my assistance was paramount to saving the Hungarian Republic! I, in turn, was enamored with the idea of saving the Hungarian people—helping them win their independence.

Here the plan became really convoluted. It seems that in the course of Kossuth and his compatriots fleeing over the border to escape the Austrians, they decided it would be wise to bury the Hungarian crown jewels they had managed to confiscate from the palace. My so-called mission abruptly changed to capturing back the jewels that Kossuth had buried for safety when he was about to escape to Turkey!"

Marion put her hand to her chest. "My lord!" she gasped. "They must have been of inestimable value. Were they itemized and recorded? How did you ever proceed with such an intrigue?"

Stillman laughed. "I'll get to that part. But now comes the part where you may doubt both my sanity *and* veracity. But to first answer your questions, Marion—the jewels were itemized, and included in the cache was the crown of St. Stephen, which was believed by the Hungarian people to be necessary for the lawful crowning of their King. Of course there were other crowns, pendants, necklaces, brooches and such. All had been buried in a secret place down the Danube. At the point I was brought on, Kossuth believed one of his former cohorts was about to divulge the secret hiding place to the Austrian government in return for favors. My mission, as unbelievable as it sounds, was to pass on the secret code and directions to his trusted colonels, who were supposedly waiting for me and the coded directions to lead them to the treasures."

Myrna was rapt…now this was quite a story!

Stillman gave pause…"As you, or any other reasonable person, might have thought at this juncture—this is complex; things could go wrong or get dangerous. I'm not saying I wasn't a little apprehensive, because I was. But the excitement of the whole mission carried me away…at first."

Myrna nodded at this revelation. It struck a true note. To a one, the Duffneys had spellbound looks.

"First off, the description of the hiding place was written in a most complicated dispatch. It was an elaborate code, the key to which was contained in a stanza of a song known to Kossuth's correspondents in Pesth. Each letter in the dispatch was represented by a fraction, of which the numerator was the number of the letter in one of the lines of the song...and so on. It was *very* complicated.

But for my part, I simply had to pose as an artist on holiday, travel at a leisurely roundabout way to Pesth, find the correspondents, pass on the code (which was sequestered in the hollowed heel of my boot) and, once that was accomplished, I was to organize an expedition to capture the jewels. And *then*, once we recovered the jewels, we were supposed to hide them in a fruit conserve—one of the regions specialties, and surreptitiously carry them to Constantinople. From there it would be my task to deliver them to Dr. S. G. Howe, the well-known philhellene, in Boston. "

Sam couldn't contain himself. He laughed tears. Wiping his nose he said, "Hidden in the heel of your shoe! So what went wrong?"

"Hush, Pa," Myrna scolded—though she saw the humor of it.

"You know, I've never told this story out loud this way. It *is* funny—and I've only told the half of it! Wrapping-up, I didn't find the people I was supposed to contact. Someone I did find, a revolutionary of sorts, was furiously outraged that I was openly bringing attention to him by my actions.

In short, things weren't working out as I expected. I began to panic. My boot heel got a hole in it, making it impossible to keep the code hidden. Suddenly, I realized, mostly due to Kossuth's incomplete planning, that I'd put myself and others in danger. I ended up tossing my boots in the river and high-tailing out of there! I caught the first train I could out of Austria. I have to say, I was both mystified and more than irritated at Kossuth. He had never even replied to any of the dispatches I sent previous to my departure."

"My word! You must have been terrified!" Marion said.

"I think I was, Marion, but belatedly. My actions back then, as I think of it, were not prompted by the courage of one who realizes his danger and faces it coolly, but reflected my constitutional inability to realize what the danger was, however clearly it may have been shown. In other words, once the actual danger had gone by, I felt very frightened. Remember, this was over six years ago. I like to think I've grown wiser since."

"What about the crown jewels, Bill...were they ever recovered?" asked Sam.

"Oh yes, having learned that Kossuth was sending an expedition to recover the jewels, someone who was in on the secret disclosed the hiding place."

Myrna was captivated by Bill's story. This cast him in a new light. Apparently, the reflective landscape painter had other facets to his person. She liked that he was willing to reveal himself as somewhat gullible and foolish—though brave and earnest, too. "What happened to Kossuth?" she asked.

Bill paused. "While back in London, I went to report to him, expecting a scene and reproaches. I was fully prepared to confront him about his communication failures. However, after a lengthy back and forth, it was apparent that he was unwilling to admit any responsibility for the failed mission—or even feel regret for putting my life in danger. We parted in mutual dissatisfaction. Later, I learned that this was characteristic of him."

"Was that the end of your intrigues with Kossuth?" Myrna couldn't help but ask.

"For a while I awaited some final word from Kossuth. I still wanted to join the ever impending—and ever postponed—insurrection. But in the meantime I was deeply involved in my painting, though I also continued to write journal dispatches for some newspapers. It was several years before I again came in contact with Kossuth. It was all very strange. When I brought up our failed mission in recovering the crown jewels, he denied any recollection of our conspiracy!"

"It is strange how the truth of memory shifts over time, is it not?" Sam said, while pondering Bill's story.

- CHAPTER 2 -
Scouting Follansbee Pond

They rose early the following morning. It took Sam and Bill most of the day to pack and complete their preparations for scouting the Follansbee Pond area. They would leave the Duffneys' next morning at daybreak. Sam decided that Myrna could join him and Stillman on their initial exploration.

Actually, Sam liked having Myrna's help in guiding the sports who came to the North Country. She was strong and quick—and a damn sight more competent then most men. Myrna had all the skills of a crack woodsman, plus was a sure shot with her Hawkins rifle. Her tackle box was always ship-shape, too. Other guides would agree.

Stillman was anxious to make an advance trip to Follansbee Pond so's he could picture the whole camp set-up before he and his Boston friends arrived the following summer. Sam agreed. Next year's expedition sounded ambitious in scope, even though 1858 seemed a long ways off.

Meanwhile, in preparation for the scout, Myrna had made arrangements for a woman named Belle-Liz to continue with reading lessons for the children at the settlement school. Belle-Liz was a newcomer to John Brown's settlement in North Elba—an experimental community established by Garrit Smith for freedmen and former slaves. Mr. Brown and his family were excellent farmers, interested in sharing their farming knowledge with their black neighbors. Some of the tenants, who had previously been in other professions, welcomed his assistance. They were also, naturally, abolitionists.

Myrna was pleased to join Pa and Bill on this exploration. Her preference was for working outdoors, even though she acknowledged her main job was schooling youngsters. Teaching paid some, which was helpful to meeting her sundry expenses. And most days Myrna liked working with the children. However, she much preferred the challenge of woods skills—and was hoping to do more serious guiding. She worked hard at building her guiding talents.

The task at hand was organizing their camping items for next day's scout. Myrna was chatting while loading her worn leather pack. She wanted Sam, and by extension Marion, to know she had found a capable woman to assume her teaching responsibilities while she was on expedition.

"Belle-Liz is a new tenant at the settlement," Myrna explained to Sam. "I judge her to be about my age — twenty years or so. I'm not sure why she's come north. Her family lives in Troy on the Hudson River. There's some gossip that her father is an activist and abolitionist. One of the Greens implied her father was a fugitive. All I really know is that she's educated and willing to do lessons with the children. I like her. We spent a pleasant afternoon together a few days ago looking for herbs on the Epps' trail."

"Well then, you'll feel better about leaving the students," Sam said, distractedly, as he checked his rifle.

Myrna was pleased that Belle-Liz was willing to take on the class lessons for a week. Actually, classes had dwindled with the onset of harvest season, but Mrs. Brown and the other mothers liked to keep the younger children occupied during the day. And they all, under Mr. Brown's encouragement, valued education—especially reading and arithmetic. Myrna thought the Browns were a bit fierce on this point. But on occasion, Mr. Brown could be kind, even light-hearted with the young students.

The following morning, they got up in the hush of early hours and set out after breakfast; their packs well prepared the evening before. They rode horses with the intent to leave them at Martin's Hotel on Saranac Lake, before the last leg of the journey by canoe. Sam had arranged for stabling the horses and letting canoes when he was out Saranac way a month past. He had a cordial business relationship with Stephen Martin and Avery Moody, and saw no reason to assume two good guide boats wouldn't be waiting there for him. Sam's horse took the lead, Bill behind him, with Myrna bringing up the rear.

Myrna was relieved that Stillman hadn't commented one way or the other on the fact that she rode in her brother's trousers and flannel shirt. It was really the only sensible outfit for exploring and guiding, still, some people made comments. Myrna thought she'd have been disappointed if Stillman had felt it necessary to call attention to what she wore on expeditions—worse yet if he were patronizing. She wished her mother could be supportive of her desire to pursue a guiding career. It rankled to face Marion's ongoing opposition. Myrna knew that her skills in the outdoors were proficient. But Marion's suggestion that she carry a comb to keep tangles in her hair at bay seemed sensible, so she'd packed one.

Myrna tied her hair back with green ribbon—the one that had been wrapped on her gift—and wore a simple broad-brimmed hat to shade her face. She supposed she did look like a boy, but felt she also looked attractive.

Myrna had never been to Follansbee Pond and was excited about exploring and making camp in a place foreign to her. Stillman had described it as a pristine, remote pond banked by maples and conifers, mostly hemlock and blue spruce. The access to it was downriver by canoe.

They had set out when it was still dark. After sunrise, the colors of the forest were gradually illuminated. The lack of conversation allowed her to observe the trail surroundings. Sumac and maples already had tinges of red or yellow at the higher elevations. She noted wild thyme in abundance, the fragrance of it rising with the mist. There were plentiful bear scat and deer droppings, indicating good hunting. The rhythm of hooves and the musky warmth of Star, her horse, left her to idle reveries. She wondered if they would spend time in the village of Saranac. Myrna found she was well-suited for traveling on horseback, though she preferred a faster pace.

They were lucky to travel on a dry, temperate day. It was agreed that they would stop in the small settlement of Lake Placid to buy some provisions and refresh the horses and themselves. Sam figured it would take most of a day to reach Martin's, where they would camp or board overnight.

They kept a steady pace, stopping occasionally to stretch their limbs and give themselves and the horses sustenance and water. They forded a shallow river. The water was clear to the stony river bottom, fast and reaching to the horse's haunches. Star tentatively side-stepped and snorted. She didn't care for the river.

When they reached Lake Placid, they had a good rest, fully quenching their thirst and sharing brown bread and apples, "I believe this is the last water we have to cross until Saranac," Sam said, addressing Myrna. Bill nodded in agreement.

"I'm relieved about that," Myrna replied, studiously cutting apple slices on a flat outcrop of granite. "Star's my favorite, but she's never taken to moving water." The men nodded, having noticed how skittish Myrna's mount was.

"We can switch horses anytime you'd like," Bill offered gallantly.

"Nope," Myrna laughed, "A favorite's a favorite, but thanks anyway." Myrna was pretty sure that Star would give Bill a *really* hard time, though she was too polite to say that.

They reached the village of Saranac by late afternoon. The roadways were sometimes rutted and difficult. The mountain vistas were lush and burnt with early fall color. They had met with no unusual obstacles or danger. But, as expected, it had been a long and arduous day. It felt good to dismount. The amber dust of the trails clung to their damp clothes and to the heated bodies of their horses. Still and all, they had reached the day's destination.

After a brief discussion between Sam and Bill, it was decided they would take rooms for the night at Martin's hotel, a few miles west of the village. Stillman said he'd be honored to treat for accommodations. And, as luck would have it, there was a young woman staying at the hotel who was looking to share a room, which would lighten the expense. Bill and Sam would share another room.

Myrna had fully expected to sleep on a pallet under the stars tonight, and had to admit that it was exciting to be staying in a proper hotel. She had heard of The Saranac Lake House, commonly called Martin's. It was elegant by mountain resident standards. The main clientele were downstate sports who were, or fancied they were, skilled hunters or fishermen. Guides, such as Pa, frequented the place, but more usually camped nearby. Myrna was glad she'd let Marion convince her to pack a dress, just in case. It was a simple dark blue patterned print, graceful, but not sophisticated. She'd wear it to dinner, which might even surprise Pa. She'd noted that he'd seemed very weary as they brushed and stabled the horses. Perhaps Stillman had also noticed, and was why he'd insisted they stay at the hotel.

Since, for the moment, Myrna had the room to herself, she unpacked her dress and freshened in the basin set out for that purpose. It felt good to scrub twenty-some miles of trail dust from her skin and hair. Once dressed and combed, she sat on the narrow cot under the eaves and took out her daily journal to make notes about the day so far.

There was a tentative knock. When Myrna opened the door, there stood an elfin blond woman with protruding ears. "I am Amalie," she said, haltingly. "Might you be Myrna?"

"Yes, yes, of course. Please come in. I was expecting you."

Amalie circled the room, then went to the window and looked at the lake view. Finally, she crossed the room and flopped on the opposite cot. "I am so relieved," she sighed. "I worried you'd be...well, different."

Amalie was from Canada and of French heritage. She had an accent, sounding 'zee' and 'zis,' and so forth. She told Myrna she had learned English from the American loggers who came across the St. Lawrence River to her small community near Quebec to chop trees. In fact, her fiancé, Edgar, whom she was to meet at Martin's, was one of them. She had no living parents and hoped to marry and have many children. She had left her uncle's home in Aumond, and made the trip here on her own, seeking a better life.

"I can speak good English, but zee reading, not so," she said, asking Myrna if she might translate a letter she had received from her beau, Edgar.

"If you like I will read it to you, though I hope it is not too personal in nature," she said as she glanced at Amalie.

Amalie shrugged, "But, I might like, as you say, personal." She smiled shyly.

Myrna liked Amelie's manner—her subdued forthrightness. She hoped this Edgar was a good, honest man. She unfolded the letter and began.

"Dearest Amalie, I miss our times together and think of you every day. I loved to hear your little bird-like heart flutter when I lay my head upon your breast..."

Myrna looked at Amalie, raising her eyebrows, inquiring, "Now it reads very personal! But, I will continue, if you wish."

"Oh, yes, please. I love to hear zee bird-like flutter!" She giggled.

Myrna continued reading the rather explicit love letter, and was relieved to know that Edgar planned to meet Amalie here at Martin's on the twenty-fifth, which was one week hence, and that they would soon be married at his family's parish near Raquette Lake.

The diminutive Amalie clapped her hands and spun in the small space between their cots. "I am so happy!"

She was flushed to the tips of her protruding ears. When she sat back on the bed she told Myrna that she was glad to have the letter read to her by a kind and sympathetic spirit. Myrna supposed this might be true, though she wondered about any likely future ties for herself. She knew at the moment she had no interest in marrying and raising a family—at least, not yet.

Myrna was taken aback when Amalie proceeded to tell her things she had learned during her courtship with Edgar—after all, she, Myrna, was barely an aquaintence. Perhaps she concluded that all unmarried women needed advice about the ways of men and women. Myrna was thinking she should interrupt Amelie's discourse. On the other hand, where else was she going to hear about these things? The information about 'French Envelopes' sounded strange and complicated. But Amelie's suggestions for what she called "playing" were intriguing. She laughed, saying to Amelie, "Unfortunately, it does not seem that I am destined for a romance."

Amelie smiled mischievously. "Ah, zees things happen when least expected!"

Looking at the pocket watch that Stillman had lent her, she abruptly rose and announced to Amalie that she had to go meet her Pa and his friend downstairs, and then closed the door behind her.

When she reached the dining room, Pa and Stillman were not to be found. A friendly desk clerk, called Pockets, said he knew that Sam Duffney, being a guide, was probably at the 'hole' with the other fellas. He walked her to the front porch facing the lake, pointing to a broad passageway under the main building that led from the roadside entrance of the hotel straight through to the lake—a handy convenience for carrying packs, supplies, and guide boats to the dock.

"Take care," he said, smiling, "Those men aren't used to seeing a pretty woman." At that cautionary utterance, he walked from the porch back to the lobby entrance.

Myrna wondered if his comment was meant in the way of being flirtatious, as she hardly thought the company of men gathered at the 'hole' would be dangerous. She expected that she might even have met some of them on her expeditions with Pa. When Myrna walked down the stairs towards the open passageway there was a large gathering of maybe thirty men. They all looked to be hunters or guides, though a few stood out from their appearance as 'sports'— that is, their clothes were clean and too refined for them to be local woodsmen. Pa spotted her first and quickly walked towards her. "You look nice. Your mother would certainly approve," he said warmly. Bill also detached himself from the larger group and joined them.

Once seated at table in the dining room, Myrna felt relaxed and able to enjoy taking in her surroundings and the hotel clientele. At first she was conscious of being noticed. A few guides who were friendly with Sam came to their table. He introduced them to her and Stillman. Gradually, she felt absorbed into the background, unnoticed. Sam and Bill did most of the talking, continuing to refine their itinerary for the last leg of the paddle to Follansbee Pond.

Myrna saw that the dining room was more in keeping with satisfying the tastes of sports and tourists than locals, not that the room could be called fancy, but it was a large room that could seat at least seventy people. There were wall sconces and paintings on the white-washed walls. Fine linens draped on tasteful oaken tables and good quality cutlery and crockery were displayed, as well as table lamps. The only comparable establishment Myrna could remember seeing was the Eagle Tavern in Albany. Perhaps she had seen the like in Cambridge, too, but didn't recollect it. As for the variety of viands, she was very impressed. Both she and Marion could be considered fine cooks and bakers. However, the assortment of foods and elaborate preparations from the hotel kitchen were a surprise. At Bill's insistence, she ordered oysters and was pleased to find them strangely delicious.

There were more men than women at table, which was not a surprise, as most had traveled specifically for fishing or hunting. The lake was known to harbor large trout and other fresh water game fish. She observed that those women in attendance were stylishly dressed. Still, she thought her own dress was attractive enough. Myrna was curious about the other guests and strained to hear any snippets of conversation around her. Marion would like it here, she thought—and, together, they'd have had fun gossiping about the other guests, too. She concluded that the couple at the adjacent table was not married (at least not to each other). When the gentleman in question introduced the woman to a fellow fisherman, "This is my wife Carrie," he winked.

When the leisurely dinner was finished and the conversation wound down, Myrna noticed that Pa looked spent. It had been a very long day for the threesome. She rose from the table.

"Shall I meet you early tomorrow at the hole?" she said. The hole being the passageway between buildings that led to the lake.

"That'd be fine," Pa said.

Myrna awoke before dawn and dressed in her comfortable clothes for continuing their expedition to Follansbee

Pond. She briefly thought of her brother, George, as she buttoned his appropriated shirt. He'd promised Marion a visit before the chilly season arrived, and they all looked forward to spending the week together with George and his family. Myrna hoped for some good stories to tell George about the Follansbee Pond outing.

Her roommate was sleeping soundly. Myrna noted the letter from Amalie's beau, Edgar, had slipped to the floor. So she lifted the precious message and set it under the water glass on the nightstand before quietly closing the bedroom door.

The kitchen provided a hearty breakfast of eggs, bacon, coffee and toast in a side room meant especially for the guides. She was first to arrive and made a quick go at breakfast. Then, after thanking the cook, Myrna set out for the hole to see if either Pa or Stillman was about. There were a few men she supposed were guides gathered under the veranda. One of them pointed at her and said, "Hey! Ain't you the girly girl we saw yesterday?"

Myrna pretended not to hear him and sat on a bench facing the lake, her back turned from the man. Not easily dissuaded, the intruder came up behind her. She felt a tap on her shoulder. A particularly keen nose was not needed for smelling the alcohol and unwashed odor he carried on him.

"Girly, I wuz speaking to you," he said. "How come yer wearing guide-boy clothes?—...don't suit ya, nope, not a bit."

Myrna preferred not to tangle with him. She didn't know an adequate response, anyway. She figured Pa and Stillman would soon appear.

"Hey! Answer me..." He was stopped from continuing by the appearance of Alvah, a guide friend of her father's. She was surprised, but relieved, that Alvah came to her assistance. She didn't know Alvah that well. He was probably seven or eight years her senior, closer to Stillman's or her brother, George's age. He made a good appearance, fit and tawny, with blondish hair and tanned skin. He and Pa did some guiding together, though Myrna had never been on those expeditions.

"Hello, Roger … you bothering Miss Myrna?" he said.

"I'm just talkin is all. I mean what's she doing in those boy clothes…and acting so haughty," he huffed.

At Alvah's stating that Myrna was indeed a qualified outdoorswoman, Roger jeered. "I'm supposin' yer telling me she's a marksman, too."

Alvah nodded, rubbing his chin. "I hear she's a fair shot."

This seemed to incense Roger. Turning directly to Myrna, he said "Two'll get you ten you can't out-shoot me. In fact, if you'll go over there to the range, I'll give you a chance to prove it." He seemed to take delight in taunting Myrna.

For her part, Myrna had gone from slightly uncomfortable to angry, but she demurred from the challenge, as her gun was packed with Pa's gear. When Alvah offered the use of his firearm she didn't hesitate, thinking, this Roger person dares to make me for a fool! As she, Alvah and Roger made their way to the shooting range— two rag-tailed hunters joined them. Once there, they set apples on posts at about a hundred yards distant. Roger shot first and missed. "All right, best out of two," he said.

Alvah's firearm felt comfortable enough, though it was heavier than her Hawkins rifle. Turning to Alvah, she said, "I presume your rifle has been well sighted, right?" He nodded affirmative, smiling encouragingly. Myrna took her time. She knew the rifle would kick, but decided to hold it firm, rather than use a rest. She took careful aim and fired, blasting the apple to sauce. The two hunters cheered.

Alvah said, "Good one, Myrna!"

Roger scowled and 'harrumphed'.

Myrna let a faint smile pass her face, but tamped down her feeling of triumph and deliberated as she reloaded. Once again she hit her mark, and once again Roger missed.

Alvah and the bystanders cheered, whooping it up to Roger's discomfort. The lanky, tall hunter said to Roger, "Guess you'll have to pay up!"

Looking impassively at Roger, Myrna said, "Not this time. I need to hurry to meet my party." Turning away from Roger and the group, she thanked Alvah for use of the gun. As she did, he grinned and tipped his hat.

Myrna walked hurriedly with a jaunty step towards the 'hole' when she saw Pa in the near distance. He was not smiling, and his jaw was set tight. "It's wise to not over-display your talents," he said with reproach in his voice. Myrna knew he was likely right, but felt elated at having put Roger in his place. It seemed better, to her, to have demonstrated her competence. It might save her from harassment later, she reasoned.

Given Pa's mood, Myrna was happy that she and Stillman would share one boat, while Pa paddled the other one on his own.

The lake was placid as they began their voyage. Stillman sat in the boat's bow, Myrna in the back seat.

It seemed like much had already happened that day, Myrna thought, as they paddled across the lower lake into another. Still, it was early morning. Gradually, civilization was far behind. The only sounds were birdsong and lapping water. The steering position from the back of the canoe kept her alert to the changes in wind and current. Since Bill didn't address her, she saw no need to promote idle conversation. Talking seemed unnecessary, even intrusive. They'd be more likely to observe wildlife near the shore if there were not foreign, human voices reverberating on the flow. When Pa turned his head to check their progress, he looked relaxed and content, which was no small matter to Myrna. They were all strong and able paddlers. At mid-day, they reached the swift flowing river that would take them into Follansbee Pond, actually more a cul-de-sac of the river than a separate body of water. For quite a while, they nimbly dodged protruding rocks and thick brush. The river was high-banked with a vast, green apron of branches hanging overhead, lending a deep tint to the clear water. They were pulled by the current, it seemed, to a deep, hidden grove. The inlet to the pond was so narrow and sheltered by foliage that they nearly missed it. "Turn sharp," Pa said. They'd almost shot by the opening. No one was disappointed. It was a magnificent, secret pond.

Stillman was pleased to see the genuine enthusiasm shown by Myrna and Sam for the place he'd chosen for them to make camp. He'd noticed earlier the disagreement between Myrna and her father, which he knew had its origins in Myrna's shooting match with one of the local guides, but Sam's temper had passed and he seemed to be mellow now.

"I'm thinking," Stillman said, to Sam in particular, "This place near the shore between these two maples is where I'd like to make camp with my friends next summer. The way I see it, is that there's a good space for a large shelter and the water access is excellent."

"Agreed," said Sam. "I'll have some men come out earlier next summer before your group arrives to make a larger clearing and a fire pit in front of the shelter. This spot you've picked is a beauty— no sir, you weren't exaggerating. I've already seen plenty of deer sign and a large trout just jumped in that cove. We'll explore around here for the next few days to see just what's what." Sam could hear Myrna already chopping some balsam branches for their bedding and shelter. It made him smile—she was competent in the outdoors, and very industrious.

For the next few hours the threesome diligently went about the business of making a comfortable campsite— constructing a rudimentary shelter, chopping firewood, and collecting kindling. Since everything seemed to be getting tidy, Myrna announced that she would take one of the boats and catch fish for dinner. "I'm thinking two or three trout would do us fine," she said.

Myrna was glad to be alone in the boat for a while. There was a burst of late afternoon sun that warmed her back. She felt sticky and grimy from her chopping and hauling. When she was around the cove and out of sight from the camp, she stripped off her clothes and swam in the cold water. She stroked and dove deep in the smooth lake, opening her eyes to look at the rocky bottom. It felt like flying through thick air. The sun's warmth on the smooth rock was intense as she exited the chilly pond. Myrna lay on the boulder until she was completely dry, then got back into her soiled clothes. Nevertheless, she felt refreshed. She spent a pleasurable time casting and reeling her line over the water. Three good sized trout were caught for dinner.

Sam had already started the fire when Myrna arrived back at camp. Stillman was feeding it twigs that were snapping and crackling. "Camp looks nice—homey," Myrna said, while she prepared the trout for their meal. She had found a bunch of peppery watercress near the cove and the ever prevalent wild thyme in the woods, figuring the herby flavors might enhance the meal.

Stillman produced some biscuits that the cheerful, matronly cook had given him after the morning's breakfast.

"You know, the cook at Martin's isn't known for her generosity. You must've made an especially favorable impression," Sam said, jokingly.

"I figure, if you've got charm, you might as well use it," Bill replied, laughing.

Myrna thought it was all true enough, as they continued amiably through dinner. She gathered the tin plates and utensils to rinse in the pond as the men made plans for scouting and exploring the area the next day. Someone had given Stillman a hand-drawn map of the area that Pa said seemed 'off' to him. She left them still puzzling over it.

Suddenly, Myrna fled back to the campsite—she was breathless. "There's a very large bear down there!" she exclaimed. "But, I don't expect it'll bother us. It's just that they don't usually come this close."

Neither Sam nor Bill was particularly perturbed by the bear's proximity. However, after some discussion it was decided they would all share the lean-to shelter at bedtime. Of course, it was usual for Myrna to sleep in outdoor shelters with Pa and her family. But, she was aware that there was an awkwardness that always needed to be addressed about sleeping arrangements when camping with men who were not family. Frankly, as a working guide the artifice of it all in these situations irked her. She saw herself as an accomplished professional.

As darkness fell, they stoked and watched the fire. It had been another long day. Bill was tempted to draw Sam and Myrna into conversation about topics, such as their neighbors, the Brown family. He'd heard his Boston friends, some of whom would be coming to camp at Follansbee next summer, praise Mr. Brown's anti-slavery speeches. However, he could see that his guide friends were ready to retire for the evening. Actually, he was feeling sleepy, too.

The following days were planned for explorations. On day one, after a full morning of trekking in various directions and making notes, Sam and Bill launched one of the canoes for circumnavigating the pond and going up-river beyond the inlet. Meanwhile, Myrna's task was to continue her inspection of the immediate area near the camp, and to find game or plants that might round out the evening meal. Myrna had some expertise in identifying edible plants and knew she'd also be able to harvest suitable game. But she thought her first order of business would be to track the large bear she'd seen the day before. The size of it, coupled with its seeming lack of fear, was worrisome. Following the animal's tracks a ways might provide clues.

She thought the best way to follow her quarry would be to walk the rim of the pond to the rocky ledge and cove where she'd first spotted the animal and then try to follow any tracks inland. It was a warm afternoon, which would make this a pleasant walk, in any case. Once Myrna was near the cove, she easily spotted the tracks of the large animal. She managed to follow the tracks for almost half a mile, she judged—and then lost sight of them. Tiring of the hunt, she backtracked to the ledge by the pond and decided to try finding some underground, lateral stems of the cattail plant. She'd never cooked them herself, but she'd gathered some recently on a foray with Belle-Liz, and had found the cooked preparation tasty. She'd filled her gathering satchel with a dozen or so roots when she sensed a presence in the brush. Sure enough, it was the large bear. When it saw her turn his way, it went opposite, crashing through the brush. She had to conclude that she and the bear were merely curious about each other.

Taking a longer route back to camp, Myrna gathered some trumpet mushrooms and shot a large jackrabbit. She had the day's dinner provisions well in hand.

There was no evidence of Pa or Stillman at the lean-to. Myrna relaxed on the pine boughs and took her journal from her pack. There was much to write about…

'Having the day to myself was especially lovely,' she wrote. 'I had a chance to do some animal tracking, a task that requires a bit of quiet concentration. Hopefully, I'll manage a suitable preparation of the cattail roots for dinner tonight. I'd hate to sicken Pa and Stillman! Belle-Liz is so clever in the way of finding edible herbs. I think next week I'll take Marion to the marshy area downhill from our house. She'll enjoy finding a new vegetable for the table. Pa seems to have forgotten about my sharpshooting incident at Martin's. Either that or he's waiting to find a private time to express himself…' Myrna drew a rough sketch of plant life she'd seen that day next to her journal notes.

After Sam and Stillman arrived, and they'd prepared and eaten dinner, they were in a mood for meandering dinner conversation.

"That rabbit dish was delicious," Bill said. "Whatever were those white tuber-like things and the dark fan shaped mushrooms?" Bill rummaged in his pack and brought out a full bottle of brandy. "I remembered that you preferred brandy to whiskey," he said, extending the bottle toward Sam. Myrna politely declined the pour offered to her. She explained about her herbal foraging.

"I'll have to say that I'd like to know more about wild plants, that is, ones safe to eat. It certainly elevates campfire cooking," Bill said.

"I think there's really not a shortcut to it. Marion has taught me a bit about mushrooms—they can be tricky, even dangerous, of course. My friend, Belle-Liz, showed me how to find and prepare the cattail tubers we had with dinner. I also have taken to carrying dried herbs in my pack, like thyme, sumac, and such. If you'd like, I'll show you about the cattails."

Bill nodded in agreement. "Is your friend, Belle-Liz, the woman you mentioned who is tending your classroom charges? I've been meaning to ask you about teaching at the Brown's—actually about Mr. Brown, too. I've heard him speak in Boston on the slavery issue—very impressive. He's sparked a lot of discussion amongst my friends. A number of them, including Waldo, have even made monetary contributions to the cause." Bill paused. "You've never mentioned your thoughts on these matters," he said, turning to Sam.

Sam was busy stoking the campfire. "It's not that I don't have opinions about slavery and politics. I certainly do. The thing is, you'll never hear me spouting about politics willy-nilly—especially on a guiding trip. I always figure most 'sports' want to hear themselves, not me." Bill looked rebuffed. Taking note, Sam said, "With you it's different.

I'm assuming you have a genuine interest, and you're wondering what Myrna and I might be thinking, so let me try to explain. First off, the Browns are helluva good neighbors. His tenants, for the most part, are dedicated to making a go at farming, too. Of course, farming is a challenge in the North Country. But whether or not they succeed at growing crops, they're sincere idealists, in my opinion. John does take pride in raising and showing his sheep. I'm supposing if he wasn't so busy otherwise, he'd enjoy spending more time at it."

Now Bill was listening carefully. The journalist part of him wanted to know more.

Myrna interrupted. "In case you're wondering, Bill, yes, we're abolitionists," she said, adding, "Most of us are, at least nominally, in these parts." She added, "Pa and Marion were completely disheartened when our government passed the Fugitive Slave Act. Once I came to understand it, I was in agreement."

Until now, Bill had not realized the clarity and strength of Sam and Myrna's opinions.

Sam said, "When word first got around about Garrit Smith's plan to foster a farming community for these folks, and hire John to tutor in planting and raising livestock, no one knew what to make of it. Truth be told, I had doubts myself. Seeing a whole group of dark skinned people arriving by wagon to North Elba made quite an impression on me. Sure, I'd seen Negros when I'd visited Albany and Boston, mostly working as tradesmen. But, to see a little village of them was a whole new experience. I know I wasn't the only one curious about them."

"Have you gotten to befriend any of the settlement folks?" Bill asked, tamping his pipe and passing the bottle again.

"Well, the first year they kept kind of private. You know, they were busy with working the land and getting settled. John, being a preacher, even held Sunday services at his place. But gradually, more of us mingled. A few of them began to go to the Methodist services in Elizabethtown. Then there were the regular interactions at the general store and such. You know, it might just be me. I don't exactly spend a lot of time socializing with any of my neighbors." Sam paused, thinking.

"What about Lyman?" Myrna said. "You and he have done some guiding together."

"True, very true. He's superb in the woods. I'm sure we both like working together. Kind of like me and Alvah. It's just that we don't visit outside of that."

Myrna scowled. "And why is that?"

"Don't rightly know, Myrna. Guess it's never occurred to us."

Myrna was perplexed. She knew Pa liked Lyman and Alvah. So why didn't they get together once in a while?

"But, you've got me thinking," Sam said. "Both Lyman and Alvah would be excellent to guide with us on next year's expedition. They've got all the skills, plus are congenial—though not overly so, if you know what I mean."

Bill laughed, "I surely do know what you mean. I'm reluctant to say that I encountered that very sort on a trip last year. It was one of my painting and sketching trips. Sanford, who you've met, and I, wanted a guide for two or three nights simply to carry easels and supplies to a place on the Ausable River near Keene Valley. A lady we'd boarded with told us this fellow was capable and needed the work. So, we met and explained what we expected of him. And he yes'd us to death. We should have been wary when he showed late the first morning. But, he had a plausible excuse about a cow getting loose and was very apologetic. So, we set out two hours late, keeping a good pace to make up the time. Well, not to go on, it went from that to worse. He'd disappear for periods and then talk aimlessly around the campfire after dinner. His stories were exaggerations about his exploits and weren't all that interesting. By the end of the second day, he became scarce to find. Luckily, we were capable of catching fish on our own. When Sanford went in his pack to take out a bottle for our traditional evening nip, it was missing—and so was our guide! In the morning, after we made breakfast, we found our guide snoring contentedly, curled under a tree by the river!"

"Hard to believe he'd treat you so!" exclaimed Myrna.

"Outrageous! I hope you didn't pay him a penny," said Sam.

"Sanford and I didn't know what to think. Sanford has a soft spot for drunks, so we gave him a minimal amount and no gratuity. Besides, we each were pleased with the sketches we'd made, and that counted for some." Bill looked at Myrna. "That guide who challenged you to a contest at Martin's looked to be of that ilk, yes?"

Myrna wished that Bill had had the good sense to not raise to mind the target shooting incident, but she replied, "I suppose that might be true, or perhaps he was just an uncouth bully out to embarrass a woman."

Since the episode was now brought to the open, Pa couldn't resist. He jumped in. "Myrna that was a foolish thing you did. Why did you need to make a spectacle of yourself? You should have ignored the lout."

Myrna looked into the fire. She could feel the discomfiting flush rising to her cheeks. Taking a deep breath she decided to hold her ground. "Pa, I knew you were angry, and I've been feeling sorry about that. However, I'm not sorry I outshot, Roger, that unpleasant man. To start with, I did turn my back and ignore him. I declined his challenge. He was relentless. Maybe I should be sorry for showing him up, but he had it coming."

Pa had that hard as nails look. "A good guide, and a woman at that, needs to have the sense to ignore ignorant behavior."

"But by winning he won't want to harass me in the future!"

"No 'buts' Myrna. I heard you and you heard me. Now, that's that."

Bill had unwittingly touched on a situation that was tenderer than he had anticipated. He didn't want to ruin the evening by causing Myrna and Sam to be uncomfortable. He addressed them, changing the topic.

"This fellow guide, Lyman, who you mentioned as joining our expedition here next year is of Negro persuasion, I presume. I'm thinking that might set especially well with the party from Boston. That is, most of those signed on are ardent abolitionists. They'd, no doubt, welcome having a Negro in our midst."

Sam mulled this for a moment before replying. "Yes, I mentioned both Lyman and Alvah for next year because they are exceptional guides. We work well together. The thing is, I don't think Lyman would like to be fawned over because he's Negro. In fact, I'd want no part in seeing him patronized because of his race. I hope you understand, as I want to be clear on this point."

"Of course, Sam, I meant for his being hired in his own right as a man with skills. Bill was beginning to realize that the Duffneys were strong, possibly obstreperous characters. They didn't mind calling you to task. He liked them.

- CHAPTER 3 -

Going Home

As the week progressed, it seemed they'd made Follansbee Pond their home. There was a rhythm and soft melody to their days. Sam, Myrna, and Stillman were each taking more time for exploring or foraging on their own, then coming together to prepare the evening meal. Sam sometimes announced at breakfast that he'd be shooting game or catching fish. Bill had taken to long walks where he'd find wood scenes to sketch. Myrna often joined Sam. They were at ease with each other in these activities.

On one particular sunny morning, Myrna decided she'd take the boat to the far side of the lake. They'd be journeying back home on the following day. She traveled by canoe to avoid the thick underbrush along the shore, to a secluded place on the water she'd noted previously. While there, she'd launder a few items and set them on the rock-face to dry. She liked the feeling and smell of clean clothes, that is, her own garments; though she was not prissy or offended by the men's lesser standards of hygiene. If it was just her and Pa, she might have offered to wash his shirt, but she wasn't about to set an expectation for washing the men's clothes.

The cove she had in mind, one with a large, flat, offshore, granite rock, was some distance from their campsite. Once there, Myrna tied her boat to a tree along the shoreline, then she swam back to the rock and shed her garments. It seemed sensible to wash the clothes she was wearing as well as those few items brought to launder. There were no particular tasks assigned to her that day, and so a leisure period of swimming and sunning on the boulder seemed a perfect way to spend a few hours. Myrna enjoyed the feeling of the hot sun on her naked body. She turned from front to back. If too warm, it was simple to slide into the cold water for refreshment...and then start over the baking process. Though she didn't burn easily, she took caution and rolled to the shade for a while. It seemed so private and relaxing staring through the dappled, green canopy above, that reveries occasionally spilled into dreams. She walked on the rock surface to the opposite side where her clothes lay drying— almost ready, she thought.

Standing poised to jump into the pond for a last swim, Myrna heard a rustling sound in the brush nearby. She paused, alert, thinking it's probably just the afternoon breeze. Then she dove and swam for a good distance. The water felt cool and smooth skimming her body. Her strokes were long and slow. There was no hurry. Returning to the granite ledge, she stood dripping. It wouldn't take too long to dry off. Her clothes were already dried. Glancing left to the shoreline there was an unmistakable flash of red plaid—it had to be Stillman. What should she do? Waving was out of the question. Then there was the dilemma of getting her boat, and paddling back naked to the boulder. She could put her garments on and *then* swim to the boat. But, what was the point of her effort to have clean, dry clothes? Certainly that was not an option. Well, she decided, stretching to a graceful arc while diving, a noisy, splashing, swim would alert him to her presence and, no doubt, cause him to do the gentlemanly thing by backtracking into the woods. Besides, she thought, there was no shame in bathing in a private cove. Nevertheless, she had to admit to feeling exposed while paddling the canoe a short distance back to the rock. Once she dressed in her clean dry clothes and folded the rest of the laundry into a small pack, she knew she'd done the sensible thing. She laughed at the thought of the incident as she began her long paddle across the lake and back to camp.

Meanwhile, Stillman, who indeed it was, remained quiet in the brush until Myrna was well along her way. He certainly hadn't intended to intrude. Actually, he was stunned to see her standing nude on the rock. As an artist he'd painted nudes while studying in Paris, but none that looked like Myrna. From the back view her slim figure looked muscular and boyish. From the front she was definitely a woman, smooth and girlish. She had well defined arm muscles as she gracefully swam. Though embarrassed by it, he felt a stirring of his manhood as he observed her. As an artist, he wished she would allow him to paint her, but knew the chances of having her pose nude were slim. In fact, he supposed Sam might punch him if he broached the subject. Hell! Myrna would probably shoot him!

That evening, after dinner, Sam thought Stillman, and even Myrna, was uncharacteristically subdued. He supposed they were anticipating packing up and leaving. But once darkness fell and they stoked the fire, all normalcies resumed. In fact, once begun there was a cheerful loquaciousness amongst them.

Sam asked if he'd done any sketches that day, as he knew Bill was itching to record the Follansbee landscape. Bill responded that he had.

"I don't know if I've done the place justice, but I'll show what's in my notebook, if you'd like."

Sam and Myrna were both agreeable to seeing the sketches and sat on either side of Bill as he turned the pages. As he displayed his drawings, Myrna was surprised at the level of detail in some of the botanical pieces. She noted he had a sure hand, especially in the smooth elliptical shapes of the mushrooms—and told him so. Pa seemed interested in the chipmunk drawing.

"I like trying to capture the spirit of the small, furry creatures," Bill said. "Unfortunately, they mostly skitter away before I finish. But, this little fellow was happy to stay nearby as long as I kept feeding him a supply of crumbs."

Bill turned the page to a pretty portrayal of woods, shoreline and an off-shore boulder. There was a fish breaking the surface in splashy ripples to the right of the boulder. Myrna recognized the scene as the very cove in which she'd spent the afternoon. She hesitated a moment. "Ah, the one that got away," she said, with a hint of a smile.

Bill gave her an uncertain look. "I especially favor the elusive trout. They are gorgeous creatures when the sun catches their colors, I think."

"That's another reason your Boston friends are going to enjoy it here," Sam said, "Excellent fishing."

They rose early next morning to dismantle the campsite and pack the canoes.

It took some time to complete the task. When they'd finished, Sam looked back from the shore. "You'd never know we'd been here," he said with satisfaction. Bill and Myrna nodded from the boat they shared. Bill thought how this magnificent wild setting would appear to Waldo and his other friends from the Saturday Club. He said to Myrna, "I can hardly wait until my return next year," as he pushed their pack-laden boat from shore.

Slowly, they navigated their boats upstream on the river, leaving the quiet pond to its wildlife inhabitants. They decided, once again, to board overnight at Martin's hotel before proceeding to the Duffneys' home.

Bill declared he was looking forward to a soft bed and a sumptuous meal. Neither Sam nor Myrna would have been as comfortable stating such. They were used to roughing it when guiding sports. Nevertheless, that didn't mean they wouldn't fully enjoy the comforts offered by Martin's.

Myrna went to the hotel reception desk to inquire about her acquaintance, Amalie, and learned that she had indeed been met by her fiancé and had boarded a coach two days ago for the town of Raquette Lake.

"Would you, by chance, be Myrna?" inquired the friendly desk clerk. "Miss Amalie left you a note," he said handing her an envelope. She thanked him, affirming that she was indeed Myrna.

Myrna took the somewhat bulky envelope to a quiet corner of the hotel's parlor to open and read the message. Surprisingly, there was a delicately embroidered handkerchief included as a gift, with the note. The note had, apparently, been penned by Edgar, who wrote: "Dear Miss Myrna, Amalie has asked me to write you this note because she is unsure of her English writing. She was so pleased to have made your acquaintance that she wishes you to have this hankie that she embroidered herself. She did not know that you were a famous trail guide until someone here mentioned it. We both think that is unusual and interesting..." The note continued to tell of their wedding plans and describe the house he was building for them on Raquette Lake. It ended with a warm invitation for Myrna to pay them a visit come spring.

Myrna was pleased to hear from Amalie. But, I'm hardly a famous guide, she thought. Maybe Pa's well known enough. She unfolded the handkerchief on her lap. The dainty embroidery, in one corner, had a tree with two birds. Miniscule hearts and flowers bordered the whole piece. Myrna smiled to think of Amalie having said "but, I like the bird fluttering heart." Myrna sighed. Whatever would she do with an item like this? Of course, Marion would like it—and would wish it might be Myrna's handiwork. She tucked the note and hankie in her skirt pocket, then decided to walk outside. She needed to stretch her leg muscles after a day in a guide-canoe. Pa and Stillman were tending to the horses. They simply wanted to be sure their mounts were ready for tomorrow's ride home.

She felt a little cautious about walking near the 'hole', but figured that since she was wearing her proper blue dress, she'd be unnoticed by the other guides.

She heard Alvah before she saw him. "Evening, Miss Myrna," he said. "I almost didn't recognize you. The dress looks nice."

"I thank you for the compliment, but you know, I got into a heap of trouble with Pa over that shooting incident last week." She paused. "Actually, it's not to do with you. I just shouldn't have taken the bait and out-shot him. Pa said I was acting too…well, maybe arrogant, though that's not exactly what he said."

Alvah looked surprised. "I don't agree with Sam on this one!" He hastily added, "Though I've a lot of respect for Sam's opinions, usually. That fella was most definitely harassing you. You're ten times the guide he is! Furthermore, he was disrespecting you and had no manners. Believe me, he needed just what he got." Alvah smiled broadly and gave her a playful punch on the arm. "Maybe I shouldn't mention it. The fellas are all talkin about you. Yep, you gained a lot of admiration by outshooting Roger—that rascal."

"Alvah, just promise me you won't mention it to Sam—at least not yet."

Alvah slightly frowned. "As you like Myrna. You know, Sam is proud of you." He supposed maybe it was natural to be protective of a daughter, but held his tongue on that one. Truth be told, Myrna was different from any woman he'd ever met. He'd always liked her, but watching her handle that woods lout…well, that was really something. She piqued his interest, but seemed distant and skittish. He said, "Sam mentioned that Bill Stillman was intending to take a large hunting party of Boston city 'sports' to some remote area of woods next year—and that he'd hire me as a guide. I assume you all were scouting a place for a camp, right?"

Myrna nodded, looking thoughtful, but didn't say a word. "I'm supposing you'll be one of the guides?"

Myrna scrunched her brows. "Hard to say," she said. Meanwhile, thinking, *of course, I mightn't be included— you nitwit. Pa will worry I'll do something 'unbecoming'.*

Alvah noticed that she looked dejected. "Did I say anything to offend you?"

Rallying, Myrna coolly turned away. "No, not at all, really. I'd best find my party." She walked quickly in the direction of the dining room. How could she explain how she felt—even to a sympathetic sort like Alvah? It was her fervent hope to become a full time guide—but the future was doubtful.

Alvah, watching her retreat, thought that his attempt to converse with Myrna didn't go so well. She wasn't just different— she was difficult, too. Still, he'd like to get to know her better.

Myrna found Pa and Stillman chatting in the hotel lobby. They escorted her, one to a side, into the dining room and sat at table. They were all hungry and of good spirit. Bill ordered a bottle of wine to celebrate what he called "an outstanding adventure."

The next day, at the end of their journey home, they saw two figures in the Duffneys' homestead garden. They were Marion, and to Myrna's surprise, Belle-Liz, who was helping Marion gather vegetables. When Marion saw them she looked both happy and relieved.

"I'm so glad to see you!" She gave them each a heartfelt hug, then introduced Belle-Liz to Sam and Bill. Sam gave Belle-Liz a welcoming smile. "Myrna says you've been helping her with teaching children at the settlement." Belle nodded.

Looking at Belle-Liz, Marion remarked that it had been a very good idea to prepare a large batch of vegetable soup—just in case.

Myrna felt energized by Belle's presence. "I'll take over in the garden while you have a sit with Pa and Bill," she told Marion, who gratefully took her offer.

Walking to the garden with a water jug in hand, Myrna asked Belle how she had come to help Marion. She'd already decided that Belle was the shorter and best appellation.

"It was quite by accident, really. I stopped by a few days ago with Lyman, thinking you were due back. Marion was working in the garden and I judged she could use a hand. So I sent Lyman back to the settlement and stayed on. Don't worry, I left the children with homework." She looked amused and laughed, linking arms with Myrna. "No more worry, worry."

The simple welcome home dinner felt festive. Bill told them more stories about his childhood in Schenectady and his studies at Union College. It so happened that Belle and her mother had spent a few enjoyable days in Schenectady before traveling to their current home in Troy. "I remember Ma and I walked in the beautiful gardens on the college campus," she said. "And I understand the library has a wonderful collection of books on botany." Belle paused, "I hope to learn more about plant life while here in North Elba."

Bill cleared his throat. "Myrna cooked some cattail roots for us on our excursion—said you'd taught her...very tasty."

Myrna noted that Bill was eager to appear at ease in talking with Belle, but displayed a tinge of awkwardness in responding to her. Was it Belle's striking beauty, or that she was of African descent? Myrna wondered.

Marion was so happy that Sam and Myrna had returned safely from their sojourn in the woods. It had only been a little over a week, still she had worried and missed them. It was a blessing to have had Belle-Liz appear on her doorstep. This evening, it was a joy to listen to their adventures. Perhaps, someday she and Sam would stay at Martin's. Marion caught Sam's eye and smiled at him. She felt a pleasant anticipation for bedding with him. They'd have to be quiet, though.

At bedtime Myrna shared her large feather-bed with Belle. They chatted through most of the night. It felt like when she was a child at her cousin's house in Jamaica Plain. Actually, it seemed fun to be girlish with a bosom friend. Though, of course, they were adults and new friends—more acquaintances, perhaps. Belle snored.

After breakfast, when they said their goodbyes to Bill, he turned to Myrna, "Promise you'll write to me when you finish reading Waldo's book. I would very much like to know your opinions on it." Myrna said she would.

- CHAPTER 4 -
Connections

The long days of summer were smoke up the chimney. September would be on their doorstep in just six days—the day George and his family were due to arrive at the Duffney homestead. George, his wife Janine, and their five-year-old daughter, Jane, had been unable to make their usual spring trip in May, due to Janine's bout of pneumonia. So, Marion, Sam, and Myrna were excitedly anticipating their visit.

Sam was pleased that George had taken so well to managing the Duffney textile mill in Charlotte. It had been a relief to hand it over to him. It had been Sam's responsibility for thirty good years, but he'd always preferred his time here at the farm, balancing the work of growing a substantial kitchen garden with his guiding business, his main source of employment. When his former business partner, Stephen, moved west to Kansas to try his hand at ranching, George offered to take over the Vermont textile business. And that had actually surprised Sam.

Marion and Myrna were busy preserving blackberries and green beans, partially in anticipation of George's visit. Belle had asked if she might help. She was experienced from her own mother's kitchen in Troy. She said it was a task she'd always enjoyed. Belle was experimenting with using beeswax as a sealant for jars. Marion said she was willing to try this method for preservation of the berries and pickled green beans.

"Past Tuesday, I helped Mrs. Epps put up some butter beans, but she has her own recipes and doesn't take to trying anything new," Belle said. "You and Marion make preserving almost fun." The kitchen was steamy with kettles for boiling and blanching. Myrna threw Belle and Marion rags as she mopped her own brow.

"Ann, though I'm used to calling her Mrs. Epps, was horrified at my suggestion we add garlic to one batch of beans. She said it would make them stinky…and that garlic was a medicine, not a flavoring."

Marion smiled at Belle's pronouncements on the culinary arts. "I'm happy to try a small batch of green beans with garlic, as you say. But, as you know, garlic can be tricky…hard to say how it'll ripen over time in a jar. Myrna and Sam do like fresh garlic, though."

"I love the paste you make from garlic and mustard seeds that you sometimes serve with roast venison," Myrna said, thinking of dinner possibilities. She was happy to help with today's preparations, but thought of preserving as more a chore than a pleasurable pursuit. On the other hand, the camaraderie and Marion's lighthearted smiles were happy notes. It was not always easy to achieve balance in Myrna's usual household interactions with her mother. Also it was good that they'd be well supplied with favorite foods in advance of George's visit. Myrna was intrigued by the bee hives being kept by Belle and the Epps family, too. She made a mental note to ask Belle to set aside some time after classes in the coming week to show her more about the workings of the bees. She wondered about the world of insects and tiny plants—small things that she often overlooked—and resolved to give forest minutia more attention.

Sam rose early the following day and sat on the porch stoop with his morning coffee. He and Lyman had made a plan to travel together to Elizabethtown for provisions. It was generous and unexpected of Epps to make the offer, though Sam's house was not out of the way. Perhaps he'd heard about Stillman's visit and hoped to secure his position on next year's guiding party, which Sam was already planning. It would be, after all, a notable Adirondack expedition.

Sam saw a cloud of dust on the road signaling Lyman's arrival, and went back in the house to see that there was a fresh pot brewing on the kitchen stove. He filled an additional blue mug and brought it to the porch, as Lyman tethered his wagon.

"Ah, there's nothing like the aroma of coffee steaming from a cup on a chilly morning," Lyman said, sipping his brew.

"I figured you might like a quick rest stop before we head to Elizabethtown...mighty nice of you to offer me a ride, by the way."

"Well, I see's we both need to get there, and usually in our separate wagons. So, last week I say to Ann that it hardly makes sense for two fellas to use two wagons and tire two horses, when only one conveyance might be needed."

"Yep, makes some sense to me." Sam topped off their cups.

Lyman hesitated, looking uncomfortable. "Truth be told, I've been looking for a chance to speak with you..."

Sam interrupted, "No need to worry about next summer's big guiding expedition. You are surely my first choice," he said.

Lyman smiled. "That I did expect. No, it's about something different altogether. It's about the young woman, Belle, a delicate situation to discuss." He paused. "She's in my charge, you know. And I've promised her father, and, John, too, for that matter, that I'd keep her safe. That'd seemed easy enough while she'd stayed around me and Ann at the settlement. But, now she's taken to visiting Myrna and you folks. I guess she's here right now." Observing Sam's puzzled expression he added, hastily..."Now that's a fine thing; It's just I can't keep an eye on her when she's away."

Meanwhile, Myrna sat out of sight by the open kitchen window. She had not intended to listen, but she had heard most of Lyman and Pa's conversation, and was wondering what possible danger could await Belle... or what other reason was concerning Lyman, as she watched them leave together in the Epps's wagon.

Belle entered the kitchen on her return from the privy. She looked wide awake, ready to start the day. "Have the men left for town yet? I thought I heard voices outside." Myrna nodded.

"Well then, I'll cook a special breakfast for you and Marion. That is, if you don't mind me messing in your kitchen," Belle said, brimming with enthusiasm. "I'll just need your help in finding this and that."

Myrna nodded— Belle's energy was contagious. "You know, the kitchen is Marion's purview. She prefers that I don't get underfoot, at least not while she's in it. Not that I can't cook," she hastily amended.

Belle frowned and tilted her head. "But, she'd like a delicious surprise...Yes?"

"I think so. It's still early, but she's not yet awake—she must be tired. Yes, your cooking will be a welcome surprise." Myrna wasn't really sure what Marion would think of them concocting breakfast, but she did know her mother would make every effort to be polite, no matter her inner thoughts.

It seemed the nimble fingered Belle had spotted and gathered mushrooms and herbs yesterday. She instructed Myrna to gather six eggs from the hen house. "Shhhh...be quiet so's we don't wake Marion," Belle said. "While you're gettin the eggs I'll start the batter for honey biscuits."

I guess this is what it'd be like having a sister, Myrna thought as she trudged to get the eggs. Actually, she rarely gathered the eggs, as that chore was part of Marion's routine. Thinking back, she realized that her brother George was usually the one to accompany Marion to the hen house. Myrna missed George and was happy that she'd be seeing him soon.

The hens were warm and a-flutter when she reached under them for eggs. But, Myrna was stealthy, fast and efficient—she came and left before they summoned a cluck.

They heard Marion making her morning ablutions, and the stairs from the second level creaked as she descended before entering the kitchen. The suspense in the air was as thick as the waft of garlic. Myrna and Belle laughed together when Marion said "Oh my! This looks appetizing, though I'll admit that the delicious fragrance of garlic simmering kept it from being a complete surprise!" She hugged both women, and gave Myrna a fervent kiss on her cheek. "Thank you," she said.

Since no men were about, Sam and Lyman having gone to Elizabethtown, they lingered over their breakfast and talked of sundry things—mostly interesting recipes using mushrooms or honey. And, of course, there was the excitement around George's imminent visit. As they chatted, Myrna's thoughts kept returning to the conversation she'd heard between Lyman and Pa about Belle. Should she broach it, or, shouldn't she?

But as the day lengthened, Myrna couldn't seem to find words for the questions she wanted to ask Belle. Even when they found time to take the long path to the river, she found it easier to discuss plants along the way than to attempt a serious personal conversation. For one thing, Myrna was reticent to reveal much in the way of her own feelings. That is, she wasn't in the habit of expressing her private thoughts and assumed others felt likewise. Also it was very pleasant to simply walk and observe the variety of plant life. Belle had brought a small magnifying glass with her so they could examine some stems and leaves closely. She had a notebook in which she entered brief sketches of those parts she found most interesting.

"I know there are formal names for these," Belle said, holding up a white lacy flower. "Someday I will learn more about this."

Seeing her determination, Myrna had no doubt that Belle could do this. "Marion calls it Queen Anne's Lace."

Belle nodded briskly. "Yes, that is one name. It is also called wild carrot because the young roots have that flavor. But," she said, wagging her finger, "they mustn't be tasted this time of year—make you very sick."

"How so, sick?" asked Myrna, out of curiosity.

"I think the tongue turns purple and green snot flows from the nose!" She giggled. "Actually, this is one I do not know. I'm just repeating admonitions about 'sick' that I've heard from the aunties—you know, elder women. But, I think it is probably stomach sickness—it won't kill you."

"Hmmm...I don't care for the idea of plants and herbs that can trick you from one day to the next."

"But," said Belle playfully, "most anything and anyone can sometimes fool you."

"And that is why I enjoy cultivating a skeptical mind," retorted Myrna, in good humor.

By the time the women had finished their woods foray, Pa and Lyman had returned from Elizabethtown with their purchases. They were sitting on the porch. Lyman rose when he saw them, and waved. When they got to the stoop, he said, "If you don't mind, Belle, we should be getting back, so's Ann won't worry."

Marion packed a satchel with a jar of beans and one of blackberry jam for Belle to bring to the Epps' household. She hugged Belle and thanked her again for her help.

Myrna stood by the wagon. "I hope you'll be able to help with arithmetic classes on Monday," she said. "You have a knack for it with the younger ones."

Belle replied, "I will surely be there."

Sam had plenty to think about after his excursion to Elizabethtown in Lyman's wagon. He'd always liked Lyman, in the way you'd admire a fellow woodsman. But, Lyman had shown a serious, thoughtful side today. Sam was taken aback by Lyman's willingness to share deep convictions and fears about political repercussions. On one hand, Sam felt honored to be included in such a discussion. On the other hand, he guessed his own liberal opinions must be more apparent than he'd meant them to be. Maybe Lyman took a gamble about expressing himself in the interest of being clear about protecting Belle. Sam was bothered that there were layers of complexity about abolitionists and slavery, which he hadn't even suspected— right here under his nose. He was left with a lot to mull over. He might have to share some of this with Marion and Myrna.

Myrna was very pleased when Pa suggested they go for an early morning hunt. She knew George and his family would appreciate fresh venison, and she'd been looking for a chance to inquire about what Lyman might have said about Belle—besides, truthfully, she felt she'd done enough kitchen work over the past few days. Being out-of-doors, scouting and hunting was more to her liking.

The morning was going well; Sam got a shot off within the hour. It looked to be a good sized buck. Judging from the blood on the trail it was, no doubt, mortally hurt. All they needed to do was track it to where it would finally fall. Myrna led the way. She was quick and agile. The wounded animal crashed through the brush for a good ways before collapsing in an oak clearing. The deer, hurt and frightened, was still breathing. Myrna, without hesitation, aimed and shot between his eyes, and then sat cross-legged beside her quarry. Shortly, Sam came to the clearing, slightly limping, holding his right side. "It's just a touch of colic," he said, noting Myrna's concerned look. "We might as well take a rest here and share this flask of tea before we field-dress him. Nicely done Myrna, there's no point letting an animal suffer." They walked to a nearby fallen log and sat.

"Pa, I've been meaning to ask you some things. Firstly, let me say I accidentally eavesdropped yesterday when Lyman started to talk to you about Belle. Is she in some kind of danger?"

"Actually, I've been going to talk to you about that—to Marion, too. But anything I tell you now can't be repeated—clear?" Myrna nodded vigorously.

"The thing is, it's complicated. Belle *might* or might not face danger. Her father is involved with some fund raising activities with Mr. Brown. Oh hell, it's likely more than that… Anyway, when Belle was on a visit with her father in New York City a few months back, a man was spotted following her. Worse yet, the man is a known slave trader. Of course, Belle and her folks have papers proving they're not slaves, but after that incident, her Ma got anxious about her walking about the streets of Troy. So, it was decided to send her to the Brown settlement to live with the Epps family where she'd likely be safer. Her Pa was worried that that scoundrel might try to take retribution on him by harming Belle. Both John Brown and Lyman are friends of her father."

Myrna took in her father's words. "That's terrible! Do you think Belle is worried about this man?"

"Apparently, not worried enough, to Lyman's thinking. She never consults him when she walks in the woods on her plant gathering forays, or when she has a mind to go somewhere with you. Then there's also the issue of a possible suitor back in Troy." Sam paused to chuckle. "Not to make light of it, but she's more than a hand-full for Lyman and Ann. As Lyman says, she's pretty enough to turn heads and get noticed even when a fellow means her no harm."

Myrna sighed. "There's a lot to think about, isn't there." She thought she needed to ponder more about slavers and abolitionists. The idea of Belle being threatened was making a personal issue of what heretofore had been an abstract political matter.

"I guess we'd better get to work field-dressing," she said. "I brought along a clean bag for the heart and liver."

Once the deer was dressed and trussed to a cedar pole, he wasn't too heavy for them to carry. Pa took a few rest stops; still, they made good time going home.

The Visit

George, and his family, arrived as expected and settled in at the Duffney homestead. Happy new routines emerged in their daily schedules. Though George would stay only a week, all were determined to make the most of the visit. In that spirit, unessential chores were neglected and ordinary routines were cast aside. After a full day of visiting, it did not take much coaxing to convince Marion and Sam to sleep-in the following morning. That day found Myrna, Janine, and Jane preparing the breakfast.

"I always say, one can carry on most of a day after a hearty breakfast," declared Janine, whipping a large bowl of pancake batter, while Myna sliced generous pieces of ham on a platter. Young Jane picked tiny errant stems from a basket of blueberries.

Myrna was enjoying getting reacquainted with her young niece, Jane. Of course, a year was a good stretch of time in a child's growth. But it was amazing to see the inevitable changes. Jane was talkative and very inquisitive. Myrna showed her niece some favorite story books that Marion had read to her as a child.

Jane was enthralled with *The Tales of Peter Parley in America* by Mr. Goodrich. It was a warm-hearted picture book about a grandfatherly gentleman telling stories about his life as a young man in Boston. Jane had never been to Boston, and after having read the book with Myrna, and knowing Grandma Marion had once lived near Boston, had no end of questions for her grandmother about the appealing city. It was obvious that Marion took enjoyment in recollecting those chapters of her life, too. After the evening meal, Jane surprised them all by proudly reading aloud several of Peter Parley's adventures. "I think someday grandmother Duffney will take me on a train to Boston," she said, giggling. They all knew that Marion had likely made no such promise. But in the spirit of the moment, Marion said, "It's altogether possible that we could take such a trip in a few years."

By Wednesday morning, Myrna felt obligated to resume her teaching responsibilities at the settlement. She left early in hopes of making it a short day. Jane teased to go with her, but in the end, it was decided that the day would proceed more smoothly if Myrna went by herself. Tucking Jane back under the covers, with a, "Shhh..." Myrna quietly closed the bedroom door.

It felt good to be back in the classroom. Clearly, Belle had put some energy into the children's arithmetic lessons. A few of the older boys proudly recited multiplication time's tables. There was a definite advantage in having two teachers.

After classes Belle and Myrna shared a quick cup of tea. They talked about how well the students were taking to having two teachers. Belle hesitantly offered that perhaps it was good for them to have one of their own skin color as a teacher. Myrna allowed that this was probably true—it made sense to her. At the end of their talk, they both acknowledged how pleased they were to be able to speak so freely to one another.

As Myrna drove the small carriage home, she thought: Yes, Belle and I are comfortable together—still, I haven't managed to ask her about the danger she may be avoiding—or need to flee from. It seemed only fair that Belle be forthright. Myrna resolved to address this matter with Belle the following Monday. She had arranged to be at the Duffney family homestead for the rest of this week.

The following day mid-morning, after breakfast, Myra was surprised to hear Pa and George chatting and laughing outside. Looking through the window she saw that Alvah Woods was with them, and wondered why he'd stopped by. Whatever was the conversation, George was all smiles. She was tempted to go join them, but then Jane called her to the living room for a reading session. It seemed that young Jane was determined to practice reading, at least for the time being.

"This one's about four orphan children from long ago in England, who are hiding in a forest from "roundheads". People think they are dead, but they've been saved by a gamekeeper—I mean, the orphans." Janie said, breathlessly. "Will you read it to me? I can help read it, but I like to listen to the words sometimes."

She was so insistent, Myrna was won over—she took the book and sat beside her niece. The well-worn book *The Children of the New Forest* by Frederick Marryat had been a favorite of her and George's. The gamekeeper of the story, Jacob Armitage, had been one of her first heroes. She could inquire later about Alvah's visit. Besides, it was good to give Marion and Janine some time for relaxing. Jane was proving to be a dear, but somewhat demanding, youngster. Upon reflection, Myrna realized, guiltily, it appeared easier to be in a classroom for a few hours, than have full time children of one's own.

The rest of the day seemed to fly by. Later, after the evening meal, and the dinner dishes dried and back in the cupboard, the women were free to join Pa and George by the parlor fireplace. Janine dutifully climbed the stairs to see that Jane was comfortably sleeping. Myrna had declined accompanying Jane and went to brew the tea instead. She thought it best to not chance having to read 'just one more chapter...pleeese'.

Myrna hoped someone would mention Alvah's morning visit, but they didn't. Pa and George talked on and on fondly about the mill, the new carding machinery George had installed and the economic problems with the escalating prices of raw cotton from the southern states. George was venturing into more wool products to offset the fluctuating cotton market.

George, like the rest of his family, was an admirer of John Brown and the settlement. He said he'd heard Brown give a rousing anti-slavery speech in Burlington and was mightily impressed—he'd even donated to the cause. Marion, sternly interjected, however, that she thought John left too much of the daily running of the farm to his wife, Mary, and that the birthing of so many children was tiring her. Sam and George always seemed surprised at Marion's strong opinions. Truthfully, they did not welcome an open forum on the subject of relations between men and women, even within the closed circle of family. Janine caught Myrna's eye and they smiled together, knowingly. "I think it must be a very good help to the Brown settlement that Myrna teaches the children," Janine offered.

Meanwhile, Myrna was still waiting for George or Pa to get around to mentioning Alvah's morning visit. Finally, her impatience got the best of her. She said, with as much diffidence as she could muster, "I saw Alvah in the yard this morning. He doesn't often pay us a visit…"

"Guess he heard I was here for a few days and wanted to say hello. We were schoolmates in Elizabethtown, back a ways. He has relatives in Charlotte nearby the mill." George stood and stretched, signaling he was ready for bed. Janine carried their teacups to the kitchen.

So, that was that, Myrna supposed. And it was, until the

next morning when Myrna and George went walking together by the river. As Marion called it, their family gossip stroll.

It was amazing how the years rolled away with their steps. As children they'd hardly been contemporaries. George was eight years older, and had definitely been the big brother. Thanks to him and Marion, Myrna had known her numbers and read at an early age. Myrna told him about her reading session with Jane. "Do you remember that book *The Children of the New Forest?* I read some of it to Jane yesterday. Actually, I'd been going to join you in the yard with Alvah, but Jane can be very persistent."

"She sure is," they both chuckled. After a moment, George said, "You know, I wanted to mention last night how admiringly Alvah speaks about you. But I wasn't sure how to frame it. I mean, he told about this incident where you bested a rogue guide by outshooting him. Clearly he was in awe of that. The thing is, Pa was proud, but slightly uncomfortable when he told the story…and Ma, well she has visions of you as a proper homemaker. So, I held my tongue." George shot her a conspiratorial look. "You know, I think Alvah might be sweet on you."

Myrna snorted. "Maybe as part of a hunting party." But then she relented. "Well, truthfully, I did enjoy having him there to see me win the competition. He has a worthy firearm he let me borrow, too"

George pierced her with another look. "I suppose sooner or later you'll be wanting to consider a beau and marriage. Though, I'll havta say there are slim pickings hereabouts." His words trailed off.

Myra abruptly sat on the boulder at the side of the trail and George took a seat beside her. She thought for a long moment. "I hear what you're saying, George, but I simply don't seem ready for that kind of life. I like teaching well enough, but I don't fancy having children of my own. I wish teaching paid better, so's I might be more independent. I like being in the woods guiding...and I'm best at that. So far, Pa seems to value my abilities. Nevertheless, I'm totally dependent on him for those jobs...and Marion is so disapproving of the idea of a lady guide that he might stop including me." Myrna stopped with a sigh. She was surprised to feel tears welling.

George looked at his sister. "I'm sorry, Myrna." He handed her a well pressed handkerchief.

"No need to be sorry. Somebody needed to bring up these things. It might as well be you," she said ruefully.

They sat, arm to arm, for a good while. George spoke first. He realized his brotherly banter had provoked deep feelings. Trying to make amends, he started, "You know, Myrna, when I offered to run the mill for Pa, I wasn't sure I'd like the work—or that I'd be any good at it. But I saw Pa wanted to spend time here. It seemed the right thing for me to do—and it turns out I'm pretty good at it. Besides, I met Janine in Charlotte—she's a fine wife. Now, I know your situation is different. And I'm sorry I treated it so lightly. But sometimes you have to make decisions you're not sure about." He saw Myrna's doubtful look. He continued. "I'm not going to placate you with chicken feathers. I do promise I'll think more about what you said before I offer any advice."

Myrna felt relieved that George seemed to have understood her predicament, though she was skeptical about finding any solution. She was sure of one thing though, she could count on George to take her thoughts seriously, and that was no small thing.

Having spoken to George about her innermost worries, and having gotten his considered opinion, lightened the mood as they continued their walk. Myrna told George more about her teaching experiences at the Browns' and he let her in on his thoughts about expanding the mill. When the trail took them to a bend in the river, she showed him a tree stand she'd built on a wooded knoll. Inevitably, their talk turned again to Pa's guiding business.

"I'd say it's all going very well," Myrna said. "I know he mentioned our big trip being planned with Bill Stillman next summer. I got to go on the maiden scout, as you know." Myrna smiled, remembering. "It was quite the adventure. Pa was in his element there. Stillman has some woods skills, too. Of course, that's the upcoming trip I'm fretting about—afraid I won't be included." Myrna felt she could speak freely to her brother now.

George looked worried. "I've been wondering about Pa's good health," he said. "I've seen him wince and favor his right side now and again. He looks a bit tired, too. Have you noticed?"

Myrna looked thoughtful. "Yes, I have noted him favoring his right side, at times. He says Doc Redfield calls it dyspepsia. You know, stomach upset. I'll let you know if he seems worse."

George patted her shoulder. "I appreciate you watching out for Ma and Pa."

The two returned from their walk. George sat in the parlor with his father and Jane, while Myrna went to the kitchen to help Marion and Janine. Grandpa Sam was enjoying reading to Jane, who sat snuggled on his lap.

Later, after dinner, and a leisurely time talking by the parlor hearth, Myrna rose to help Janine gather Jane's books and scattered items. They were packing their belongings in preparation for leaving the next morning, Myrna realized that she would truly miss George and his family when they left.

Even young Jane had managed to insinuate herself into Myrna's affections, enough so that she decided to give her the pretty embroidered handkerchief from Amelie. She hesitated a moment, thinking about Amelie—how generous she had been. Also she'd thought originally to gift Marion with it, hadn't she? But when she saw how Jane admired it, she knew it had been a good decision.

"You are the very best aunt!" Jane exclaimed, hugging Myrna. "I hope you can visit us soon."

- CHAPTER 5 -
Stillman's Idea

Stillman awoke instantly. It had been a dream, he thought. But pulling back the wisps of it was like watching a rainbow dissolve in the sun. He closed his eyes to think. Yes, Myrna had been there, naked at the end of his fish line, laughing and arching her back as she exited from the lake in a high leap, then quickly submerged to the bottom. In the receding vision he had reeled with exacting strength; a supple trout landing in his creel. But was that it? Could he bring more images to his awake state? He envisioned the crest of the azure water, green foliage and rippling fish were intensely saturated with color. He was tempted to bring out his paints and easel. He realized momentarily that his pole was up, and snorted a laugh!

Once he finished his morning wash-up, and had made a strong cup of breakfast tea, his day took focus. It was October. He still felt a chill. And was glad, Bridget, his housekeeper, had stoked the fire.

It really was not so odd that Myrna had appeared in a dream, he thought. After all, it was this evening that he would present his proposed Adirondack adventure to his Boston friends at the Saturday Club. His plan for the challenging outing had crystallized since his latest explorations with the Duffneys. He knew Waldo was keen on the trip, as was James Lowell and John Holmes. Lowell had already been trekking with him in the Adirondacks and was quite taken with the restorative effect it had had upon him——

and he was brilliant in his use of descriptive words. Lowell was renowned as a poet, and a gifted wordsmith. Others also liked the idea of it. But would they be willing to make what was, admittedly, an arduous trip? He hoped his words would suffice in reflecting all he saw and felt in that secluded place. Follansbee Pond—the canoe trip through the breathing dappled greenery was an unparalleled experience. They would feel transported to a more natural, purer, time at the pond. Was not that the experience they all sought?

Instinctively, he turned to his journal and jotted some fresh notes. Tonight, perhaps he would read to them from his journal—his musings about the place, or show them sketches of the shelter that he and Sam had constructed. After all, these men were Transcendentalists. They were keen to espouse on their thoughts about man and nature. Waldo, in particular, had captured the Country's imagination in his writings on the subject. Lowell and Holmes were well spoken on these topics, too. At last, Bill set aside his journal and put on a worsted jacket. It was time to leave for the Saturday Club—that exclusive gathering of Boston's most esteemed intellectuals.

Walking in the crisp air through Cambridge always settled his thoughts. As he passed the brick walls of Harvard Yard, there were students assembled. One of their fellows was excitedly orating on the need to abolish slavery. It seemed some in the crowd planned to march to the State House with petitions. Stillman stood by for a while to watch. He did not disagree with their sentiments. In fact, he'd call himself an abolitionist. The quandary is, he thought, what manner of action should I take? writing, speaking, or fighting were possibilities, he supposed. In spite of watching the incipient fray, he felt removed from the issues. The only time, of late, his blood had stirred in empathy for African persons was around the campfire with the Duffneys. The way Sam spoke about his black neighbors as resourceful farmers and friends—fine friends who deserved support—had cast the problems in human terms. In those moments Stillman's embers of conscience flickered. Yet, life made him wary of premature actions. He knew that when he became clear in his thinking he would do *something*. That much was inevitable.

He'd been fascinated by Myrna's description of her students in school at the Brown settlement, mostly black and a few white. Her fond ease with parents and children was evident. She chided him for his characterizations of the settlers as former slaves, saying, in truth, most of the tenant farmers were never slaves, and had come from cities where they had other professions. Their intent on going north was to take advantage of free land and an opportunity to try farming. Myrna said that she suspected a few were there to avoid the sense of turbulence in the cities—and fear of being targets of pro-slavery violence or capture. In response, he'd told her of incidences of that very kind of behavior in Boston. They agreed that there had been some nasty business in cities, even in the north.

In musing, Stillman thought that without a doubt, he loved the woods. It felt peaceful in the North Country. If it was not for the fierce winters, he might even consider living in a place like Elizabethtown. But, then again, he did value consorting with learned and accomplished individuals, and enjoyed the concomitant institutions they established. He wrapped his scarf higher against the wind. He was young enough to embrace many experiences yet.

When Stillman arrived at the Club meeting room, Waldo Emerson was already holding sway on transcendental ideology. He cordially smiled, nodding to Stillman. "Come sit here, Bill" he said. There was an empty seat to Waldo's right.

There was good attendance tonight of the Saturday Club. As usual, it took a while for the assemblage to settle.

Waldo and Oliver Holmes sparred on political themes. Several had comments about the ruckus in Harvard Yard, causing Emerson to remind the others that it is important to keep an independent mind in the midst of a crowd. Stillman thought it a contrary comment on his part, much as Waldo espoused the antislavery credo. But then again, Emerson liked to make the group stop and take pause. Holmes gave a chuckle and shook his head. He had a tolerant fondness for Waldo. Lowell complimented Holmes for giving the suggestion of a title for their new literary magazine, "The Atlantic Monthly". He then turned to Bill saying he hoped it would attract as much positive attention as Bill's graphic art magazine, "The Crayon".

Stillman tried to take these comments in a favorable light, as Lowell would be the last to cast an unkind barb. Yet, it felt uncomfortable. The Crayon, in fact, was behind its publishing schedule and wasn't making the expected profit. Surely, there were some at the table who already gleaned as much. Lowell was such a close and dear friend that the brief flush of embarrassment Bill felt was fleeting. Bill soon realized that he might indeed be suffering from a head cold. However, he persevered with his presentation about his latest excursion to the Adirondacks. Once he began to describe his adventure in the Saranac's, and showed the group sketches of the magnificent shelter and scenery around Follansbee Pond, he felt spirited. His proposal that they mount an expedition to Follansbee Pond the following summer—as a group— was met with a chorus of approval. The group grew animated and asked questions about the overland trip from Boston, what kind of inns they'd stay at, the nature of the paddle on the rivers, would they hunt and fish, and what could they expect of the guides, and so on. Henry Thoreau wondered about the dangers they might encounter; Louis Agassiz and John Holmes talked about the possibility of collecting samples of plants and fauna. As an aside, Waldo asked Bill about John

Brown and his nearby settlement. He seemed pleased to know that the lead guide was a friend of the Browns. By evening's end, it was clear that a core group was planning on the Adirondack adventure next summer. They would leave the arrangements to Bill.

Bill continued feeling the effects of an illness. Speaking to Waldo after the meeting, he said "I feared this blasted cold that's coming on was ruining my presentation about the trip. I hope I managed to convey at least some of Follansbee Pond's and the Adirondacks' awesome beauty."

"Yes, you did indeed." Waldo said warmly. "Every great achievement is the victory of a flaming heart," he said.

The next morning, Stillman got on the train for New York City, as planned. By the time he disembarked and took a coach to the residence where he'd be staying, he was feverish. Truly, he was very ill, near collapse. His only solace was that he might be on the shores of Follansbee Pond by the following summer.

- CHAPTER 6 -

Dilemmas

Myrna was free to resume her teaching schedule at the Browns' now that George and his family were gone from the Duffney homestead. The house that had happily expanded to accommodate the larger number was slowly contracting back to its ribs; extra chairs were once more stored in the barn loft; comforters were back in the attic chest and the two table-leaf extensions stored in the back pantry. It seemed the house had exhaled a measure of its liveliness.

Myrna could see that Marion was most affected by the absence of George and Janie. But Myrna missed George, too. This particular visit had been a milestone of sorts for them. Myrna realized that in spite of the age gap she and George were finally adults on equal footing. She fondly looked back on their serious talk by the river. George had been attentive in listening to her dilemma about future prospects. And he'd shared some quandaries about his own life decisions. It felt good to know he might be willing, up ahead, to hear any personal ideas she had, if need be. She was so used to going alone, within herself, that she'd forgotten about the possibility of outside support. Of course, it was true that Pa and Marion wanted the best for her…but, 'the best' was so tangled with their expectations for her. And then there was the fact that neither of them could quite get comfortable with Myrna's ideas for a future.

She was thinking about all these things as she rode Star to the Browns'. She'd promised Belle that she would stay after classes to review lessons. Maybe they'd find time for a walk and talk. Myrna looked forward to some simple conversation with a friend.

This morning one of the older youngsters asked if they could try singing and playing music at the end of their studies. Myrna looked to Belle for help. She said to the boy, Phillip, "I think that's a fine idea. The problem is that my musical talents are limited, though surely we can sing some songs." There was an old piano along the back wall of the one room schoolhouse, but neither Myrna nor Belle played.

"I've heard Mr. Epps play tunes on his banjo. Could we maybe ask him?" Phillip said. Belle told them that she would check at lunch time with Mr. Epps. Several children clapped their hands. Myrna cautioned them that all the reading and math would be completed first, and that there was no telling if Mr. Epps would agree. Myrna and Belle allowed a conspirators' smile between them. Phillip was a quick-witted boy who easily grew restless. And he was impatient with the younger or uninterested students. Belle had initiated a plan where he was a teacher assistant. Once he had mastered a subject, his job was to teach it to a select few who needed coaxing.

At lunchtime, a quick break really, Belle said, sotto voce to Myrna, that Phillip deserved something in order to maintain his interest in school. Hurriedly she left to find Lyman—Mr. Epps. Also they agreed that if worse came to worst, together they'd try some songs before class dismissal.

Lyman Epps was a kindly sort. Myrna expected that he'd likely be willing to pause at whatever task he'd been doing in order to give the children a treat, and that turned out to be the case. He brought his banjo with him and was also able to plink out tunes on the worn piano. Phillip beamed throughout the musical exercises. Myrna and Belle effusively thanked Lyman at the end of classes. He said that now the harvest was about completed he would try to teach a little music every two weeks. That is, if he wasn't guiding clients. "You know," he paused, "I'll always be grateful for the lessons I got when I lived down Troy way. Once you know some good music you're never lonely." He tipped his hat, "ladies," he smiled cordially, and left.

"I cannot believe how wonderfully well that went!" Belle enthused. "And to think he'll be coming back, too! Also, Myrna, you have such a clear, strong voice." Seeing Myrna's skeptical expression, "No, really." She said.

"Well, I guess we all enjoyed it. A bit of very good luck, I'd say. Your voice is good, too, pure and tinkly."

"Tinkly?" Belle wrinkled her nose. "I'll try for better than that."

They were in the mood for a good walk in the cool mid-afternoon. On the way back they took a path skirting the Browns' farm. They stopped to rest on a large boulder that had a beautiful view of mountains to the south. The curve of grey granite was smooth and comfortable.

They'd exhausted talk about students and plans for lessons. For a while they crunched on the apples Belle had brought for sharing and admired the view of the peaks in the near distance. But Myrna was itching to talk about Belle—that is, about the conversation she had overheard between Pa and Lyman, and the subsequent talk with Pa about Belle being in possible danger. She'd been trying to think of a way to bring Belle to the subject without saying she'd overheard conversations.

"You know, you've never told me much about when you lived in Troy," Myrna prompted. "Surely, it must have been far different from living here in the woods."

"Yes, in some ways it was different. There we have close-by neighbors and can walk to stores and churches. Mama's a seamstress, so the downstairs front room of our house is actually her shop. She has some basic dresses on display there and has a machine that she uses for sewing. Bolts of cloth are on shelves all along the back wall. When I was a young girl I loved to play with the colorful scraps. People are regularly coming and going. Mama does a lot of business. After I finished my schooling, it was thought I'd work with her. And I did for a short while…" Belle paused. "Then she and my father had other thoughts." Belle shrugged and looked at Myrna.

"Other thoughts?" echoed Myrna. "Did they find Troy an unsuitable home?"

"I hesitate to tell you these things, but I do need to talk. The cities in the Hudson Valley, especially those along the river, are heavy with boat traffic. Every day, all kinds of traded goods arrive and all types of people drift along the shores of Troy. This has mostly been a very good thing for local merchants. But the fractious political climate in Albany and Troy is stirring a gale of upheaval. There have been instances where ruffians have come to the city disguised as honest merchants and captured people of my race and sold them to slave traders." Belle grew heated. "They've even taken some freemen who have papers!"

Myrna had read of such things, even though in many ways she was insulated from the reality of these instances. She did not want to appear to Belle as ignorant as she felt. "I did read about one horrible account of this sort of thing in a news periodical. The man who told the story was a musician named Solomon Northrup."

"Exactly!" exclaimed Belle. "Solomon is a friend of my father's. He was spirited away by bounty hunters and enslaved for over ten years. His family had about given up hope of ever knowing what happened to him. It was terrible—terrible all around." Belle shook her head in exasperation. "Solomon has had the courage to record everything that happened in a book—a very good thing," she said with satisfaction.

Myrna thought that, once again, she felt in touch with only the woods and its creatures. She was shielded by the mountains and vast tracts of greenery. How in God's name could she be teaching at the Brown settlement and realize so little of the world? She held her silence for a moment.

Finally she asked Belle, "But, are you in danger? Do you feel frightened…I mean for yourself?"

"No. I can't say that that's really the case. I know, in theory, when I lived down in Troy there *might* have been the possibility someone could grab me while I was unawares, but no one ever tried to harm me. It was just that my parents were fearful—and I am their only child. You could say that they dote on me." Belle continued to twist a lock of her tight curls. "They also were not happy with my choice of a beau. His name is Joachim. He was thinking to ask for my hand, but knew there wasn't a chance Papa would approve—though I'm of an age to consider marrying."

Myrna was curious. "I can't imagine you caring about Joachim if he wasn't acceptable."

"Yes, that is true. The problem was they didn't find his family—more accurately, his father, to be a wholesome sort. It is rumored that Mr. Gant has been dishonest in business. I'm not sure that's true, but it is common knowledge that he's dishonest to his wife," Belle added hesitantly, "Mr. Gant is white. Joachim is mulatto." Perhaps Myrna looked puzzled. "Really, Papa is not ordinarily disapproving of these situations," Belle said.

Myrna knew she was on unfamiliar ground. She was unsure of how to proceed. Belle simply asked for her thoughts.

"My thoughts," she said. "Well, I think you have more drama in your life than I could imagine. I think my life is staid in comparison."

"Staid! Not you, the famous woman guide who can out-shoot most men," exclaimed Belle.

"I'm hardly famous…and I've no intriguing beau trying to court me. However, it's true that I'm a damn good shot with a rifle." This set them both to laughing.

Belle jumped from the boulder where they sat. "Come with me to the Epps' house. I'll show you the cottage where I stay before you set out." They made haste so that Myrna would not have to ride home in the dark.

Myrna had admired the Epps' house, but had never been invited inside. It set back a ways from the road on a rounded knoll. There were two large maple trees framing the path to the front porch of the house, and daylilies bordered the fence surrounding the kitchen garden. Myrna had noted the symmetrical and tidy kitchen gardens, supposing Ann and Belle carefully tended them.

Belle opened the front door and helloed...and then paused. The Epps were apparently elsewhere. Belle gestured to the doorway beyond the main room. "That leads to my room," she said.

Myrna was taken by the attractive hominess of the house. The kitchen was whitewashed, with red stencil work on the wooden floors. There was a very large oak table in the center and tied bundles of drying herbs hung from the ceiling. The room smelled of lavender, sage, and some unidentified leaves. Most peculiarly, the wooden chairs for the table hung on pegs along the wall. Belle told her that she too had thought it odd when first she'd seen it, but it seemed most efficient. Each family member took a chair from the wall peg at dinnertime and then returned it to the wall after the meal. The practicality of it left the table open and unencumbered for the various workday tasks. Also it made sweeping the floor an easy chore. The main room of the house had a fieldstone fireplace at one end. Myrna was interested in the exotic wall pieces that Belle said were African art carvings. The chairs beside the fireplace were roughhewn in the Adirondack style. The wooden sofa in front of the fireplace was filled with colorful patchwork covered pillows. There was a table under the only window in the room. It was a large oblong piece of polished oak standing on bent birch legs covered with white bark. Myrna thought it one of the most beautiful of its kind, and said so. The room as a whole was simple, but elegant.

Belle's room was an addition to the original house. There was a heavy velvet curtain draped across the doorway, separating it from the main room. Upon crossing the threshold beyond the doorway was a wholly different world. Myrna presumed the furniture in this room had been brought from Belle's home in Troy. The pieces were of finely carved Birdseye maple. The plush, earthen-toned rugs were scattered by her posted bed, which was covered with an intricate quilt of flying-geese design in cream and blue shades. The wall over the bed featured an array of hand-colored botanical prints. Belle acknowledged that these were from her own drawings. The corner writing desk and book shelf was partitioned from the room by a silk screen with oriental scenes of trees and water. There were two windows in the room, both set high on the outer wall. The room furnishings were more likely to be found in a city house. Belle offered Myrna the small rocking chair, while she sat cross-legged on the bed quilt. "So, this is where I stay," she said. "My room at home in Troy is on the second level of the house—more like the arrangement of your house. This furniture," Belle gestured, "is from my home, as you no doubt gathered. I appreciate my Papa and his friends bringing it this long way. Still, I'd have rather they'd left some in Troy, so's it would be there when I returned—or, that I might now be free to imagine my home as it was." Belle appeared to study the pattern of her quilt.

"Nonetheless, it is an especially pretty room," Myrna said.

Belle nodded, "As long as we remember I'm somewhat a captive," she said.

Myrna could think of no placating or intelligent reply, so she simply nodded in what she hoped was an understanding response.

On her ride home Myrna reflected on all the events of the day, including Belle's revelation of the dilemmas she faced. Her new friend's life was very complex. She could barely imagine it.

- CHAPTER 7 -
Frozen in Time

Marion stood at the stove stirring oat breakfast porridge. Seeing Myrna, she smiled—then asked if she'd mind gathering the eggs.

Myrna finished that task quickly and then went back outside to bring in some extra firewood. "Brrr...it feels like it could almost snow!" she exclaimed. She couldn't help but think of the benefit a coating of snow was to tracking game. Hopefully, she and Pa would get a chance to hunt sometime this week. Now that November was near, classes were reduced to twice a week, giving students and teachers more time for winter chores.

No sooner were they seated at breakfast, when there was a knock at the door. Sam clattered his chair back on the floorboards, and rose from table.

"Alvah," he said, opening the door. "Come sit down—you're just in time for Marion's special porridge." Marion waved her hand dismissively, reaching for another blue bowl. Alvah seemed happy to join them after first politely saying not to "bother."

They talked aimlessly a bit about George's recent visit and the weather. Marion kept filling their coffee cups and ladling oatmeal. Myrna quietly observed and listened. Apparently, Alvah was hoping Pa would be free that day to scout the area beyond their meadow and across the stream that flowed below it. He'd heard there was a large herd of deer that may have decided to bed for the winter in that area.

"Now, I haven't scouted back in there this year," Pa said, "partially because I'm not clear on the property boundaries...and, of course, I harvest enough around here. But, I see no harm in exploring the territory—looks to be a good day for it, weather-wise." He glanced at Marion and rose from the table.

Myrna sat at table staring into her half-cup of coffee, thinking that her hopes for a hunt with Pa this week would now surely be dismissed. She was startled when Alvah asked if she would be joining them. She saw a quick flicker between Pa and Marion. Pa said she might as well come along if she hadn't other chores.

Myrna quickly cleared the breakfast leavings. "Just give me a moment to change into my hunting clothes," she said, rushing up the staircase. She quickly grabbed the clothes on a hook in the closet. The pants were of good quality worsted and fit her well. The shirts and red checked woolen jacket were a bit large, but that was fine with Myrna; she liked the roominess for hiking. Since it would be chilly outside, she pulled on a woolen cap. But, then she remembered Belle saying how unflattering it was, and, when pressed, had said it highlighted her beak and close-set eyes. In the end, Myrna put the hat in her pack, laughing at herself. She also combed her curly hair, her best feature.

Pa was stuffing apples and cheese in his knapsack when she joined them in the kitchen. Marion couldn't help a brief look of distress in seeing her only daughter dressed like a boy. Myrna wondered that Marion never seemed to accept the logic of dressing to meet the task. It was damned irritating, she thought. At least Alvah seemed happy that they'd be a threesome.

Once they closed the kitchen door on Marion and geared-up for day's adventure, Myrna felt back in her element. She liked to travel light; her knapsack contained a change of shirt, canteen, venison jerky, black powder, and, of course, her woolen cap. Her Hawkins rifle was slung cross-strapped over her shoulder. She took pride in keeping her favorite firearm well-oiled and polished. She noticed Alvah looking at it. It was a very nice piece. He joked if that was the one she'd have preferred using in the competition at Martin's hotel, making her escapade sound like a major event. She smiled and nodded affirmatively. She noticed that Pa looked relaxed about the whole thing. Maybe he was beginning to be comfortable with her talents. She thought, nevertheless, he probably wouldn't have included her today if Alvah hadn't asked. But it felt like some kind of progress.

For his part, Sam felt good about the day, so far. It was unusual for Alvah to spontaneously drop by. He supposed that Alvah's visit with George a few weeks back made him feel comfortable again with the household—that and as a youngster he and George spent hours at the house on their various projects. Sam had had a brief cordial acquaintance with Alvah's father, who was ailing for a few years before succumbing to consumption. It was good of Alvah to take account of Myrna today. Sometimes it was hard to know what to do with Myrna in these situations, he thought.

It seemed they reached the stream beyond the hills in no time. The water was high and swift due to heavy rains over the week, making crossing it a challenge. Ordinarily, getting wet would not be a problem. But it was chilly and windy, which could lead to uncomfortable or even dire consequences. Myrna crossed first, before she could lose confidence. Sam and Alvah followed the crossing she'd chosen. "Whew!" Sam exclaimed, "That one isn't usually so tricky."

It was still another hour or so to where Alvah speculated there'd be a large deer yard. They tried to cut a rough trail through the densest brush and Sam used a compass for the major markings. To a one, they used the position of the sun to get their bearing; its light was cool and pale now. If the area showed promise, they'd come back another day to blaze the trail. They proceeded at a fast, but enjoyable pace in order to make best use of the day. Myrna noted some interesting mushrooms, but didn't stop to gather them. It was quiet except for their footfall and breathing.

Alvah, at this point leading, suddenly stopped. "You hear it?" They all heard the thrashing in the brush to the west. The noise continued. There were no animal calls to the commotion. Cautiously, they continued toward the sound. It was a young doe, tangled in what appeared to be the remains of an old wooden fence. She was desperate to get freed. Instinctively, Myrna approached to calm the now quivering animal, to some good effect. She kneeled near the doe to assess its predicament. Alvah grasped the snarled wood in order to loosen it, while Myrna stroked and tried to hold the animal's leg. The doe bounded free, but in the process gave a sharp kick to Myrna's forearm, tearing her coat and breaking the skin. She fell back, grimacing in pain, blood running down her arm.

"Ugh, this really smarts," she winced. Alvah was quick to search in his pack for a suitable bandage.

He sat on the ground beside her and began to apply his remedies. First, he poured whiskey generously over the cut part and then wrapped and tied her arm with clean muslin. They decided her arm was bruised, but not broken.

In the process, Alvah sat close to Myrna and held her arm elevated across his knee. "This will help stanch the bleeding," he said.

Myrna quietly marveled at Alvah's gentleness. His hands were strong and warm. She was secretly chiding herself for enjoying his touch when Pa said, "Well, you seem no the worse for it. We might as well rest here and have some lunch." He began rummaging in his pack for food.

Meanwhile, Myrna looked directly into Alvah's eyes and thanked him for his ministrations. For a few seconds their eyes held—faces close together. Myrna dropped her gaze first, but she didn't move her body from the pleasant sensation of his touch.

Both Pa and Alvah fussed over her at lunch, Pa saying he was glad the injury wasn't worse; Alvah saying he was glad he'd been prepared to help.

Myrna said, "I'm glad we managed to free the doe... she was so scared." Then, at the thought of Alvah sitting so close to her, Myrna felt her cheeks color. Damn it all to hell! What's wrong with me, she thought.

"Those young does can be high spirited alright," commented Alvah.

Sam wondered at the liberal use of whiskey over a cut. He said he usually used just water to wash off the dirt, unless there was deepness to it. Alvah talked about something called antisepsis. "Also, my Gramma always said whiskey on a cut curbed infection. Turns out she was ahead of her time."

Sam was puzzled by finding a fence this far into the woods, albeit roughhewn. He said he didn't know who would have built it, or when. It was possible someone had recently acquired the property, but it was definitely old fencing. He thought he'd ask in town next chance he got...one of those curious things, he supposed.

Their talk then turned to Follansbee Pond and next summer's excursion. They all were enthusiastic about the prospect of it. However, Myrna did not dare to assume she would ever be included in the trip, so she couched her comments accordingly. Alvah was most curious about the Boston men who would comprise the party, especially Stillman. Sam and Myrna both enjoyed telling tales about Stillman. They exaggerated his foibles somewhat but, in the end, credited him with being a good woodsman. Sam said, "I think you'll like his company well enough, Alvah."

It turned out the deeryard they were looking for was only another hour away. They saw a lot of deer-sign. The deer were bedded on a rocky side below a steep hillock. They approached downwind so as not to startle them.

There must have been at least fifty of them. It was a marvelous sight. They'd come back another time for harvesting. It was early afternoon, but the days were short. There was no point risking getting lost in unfamiliar territory. Going back they managed to skirt the turbulent creek at a narrower crossing upstream. Alvah and Myrna each shot a turkey on the way home. It had been a very satisfying day.

As he was leaving their kitchen, Alvah shook Sam's hand and bowed slightly to Myrna. They all agreed it had been a worthwhile scout.

- CHAPTER 8 -
Trip to Keene

Neither Myrna nor Belle were regular churchgoers. In Myrna's case, it was mostly lack of proximity to St Mary's, the nearest Catholic Church. Her mother, Marion, had attended services there when she lived in Irishtown. She sometimes said she missed being active in the women's blessings society. However, encouraging church activities on Myrna was yet another battle Marion had surrendered.

Belle said she had attended the Baptist Church in Troy. But now that she was with the Browns she simply went to the family sermons and prayer meetings.

Today was a special occasion for Belle and Myrna and some of the North Elba residents. Lyman and his son were presenting a music program at the Calvary Methodist Church in Keene. It was a special Saturday Harvest service; not the traditional somber Sunday service—or so they hoped. Lunch would be served at the nearby Grave's Hotel. And there was speculation that there would be more music and even dancing at the hotel—that is, if the Methodists didn't object. It was an event that both women had looked forward to all week.

It was barely daylight. The Epps' wagon was full by the time it reached the Duffney homestead. Mary Brown and Ann Epps sat in the back with an assortment of people from the settlement. Belle, Phillip, and Lyman Jr. hopped off the wagon and joined the Duffneys in their wagon. Ann waved to Marion. The two wagons would travel in tandem to the church. They moved slowly on the corduroy road due to the heavy loads. It was early morning and cold. Steam rose off the horses and puffs of breath circled their noses. They spread lap robes and shared shawls, but it seemed, altogether, a festive occasion. It was Saturday morning, in deference to the Methodists who were severe in their observations at Sunday services.

Myrna reckoned it had taken several hours to reach the church in Keene. It would have been faster on horseback. Nevertheless, it was fun traveling piled together in the wagon. Marion and Ann had made molasses biscuits and apple bread for the trip, which served them all well. Phillip said Lyman had let him practice some hymns in preparation for the event, but he felt shy about singing before a congregation of strangers. Both Myrna and Belle coaxed him to give it a try. At their urging he sang the hymn *Rock of Ages* ... On the third try, he did not hesitate and sang with assurance. He beamed when Marion complimented him, saying his pitch and tone were perfect.

Belle and Myrna took the youngsters aside in the churchyard before entering the building. They straightened jackets and wiped a few faces, admonishing each one to remember to sit quietly with hands folded during the preacher's homily. Phillip scowled. "We know what to do," he said. Belle cocked her head. "Did I ask for comments?" she replied sternly. Lyman intervened, lining the boys in a row before proceeding along the walk to the front door.

Myrna and Belle took a moment before leading the two young girls, Hannah and Suzanna, a few paces behind. They noted softly to each other that Keene looked a bit forlorn under the grey skies. Some of the town women who spoke to them, by way of introductions, were clearly in their best garments, others entering the church seemed downcast and looked a bit shabby. Belle whispered. "I hope our luncheon at the hotel will be adequate. The main street has a meager look about it."

Myrna nodded. "Let's hope for the best," she said.

As Myrna expected, the service was insufferably long. It was a wonder to her that their young charges were managing to remain quietly seated and well behaved, when she could feel her own lids heavy and her restless toes wiggling. It seemed the whole throng sighed and exhaled together when the preacher announced that the program of liturgical music would commence. The music resounded off the walls of the church. Lyman and his son sang many selections in a-cappella harmony. A guitar and penny whistle were featured on some tunes. Their closing hymn was *Blow Ye Trumpets Blow*, one of their mentor, John Brown's, favorites. Phillip proudly sang along with them on that one. The mood of the congregation was greatly buoyed by the music. It was understood that at close of service, all would be welcome at Graves Hotel for lunch.

A number of folks came up to the Epps to thank them for the beautiful music. And they modestly received the accolades. Belle thought they might take the young people for a quick walk to dispel any restlessness. But Phillip spoke-up politely and said he preferred to go straightaway to lunch. Then grinning he added "I'd hate for Miss Belle and Miss Myrna to only be getting the lunch leavings."

The hotel wasn't much compared to Martin's, Myrna confided to Belle. Still, the dining room with its dark wood and low ceilings was cozy, and a robust fireplace exuded warmth. Mr. Graves, a large man whose top hairs grazed the rafters, was outgoing and friendly. The place had a warm cheery feel in contrast to the sparsely heated church. Mr. Graves shook Lyman's hand and said he was pleased he was able to get away to hear the music portion of the service. "Listening to that hell and damnation part gets me nerved up," he chortled.

There was a long wooden table along the back wall of the dining room set buffet-style with casseroles of baked beans, pumpkin custards and apple puddings. There was a large platter of baked ham and a variety of breads. Marion and Ann had each brought extra loaves of apple and molasses breads that they contributed to the meal. Jugs of cider were set out for drink.

The Methodists were known to advocate temperance, so for the most part liquor was to be avoided. However, Mr. Graves was quick to say he was not a Methodist. He said he was an old-fashioned Irish Catholic from St. Patrick's in Port Henry, brought up on papal wine. "Besides," he said, "Don't make sense for a tavern keeper to be of the temperance persuasion, does it."

There were some long benches and stools scattered about and a few smaller tables to sit at. Marion and Ann made a point to mingle with the church women. Myrna and Belle followed suit. Of course, Mary Brown couldn't avoid her celebrity. She sat reserved and friendly in a comfortable chair by the fireplace. Ann said to Marion, that getting out more would do Mrs. Brown a world of good.

The large fieldstone fireplace with a polished split-log mantle was at the opposite end of the room, where a crackling fire had been laid. The group from North Elba felt warmly received by the town folk gathered there. Myrna realized from their conversation that at least some were abolitionists, including the preacher, Mr. Bartholomew. Belle had whispered earlier that the Graves' homestead was one of the lesser known stops on the Underground Railroad. Later in their talks together, Myrna realized that several families known to her were involved in sheltering escaped slaves on their way to Canada. As Belle noted cynically, but not unkindly, that was the easy part. Mustering the courage and energy to overturn the Fugitive Slave Act would be much harder.

Since they more usually traveled to Elizabethtown (known to all as E-Town) for supplies, the women and men seated with them were not familiar to Myrna or Marion and presumably not to Mary or Ann either. On the other hand, Sam and Lyman seemed to know some of the men, presumably from guiding activities or meetings in E-town.

After the hearty meal and animated conversation, there was a sense of relaxation. It did not take much coaxing to get Lyman and his son to agree to play some tunes. As luck would have it, there was a fiddle player in residence who happily agreed to join them. Through the doorway to the tavern proper, Myrna saw Alvah smile and walk towards her. "May I sit here?" he asked, pulling a stool near her. Belle, sitting to her other side, subtly kicked Myrna with her dainty foot. Introductions were made. Belle said, boldly "Myrna tells me you are one of the most accomplished guides in the North Country."

Alvah laughed. "Her sayin' that would be quite the compliment." The beginning music quieted their conversation.

It was enjoyable sitting and listening to the music. And, Myrna thought, one of its supreme pleasures was that it negated the need for aimless conversation. So, she simply tapped her feet and occasionally smiled at the musicians. After playing a few staid numbers, there were requests for lively fast-paced tunes. Some town folk rose to their feet and began a dance while those seated clapped their hands in time to the music. A few of the more dignified Methodists sat quietly, but didn't leave the gathering. A small group organized a reel. Alvah nudged Myrna at a tuning break. "Shall we give it a try?" he said.

"Oh, I don't know how...really," she stammered. Belle, surreptitiously, gave her a good pinch to her thigh, causing her to rise to her feet.

"Don't worry," Alvah said, "This is the kind of group dance where they show you all the steps before it begins."

True enough, it seemed. Myrna quickly lost her self-consciousness in responding to the music. The spins made her feel a little dizzy, she confided to Alvah. "Oh, the remedy for that is to keep a steady look into my eyes during the swings. Focusing like that stops the room spinning feeling."

"I'll be darned. That works!"

Alvah smiled, and in a daring moment, pulled her closer on the next swing. At that, Myrna felt a bit giddy, but had no words of complaint. Thank goodness, she could claim her rising color on the dance exertions. She glanced at Belle, who was dancing sedately with Phillip's widowed father. As was the general custom, the folks from the Brown settlement tended to gather together at separate tables. However, Belle and the Epps mingled more freely, Lyman being a musician and Belle a cosmopolitan beauty.

In preparation for leaving, Belle and Myrna walked the girls to the outhouse back of the hotel. As she returned, she spotted the obstreperous guide she had bested at Martin's sitting in the tavern. He jumped to his feet and walked toward her, but was cut off by Alvah. "Aw, come on Al, I wuz just going to ask the pretty sharpshooter for a dance," he said. Myrna nodded politely and turned on her heels. She then gathered the youngsters to load the wagons for the trip home. She wondered what Alvah was saying to Roger, the troublesome guide. It took them awhile for Lyman, Pastor Bartholomew, Mr. Graves, Sam, and the rest to say their mutual thanks and good-byes.

As Belle, Myrna, and Sam set about the task of loading the wagons, counting noses and getting everyone comfortably settled, Alvah appeared. Addressing Sam, he said, "I was wondering if you might like to continue our hunting explorations next week sometime."

"Sure, Tuesday is good for me…long as the weather is decent. Should we include Myrna?" Sam remained straight-faced.

"Don't see why not." Alvah smiled and tipped his hat to Marion, somehow including Myrna and Belle in the gesture. "Ladies," he said.

As they pulled away from the hotel, Ann Epps said she thought that Alvah had lovely manners.

The ride back, as expected, was long and bumpy. When they arrived at the Epps' house, it was agreed that Myrna would stay overnight with Belle. She told Marion that she'd be home by dinner, Sunday.

Once settled in the Epps' home after the long ride, Ann Epps insisted on brewing them a cup of tea. It was a fragrant herbal concoction. Initially, Myrna demurred, thinking Ann looked weary, but holding the steaming cup in her hands felt soothing after riding several hours in the cold. Ann said she was retiring to the bedroom, leaving Belle and Myrna, to their relief, to do likewise. After a quick wash-up, Belle lent Myrna one of her flannel gowns. The room was chilly, but once they lit the coals in the brazier and turned the lamps up, they began to feel comfortable enough under the piled quilts. It had been an exciting day for the women, with some incidents worthy of a private conversation.

"You never said how handsome Alvah is!" exclaimed Belle. She cocked her head and looked thoughtful. "And, I believe he is drawn to you."

"Drawn... How so?"

"Oh, Myrna, don't be so obtuse...drawn in the way of men and women. Surely, you understand." Belle sounded perplexed.

"Yes and no," Myrna countered. "I know most everything in a theoretical way. I've observed...I've read stories. But, I've not had personal experience of the sort." Thinking more, she said "I've probably rebuffed any efforts on Marion's part to talk about these things." Pausing, she added, "When Pa and Marion bring up the subject, it's always in the context of marriage. That is, of finding someone to take me off their concern...and that has not been an appealing thought for me. I know Marion thinks I'm not pretty enough—that, and her dislike of my interest in hunting and fishing, which she calls 'unfeminine'. I'm the worrisome daughter, I guess." Myrna shrugged.

"But, if I may say, you did seem to enjoy dancing with Alvah…I'd say you looked equally drawn to each other. Could that be correct?" Belle's eyes peered wide over the top of her teacup.

Myrna laughed. "Let's talk awhile about you and Joachim, shall we?"

"No, no, no…let us complete one thought at a time. Isn't that what we tell the children in class?"

In some way, Myrna enjoyed this mischievous quality in Belle. She felt free to entertain honest answers. "Let me think" she said. "Yes, I enjoyed dancing with Alvah. It was an unexpected thing. Being near him does elicit new feelings. I've never considered the possibility of him being drawn to me. That is, to me, a novel idea. I've come to accept the fact that I'm not what people call 'pretty'. But I'm comfortable with myself. I feel confident and competent in the woods, and even in the classroom. My assumption would be that Alvah admires me for my woods skills. And one more thing has crossed my mind. I worry that a marriage relationship would limit, rather than expand, my possibilities. Though, truthfully, I'm not sure how I'd proceed in those ways or what exactly are possibilities."

"Let me consider this," Belle said. "First of all, you are very attractive, if not conventionally pretty."

"But, my ugly nose…" interjected Myrna.

"Aquiline, majestic, and your cheekbones are enviable. Then there is your bearing, as a whole; erect, slim, graceful. Let me tell you, you and Alvah looked beautiful dancing together. That other unpleasant fellow in the barroom found you attractive also. As for your general thoughts on marriage, I understand your opinions about that. Now that I'm separated from Joachim, some doubts have crept into my mind. But I expect I'll eventually marry."

Myrna paused a moment. "You do help me see things in a new light, though you may flatter me. Now let's talk about your beau Joachim."

"As I mentioned earlier, he is a good person, and handsome, too. As we had assumed we'd soon be married, I'd allowed for some physical closeness. Not complete, of course...But enough to develop ties," she said, delicately. "I enjoy receiving letters from him, almost weekly. But my current situation does not allow for much freedom, as you know. He is apprenticed to a mason in West Troy, a wonderful opportunity, but one that would make it unlikely for him to be able to travel here. Since I'm forbidden, for the moment, to travel back to Troy, it is unclear what our future might be." Belle sighed. "I do miss city life, but, I'm lucky to, at least, be here in North Elba surround by kind friends and beautiful scenery."

"It is good to hold positive thoughts," Myrna offered. "And it is equally good to be able to share our uncertainties about the future. Parents are not the same as friends," she said. They talked on a bit more, and then Belle rose to add fresh coals to the stove and darkened the lamps. They said goodnight, each turning to opposite sides and arranging the covers around them.

- CHAPTER 9 -
Family Ties

Tuesday's hunting expedition with Alvah and his cousin, Carson, was going well. Clearly, Pa enjoyed Alvah's company, thought Myrna. She was becoming more comfortable, or less self-conscious, around Alvah, too. Talking with Belle had proved helpful. Myrna found that she was more alert now to Alvah's interactions with her. During lunch, when he tossed an apple her way, she neatly caught it, and then playfully tossed it back. A few weeks before, she could imagine herself either missing the catch or mumbling thanks without meeting his eye. She still didn't know what kind of attraction he might have to her, or what the extent was of her feelings. But she did think they genuinely liked each other.

Alvah's cousin, Carson, was a happy-go-lucky sort. Sam seemed to have inklings as to his kinfolk and made polite inquiries about them. Carson said most of them had moved back to Vermont, but he was trying his hand at logging north of E-town. He was light-haired, burley and muscular, and told them he'd just turned sixteen. Carson and Sam each shot a deer, an eight and ten pointer, respectively. After Sam brought down the second buck, they thought to call it a day. It took some time to track and field dress their harvest. The dead weight of the animals was a burden to carry, even when roped to poles with a hunter on each end. Carson, to their amazement, carried his deer for over a mile, slung over his shoulder, before conceding a pole carry would be easier. Alvah and Sam, pole-carried Sam's heavier deer, until Myrna noticed Sam limping. After a short break,

Myrna wordlessly grabbed an end of the pole and marched forward with Alvah. She jokingly said she didn't want to be left out. Sam fussed a bit, but truthfully, was happy to be relieved. The trail from then on was wide and flat, as it had been used for logging in the spring. Carson declared he'd gotten his energy back and, once again, hoisted his deer. After completing their wearying task of getting the carcasses to the main road, Myrna volunteered to run to the barn and fetch a wagon. It seemed she'd run the loop in no time. By the time she returned, the ragged bunch was relaxed under a maple tree, but glad to see her. Sam said, "Today's near perfect huntin' weather. Carson was good luck, mighty helpful, too. Once we get them butchered, they'll keep a good while in the cooler-shed." They each nodded agreement. Myrna told them to hurry along, Marion would have dinner on the table in about an hour. Alvah and Carson slung the deer into the back of the wagon. Carson rode up front with Sam at the reins. Alvah and Myrna sat in back with the carcasses. Along the way back, Alvah caught Myrna's eye. "Miss Myrna, you are one amazing lady," he said.

"Coming from you, that's a real compliment," she parried. For a long moment their eyes held. Then they laughed. Myrna wasn't sure why that was.

THE STATLER HOTEL
AT CORNELL UNIVERSITY

- CHAPTER 10 -
Heartbreak

As Sam, Marion and Myrna were having a cup of tea around the fire later in the week, Sam said he'd like to go on a scouting excursion the next morning. Myrna was surprised that he'd want to venture out so soon after their hunt with Alvah and Carson—that trip had been only three days back. She also worried about his limp. Nevertheless, she always liked being in the woods with Pa. He went to the door and looked out at the sky, saying he thought the weather'ed be good next day. Myrna dutifully laid her pack and fresh hunting clothes on a chair in the kitchen, ready for the next morning. They agreed that there was no reason to rise especially early, as this was to be what Sam termed a leisurely scout. They would have breakfast with Marion before setting out.

When Myrna awoke, she heard Marion downstairs bustling in the kitchen. She hurried with her morning wash-up in order to help with breakfast. Entering the kitchen, she smiled at Marion who was humming a dance tune that Lyman had played at Graves' Hotel. Apparently, Pa was still sleeping. When Myrna asked Marion about the tune, she said she had no idea of the name of it…"It's one of those pieces that just stick in your head," she replied. Myrna liked the tune, she thought Lyman might have the words to it. "Next time I'm at the Epps house I'll ask for the words to the music."

Cautiously, and unexpectedly, Marion asked what she thought of Alvah. At first, Myrna continued peeling apples for the porridge and pretended not to hear. Then she looked up at Marion. "He's alright…actually, I like him. Pa and I think he's excellent in the woods." Seeing Marion wanted to say more, Myrna interjected. "Honestly, Ma, if there's more to tell, I'll let you know." She rarely used the term 'Ma' and saw it pleased Marion.

Breakfast was so pleasant and leisurely, it seemed they'd never get out the door, but they did. It was another crisp, blue sky day. Most of the maple leaves had fallen, but yellow birch leaves still clung tenaciously to branches. They kept a good pace, in spite of whatever physical problem was bothering Sam. After about two hours or so, they came to a pond where some beaver traps were set. Sam said it bothered him to see them so far into the forest. "It's not fair to the creatures when they are set this distant from anyone's property—could cause unnecessary suffering. I doubt these are checked very often." Having said that, he sprung two of the traps. "There!" he said with satisfaction.

After climbing the rocky shoulder of a mountain, Sam said he'd like to take a break before proceeding. They sat in the afternoon sun under a substantial oak tree. Sam took off his pack to look for the lunch items Marion had placed in it. "Marion always packs something tasty," he said. They quietly shared some cheese with cups of cider.

Sam suggested that Myrna go ahead and explore the other side of the mountain. "I'll just poke around this area a bit—meet you back here under the tree."

Myrna was happy to go at her own speed. She liked solitary observations, often making notes in her journal along the way. She knew it was early afternoon and needed to pace herself accordingly. At some point, she judged it to be nearing mid-afternoon, and thought to head back when she heard a gunshot ring in the distance. It explosively ended her reverie. Was it Pa? Was it another hunter? She fairly leapt her way back to the oak clearing. Pa wasn't there.

She called, listening hard. There was a weak sound from the gully. It was Pa, and he was wounded. He was bleeding from his right side and in pain. Apparently, he had tripped going downhill and his gun discharged. Myrna knew that the first thing she needed to do was examine the wound and stanch the bleeding. The second thing would be to keep Pa warm and comfortable while she went for help.

In theory that was fine, but the wound was a deep one. It was getting to be late in the day, and the gully where he lay was damp and inhospitable. Once Myrna had cleaned and applied a compress to the injury, they decided to attempt hiking out. With excruciating difficulty, they managed to walk nearly a mile before Pa's legs began to buckle. Myrna was strong, but Pa was heavy. They were both straining and sweating profusely. They needed to stop moving. Myrna knew they were not too far from a place where they sometimes camped. It was a dry spot backed by a wall of rock shelter, and a stream of fresh water flowed below it. It was a plan, and Pa nodded his assent. Under the circumstance, it was the best of their limited choices. They struggled to it.

Myrna was vexed that it had taken so long to reach their destination. It felt that time had stopped, but the lowering sun told otherwise. She would need to work very fast to make a rudimentary camp before sundown. Pa knew this. He spoke weakly with his suggestions. Myrna piled pine boughs under the rock overhang like they had done other times. She built a fire in the pit they had made at an earlier encampment. She carefully checked his wound, redressed it, and helped him change to a dry shirt. She also changed to a dry garment. She went back to the creek below and got a pot of water to brew some tea. There were still biscuits, apples and cheese for a meal, though hunger had left them. They knew they were there for the night… no matter what. It was a slow realization that they quickly accepted. Once settled and relatively comfortable, Sam wanted to talk. Myrna, at first, was optimistic about the well of energy he summoned. The thought he might die filled her with dread and despair. Perhaps the injury was not as deep as it seemed. Pa asked her to fetch some laudanum from his pack. "Laudanum?" she said.

"Yes, I sometimes take that for the pain in my gut," he said, as a matter of fact. "I've been having a bout of it lately." Myrna noted he took a swig, not bothering to measure it. She wondered if it was pain that had been causing his limp. But, of course, that was irrelevant at the moment. He seemed to want to talk about other times they'd camped out and the successful hunt they'd had a few days earlier. Then he talked about her and George when they were children, about how much he appreciated Marion. He rambled. Myrna let him lead the conversation wherever he wanted to take it. Suddenly, he asked, "Have I been a good father?"

"Of course, Pa! Why do you ask?"

"Well, it's a good thing I've been adequate, cause I might not have time to make amends." He chuckled, asking if there was, by chance, any whiskey in his pack. Myrna fished out a pint flask, her hands shaking. There were tears in her eyes. "Pa, please don't talk this way. You can't leave us," she wailed, realizing what he meant by his words. Pa took her hand and held it to his heart.

"Myrna, I want you to listen to me. It's important to me that you calm down and do so. This is a bad injury I've got here. We've watched other animals die in the woods… we don't give them much chance if it's a gut shot, do we?" He wasn't looking for an answer, and she didn't render one. "I'm thinking, however this thing turns out, I'd like, right now, to tell you some things while I've the chance. First thing, when I expire, you and George will have to help your Ma reach good decisions. I was so pleased to see how well you and George got along his last visit—really, it made me proud of you both. Another important thing is that you make sure the guiding excursion with Stillman and his crew goes just perfect." Myrna tried to interrupt. How could she manage such an endeavor? Sam over-talked her. "You are very capable. I think you will need some assistance getting a guiding project of this scope organized—George and Alvah are certain to help you. I'd hate to see Stillman disappointed...besides, you and Marion will greatly benefit from the considerable income of that venture." He turned towards her. "What do you think?" he asked.

Myrna took a deep, audible breath. "Think? How can I think?" But, she knew Pa expected real answers, so she looked directly through her tears. "You know I'll always do my best for you," she said. Pa squeezed her hand saying, even if worse wasn't to come, it was a great relief to him to have gotten his deepest wishes granted. Then he told her they should feel free to talk of other things—to ask him any questions she might harbor.

She asked him if he thought there was such a thing as an 'afterlife'.

"Jeezus, Myrna! It's a little late for me to cogitate on thoughts like that...but no, no I don't. How about we talk about you...what your plans are for the near future, for instance. I'd be interested in what you think of Stillman and Alvah, too—especially about Alvah." He took another slug of whiskey and adjusted the makeshift pine pillow behind his head. He offered some of the strong amber brew to Myrna, and she decided to join him in a drink. He alternated between the laudanum and whiskey. Sometimes he dropped threads of the conversation or rambled. He said time was not linear; he would always exist in their mutual past—also in her imagination. She told him she understood what he said. At some point, he said that if she were anyone else, he'd ask that she shoot him now to end his painful misery.

"But you know that is too much to ask," she said.

"I do, that," he said, wearily.

Before dawn, they both slept huddled under one spare cover. When Myrna woke, Sam was gone, though he still appeared to be asleep. His hand and cheek was cold. Vainly, she listened for the faintest beat…the lightest breath.

She felt wounded and hollow, knowing she would live through this incident. And then she thought of her mother… how painful this day was going to be for her.

- CHAPTER 11 -
The Aftermath

It had been almost a month since Sam's burial. Truthfully, Myrna had lost all sense of time since she had strapped Sam to a bier crafted of pine branches and brought him through the woods. It was terrible losing Pa, but when she saw the ashen, stricken face of Marion, she knew she'd lost her Ma, too—at least in some indescribable part.

So many people were being kind and caring, but they all seemed to be in another world, while she existed separate in a closed impenetrable fog.

She tried to remember to do her best for Marion, but knew she faltered. Sometimes upon waking in the early hours, they could hear each other sobbing. Many friends and neighbors arrived to take on the homestead chores and bring food. Belle, Ann, Lyman and Mary Brown were constant as a daily presence. Alvah, too, was often at her side. George, heartbroken and crestfallen had arrived and stayed for several weeks. They all avoided asking Myrna directly about the day of Sam's demise. Even Marion held back any questions after Myrna's first accounting of the accident. It seemed too terrible for repeating.

Then there was the day that Myrna saw a facsimile of herself in the upstairs hallway mirror. The image was not slim, but gaunt. The eyes were rimmed with darkened circles set in a pallid face. Her unbrushed hair was tangled. Grief surrounded her visage. She wondered if she would always look forlorn.

One day, several weeks after Sam's burial, Belle and Ann were on their way to the Duffneys' home. It was Ann's idea that Belle and Alvah walk to Sam's grave with Myrna and George. Ann had told Belle she thought it might help them. "Saying prayers can help even if you don't usually pay it much mind," she said. Belle, nodded. She thought any reason to get Myrna out in the fresh air would be better than seeing her sitting in her darkened room.

Myrna heard them downstairs. She'd freshened a bit and was ready to dress for her walk to the grave. She looked in her closet for a dress, then saw that her hunting clothes had been freshly laundered and folded at the floor of the closet. Yes, she thought, this is what Pa would expect. Once dressed, she realized the clothes hung loose on her slight frame, but it couldn't be helped. She added Pa's tan hunting suspenders to her outfit and brushed her hair.

Alvah was with George in the living room. Belle, Ann and Marion were in the kitchen. The women turned to Myrna as she entered the room. "Ma, would you mind terribly if I walked to…the woods before having tea?" she said. Marion said nothing about her outfit.

It was decided that Marion and Ann would remain home until they returned. Marion preferred solitary visits to Sam's grave—she would visit next morning, she thought.

It was a quiet half mile or so to the grave site, which was in a small clearing in the woods on the Duffney property. They were a somber procession in the cold afternoon air. The sun actually hurt Myrna's eyes. There was a beautifully marbled granite boulder that had been placed at the head of the grave site as a tombstone. Myrna felt compelled to talk. "I'm glad you came with me…" her unused voice caught. "I mean, I'm glad the four of us are here together. The monument rock is beautiful. Pa would have appreciated the natural memorial" She ran her un-mittened hand over the deep vein of marble. It seemed George and Alvah had found and carted the boulder to where it now rested. "Yes, Pa, would be honored, I think." She smiled at George. He put his arm around her. Alvah said, "Sam was one of the finest guides... best of men. I'll miss him, forever." His eyes welled tears.

Belle, not sure if Myrna was a firm believer, suggested they hold hands and say silent prayers. They stood semicircle in this fashion for a while, before walking back to the homestead. Belle pointed to a cardinal, secreted in pine branches ahead of them. "My mom says cardinals carry great spirits," she offered. Myrna felt these kinds of thoughts were comforting, not that she wished to speak aloud about it—that might dispel the magic.

Tea and apple bread were ready when they returned to the house, served in the living room by the fireplace. Marion smiled at Myrna. "The air has done you some good—you don't look so peaked." Ann and Marion returned to the kitchen. They said they would continue their conversation there, leaving the four friends to talk separately.

Initially, the friends tried for lighter talk.

But then Myrna said, unexpectedly, "There are some things I've been thinking that we might as well talk about... things Pa told me. Some of it pertains just to me and George, but I'd like Alvah to hear, as some involves him. Belle is my valued friend, so her wise thoughts are welcome, too." To a one, they all turned expectantly to her.

Myrna carefully tried to convey what Sam had said about Bill Stillman's summer expedition to Follansbee Pond; how he wanted to be sure we wouldn't let Bill down, that good money was in it for them and the rest of the guides, and that, he, Pa, expected the whole thing to be no less than perfect. Sadly, the explanation of Pa's wishes vividly brought back the colors and sound, the weight of Myrna's last day with her Pa. She began to falter and sob with the recollection. George crossed the room and sat next to her. He took her hand. Taking a handkerchief from his pocket and wiping his nose, he said perhaps they might continue later. Myrna shook her head. "No, I want to finish this...it was so important to Pa. Really, I'm fine now."

Belle, sensing they might talk for quite a while, went to the kitchen to join Ann and Marion. She told Marion the gist of the living room discussions. That is, Myrna's thoughts about continuing with Stillman's expedition to Follansbee Pond. Marion looked thoughtful…contemplating. She asked Ann if she'd mind waiting dinner for a while. "Of course not," Ann replied. "These things are difficult… but good."

By the time Belle returned to Myrna and the others they were in the thick of discussion, excited, too. George wondered if it was realistic to carry on without Pa. It was a complex guiding venture that required many details: informing the clients of the particulars, arranging for guides and transportation from Keeseville to Martin's Hotel, buying and packing food and supplies, securing and having ready boats at the landing.

"Really, Myrna, I can't take time from the mill to do this. So how's it going to happen? Surely, you can't manage an expedition on your own." he said, heatedly. Belle sat quietly, glancing from one to the other. She found George's words intimidating—at first.

Myrna was quiet after George's outburst, but she looked resolute. Calmly, she retorted, "I do believe I'll be able to accomplish a worthy expedition." George began to interrupt, "No"…Myrna held up her hands. "Please, hear me out—at the very least. It is true that I will need help. But Pa has already talked with the guides he wants and they're all experienced— looking to get the work, too. I've already scouted the Follansbee area with Pa and Stillman. I've got good maps and notes from that trip. Stillman is comfortable with me. I'm strong, knowledgeable and skilled … Pa did say he thought you and Alvah would give me a hand, though I realize your contribution would be limited." She hoped she wasn't overstating Pa's expectations of her.

George frowned and paced, mulling it over. Myrna was watchfully silent. She felt anxious and desperate—she hadn't thought George would be this resistant. Turning to Alvah, George asked, "What are your thoughts about Myrna's scheme?"

"Myrna's one of the most accomplished woodsmen in these parts. She's been making a name for herself as a sharpshooter this past year. The other guides, the ones Sam picked for the expedition, think she's competent and reserved—kinda lady-like, ya know? Truthfully, I'd as soon scout with her as most anybody. Yep, Sam was proud of her." He beamed at Myrna. "I mean it, too—every word." Alvah's compliments eased the tension. In fact, made them laugh.

George laughed with them. Alvah was in Myrna's corner, no doubt about it. George felt he had ignored the extent of Myrna's maturity. He supposed their age difference would account for it. Now he recollected how serious she was when they talked earlier in the fall.

Regardless of her skills, he wondered what the Boston clientele would be thinking of her role. Would they accept her? Looking to the group, he said, "I'm stymied as to how to proceed."

Marion was hovering in the doorway. Initially, she had approached simply to ask about dinner, but the conversation held her fast.

Quietly, she spoke. "If Sam believed Myrna capable of leading this expedition, then she must be given that chance. And that is my wish, too," she added. Myrna hadn't expected Marion's support; it felt immensely gratifying. Myrna knew it wouldn't be easy, but was determined to succeed.

At that, they all filed into the dining room, where the conversation turned to lighter subjects over their meal. If there were lingering reservations about Myrna's intentions, none were voiced. Emboldened, Myrna decided to move forward on the Follansbee Pond expedition. She knew Pa was a great believer in carpe diem moments.

After dinner, Myrna brought out her notebook so that they could begin planning. In the end, it was decided that Myrna would draft a letter to Bill Stillman, and it would be signed by her and George. The letter would announce the sad news about Sam, and offer the revised plan for leading the esteemed Boston coterie to a camping expedition on Follansbee Pond. Myrna thought the odds were good that he'd accept the camping revisions with grace.

- CHAPTER 12 -
Stillman Reconfigures

New York was chilled by wintery weather. Stillman was sitting in the blue, damask, overstuffed chair in his room. The odious pleurisy that had sat in his chest for over a month now seemed to be clearing. He might even consider a small walk in the afternoon, though the prospect of a jaunt out on the New York City streets in mid-December was not inviting. There was also his obligation to the *Crayon*, a promising literary venture that appeared to be faltering financially. He really needed a heart-to-heart talk with John Durand, his able publishing partner. Perhaps he could walk to the magazine's offices, and perchance find John there. At the very least, that'd give him the opportunity to drop off some edited pieces he'd just reviewed. Admittedly, the combination of his chest congestion, along with the burden of his concerns about the *Crayon*, was leaving him in a heavy funk. Even last evening's highly anticipated attendance at a séance with a famous medium did little to lift his spirits, (He snorted at his feeble joke). If he knew anything about himself, it was clear that sitting in the gloom, brooding, never helped. Yes, he thought, I'll take a cup of tea—then on to the office. He stood, stretched, then went to his desk for Lowell's copy and returned to the chair and sat. He lifted the cozy from the teapot and poured another cup of breakfast tea. He always enjoyed reviewing a piece by Lowell—a fine writer, as well as a good friend.

At first, he did not hear the soft knock—he was that engrossed in reading the manuscript. It was his landlady, Mrs. Sarah Palmer, with the morning mail. She smiled pleasantly, as she handed him two letters, saying she thought his color was better today.

After she left, he sat and opened the unexpected letter from the Duffneys. He re-read the letter three times, and then set it, opened, on the desk. It was terribly sad to think of Sam's death. He had thought of him as his most esteemed North Country friend. After his last visit in the Adirondacks, he'd come to a deeper appreciation of Marion and Myrna, too. On their mutual trek to Follansbee, he felt bonded and comfortable with both Sam and Myrna. They were congenial, well-read, thoughtful types. It was a pleasure to while-away the evening hours around the campfire with them. He also realized on that trip that Myrna was an accomplished hunter and guide. But now, under the new circumstances: What was he to make of George and Myrna's proposal?

The letter to him was drafted by Myrna and her brother, George. In it, they proposed that they'd continue the planning for next summer's, August 1858, expedition to Follansbee Pond. They pointed out that Sam had already lined up a selection of worthy, experienced guides to attend to the clients. Myrna, George, and a fellow mentioned as Alvah, would tend to ordering supplies. If Bill found the plan agreeable, Myrna would send a list of what each client should pack for the trip… Bill smiled at this—so like Myrna, the efficient schoolmarm. He sighed, could this possibly work? What would his Boston friends think of Myrna? Surely, she is capable, but she is a woman. On the other hand, he felt he owed something to his honorable friend, Sam. And then, he imagined the family had counted on the proceeds from the expedition, too. Well, he'd spend some time thinking on his afternoon walk—perhaps discuss it over a drink with Durand this afternoon. He'd write a reply tomorrow morning. He was still feeling the shock of Sam's unexpected death.

The second letter on his desk was from Waldo, he knew from the handwriting on the envelope. Bill figured he might as well open it now. After all, it was bound to bring cheerier news than had the Duffney letter.

It was a typical Emerson letter, full of Boston news and interesting exposition. His recounting of incidents at the Saturday Club made Bill long for the convivial conversation of his comrades. On a positive note, Waldo said he and Lowell were already in high anticipation of their upcoming trip to the Adirondacks. They'd even practiced with rifles out by Thoreau's woods. Waldo also mentioned he'd heard John Brown give a wonderful anti-slavery speech and wondered if they'd be near Brown's settlement on their summer encampment. He said he was curious about Garrit Smith's experimental community. Bill wondered about this, as he often did about Emerson's musings. In the final paragraph of the letter, in his kind, brotherly way, he suggested that Bill not despair over the finances of the *Crayon*, saying that society's views of failure and success were skewed. Bill always felt encouraged by Waldo's words, even if the sentiments were often familiar—a page from Emerson's treatise "Self-Reliance".

Bill carefully folded both letters, and placed them on his desk for a second reading when he returned from his walk. The interrelated contents gave him much to think about. He wrapped a green knit muffler around his neck and buttoned his long tweed coat. At the bottom of the stairs he called to his landlady as he pulled on his deerskin gloves. "Sarah, I'll be dining out tonight…no need to save me a plate."

As Stillman walked along Irving Place, the wind whipped and snow began to swirl. He pulled down his cap and turned up his collar. The air was bracing, but the flow of energy from the crowds almost warmed him. When he arrived at the Crayon's offices, John Durand was at his desk, lamp lit and surrounded by papers—he was in a fine mood. "I hope I'm not interrupting," Bill said, shaking snow off his hat.

"Good God, no! I'm happy to put my pen back in the well. You're looking much, much better…of course, there's nothing like snow and wind biting your cheeks to give some color."

Bill took the liberty of adding more coal to the stove. Within minutes, they settled into their good-natured camaraderie, discussing articles and gossiping about authors. Bill handed Lowell's latest manuscript to John, saying, "I think this piece by James should definitely be in our next issue."

"But, what about the poem by Bryant?"

"Yes, I like that one very much. In fact, I think with that addition we have a full issue. What do you think?" he said deferentially.

John agreed. They decided to spend a few more hours reviewing and editing what they considered final copy and then go someplace for a proper dinner. They were in their element as editors. They worked later than they had anticipated, satisfied that they could get it to the printer by week's end. At the moment, the idea of dinner and drink were uppermost on their minds, and they hurried out into the bracing air towards a nearby pub called Bushnell's.

Once at the tavern, they were pleased to get a table near the blazing hearth. The neighborhood pub was filled with amiable imbibers, many of them acquaintances—writers or publishers. They ordered chops and ale, and settled in for a companionable evening.

Bill told John about the two letters he'd received that morning. John was easy to talk with—a very good listener.

Bill mentioned that Emerson continued to offer encouragement for the *Crayon*, but disturbingly, noted that it might not be a financial success. "The thing is," Bill said, "it is annoying to think our Boston friends are gossiping about us." John made a dismissive gesture, waving his hand. "I'm not so concerned about Waldo, he hasn't even offered to contribute a piece."

Bill nodded his assent. In many ways they were gaining recognition and making good progress. John was intelligent and diligent, factors that boosted Bill's confidence about the magazine. As they parted outside the tavern, it was decided they'd meet at the office again the next day... just to give the issue a final polish.

The trip back to his rooms seemed long. The temperature had dropped and snow was blowing towards him; the wind had shifted, so that he was heading into it. Bill noticed his cough had returned as he bounded up the front stoop. The rush of warm air when he opened the front door was welcome, indeed. Mrs. Palmer greeted him, saying, "Oh, my...your coat is covered with snow, let me hang it by the stove. I'll bring up a fresh pot of tea, too." Bill did not protest her offer. He was grateful when she delivered the tea with some biscuits to his room, and he told her so.

He reread the Duffney letter and decided; yes, he would proceed with the plan offered by Myrna and her brother. He had meant to raise, over dinner with John, some concerns he had about the reconfigured expedition, but, in the end, hadn't. They had spent a good while in discussing Waldo and the Boston crowd. Bill realized that it would never do to cancel the trip at this point. And he did believe Myrna capable of carrying Sam's preparations forward. He continued to sip the tea, and ate another biscuit. He felt positive about his decision. First thing in the morning, he'd draft a letter of accord.

It was barely dawn when he awoke. He had a satisfactory letter of agreement written in less than half an hour. He decided to write a separate letter of condolence, which took him several tries. He would sincerely miss Sam. He posted the two Duffney letters before going to the Crayon's offices. He could respond to Waldo later.

Another week had passed. His recuperation was uneven. It was decided that he'd return to Boston and stay there until, at least, after the Christmas holidays. John had encouraged him to do so. He would leave by train tomorrow morning.

– CHAPTER 13 –

Staying the Course

Marion and Myrna sat at the kitchen table. The two letters from Bill Stillman were spread between them. Marion fingered the condolence letter, tears in her eyes. "He writes of his affection for Sam so beautifully," she said, softly.

Myrna nodded, taking a hankie from her pocket and handing it to Marion. She took a breath and pressed her lips together, willing herself not to cry. She needed to be strong so they could get through the winter. She resolved that her strength would be Marion's comfort. There were chores that needed doing, and she had no intention of expecting the neighboring menfolk to assume them all. As it were, she and her mother had been shown great kindness from the community. She ruefully smiled—Pa had made the barn work look almost effortless. Of course, she'd been there to give him a hand. Thankfully, Pa had stacked two cords of wood before…the incident. Yesterday, Alvah had helped her chop and stack another cord. Myrna thought the worrisome thing was figuring out new routines for getting the various tasks done. Marion would help, but right now it didn't seem fair to make an issue of it.

But then there was the excellent news from Stillman about next summer's guiding expedition. His letter said that he was in total agreement with her plan for proceeding, and that he had full confidence in her abilities as an outstanding guide. He even asked how much money he should send to guarantee the outfitters for the trip and to buy initial supplies. Myrna realized that this expedition meant that she and Marion would have ample savings well into the following year.

Marion looked up from the page. She had begun perusing Stillman's response letter. "Do you think you'll be able to manage this?" Although Marion said this in a neutral tone, Myrna bristled.

"And why shouldn't I succeed with this expedition?" She said archly.

"Oh, dear…I do seem wrong-footed in speaking with you. May I start again?" Marion plowed forward without waiting a response. "I simply meant that it is a rather grand project. I would have made the same comment to Sam, were he sitting across from me." Her sigh was audible. "Myrna, this feels awkward to say, but I want us to try harder to understand each other. Your Pa often acted as a buffer to smooth things…in our new situation I'd like us to learn how to appreciate each other. I do think you are capable. Bill Stillman thinks so, too. I think my question to you was an honest one. George can advise you, but the brunt of the work will be on you."

Myrna was surprised, but not displeased, by her mother's expressiveness. In truth, she knew there'd be obstacles in getting everything in place and then other problems once they got to Follansbee Pond. Actually, in some way it was a relief to hear Marion voice some apprehension.

"You're right Ma. I apologize for assuming the worst. Really, I'm glad for you to acknowledge that this won't be easy for me." She took another handkerchief from her pocket and blew her nose. "But I will make good on this—and we can talk over some of the things that might be problems." Marion had a quizzical look, but Myrna thought they'd said enough about it for the time being. For now, it was enough that they agreed it was an important business venture for them, one that Pa wanted to come to fruition. Myrna walked to the stove and brewed a pot of blackberry herbal tea, Marion's favorite. She set out two of the good, rose-patterned cups and filled them. It felt like a peace offering.

Sunday morning was sunny. Belle had suggested they go hear the visiting minister at the Methodist Society in North Elba, weather permitting. Supposedly, he was a good talker of a liberal bent. Marion agreed to give it a try, though they were still in mourning.

When they arrived at the church, Anne and Lyman were there with Phillip and others from the settlement. Surprisingly, Alvah was there with his mother, Delia, and nephew, Carson. Carson whispered hello to Myrna. Myrna smiled in response. She, Marion, and Belle sat together on a bench towards the back of the simple rectangular room. Up front was a shallow alcove with a large wooden cross. Below the cross was a polished oak table with a pottery jar of fragrant spruce boughs and a bible set beside it. A lectern, presumably with the preacher's notes, was to the right. The large room served as a church for the Methodists and a general assembly room for the community. On this day, Myrna judged there were around sixty people in attendance. She wondered how many of the crowd belonged to this congregation, and what portion of the audience were visitors—like her and Marion.

Marion was dressed in full black mourning regalia. Myrna wore a simple dark-blue worsted dress covered with a matching cape. Belle's outfit was of green wool, a becoming color on her. The new dresses were Belle's idea. Together they had sewn them over a period of weeks. That is, Belle and Marion did most of the work. Myrna could see that the sewing had been a positive distraction for Marion, and Belle enjoyed it, too. She hoped their enthusiasm for stitching dresses would dwindle soon, as she found it to be tedious work. It was December, and the dresses were warm, a good thing.

The Reverend Horace Barnes walked to the lectern, briefly introducing himself. He was a dark-haired, stocky fellow with bright blue, expressive eyes, overhung with bushy brows. His voice boomed and his feet paced restlessly. He was energetic enough to wake any dozers. Reverend Barnes played strong to the receptive audience. His message was simple and compelling: slavery was wrong; God thought it was wrong; anyone with compassion and decency knew it was wrong; and anyone who didn't speak out against it was slacking their duty. He went on in this vein, exciting the crowd (that already agreed with him). Myrna was spellbound by his oration, and glancing Alvah's way, she knew he was fascinated as well.

After the lecture, some church women sat with Marion during the social hour. One woman, Harriet Wells, was a stranger in their midst. She was not local but gave forth freely on subjects of abolition and women's rights. Myrna thought she seemed independent and interesting. Marion was acquainted with many of the other women, but as a married woman had not taken time to socialize with them. Some were widows, slightly older, who meant to provide comfort to Marion. They belonged to a loosely organized auxiliary that met to sew and do good deeds for the community. They delivered food to the homebound or warm clothes to the needy. One of their current projects was to knit mittens for school children. Marion liked to knit, and said she might attend their next session. Myrna could see that her mother was making a game to try to create new experiences for herself. She'd not have expected such determined resolve by Marion, if she'd thought at all about it. But then, who'd bother with such a thought unless faced by unexpected circumstances—like Sam's death.

Alvah gravitated towards Belle and Myrna, a cookie in hand. There was now an offhand ease in their relationship. The threesome was comfortable together. Myrna told Alvah about Stillman's letter. He said he'd stop by on Tuesday to discuss it. "I'd been thinking to pay you and Marion a visit that day, anyway." He smiled, looking at Myrna, before leaving with Carson.

Belle sat on a bench at the back wall, and motioned for Myrna to join her. "I got a letter this week, too" she whispered, "It was from Joachim." Myrna sat next to Belle, leaning her head closer. "Were you pleased with what he said?"

Belle nodded. "I'd like to talk more about it, but not here. I'll come to your house tomorrow, where we can talk freely." Myrna agreed that would be fine. She was curious as to why Belle wished to be secretive—and was also pleased they were able to confide in each other.

That evening, upon returning from their outing, Marion and Myrna sat comfortably by the hearth and reviewed their interesting afternoon at the church. Marion said she had decided to join the ladies social club, even though she didn't expect to become a Methodist. Apparently, the club-women didn't think church membership was absolutely necessary to partake of the knitting circle. Though they'd added that pastor Barnes would probably try to enlist her. Marion was excited to hear that the club was providing the knitting wool, contributed by Henry and Ruth Thompson's farm. Looking out the side window at the light snow falling, she said she hated to think of little children without proper mittens. It was good to see Marion looking to the needs of others.

Late next morning there was a knock at the front door. It was Belle, light snowflakes on her coat and red woolen kerchief. She stomped her feet and brushed snow from her garments before entering the foyer. "Lyman let me take the one-horse sleigh…said it was a fine skill for me to learn while the snow was still light. I think Ann would've come along, but sensed I was bent on 'girl talk' with you." Belle emitted her silvery laugh.

Marion couldn't help but overhear her. "Am I required to stuff cotton in my ears?" she said, good-naturedly. Belle was discomfited and protested, but Marion laughed and assured her that she actually did have some kitchen chores to attend to. Myrna and Belle made themselves comfortable in a far corner of the parlor.

Belle had Joachim's letter in her pocket. She carefully unfolded the envelope and handed it to Myrna, asking her to read it. Myrna, in her deliberate manner, read it twice before responding. The gist of the letter was that Joachim wanted to plan a visit for early spring, though it rambled on about a good deal else. Myrna looked up from the letter. "So?" she said.

Belle sighed. "I'm not sure what to do. If he visits, he'll no doubt press for marriage—and it'd have to be one without my father's approval. Also Lyman would be furious, should he be caught in the middle. Whether we tried to live here or back in Troy, my life would be in turmoil. Truthfully, the closer Joachim reaches towards me, the further I seem to withdraw. And yet, I do love him. Perhaps I'm simply not ready for a marriage commitment. What would you do?" Belle asked Myrna.

Myrna looked perplexed. "I'm a fine one to ask about these kinds of things. In fact, I'm not sure what you are asking." Belle appeared dismayed. "But wait, Belle, I'll tell you my best…just give me a moment to think. Let's sort this out. Hmm…You say you're in love with Joachim, but unsure of when or where you might be willing to be his wife. You are also unwilling to cross your father or mother in this instance—or the Epps for that matter. You think if Joachim comes here you will need to be prepared to accept or reject his marriage proposal." Myrna smiled. "Am I correct, so far? Would it be better if he didn't visit?"

"Yes, you are right in your surmise. From what you glean, you'd think that might be the case. However, if I don't see him, spend time with him, I'll never know if I'm willing to endure the trouble of marrying him. I'm not clear on that. It occurs to me that I also might want to experience a few more years of freedom, too, but I really do want to see him. Still, early spring seems soon…" Belle curled in her shawl on the sofa. She was perplexed.

"Alright, he should visit." Myrna said, decisively. "You could tell him not to come in the spring. Truthfully, it is wet and muddy here in the mountains—not a good time to travel. You could also be forthright about his not getting expectations too high for the visit. Maybe even something about wanting to continue your teaching commitments for another year. Saying these things might dampen his enthusiasm." Myrna peered over the letter. "You know I'm a novice at this, right?"

Belle sighed, "No, honestly, you are being helpful. The spring would be a bad time, all around—wet ground, bugs, school in session, which I truly enjoy teaching with you. Summer is definitely the better season. And even if it's difficult, I should be honest with him about not being ready for a marriage commitment. If I tell him these things, and he still wishes to visit, I'll feel comfortable telling Lyman and Ann that I'm expecting a visitor."

Myrna nodded. She knew these proposed situations never went quite as planned. She also felt concerned about other issues raised in Joachim's letter, especially the political tension surrounding the southern merchants who traded on the Hudson River. Apparently, there'd been more skirmishes between abolitionists and pro-slavery traders in both Troy and Albany. She asked Belle if she thought the political climate was getting more heated in Albany.

"I do not know, Myrna. Certainly, Joachim makes it sound so. Mother didn't mention anything like that in her last letter, but then she doesn't wish to worry me, I suppose. My pa is usually on the road rabble-rousing, so he and I don't get to talk much. But I do miss having conversations with my ma—you know, one-on-one like you and Marion." Myrna nodded.

Belle arose abruptly from the rocker and walked to the window, peering out at the horse and sleigh." She paced a bit more and folded the letter back to her pocket. "I do have a project in mind that will be enjoyable for us, that is, if you'll give it a chance. Just let me explain it before you say no."

Myrna truly had her doubts about quilting, but Belle was excited to try it. She said she had a bag of sewing scraps that her mother had given her. It contained various kinds of materials left over from her seamstress business. The first steps were interesting enough. They would draw an overall design for the face of the quilt. Once they were satisfied with that, they would create a pattern with precise measurements—that being the 'tricky' part, Belle said. Next, they'd select colors and materials from Belle's stash, and maybe from Marion's cloth scraps, and then assemble and cut materials to match the pattern. "Of course," Belle said "We could just cut squares of various colors and stitch them together."

"I think I'd like to start with something simple—like squares. Why don't we decide how big the quilt will be and the size of the squares, and then decide a pattern based on the color of the squares. Does that make sense?" Myrna offered. She was thinking this might, after all, be interesting. She asked Belle to wait while she went upstairs for paper and pen to draw a design of light and dark squares. She returned momentarily and sat in her chair. "Is it a silly question to ask who will use this quilt?"

Belle replied "I think we haven't hatched that part of the project." Jokingly, she said they could make it, and then the first to marry would have the quilt as a wedding gift. Myrna said that was hardly fair, as she hadn't even a beau.

"But, what about Alvah?" teased Belle "You know he has a certain interest. You like to pretend you're merely companion hunting guides, but I see more than that."

"If that were true, he's never said words to indicate it—not that I've a particular interest," Myrna was quick to say.

"Of course he's said nothing!" Belle exclaimed, "You are officially in a period of mourning…an expression of affection would be unseemly."

"I would call that a high piece of speculation, Belle. Besides, I'm beginning to think you and I both have our reservations about marrying. By the way, what did you think about what Harriet Wells said at the Methodist meeting?"

Harriet was an avowed suffragist who talked about having attended the famous meeting of women at Seneca Falls. The meeting had been held in 1848, almost ten years ago, but Harriet said she'd been inspired ever since, and always made it a point to hear lectures by Mrs. Stanton and Miss Anthony whenever possible. She had come to hear Horace Barnes speak because she'd heard he was not only an abolitionist, but also sympathetic to woman's suffrage.

"We don't know Harriet, but she makes sense." Belle answered. "She seems a zealot for women's causes. I would say she's well into her thirties, but acts younger. I understand she makes her home in Vermont. I did notice that Reverend Barnes caught her eye a few times. I wonder where she's staying."

Marion came into the parlor. "Oh, lordy! I think that Wells woman is a crackpot," she said. "And I do believe she's married. I hear she leaves her poor husband back in Rochester, or wherever, while she goes traipsing around and spouting words about women's rights." Marion sensed they were done with private gossip and decided to join them.

"But do you agree with some things she said?" Myrna asked, wondering just what her mother's opinions were.

"Truthfully? Yes, I believe that someday women will be able to vote. Only that Wells woman is so blatant and outspoken...not a person I'd feel comfortable standing behind." She noticed that Myrna and Belle had paper and pens before them and was curious about what they were writing. Upon hearing they were planning a quilt, she suggested they use the kitchen table. "That sounds like a grand winter project," she said with some satisfaction. "I have some remnants of materials if you'd care to look through them."

Belle and Myrna both said they'd like to pick through the scraps later in the week. They agreed to pursue the quilt project. Then, Belle said her goodbyes, saying it was time she take the sleigh home. Marion peered out the doorway at the conveyance. "That sleigh is perfect for one or two passengers," she said. "We should look into getting one."

Tuesday, after morning chores, Myrna mentioned to Marion that she thought Alvah might be stopping by to talk about next summer's guiding trip. Marion said she was glad that they were able to get the plans for the trip sorted out. Myrna set a notebook on the dining table. She was listing all that she needed to do before August. Actually, she'd have to put everything in order well before then.

Myrna walked to the barn to feed the cow and three horses. Being there always brought back memories of Sam. His hat and jacket still hung on a peg, and his muddy barn boots lay lopsided in a corner. She couldn't bring herself to remove these items. Seeing these lived-in looking clothes comforted her. Daisy, the cow, gave a long sonorous moo when Myrna pulled the stool and placed a bucket. Pa had taught her how to milk. The barn enclosure and fields were his landscape, enough so that as a young child she had felt like a visitor. Of course, as she matured and grew strong enough to help, that had changed.

Myrna wondered if the speechless creatures missed Sam's presence. As for the horses, always alert to her presence, watchful and affectionate, she was sure they noted changes in their handlers. Her personal horse, Star, nuzzled and snorted as Myrna filled the hay bucket. It was cold in the barn, but light seeped through the cracks from the reflection of the sun on the white snow outside. It was the kind of bright winter's day when she would let the animals roam in the pasture. She spoke aloud to Star, "If the weather holds we'll go for a ride tomorrow, girly, but not today." Star pawed the hay and neighed. Myrna stopped by the wood shed and filled the utility sled to carry more logs to add to the pile on the porch, and then returned to the barn for the milk pail.

When she opened the front door, she heard conversation in the kitchen—Alvah had arrived. He was sitting with Marion; then rose, slightly scraping his chair, when she entered the room. Myrna observed that the two were relaxed and comfortable. Alvah's combed hair caught a shaft of light from the window that also fell on Marion's blue gingham apron. Alvah continued talking with Marion for a short while about the snowfall being light for this late in the season, and about the Epps's new one horse sleigh. Alvah said that Lyman had built much of it himself—with a blacksmith from Elizabethtown fashioning the runners. Lyman had sent for a pattern, originally thinking that Jim, the blacksmith, would take on the whole thing. "But, you know Lyman—he likes to tinker with something new. He built it for Ann because he wanted her to have a small conveyance that was easy to handle." Myrna knew that Marion was already calculating how they might purchase one.

At the next lull, Myrna stood. "I've piled all the notes about our summer trip on the table in the alcove," she said, gesturing that way.

Alvah thumbed through the many notations, clearly impressed, and said as much. He knew Sam to have been organized and meticulous. Myrna, as a school teacher, was probably likewise. Myrna was certainly intent on the success of their venture. She scowled and bit her lower lip as she looked for Sam's supplies list. Alvah liked the way she unselfconsciously pulled at her dark auburn curls. He was especially drawn to her when her guard was down. She was very attractive when her expressions softened. He expected that some of the fellow guides found her intimidating when she was in her standoffish sharpshooter mode—though they did speak well of her. At times she was haughty and quiet, too. Myrna was an original, alright. She might need someone to champion her. I guess that'll be me, he thought.

"Apparently, I've not got this in complete order," she commented in frustration. "Could you please hand me that other pile?" Myrna pointed to his left. He passed the folio silently. In a few moments she exclaimed, "Aha! Here it is. I thought we could start with the supply list and the notes about the guides—that's what Pa mentioned doing. What do you think?"

"Makes sense to me…it's a bigger excursion than most of us have led. Sam talked about it freely with you and me, so we've got the general shape of it. Luckily, you've been to Follansbee Pond with Sam and Stillman, so you've already got a picture of what our final destination looks like, and know the quirks in the river leading to it. I'll say, without your knowledge I wouldn't even attempt this. By the way, have you written to George?"

"Not yet, I thought we'd write a letter after we finish our work today."

Myrna was finding Alvah open and easy to work with. She could see why Pa had enjoyed guiding with him. In roughly an hour's time they had put together a detailed supply list for the ten prospective sports; those things that Duffney Guiding Service would provide, and the items the clients would be expected to bring with them.

"Do we have any particulars about the men who've signed on for the trip?" Alvah asked.

"Let me see my notes I made back with Pa," Myrna replied, rummaging in another folder. She located the papers she was looking for. "It seems there are a number who favor fishing. In particular, Jeffries Wyman, Professor Agassiz, and, of course, Bill Stillman. I know for a fact that Bill is skilled with a rod, and he mentioned Wyman and Agassiz enjoyed fishing — they're the fellows who are also naturalists, and who expect to spend time at Follansbee studying plants, fish, and the like. Stillman said they are famous professors, but good sports. Let me see…James Lowell is also a professor and writer. He's done hiking and exploring here in the Adirondacks before—supposedly, he has very good woodsman camping skills. Doesn't say here about his preference for hunting though. Bill said his friend, Waldo Emerson, the one whose book I got, was fairly fit, and enjoyed being in the woods—but didn't care so much about being a sportsman."

"So, what's this Emerson fellow gonna do?" Alvah asked.

"I guess he'll hike and paddle a boat…you know, look around, explore—relax and enjoy the woods. Anyway, we're there to help him do whatever he fancies."

"Well this may be a different kind of group," Alvah speculated.

Myrna agreed, saying, "The important thing is that we make sure that they have a good time. As Bill says, he wants it to be an excellent and memorable experience."

Alvah offered to approach Moody's Boat and Livery to negotiate a fair price for renting ten boats, one per team of guide and patron (or sport). Myrna agreed. "I know Pa was in touch with Mr. Moody about the trip, but I don't have a personal relationship with him, so it's best you go ahead with it."

"I'll do it soon's the weather allows. Why don't you draft a letter to Walt Moody from you and George to the effect that the trip is still going as planned by the Duffneys—assuming George is in agreement." Myrna wrote this in her meticulous notes. "Tell me," Alvah said, "Are there any personal concerns you have about leading this excursion?"

Myrna slightly frowned and pursed her lips. "Oh, yes—I have many issues to resolve that I've been hesitant to ask you about, some of an embarrassing nature. I mean, I've thought about solutions, but would like your opinion." She paused. "Most times I've guided day hunts that don't present problems of personal proximity. And when Pa and I went to Follansbee with Stillman, we all shared sleeping arrangements in the same shelter, but, of course, I was with my father, and Bill is a family friend. What I'm saying is, that I want you to know I'm aware of some of the awkwardness of me being a woman on the trip and I'd like you to give your honest opinion as to my possible solutions—before I bring up any of this with George...or for that matter, Bill Stillman." Myrna took a deep intake of breath, looking directly into his eyes.

Alvah nodded and cleared his throat, trying to buy some time. He hadn't given this part much thought, but he did realize the awkwardness of it. Maybe he'd thought she'd stay at Martin's Hotel, as sort of an outpost. He didn't want to offend her. There was no graceful retreat from this conversation. "You might as well tell me your thoughts," he said.

Myra smiled. "Now, just hear me out completely before you toss out objections. Alright?" He nodded, faintly.

Myrna told him that she suspected George and he probably thought she'd do the planning and the communication with Stillman, meet the clients in Keeseville, and perhaps journey as far as Martin's. She figured George didn't think she'd go as far as Follansbee Pond, and maybe Alvah had just pushed it from his mind—or was in a quandary, reticent about saying anything. Alvah started to interrupt, but Myrna held up her hand. "Not yet," she said, continuing. "What I'm proposing for the awkward part about my accommodations at Follansbee is this—that I don't camp with the men, but that I make my campsite across the pond. I know a perfect, secluded spot in a cove about a mile from the main camp. That way, I'd be available to oversee the operation as Pa intended, and perform guide services or foraging, as need be. I figure I'd leave you, the other guides, and the sports to your own devices during the evening, and check to see if my services were needed in the morning, after breakfast." She looked up from her papers at Alvah. "How does this sound, so far?" she said, cautiously.

Alvah could see the sense of it. Myrna was a flawless guide who could execute Sam's wishes. Stillman hadn't raised it as a concern. Foolishly, Alvah hadn't gotten as far in his thinking as to wonder about Myrna's sleeping arrangements. "What do you think George expects?" he asked.

"Well, I think George won't join us any further than Keeseville, at best. He'll probably do that just to represent Pa's efforts. He'll want to get back to the mill and Janine. If I don't go on this trip, there'll be no one representing Duffney Guiding Services. Honest, Alvah, I think I can make this work, now that I've figured out how to deal with the problems."

Myrna at her best was very persuasive. She was looking at him with such seriousness. "You've convinced me," he said. "But, we'll no doubt have to convince some of the others—starting with George—eventually." Myrna beamed a happy smile.

"Alvah, you've no idea what a great relief it is having your support. I've been worrying about this aspect for weeks. Now I'm able to feel free in writing to George and Bill, telling them our plan."

Well, fair enough, Alvah thought. It would be *their* plan. He observed her countenance had changed. Her face was flushed with excitement, and she looked damned attractive. He thought he might like to ask her to a dance once her mourning was done. He impulsively reached across the table and took her hand. "I'm glad you brought up what was bothering you," he said, lightly squeezing her hand, before awkwardly pulling away. Marion, to the rescue, entered the alcove and asked them to come to the kitchen for tea and scones. She noted they looked happy...and wondered what she may have missed.

After tea with Marion they drafted a letter to George outlining their latest plans. Marion read it and nodded, saying it was a good letter. As Alvah was putting on his coat, he asked if they might talk again next week. Myrna smiled and nodded.

- CHAPTER 14 -
Back in Boston

Once back in Boston, Bill Stillman needed to find ways to augment his income, if he were to maintain his bon vivant lifestyle. Portraits of well-to-do maidens were profitable.

He settled Miss Almay in a chair by the parlor window. He'd taken a commission to paint the young woman's portrait. Indoor, winter light was watery, but Jayne Almay's thick features might benefit from it. All in all, he was pleased to get these commissions channeled to him by the Binneys, the prosperous friends he was staying with. Stillman thought his portraits were not as excellent as his landscapes, but he'd gotten good reviews from the Binneys and Mr. Alcott. Besides, now that his ties with the *Crayon* were minimal, he needed to have a decent source of income.

Miss Jayne was a restless model. And the dress her mother had selected for her didn't show her to advantage. It was made of white batiste, trimmed with lace. It highlighted, in an unflattering way, her pasty complexion and doughy features. He told her to take a few minutes to walk about, stretch her muscles, as it were. Lily, her mother, peered into the room to note their progress and ask when they'd care for a break in the session. Stillman suggested they continue for another hour, but first he thought she might change into the rose colored outfit he'd seen earlier, telling Lily that a colorful dress added interest to a portrait. Lily frowned and asked Jayne to come with her. Upon returning, Jayne was wearing not the rose dress, but a pastel pink one, an improvement nevertheless. Lily whisked from the room saying the tea bell would ring in an hour.

Bill rearranged Jayne in the grey damask chair and set a small table with a vase of blue and white paper flowers to the right, behind her. It was a pretty composition, and he told her so. She smiled mischievously. "Mother thought the rose dress to be a bit vulgar. She thinks the pink one looks demure, or virginal," she laughed, with a hint of coquetry.

Bill smiled and said that pink was a pleasing color on her. He had the good sense not to flirt with young women. At the moment, painting was his bread and butter and she did not appeal to him. On the other hand, her mother, Lily, was an outrageous flirt. She was his Honor Judge Almay's young second wife, stepmother to Jayne.

He was very much enjoying mixing and applying color from his palette to the canvas when the tea bell rang. Jayne ran over to see his work, enthusing over the colors. Of course, he hadn't yet painted her face in the composition, that being the tricky part.

Apparently, the judge was still in court, as just three places had been set at the round, linen covered table in the sunroom. Bill had not been in this room, which was elegant without being ostentatious. The pale, yellow walls shimmered in the light absorbed from the many paned windows, and the tied-back, cobalt curtains were a tasteful frame for the scenery beyond. Logs had been lit in the corner fireplace. It was early April and there were still traces of ice on the ponds and rivers outdoors, but the bright surface reflections and golden fire made the room seem warm. Lily replied to his genuine compliments by saying it was the one room she'd had a free hand in decorating. "You know," she said, daintily sipping, "Marjorie, Judge Almay's first wife, had planned most of the other rooms to his satisfaction. It was his wish that they remain as they were. But, this room," she gracefully gestured, "along with my sitting room and Jayne's bedroom, has been redecorated to our liking." She smiled at Jayne.

There seemed a refreshing camaraderie between the two women. Of course, Lily was not old enough to be Jayne's actual mother; pity that, as she'd not had the opportunity to inherit Lily's delicate features. Bill's observations about Jayne wandered as they chatted. She did have some pretty features. Her blue eyes were lively, her smile winning, even if her mouth was a tad large—perhaps too sensual. Of course, she was of an age where her features might grow or change. He realized the idealized countenance, for him, was a finely chiseled face with symmetrical planes. He would try to broaden his scope. Jayne would look pretty in his painting. He hoped to be offered a commission to paint Lily's portrait, too. He'd already made some preliminary sketches.

"Ruskin?" he said, alerting from his reverie, "You've read Ruskin, you say."

"Yes, Jayne and I have both read his essays in your fine journal, *The Crayon*. That is one of the reasons we are so pleased you have agreed to paint Jayne's portrait. In fact," she blushed becomingly, "I'm hoping you might find time for my portrait in the near future."

This was welcome news for Bill. He knew he lacked the skills of a businessman; however, he was an excellent fisherman. "I will have to consult my schedule," he said, noncommittally—playing out his line a bit, before setting the hook.

When the maid came to clear the tea setting it was his cue to leave. He politely praised the scones, folded his napkin, and rose from table. "I will need to cover my paints," he said.

"Then we'll see you tomorrow, same time?" Bill returned Lily's warm smile and nodded to Miss Jayne. "I look forward to it," he said with some enthusiasm.

After being shown out by the valet, he fairly skipped down the hill, thinking how well the session had gone. Both Lily and Jayne struck him as intelligent persons, perhaps unfairly judged by Boston's staid society, but he would need to keep himself in check. Unfairly, or not, the Binneys were slightly critical of the attractive Mrs. Almay, and it would be against his interest to raise their eyebrows—even if Lily were to eventually invite liberties. Besides, he'd met an eligible young woman, Juliette, he hoped to court, but so far, he'd not been invited to her home—leaving him wondering whether she was hesitant or her parents didn't wish to encourage him. Perhaps he'd glean more information at the upcoming concert in Cambridge Hall. Surely she'd be there.

He took the long route around the Commons back to the Binneys. He was grateful for their kindness in offering him ongoing accommodations, and didn't want to be late for dinner.

A few days later, his friend Louis Agassiz invited him to go walking. Bill missed being out of doors. Although the painting sessions at the Almay's were going splendidly, he was pleased that he'd agreed to walk out from Concord today with Longfellow and Agassiz. It also seemed wise to let the oils dry on Jayne's portrait before adding the finishing touches. Smudges at this stage could be a painting's undoing. Judge Almay was quite taken with Jayne's picture and liked the sketches of Lily, saying he was enthused to see her portrait come to fruition. A frank and honest man, he'd declined to be included in the picture, saying he'd likely be mistaken for her father. "Oh, tush now," Lily said, diplomatically. But he was omitted.

When Bill arrived in Concord, Henry Longfellow and Louis were already there waiting for him, sitting on a bench, amiably chatting. "There you are," exclaimed Louis, "We have picked a fine day for our stroll." Bill expected the stroll would be very leisurely.

As they adjusted their packs and took up their walking sticks, Longfellow said that his wife, Fanny, had insisted on wrapping some bread, cheese, and wine for a lunch, knowing that it'd be poor pickings at Thoreau's cottage, should he be there. He chuckled at the thought. "He's something of an ascetic," Longfellow said. Thoreau now lived fulltime at his home in Concord, but often retired to his small cottage on Walden Pond, either on a whim, or for the peace of it.

It was, indeed, a mellow day. The late April sun had gained enough strength to pull the early blooms up to the surface. As they progressed through the woods, they stopped by spring flowers named by Professor Agassiz; Trout Lily, Foam Flower, Marsh Marigold and, of course, a plethora of violets. There were Latin names for the mosses, not of as much interest to Bill. All three took time to make and label sketches.

Truthfully, Bill was glad to be in their company—without Waldo. Since Mr. Brown's antislavery lectures in Concord, past March, the various recourses posed to abolitionists were an incessant topic of conversation by Waldo and Ted Parker. That was well and good, thought Bill, but he personally grew bored with stalled rhetoric. He supposed that all in the Saturday Club were to one degree or another, abolitionists, but Waldo was becoming obsessively outspoken. Bill wondered if his own earlier experiences as an activist in the cause of Kossuth in Hungary had soured him on the antislavery political speeches. To his great relief, he saw that Louis and Henry's interest seemed to rest on flora and fauna for today. As a naturalist of note, Agassiz could easily become immersed in his scientific observations. Hopefully, this trait wouldn't make the day's walk tedious.

They decided that even if Thoreau were not there, they would take a small respite at his cabin. Bill had met, but never visited Thoreau; he was exceedingly interested in seeing the famous rustic abode.

They were in luck, Henry David was on his sliver of porch when they arrived, whittling a bird creature from wood. He nodded pleasantly, by way of greeting.

Thoreau was slim to the point of emaciation. He seemed famished and eager to get to the lunch, which Longfellow laid on a smooth rock in the yard. Bill was surprised at the sparseness of the tiny cabin, though he'd read Henry's treatise *On Walden Pond*. He could well understand the call for solitude, and wished Thoreau could join the compatriots going to Follansbee Pond, knowing how much he would enjoy that pond in its remote, lush setting. But he knew cajoling Henry David to join them was a ticklish thing, given the vicissitudes of Thoreau's health. Instead, he waxed on about the *Walden* piece and said, sincerely, that it had been an inspiration to him.

After their lunch, to which Thoreau contributed a store of wonderful black walnuts, he rose, offering to lead them on a walk around the pond. "I'll give you my favorite botanical tour," he said, with a bow to Louis.

It was a thoroughly enjoyable afternoon. Upon completing the circuit back to the cabin, they left Henry David to his quiet while they returned to Concord. To a one, they felt energized by the outing—walking, sketching, and talking on a range of subjects. At dinner, after a pint or two, they talked about Bill's success in painting the Boston crowd. In the flush of good cheer, Stillman offered to do a portrait of Longfellow, saying; "I'm thinking it should be drafted in the out of doors—and I've the perfect place." He went on to describe a familiar woodland setting with two prominent oak trees. "Would you find that to be agreeable?" he asked, with enthusiasm.

Henry Wadsworth agreed. He no doubt felt a bit flattered. Stillman had a growing clientele among the town's notables. Then again, Longfellow was known for his easygoing generous compliance. "Yes, I know the place you have in mind. At least the trees will make an attractive picture," he joked.

They decided to meet for the initial sketch in about a week hence, as soon as Jayne Almay's painting was completed. Bill figured he could handle working on Lily's painting tandem to Longfellow's.

Back in his rooms at the Binneys was a letter from the Duffneys. It was a thoughtful, detailed letter explaining the progress on their end, as well as the clothing and personal items the Boston clients should consider bringing. It was such a comprehensive list—he'd bring it to the next Club meeting. Bill breathed with satisfaction. He felt he and his compatriots were in good hands with Myrna, her brother George, and their guide friend, Alvah.

Bill had to say, his life in Cambridge suited him very well. The Binneys were dear friends who insisted he stay with them until he settled his profession—or as long as he wished. They were eager that he establish himself as either an artist or journalist. And their home was as expansive as their generosity. His rooms, a suite really, were tastefully decorated and private. The sitting area was done-up in Moroccan leather and dark wood, a nod to masculinity. A large oak desk and chair sat opposite, and an easel was placed in the corner. A doorway led to his bedroom with its mahogany, four-poster and matching wardrobe and nightstands. Marie Binney was proving to be a much appreciated personal confidant, too. Bill sought her out for advice on affairs of the heart, and welcomed her good humored opinion. Unfortunately, his latest courtship of Juliette Bristol was not progressing as he had hoped. Juliette was willing, but her father did not give consent for an engagement. He managed to sit with her briefly at the concert hall, but her parents were reserved to the edge of forbearance. So far, his interactions with them were a disappointment. Nevertheless, Bill immensely enjoyed his good standing in the Saturday Club, as well as his growing reputation as a portrait painter of note. He also felt damned lucky to have fully recovered from his bout with pneumonia. These were his thoughts as he rode in a carriage to the Almays' home.

The maid led him to the parlor where his easel was set with Jayne's portrait. Lily and Jayne were already in the room, fixated on Jayne's flattering visage. Flush with excitement, Jayne was nearly as pretty as the image before her. "It is quite perfect," she declared, "though perhaps I'm not *that* pretty," she added with good humor.

Lily hugged her saying, "Why you are just as pretty! I think we should place it here in the drawing room...or perhaps the dining room. We'll see what your father has to say."

Bill nodded, while thinking that Jayne already had a fair assessment of herself—an invaluable character trait. He also had to admit it was a richly colored, nicely composed portrait, one he'd be proud to have hung.

Lily turned her pert face to him, clasping both hands. "I do hope you'll begin my portrait soon." Bill replied that he'd begin when she wished, and he could even make some sketches today, if she desired. After some back and forth, they thought they'd try a few sketches in the sunroom, for a variety in setting. All three walked to the downstairs yellow-colored room and surveyed it. If anything, it was more beautiful in the late morning sun. Lily rang for lunch to be served there. "Yes, this room feels right to me. What do you think?" She looked from Bill to Jayne. They all agreed to the setting. "I think the colors will make a nice contrast to Jayne's picture," she said.

After lunch, Lily sat in a hard-backed chair, which they tried at various angles by the broad windows. Stillman wanted to see how her face caught the light. They were only quick sketches. Jayne lolled casually on a chintz settee, in the role of observer. She noted that the forsythia was near blooming. "Yes, with luck I may use that for the background," Bill said. They were becoming very comfortable with each other and free in their comments. Jayne worked on a needlepoint piece while Bill sketched. He drew a variety of poses. When he was done, he laid the drawings on the table for review, explaining that at this point he was most interested in composition; the rest would come later. Actually, he usually didn't involve his subjects in this part of the portrait process, but Lily and Jayne were so genuinely enthralled...and truthfully, he was flattered by their level of interest. He even let slip that he had been commissioned to begin a portrait of Henry Wadsworth Longfellow the following week. That was perhaps a slight exaggeration, the commission part anyway—but Longfellow *had* agreed to a sitting. As Bill was taking his leave, Lily lightly touched his arm and looked into his eyes in her flirtatious manner. It was difficult to not encourage her.

On his way back to Cambridge, his spirits were high. No doubt, he'd make a firm appointment with Longfellow when they were at Saturday Club this evening. He very much wanted Henry's portrait to do the great man justice. Bill also looked forward to the chance to paint outdoors again.

Tonight, the Saturday Club was meeting at the affable Tom Appleton's residence instead of the Parker House, where they usually met. Stillman thought it a pity that Tom chose not to sign-on for their Adirondack excursion. He was such jolly good company he'd surely have been an asset.

By the time Bill's carriage dropped him at the door of the Appleton residence, he saw that many of the others had arrived. As usual, it was an impressive roster. After a nod to the casually assembled, he walked to the buffet along the inside wall to receive a drink. This gave him a moment to decide where to sit—and next to whom. He took a seat by his friend, James Lowell. There were a variety of leather club chairs and a few upholstered high-backs. He was pleased to land in a comfortable chair, as he had stood sketching for most of the day. Lowell graciously asked him how he was faring at the Almays'. Bill thought he may have seen some amusement in James's eyes when he described Lily's enthusiasm for works of art, but then Tom called the meeting to order. George Ripley asked that he and Charles Dana might have some time on the agenda to talk about their New American Cyclopedia. Bill had always been curious about George's bygone effort to establish Brook Farm, but understood that since its demise it had become a sore subject for Ripley. As George and Charles, in turn, expounded on their new venture termed a 'cyclopedia', Bill took rapt notice with the rest of the group. It was going to involve a series of books devoted to American topics, the kind of thing Bill would like to be involved with. He'd listen carefully tonight, and then perhaps find a way to offer his services. Longfellow was close to George too. Bill could feel a plan hatching. Next week during his portrait sessions with Henry, he'd ask some subtle questions, and make some forays on his own behalf—he thought, yes, there could be possibilities. Bill's pockets tended to be shallow—he was always hopeful to latch onto a profitable venture.

Stillman startled from his reverie by Waldo's sudden request. "Bill, he said, "tell us the latest news about our Adirondack expedition. The fellows are eager to hear about it."

As Bill spoke, he became animated. Truly, there was plenty to expound upon when it came to the wild Adirondacks. He also shared, for those interested, the Duffneys' list of items required for the expedition. Agassiz, who was famous for his studies in ichthyology, asked about what species of fish Bill had seen in the pond. He responded to Louis by telling him his experience in catching large lake trout and bass there.

"I do like the prospect of a broiled trout dinner. I'm supposing the pond supports an active number of other aquatic species, too." Agassiz was apparently keen on fishing the pond.

Bill realized he and Louis were, no doubt, the most serious anglers in the group. Louis was easygoing and even tempered. He also was a thoughtful naturalist, used to spending long hours collecting and dissecting specimens.

Bill knew he'd enjoy the pond, and couldn't wait to show it to him. The one aspect of Agassiz that Bill didn't understand was his views on human species, not that Bill concerned himself much about it. But he knew Waldo and Ted Parker felt Louis was in error postulating Caucasians and Negros were separate species. He would ask Lowell more about this theory of Agassiz's the next time they were together. This also set him to wondering if Emerson had any hidden agenda about visiting the Brown community in North Elba on their Follansbee Pond trip. Waldo was surely taken with Mr. Brown and his abolitionist activities. He expected Waldo would want, at the very least, to spend time with Mr. Epps, one of the likely guides.

As the evening progressed and more drinks were poured, a boisterous informality set in along with the swirling curls of cigar smoke, sentences were clipped and then wantonly trod over. Any fruitful discussion quickly meandered into conversational byways. But nobody really minded. They'd raised some serious matters early in the evening; now it was time to relax and speak freely.

As Bill gathered his wraps to leave, he managed to catch Longfellow at the doorway. They agreed to meet in the Harvard Yard on Thursday morning. Tipping his hat to Tom, he took his leave, bounding down the outside steps in hopes of hailing a coach. He slept soundly that evening.

After breakfast, before he set out to the Almays', he had a chance to speak alone with Marie Binney. Bill poured his feeling of frustration about his attempted courtship of Miss Juliette, as the second pot of breakfast tea was brewing. He hadn't meant to be so voluble, but Marie had proven to be a discreet and receptive ear. And she didn't mind giving him a forthright opinion on such matters either.

"The way I see it," she said, "is that you are not a man of means. Certainly, you are beginning to establish a reputation as journalist and painter. In other words, you are promising and educated, but perhaps not able to support a wife from a rich background up to her expectations." Marie saw he was about to interject and held up her hand. "Now you may think that her father would supply a dowry…and perhaps in time he might—he could well afford to. However, Juliette is quite young and very attractive. To put it crassly, she has a high market value. In my opinion, Mr. Bristol feels it is worth waiting for other prospects to seek Juliette's hand." Marie poured the tea while giving him a sympathetic look. "I hate to see you so dejected. After all, it is only one view."

Bill laughed, regretfully. "No, Marie, I do appreciate that you are plainspoken. I know Juliette is attracted to me. Yet, she is sometimes distant, too. Perhaps I've tried to hurry our friendship beyond its natural course." He hesitated. "Do you have any advice for my situation?"

"I think, yes and no. After all, matters of the heart are mysterious, even inexplicable. How could I possibly guarantee an optimal solution? Having said that, my advice would be to continue your friendship with Juliette—be clear that you respect her father's wishes regarding an engagement. If, over time, you see a change in her level of feeling or in her father's attitude, make another approach. Meanwhile, continue to work hard and enjoy life. Really, I'm confident you have it within you to succeed." Marie patted his hand affectionately, telling him they'd see to it that he was invited to the summer season socials where he'd likely meet other attractive eligible women.

Bill thanked Marie for her candid advice. She was a good friend. At the same time, he wondered if he hadn't been found out. He was quite taken with Juliette while also conscious of her family's wealth. Was Marie saying in a lightly veiled way that she suspected him of trying to secure a financially advantageous marriage? Well, he knew Marie sincerely supported his talents and entrepreneurial efforts—he'd leave it at that. He rose from the table, saying he'd best get on his way to the Almays'. He was anxious to complete Lily's portrait.

He was lucky to quickly catch a coach at the corner. He took that as a good omen as the horses trotted along the roadway. He enjoyed looking at the river and the spring greenery along the water. He often walked to the Almays' on a fine day such as this. But an occasional splurge raised his spirits.

The house servant led him to the sunroom where Lily was waiting for him. She rose from the blue settee and set her book on a side table to welcome him. She was in the becoming dress they'd selected for her portrait—pale blue with considerable décolleté. Actually, the gown was more revealing than it had seemed on the hanger.

"Where's Jayne?" he said lightly. Lily replied, cheerfully, that Jayne was visiting a friend in the country for the day. Bill joked that he was used to them both criticizing his work. He realized there was awkwardness in being alone with Lily, at least on his part. However, Lily seemed comfortable and anxious to put him at ease, asking where he'd like her to sit and pose. She asked if they could open the French doors at the end of the room to let in the spring air and bird song. Once they settled in, it went pleasantly well. The forsythia outside the window had started to bloom. They decided to pose Lily in the cream-colored damask chair holding her book. That lent some gravity to her pose, while providing her entertainment as she glanced down.

"Once I start to paint your face you'll have to dispense with looking down at the book in your lap," Bill said. At first he did a quick pencil sketch on paper for consideration before outlining images on canvas. It helped him see the composition and loosened his hand before drawing the similar image on canvas. Once he finished a paper sketch, he became immersed in a painting. Of course, at some point he and his subject needed to take a break from the project. He did several finished sketches and set them on the floor. After an hour or so, he suggested that Lily move about a bit, change position. "I don't want you to feel cramped or tired," he said.

Lily looked at the sketches approvingly. "Might we have a cup of tea before proceeding?" she said. Lily rang for tea and when it arrived, they sat at the small table for that purpose. She showed him the book she was reading, *Way Down East* by Saba Smith, a humorous book. . Then Lily asked if she could show Bill the garden she'd been working on. "It won't take long, and some perennials have already started to bloom."

It was pleasant to meander on the paths through the rows. There were plenty of violets and jonquils in evidence as well as buds of tulips getting ready to bloom. Way back, there were leafy grape arbors. And benches were set here and there. Behind a large oak in a grove of lilacs was a bench that Lily declared her favorite. Taking his hand she declared, "I need to sit a moment." Laughing, she said, "I think my corset is cinched too tightly." Taking his hand and pressing it to her bosom, she added, "Is my heart beating too fast?" Bill felt both aghast and aroused. But he thought, under the circumstances, it might seem ungallant to not kiss her. So they gave in to the delicious moment...a few moments.

Once back in the sunroom, he again arranged her on the damask chair. She smoothed her hair and skirt a bit and picked up her book. Her face was radiant and her daring cleavage rosy. He could not help but tell her she was beautiful. "Thank you," she said. "Please do not give this afternoon a worry. I am young and my husband is not," she said frankly. "I think you are trustworthy and will not make light of me. I hope, in that, I'm correct."

He promised her that was true, and knew he would protect her. He did care about her and would not have her become part of some entertaining gossip. He sketched and painted for the rest of the afternoon and was pleased with the results. But he didn't want this assignment to end too soon.

At the door she said mischievously, "Perhaps I should be sure Jayne is with us next time, yes?" He agreed and smiled. In some way, they were conspirators.

It was not usual for Stillman to consider the various dilemmas facing women or other disenfranchised groups, but tonight, before sleep, he had serious thoughts about the unfairness of the social structure.

A few days later, Bill was pleased to begin his portrait of Longfellow at Waverly Oaks, the favorite outdoor place under two stately oaks. The setting was indeed beautiful. Lowell accompanied them on several days of the sittings. They were an especially congenial group and enjoyed spending time together in the forest. But Stillman so hoped that this portrait would be a masterpiece that the group presence impeded his progress on it. He fussed over it to such an extent that after the fourth sitting, Lowell said, "For God's sake, my man, finish and be done with it!"

Of course, there is always a danger of overworking a piece and ruining the likeness. But it dawned on Bill, finally, that Longfellow was being very patient in sitting for hours on the large boulder. He, once again, had forgotten to bring a cushion for Henry to sit on. Realizing the discomfort, Bill took off his jacket and folded it into a pillow for his uncomplaining friend — Longfellow had an especially kindly nature. Bill was pleased when Lowell complimented him on the finished portrait and offered to pay him for it. Stillman was adamant about it being a gift. He would never take compensation for it. As he said later to Lowell, it was his good fortune to be able to paint a favorite landscape—a bonus to include Henry in it.

Lowell was curious about Bill's painting commissions for the Almays. He finally got around to asking about Lily.

"What do you think of her? I hear she's something of a jezebel," he said with a knowing look.

"You know, I find her and her stepdaughter to be quite intelligent and refined. I'm enjoying painting their portraits. People tend to gossip about pretty young women married to old men—don't you think?"

"Maybe...but I've heard it from more than one source."

Bill shrugged. No one would hear slander from him. Sometimes Lowell's inquisitiveness irked him.

Bill rose early, looking forward to completing Lily's portrait. Today would be his last session at the Almays'. He could not seem to help his mind flooding with divergent thoughts. Who would be there: Lily? Jayne? Judge Almay? Would he resist Lily if they were alone? Bill felt a keen sense of anticipation. He finally decided he was more curious than nervous.

Once more he was shown to the sunroom. "Ahh...the forsythia are finally in full bloom," he exclaimed. Lily and Jayne rose together from the blue settee. Both smiled merrily and took his hand. They were wearing demure white lawn dresses—soft, comfortable looking outfits. "Daddy loves our pictures," Jayne enthused. "He says to keep you here until teatime. Please say you can stay." She clasped her hands in her girlish way.

Bill thought, why not? He saw that Lily's cheeks were blushing, but she was smiling easily. "I would like to have one closer look at your paintings, just in case there are minor touch-ups needed," he said. The paintings were still set on easels along the sunroom wall. Noting that the forsythia was now in full bloom, he decided that he'd add some minor golden highlights to Lily's picture. But, he was mindful not to over-paint it. Jayne's picture was fine. The paints on that one were completely dried; the colors were vibrant.

Jayne said she thought they'd have time for a game of croquet before tea. She'd set the game up in the side yard beyond the sunroom window. "Please...would they?" she pleaded, girlishly.

Lily and Bill agreed to it. Actually, it was a perfect activity for a warm, sunny afternoon. It was the kind of game that took just enough concentration to keep one's mind from wandering to thoughts of a tryst on the bench in the grape arbor. Bill did notice Lily glancing towards the arbor—and then she saw him catch the glance. He loved her light laugh at getting caught-out. Today she seemed such a good-natured soul.

Tea with the four of them went very well. Judge Almay was easygoing and affable. His Honor was well traveled and well connected, which Bill knew were factors to keep in mind. Lily and Jayne seemed to have sincere affection for him, too. Bill felt an uncomfortable twinge of envy towards the man. As Bill was ready to leave, the judge handed him an envelope. At the door both women kissed him chastely on his cheek. Lily smiled. She said, "You must come again in the pleasant weather. We so loved playing croquet in the garden with you."

"I would enjoy that," Stillman said, bowing to the women and taking the judges hand.

Back in his rooms, Bill sat in the leather armchair and opened the envelope Judge Almay had given to him. The check was for an amount much larger than the commission agreed upon. The enclosed note thanked him for capturing beautiful images of his girls 'at their best'.

For many days afterwards, he wondered 'if' or 'when' he'd hear from Lily. He wondered how he might respond if she contacted him. He dreamed of Lily. He did not dream of Juliette. By June he became focused on his upcoming venture to Follansbee Pond with his friends. He kept up a weekly correspondence with Myrna and George. Waldo, Louis, James and the rest were in high anticipation. Follansbee Pond now consumed Bill's thoughts.

- CHAPTER 15 -

Adirondack Spring

Meanwhile, the days in North Elba were growing longer; spring would be very welcome when it truly arrived. There were still piles of snow about, but the sun was slowly scrubbing it away. The Duffney household was keeping to its winter patterns, though with cheer in knowing that the frigid temperatures, wild snow storms, and long black nights, were ebbing to the perimeter of golden dawns. Even the inevitable mud season was welcome.

Today, the women hoped to complete their sewing. Myrna and Belle were almost done with the quilt that had occupied many winter afternoons. Marion would help them with the binding in order to finish it faster.

It seemed like a good day to devote their energy to quilting. Myrna had Carson help clean the stables and lay down fresh hay yesterday. Belle had stayed overnight to help do early chores and milking. Marion made brown bread and had beans with salt pork and molasses simmering in the oven. It was still early morning when they stretched out the quilt on the floor to survey their progress.

"I love the mixture of colors," Marion said. "The dark blue triangles of velvet mixed with the gold gingham triangles at the border just make it look fancy and finished. It was a lot of work stitching it, though."

Except for the border, the quilt was made of colorful, random squares. Belle and Myrna had decided on that pattern before gathering material scraps—partially in deference to Myrna's reluctance to sew. Belle, who had sewing experience, had never quilted. Once Marion became involved, the project went smoothly. All three women had a bent towards precision, so the quilt as it stood was a fine piece of work. They laid the muslin backing and attached batting, which had been stitched together, on the clean wooden floor. They set the front piece, to which they'd stitched half the border binding, on top of the batting. After carefully patting and smoothing, they placed pins where they'd stitch the layers together. It was a simple pull and tie method, pretty rather than elegant. It was a pains-taking project, but the women were of a mind about it—their quilt.

They were so focused on stitching that Myrna didn't hear anyone outside until there was a sharp knock on the door. She set her pins aside and quickly rose to answer it. Alvah stood there smiling. "I was in E-town at the store and there was a letter for you from Mr. Stillman, so I thought I'd come by with it," he said, holding it in his hand.

"You may come in for a moment. As you can see, we're hard at work on our quilt sewing." Alvah wiped his boots on the doormat. Then, seeing the quilt on the floor, took them off altogether.

Myrna sat back on the floor, leaving her pins in the bowl set out for that purpose. "I think we women are allowed a quick break," she said, smiling at Alvah.

Alvah walked closer to the sewing. Marion went to the kitchen to brew tea. She decided against slicing bread for the moment, knowing Myrna and Belle were serious about finishing.

Alvah bent close to the quilt, inspecting it. "This is a beautiful thing," he said, impressed. "Who's it for?"

Belle replied, with a mischievous glance, "We're thinking of giving it to the first one of us gets married."

"Any good prospects?" parried Alvah, amused to see Myrna blush.

She hastily interjected, "Belle's hoping Joachim might ask for her hand when he visits."

"We'll just have to see, won't we," Belle replied, easily.

Myrna was immensely relieved to see Marion enter the room with the tea tray and cups. The women arose from the floor and sat in chairs, leaving their quilting aside. Myrna used the opportunity to eagerly open the envelope with Stillman's letter.

"Very good news," she said. "Stillman says there are ten fellows solidly committed to our venture, and one other chap who hasn't yet committed. Bill says he read our list of personal items needed for trekking to his club members—says it became a topic of great discussion." She scanned down the page, and then looked up at Alvah with satisfaction. "He says all the men going can well afford to pay a fair share, so we shouldn't skimp on our costs." Marion nodded with interest. Myrna distractedly ran her fingers through her tangled hair. "I think next week we do a detailed budget," she said.

"I can help with some chores if I come over early next Monday," Alvah offered.

Myrna was pleased that they had a plan, and that she could rely on Alvah. She knew he had plenty to do at his own place, now that spring had arrived, and appreciated that he'd give her and Marion a hand. Apparently, he'd finished the logging job in the Saranac region.

"So, when is your beau, Joachim, going to visit?" Alvah asked.

Belle shrugged, then said, "It's a little complicated. I haven't agreed on a time he might come, but he says he may travel as far as Elizabethtown in June or July, anyway. If that happens, Myrna and Marion can chaperone me for a few afternoons." What Belle didn't express was her growing ambivalence about Joachim, and about marriage in general.

Alvah laughed. "Seems to me that quilt might set on a shelf awhile."

Myrna liked his lightheartedness. "Nevertheless, we do plan to finish today, so no more distractions from you," she said, gathering the cups and taking them to the kitchen. When she returned, she sat on the floor, picked up her needle, and continued where she left off.

Alvah rose from his chair and walked to the door. He gingerly tied his boots. "I believe I'm being dismissed," he said, thanking Marion for the tea. Walking to where he'd tied his horse and cart he thought how he liked the 'no nonsense' aspect of Myrna.

For her part, Myrna reflected on how limber and strong Alvah had looked standing in the door jam. They were equally to the task of leading a complex guiding trip, she thought. But she firmly kept away any personal thoughts about him.

The three women managed to focus and work fast for the rest of the afternoon. Any frivolous conversation could wait. As twilight began to gather, Belle exclaimed, "Finished! We are finally done!" They smoothed the colorful quilt flat to the floor once more, circling and inspecting it. The finished piece met with their unanimous approval.

"I suppose we might make another one next winter." Belle clapped her hands and spun circles. Myrna groaned in mock dismay, her fingers sore from accidental needle jabs. But she was pleased to have made something both beautiful and useful. She could believe they would sew another one. Myrna and Belle each took a corner of the quilt. Raising and shaking loose threads from it, they draped it over the living room settee.

"Looks pretty there," Marion said.

Having afternoon tea without cakes had honed their appetites. At table, Marion ladled beans from her earthenware baking pot and sliced generous slabs of freshly baked bread; churned butter was in a bowl to the side. There was a pitcher of cold spring water and glasses on the table.

Marion went to the pantry and brought out a bottle of dandelion wine. "No point keeping this in storage. This is as special an occasion as is likely to happen," she said. She rummaged in the cupboard and took out small etched glasses. "These are cordial glasses. We'll have the wine as a kind of dessert."

Myrna didn't think they'd ever used these particular glasses, and she wondered why.

Belle was full of chatter about the meal. "Marion, these are the best baked beans I've ever tasted, no lie. What do you put in em?"

Marion was in a teasing mood. "It's a secret recipe," she began, "but seeing as you might be getting ready to start a household I'll divulge it. Basically, the secret ingredients are plenty of salt pork, black pepper, grated horseradish and a dollop of molasses. Then you cook it a good while in an oven with low coals. And that's about it. Oh, it's important to soak the dry beans at least overnight, too."

"Don't know how soon I'll be starting a household, but I will be cooking this recipe!"

"Been meaning to ask," Myrna said, "When did you decide me and Ma would chaperone you in Elizabethtown. I thought you liked being independent." Myrna realized her friend had shifted further away from Joachim. At this point, Marion poured a round of dandelion wine. For a moment they sat quietly and sipped. The wine was amber colored and sweet with a hint of spice.

"Very nice, much better than expected," Myrna recalled picking the dandelion blossoms, the major ingredient, a year ago with Marion and Sam.

"I like the spicy taste," Belle said. Clearing her throat, she added, "I might as well get some advice on this prospective visit of Joachim's. As Myrna knows, I'm feeling confused about what I want in my future, though these thoughts are truly colored by my family's reservations about this particular relationship. About the chaperone idea…I worry about being alone with him because I've already allowed him liberties…small ones. But he may expect more. We could let our feelings cloud good sense." Belle looked directly at Marion to judge whether or not to continue—and saw she was sympathetically listening. "If I was sure I wanted to marry him, I would not worry about this. But what if I wish to travel or study more subjects to teach? Actually, I like being here on my own doing what interests me. When I hear older women like Harriet Wells talk, I'm inspired to become more independent."

Marion patted Belle's hand. "I completely understand. No woman should feel forced to marry. You are young and your family is willing to support you. Anne and Lyman say you do more than enough at their place to earn your keep. I would say you are wise to not succumb to physical feelings, tempting as that might be." Marion laughed. "I'm willing to act as chaperone, though you may regret it."

Myrna added, "Yep, one little nuzzle or snuggle and we'll pull you apart." Truthfully, Myrna was curious about Belle's thoughts about her future. She saw Marion was giving her a bemused look.

"Why, this is the first I've heard you expound on these things, Myrna. I'd not thought you encountered such ideas," Marion joshed.

"Sadly, so far my encounters with ideas about relationships between men and women come from books. I do read, you know." They laughed together at Myrna's honest pronouncement.

Myrna asked Marion about the etched cordial glasses. It seemed they had been a wedding gift from her grandmother, Alma. Myrna had been born after she died. Grandmother Alma had lived in Boston and been a distant relative of the Peabody's—the cousins they'd visited a few years ago. Marion said that she'd always planned on using the cordial glasses, but didn't have much occasion to. Her voice faltered in telling how one of the reasons they'd made the wine was so she'd get to use grandma's glasses. "That's why Sam went with us that day we picked the blossoms. It was a kind of joke between us—saving the good glasses." Then she added softly, "You just never know, do you." For a long moment they sipped soberly. Myrna clearly recalled the day they'd all gathered the dandelion blossoms. She knew her mother was probably thinking about it, too.

When they resumed conversation, they talked some about Harriet Wells. Marion shared additional gossip she'd heard at the church, adding it was *only gossip*. Belle said she thought Mrs. Wells was, nevertheless, a very spirited zealot for women's causes, and hoped she'd give another talk on suffrage soon. Myrna mostly agreed with Belle, but decided not to join in. It had been a wonderful day in several ways, Myrna thought. Belle slept over as planned. Myrna contemplated the day as she drifted towards sleep. She thought about Sam and Marion, Pa and Ma, but not sadly. She marveled at having missed the story behind the picking of dandelions, and the unexpected revelation that had come about at dinner. She could tell by Belle's breathing that she was already asleep.

On Tuesday morning Alvah arrived early, as promised. Carson was with him. After a quick coffee they headed to the barn for what they termed a 'spring cleaning'. Myrna hadn't known Carson was coming. She was mildly disappointed to not have some time alone with Alvah. Clearing the stalls of winter animal refuse and dragging and organizing large bundles of hay was hard work—even for three strong people. Myrna's hair was plastered to her brow and neck with sweat. Alvah and Carson were equally grimy. The cow eyed them warily as they led her from her stall. The frisky horses looked hopeful to ride, but were settled in the pasture. The three work mates had raised clouds of dust in the barn, but it was swept and fresh. The refuse was barrowed to the edge of the kitchen garden to be plowed in later.

When he finished cleaning the last stall, Alvah inspected the tools—rakes, scythes, plow blades, and the like. "I'll take some of these to town to have them sharpened next time I go," he said. Myrna shook her head in agreement. Once again, she wondered at how Pa had managed with so little help.

After they finished, they washed their faces and hands outside at the pump. Carson dunked his whole head saying, "very refreshing". Myrna settled for a full face-dip and washed to the elbows. They trod wearily to the back door, leaving their mucked boots outside. Myrna had inside-slippers tucked behind the summer-kitchen door; Alvah and Carson entered the room bare-foot.

Marion had bread and what she called 'hodge-podge' soup ready. She said all their hard outside work had inspired her to freshen the hen-house, though there was a pile of clearings that she'd dump later.

They sat at the kitchen table, eating with gusto. Carson noisily slurped his soup. Marion didn't exactly mind it, but in her motherly way wished he'd been taught some table manners. She also wished Myrna didn't look so much the rumpled farmhand, though she was pleased that the hard work was done. But she also noted that Alvah looked at Myrna in a way that said he didn't mind seeing her bedraggled. In fact, once Myrna and her companions were fed and rested, they sat-up straight and became more animated in their expressions and gestures—sort of like plants watered and set out in the sun, Marion thought.

"I've been thinkin, Mrs. Duffney, I could come here every week to help out, at least until fall logging," Carson said. "I'd settle just for meals and a small amount of change."

Marion liked his simple directness. "Let me think about it and see what we can work out," she said.

Myrna and Alvah adjourned to the dining area, where Myrna had in advance set out her papers and notes for them to draft the Follansbee Pond trip budget. Myrna ran her fingers through her hair in an attempt to untangle her auburn curls.

"Your hair always looks pretty, no matter," Alvah said. Myrna returned a skeptical look, but smiled anyway. She was pleased at how well they were working together on planning the guide trip. Truly, whatever made her think she could manage a trip of this scope on her own? Of course, George would have helped her, but realistically, he was too far away to be involved in the day-to-day planning. Also Alvah had accepted her as an equal from the beginning. Family, she realized, came with a history of preconceived notions.

They worked on their lists and paperwork until they were both satisfied. Alvah suggested they draft a short letter to Stillman. He thought they should confirm that ten boats would be needed, in addition to the guides already hired, and that the budget included with the letter should clearly enumerate each client's cost for that, as well as sundry other items. "These sports may have ample means, but in my experience those are the kind that balks at spending money," he said.

Alvah contemplated the paper before him, chewing his bottom lip. He was done with figures. Now he was trying to decide whether or not to tell Myrna what he'd seen at the post office. In general, he liked to stay out of other people's business. His main occupation, guiding, put a high value on not confiding personal information. Sure, some fellows liked to tell stories around the camp, but that didn't have much to do with truth. On the other hand, his friends Myrna and Belle did tell their concerns—Well, Belle did, anyway. Alvah hoped spending time with the women wasn't turning him into a pussy. He cleared his throat. "When I picked up your letter at Matthew's store there was also a letter there for Belle. I would have brought it with me, assuming you'd get it to Belle, but Lyman came in and took it. I'm pretty sure the letter was from the man she mentioned named Joachim…Lyman looked displeased and tossed the envelope in his satchel, almost like he was throwing it away." He looked expectantly at Myrna.

"Lyman's too ethical to deliberately throw it away, that's my impression from how Pa talked." Myrna furrowed her brows. "I do believe, depending on what the letter says, that there may be some angry discussion between Belle and the Epps."

Alvah shook his head. "That's too bad. Especially since Belle may not care so much for Joachim in the end."

"Yep, these relationships can be complicated."

Alvah nodded again. Then they both chuckled.

"I'm thinking," Myrna said, "you can help me and Marion chaperone Belle; that is, if there's a visit."

"I'm thinking I may be lacking those kinds of skills." He knew Myrna was joking, but it never hurt to be clear about what you didn't plan on doing. There was something about Myrna that drew him in. Maybe he'd ask her to go fishing next week—just the two of them. She did like to hunt and fish.

After Alvah and Carson left, Marion and Myrna sat in the living room. They were discussing the idea of hiring Carson for the summer. "I thought it best we think together on this," Marion said. "I know we've both been trying to pick up the jobs Sam ordinarily did…well, more you than me. And, of course, folks have been willing to give us a hand. But, it would be nice to just out and out hire someone." Marion looked expectantly at Myrna.

"You know, the truth is I've just been plodding along getting the work done. Mostly, things are going alright. I realized today, when Alvah and Carson helped me clear the stalls and clean the barn, that it would take me most of a week to get done what we did together in a day—and, while I appreciate what they did, I can't grow to rely on it. Also there's my teaching job, which Belle has nicely taken on at the settlement. And then there's the Follansbee Pond trip, which will make us the most money..." Myrna took a deep breath. "Damn! We sure could use two more hands and a back around here! Let's try to figure out this possibility with Carson." Myrna rose from her chair and briskly went to the desk for pencil and paper. "Let's see what we'd need to do for this to work."

It didn't take them long to come up with a reasonable plan. Marion thought they could clear out the downstairs back storeroom. It was a small room that Marion had once intended as a summer kitchen, but in recent years it had become a catch-all for clutter. It was filled with slightly broken or almost useful items. "Sam and I just never could get around to clearing that room. Sometimes I look in there, pause, and then shut the door again. Tomorrow let's drag out all that useless stuff to the backyard and see what we think. I'm ready." They both agreed. Since Carson himself had raised the idea of becoming a hand on the property, and asked for only modest remuneration, they were fair in what they would offer him—room and board, plus a small wage.

Marion seemed to be gaining back her old energy, Myrna observed. She realized that she had been so preoccupied with maintaining the household that she'd failed to notice her mother's lingering grief. It gave her pause to think she and Marion had both missed the obvious need for hired help. And Carson would be so suitable for the two women to live with. He was still a boy, really—they might seem like mother and sister to him. Carson had a sunny disposition and was strong. He was also Alvah's nephew, a fact that both women silently noted. Myrna, for her part, was realizing a friendship with Alvah. Marion saw Alvah as a potential suitor for Myrna. They both recognized that Myrna was ambitious and highly disciplined. It was hard to say what might tip the balance into courtship. Marion wasn't ready to bet on it.

Sam had always supported, even fostered Myrna's independence, leaving Marion's part of the parenting to lean towards criticism and exasperation over Myrna's unfeminine choices. But the vacuum created by Sam's absence was drawing Marion to a new appreciation of her daughter. At the same time she felt a prickle of guilt, knowing this was at the cost of losing Sam.

"Then it's settled," Marion said. "I told Carson to stop by in a few days; we'll tell him then."

- CHAPTER 16 -

Casting a line

The Ausable ran swift, but considerably tamed now that the spring snow melt had passed. There were marsh marigold nestled in the shade of hemlocks along the banks. Myrna spotted swirling eddies downstream that looked promising as haunts for trout. She and Alvah had set out in the early morning, leaving Carson at the kitchen table with Marion. He looked disappointed at not being included. Myrna had thought to invite him, but Alvah had already told Carson that he'd bring him to Round Pond next weekend, adding that trout fishing required particular skills. Carson was mollified by the prospect of pond fishing. He was usually quick to agree with Alvah, whom he admired as close to an older brother.

Alvah walked a ways upstream from Myrna, as to not crowd her space—necessary trout fishing etiquette. He turned to look her way. She took no notice of him; her absorption in the sport was complete. The grace of her cast caused a perfect arc of line before her midge grazed the surface of the rippling eddy. He was momentarily mesmerized watching her lithe movements, jealous of her easy solitude. He saw himself as a serious fisherman. He would not try for her attention—walking another hundred yards upstream. After he'd played and landed two respectable brookies and laid them in grasses in his basket, he walked downstream to where he thought Myrna would be. But apparently, she'd ventured even further down river. At first he didn't see her. Then, rounding a bend, there Myrna was—in water nearly to her waist, her line doubly bent. The current was swift.

Whatever was attached to the end of her line was causing a mighty struggle. Alvah knew there were deep pools that could be dangerous footing, and there were falls beyond the rapids. Instinctively, he rummaged in his pack for a skein of rope, just in case. But Myrna started to inch carefully back to the river-bank, her rod and line at enough tension to keep the fish securely hooked. She saw Alvah on the shore. "Hey! Can you help me land this big fellow," she said, "don't think I can hold both the line and the net!"

With Alvah's assistance, they landed an exceedingly large rainbow trout. "He's a beauty," Alvah exclaimed, as Myrna unhooked the fish and laid it in her creel. They walked a few hundred yards back to where they'd tied their horses and left their packs and gear. Myrna felt weary from her struggle. Once she sat on the grass she also felt chilled. The fire Alvah was making would be welcome. She knew the extra pack on her horse held dry clothes of some sort. She excused herself to change.

Alvah agreed that it would be sensible to get into dry clothes. However, in her momentary absence, he found himself fantasizing about how Myrna might look without clothes—her small round breasts, her shapely legs, and possibly auburn hair at her nether parts. When she returned and stepped near the fire, which was now leaping merrily, she was wearing a dry version of her usual baggy castoffs from her brother.

"Why don't we cook up one or two of the smaller ones?" She held up an old dented pan and a chunk of butter wrapped in paper. She'd picked wild ramp, which was in season, to add to the pan. They agreed they were famished. Myrna said she'd bring the 'big boy' home for dinner. Alvah said he thought that one weighed easily over six pounds. "I was a little worried when I saw you wading out to the deep water." He said.

"Yep, I got carried away, but I still felt safe. Generally, I do take care—those huge fish are a challenge, I'll admit. I was using Pa's favorite midge for a lure. I almost felt he was with us...you know?"

"Yeah, Sam was a great fisherman. You must take after him. How many did you catch today?"

"Three, but I threw one back. Pa always said we should keep only as much as we were going to eat. How many did you catch?" she asked.

"I caught two altogether. Is that Sam's creel?" Alvah gestured to it. It was basket-woven, trimmed with leather and fitted with brass hinges and closure—superbly crafted.

Myrna nodded. "This is the first time I've used Pa's stuff. He always bought the very best gear. He took pride in it. I know he'd want me to put it to good use."

They felt comfortable sitting quietly awhile, staring at the hastily built fire. Finally, Alvah mentioned that he heard that Harriet Wells had bought a cabin near Ausable Forks. "Some say it's become a stop on the Underground Railroad. They say Pastor Horace Barnes is part of it, too."

Myrna nodded. "People do love to gossip about Mrs. Wells and Pastor Barnes. Belle's quite taken by the speeches Harriet's given on a woman's need for independence, and the possibility of us getting the vote. Of course, I'm in agreement on that," she quickly added. "But the Underground Railroad business is not something to be casually bandied about. I mean 'underground' is supposed to mean secret...right? I think the part about Harriet I don't like is that she's not discreet." Myrna looked like she was trying to find more words.

Alvah was interested in what Myrna had to say. He interjected mischievously. "And is that your concern about the coziness between Harriet Wells and Pastor Barnes...lack of discretion?"

"Can't say much about that. Reverend Barnes is single and Mrs. Wells is a highly independent woman of means. Unless someone's peeking in their windows, we'll never know for sure who is doing what. I have to say, it is the kind of gossip the lady's church society is currently enjoying—so Marion says." They laughed at the thought.

As they packed to leave and untether their horses, Alvah asked Myrna if she'd like to go to the dance in town with him on the weekend. "I'm playing guitar with the fellas on some of the pieces, so we'd havta go a bit early," he said.

"That would be nice. I do like to hear lively music." She hesitated to say more, but wondered if Belle and Marion could go with them. Then Alvah mentioned inviting Marion and Carson.

When they arrived at the Duffney homestead, Myrna presented her majestic trout to Marion, who characteristically, and warmly, invited Alvah to share dinner and catch-up on how his nephew, Carson, was doing. As for Carson, he was quick to tell about the work he'd been doing for the Duffneys, adding how comfortable his room was and what delicious dinners Marion provided. "I just white-washed my room in the back and built two shelves for my stuff," he said.

After dinner, Alvah took some time to look at Carson's handiwork. He was a strong, cheerful, round-faced boy. His freckles and tousled blond hair made him appear younger than his years. It seemed to him that Carson fit very well with the two women. It set his mind at ease knowing that Marion wouldn't be alone while he and Myrna were in the woods with the group from Boston. And that thought had him wondering about some of the men in the party. Myrna said Stillman had wood skills and was fit—but what did they really know about the skills of the other men in the party? They were doing excellent work as far as preparation for the camp. However, good preparation could never compensate if a few in the party were weaklings, or took ill. Alvah guessed Myrna had faith in Stillman's judgment on these matters, but he had a few niggling reservations—he remembered Sam had said the group was city smart, but that didn't mean they were especially able to handle tricky situations that could happen at camp. Then he looked at Myrna—strong in heart and strong in mind, he thought. Seeing him looking, Myrna returned his smile. As she walked him to the doorway, he said he'd pick them all up on Friday for the community gathering.

Myrna liked that she was free, once again, to resume teaching duties at the Brown settlement. Before Carson was hired, Myrna had prepared only basic writing and math for her advanced students. Since the students would recess for the summer months, she was now anxious to have them do their lessons at a faster pace, so they might be prepared for new subjects in the fall.

She knew there were a few students who'd enjoy reading over the summer, though the books on the school shelves were sparse—an ongoing concern. Harriet Wells had offered to buy some books to contribute to the school library. Myrna was trying to figure how to say, "Yes" without ceding too much control to Mrs. Wells over which books were to be purchased. Unfortunately, Harriet could be meddlesome while being generous. Even Marion, who was critical of Harriet's flamboyant disregard of proper appearances for married women, thought Myrna and Belle should accept the woman's generosity regarding the community school. In the end, Myrna and Belle drew up a list of books they needed for the classroom and a few story books they'd like for a lending library, and hoped for the best. But in the process of garnering supplies for the school children, an interesting turn of events happened.

The other church women, including Marion, began to take an interest in providing school supplies. They were all part of the sewing and knitting group that met in the community parlor of Reverend Barnes' church. Marion found the group surprisingly enjoyable, and was now engaged with them in sewing infant clothes. Harriet, who was also a newcomer, was beginning to fit in. When Harriet wasn't trying to enlist women in the causes of women's suffrage, or abolition of slavery, she happily sat and knit or sewed with the group. Gradually, over time, most of the women had come to accept her. As Marion confided to Myrna and Belle, many of the active church women were not necessarily content within their personal lives, having little say over their household finances or relations with their spouses,

"And the poorer she is, the less chance a woman has to influence her household's destiny," Marion said.

"Wouldn't surprise me if some weren't secretly envious of Harriet's goings on," Belle said.

Marion nodded. "You must remember, she has money of her own…and a husband that doesn't require much attention. Evidently they are in a mutually satisfactory situation."

Myrna was busy trying to make a list of school supplies. She looked up at Belle.

"I guess we're going to have to become rich and independent."

Belle smiled. "Or find a handsome, rich husband that dotes on us."

Marion added, "I'm not intending to give advice, but choosing someone who admires you and is of good character is always a consideration."

"So, when we meet Joachim on Friday, should Marion and I assess his character?" Myrna teased Belle.

"Oh, I already know the two of you will give him a thorough inspection." Amidst all of the jocular jousting, that was the truth. Belle had always known that Myrna would listen and watch and then be unsparing in her opinions. She now felt Marion also had her best interests at heart. And Ann and Lyman would be even harder judges. Poor Joachim, she thought, will be tested on all fronts.

- CHAPTER 17 -

Dancing

Belle was nervous at the prospect of seeing Joachim. Though they exchanged letters every few weeks, it had been over a year since they'd been in each other's presence. Belle had Lyman drop her at the Duffney homestead so that she could ride to town with Myrna and her family. . She appreciated Lyman being kindly this morning, given the circumstances. As she alighted from the wagon, Lyman said, "Take care and have a nice day." He handed her some small coins for spending. "We expect you'll be staying in town with the Duffneys tonight." He gave her a penetrating look and went on his way. Belle knew Lyman was going to Elizabethtown, but probably didn't wish the awkwardness of meeting Joachim. However, she suspected he'd find a way to observe him. After all, E-town was not large. Joachim had said he was staying at the Deershead Hotel.

Belle knocked lightly and Carson answered the door, looking spruced for town. "You look especially pretty today Miss Belle," he said. Belle could hear the Duffney women squabbling. Poking her head in the kitchen she saw Myrna sitting fidgety on a chair, while Marion stood scowling, combing and arranging her hair.

Myrna looked up upon seeing Belle. "Ma's treating me like a prize pony going to a show," she said. "You'd think I was the one out to impress a beau. By the way, Belle, you do look very nice. Joachim will be smitten."

Carson looked at the female tableau, not sure how to interpret their joshing. Being around women in a domestic atmosphere was a novelty for him. He liked that they accepted him, almost like family. He was pleased that Alvah had suggested he join them for the trip to town, too. He couldn't help but wonder about Alvah and Myrna. Alvah seemed to listen and look at Myrna with certain intensity—like he was studying her. He couldn't ever gauge what Miss Myrna might be thinking, though. It was a pleasant thought that if Alvah and Myrna got hitched, he'd be part of their family. When Carson heard another knock, it felt like he had summoned Alvah. And he noticed that Myrna was the first one in the room whom Alvah smiled at.

They made their way to town in Alvah's wagon at a leisurely pace. Belle and Myrna rode in front with Alvah, one to a side. Marion demurred, she sat in back with Carson.

Alvah noticed that Belle seemed increasingly anxious as they got closer to town. Finally, he asked her lightly, "Just how much chaperoning would you like us to provide?"

"Oh, dear…I can hardly bear it. I think we should all stay together, at least you and Myrna, if you don't mind. I can let you know if I'd like to be alone with him." She looked from Alvah to Myrna, "Is that alright?" Myrna and Alvah, almost in unison said, "Of course!"

The women stopped briefly to leave their small overnight valises at Mrs. Best's, a knitting circle friend of Marion's. It was decided that they'd then tie-up in front of the Deershead Hotel. Belle, Myrna, and Marion proceeded to the hotel lobby. Alvah said to wait there. He'd join them in a moment, after he dropped his fiddle at the church hall. Carson said he'd find them all later. Marion felt that as a person of Belle's parent's age, she was obligated to meet Joachim. Though she didn't say so, she'd want a motherly figure to accompany Myrna, if she were ever in similar circumstances.

Belle walked to the hotel reception desk to ask for Mr. Joachim Webb, but then spied him sitting in the lobby with another gentleman. Seeing him gave her a start. He looked older and heavier than she remembered. He was slouched in a green, wing-back chair, engaged in conversation with a man opposite him in a matching chair, who appeared to be a drummer or businessman of sorts, though his clothes were somewhat threadbare. Joachim and the man seemed to know each other. Belle leaned into Marion and whispered, nodding toward the lobby. "Joachim is the one in the cream colored shirt," she said. "Perhaps we should all walk over—I can make introductions."

Joachim spotted them across the lobby. Excusing himself from the man in the chair, he rose and walked quickly towards them, smiling. They exchanged introductions and awkward pleasantries, Joachim, saying they should call him Joe. Marion suggested they adjourn to the tavern area where they might order a pot of tea. She figured Alvah would find them there. To Belle's surprise, the man Joachim had been conversing with hurried to intercept them. "Hello, my name's Jesse. Yor every bit as purty as Joe said." He smiled, showing stained crooked teeth. "Come to think...Yer all purty as flowers," he said rocking on his heels, extending a sweaty hand.

Belle looked flustered and dismayed. Nevertheless, they continued to the tavern. As Jesse's words spooled on, it became apparent that he was, at very least, an acquaintance of Joachim's. He was from Troy and worked on the canal boats with Joachim's father. Myrna thought Jesse looked older than Joe, but younger than Marion. She and Marion conspired to talk to Jesse so that Belle and Joe might ease into their own conversation. And Jesse did like to talk. Taking the Duffney women's questions about traveling on the canals as an interest in his person, Jesse became flirtatious, and more so after imbibing several glasses of whisky. "I wouldn't mind steppin out with either of yez; the young one or the slightly older one—no matter to me" (apparently, he'd already forgotten their names). Marion pursed her lips in distaste. Myrna's nostrils flared and she was about to put Jesse hard in his place, when she felt a warm hand on her shoulder. It was Alvah. His flinty smile sobered the errant Jesse. "I'm hoping you're not Joachim," he said to Jesse, who looked confused. Turning to Belle, he warmly extended his hand to Joachim, saying "I've heard favorable comments about you from Belle." He pulled a chair between Jesse and Myrna. "I hope I haven't kept you waiting too long," he said, addressing Myrna and Marion.

For his part, Jesse was a little drunk and felt disappointed, but he knew when to back off. He excused himself, telling Joe he'd find him later in the day—at the community dance.

Joe apologized to Belle, including the rest of the table. He admitted that Jesse was a friend, saying that he was actually more a friend of his father's. Smiling sheepishly at Marion and Myrna, he said, "I can see his hopes of meeting a lady friend of Belle's were mistaken."

Marion, sensing Joe's discomfort, told him now that things were settled there was no harm done. Myrna, for her part, glowered, arms crossed on her chest, but she held her words. Belle sighed and chided Joe good naturedly, "I hope you won't let this fellow spoil our time together." Then, with her most charming smile, added, "I'm afraid I simply could not tolerate having him join us in any activities." She paused, biting her bottom lip. "I do look forward to spending time with you, and having you get to know my friends. You understand?"

"Yes, I'll do my best." Joe looked somewhat dejected, but soon rallied at the thought that Belle wished to have them all walk through the town. The couple set out ahead—Myrna, Marion and Alvah following a ways behind. Alvah was humming a tune, one he said he was trying to remember so as he might play it this evening. When they got as far as the general store, Marion asked if they'd mind going ahead without her. Alvah tipped his hat saying he and

Myrna would continue their duties as chaperones. Marion gave him one of her colluding glances.

After a turn around the town, Belle suggested they sit on benches in the small park by the river. Belle and Joe sat on one bench and Myrna and Alvah on a second bench nearby. The benches were positioned just far enough apart to allow a modicum of privacy, if words were spoken softly.

The late afternoon was warm and humid, close but not oppressive. Occasionally, a cool breeze drifted up from the river. "Trout have been active this week." Alvah bent forward looking over the river. "I don't get to fish the Bouquet so often…hear there's plenty of brown trout here. Would you like to fish the Ausable with me later this week?" He turned his head and smiled at Myrna.

"We might be called on to chaperone Belle and her beau…otherwise, yes. At the moment, I'd say they are getting on fairly well…wouldn't you say?"

"Considering they've been alone less than an hour." Alvah replied.

Myrna nodded. She decided not to ask Alvah what he thought of Joe—not yet. Maybe he'd give an opinion later. Myrna wasn't sure what she thought about Joe. Frankly, he didn't make a strong impression, though he was handsome and reflected his combined African/white heritage. Her instincts told her he might not be worthy of her dear friend. Belle was pretty, vivacious and smart. Joe seemed, well, ordinary, then there was his horrible friend, Jesse. Why had he even considered letting him tag along? She supposed her best course of action was to hold back her words and give him a chance…or sleuth him out. "So what was that catchy song you were humming?" she asked Alvah..

"Oh, just a dance tune I made up. I was humming so I won't forget it." He hummed a few bars and stopped. "You're a surprisingly good dancer. Hope you'll save me a dance when I'm done playing."

"Surprisingly?" Myrna raised her eyebrows.

"I used to think of you as purely a sharp-shooting guide until we got to dance back in Keene. You know what I mean."

"And now you don't see me as a sharp shot?"

"Myrna, you love to give me a hard time, don't you." He shifted on the bench so their shoulders touched. Then he turned his head close and squinted at her. She could feel his breath when their eyes met directly. She raised her chin and thought…I'll never be the prey. Upon a second thought, she silently amended her quick unspoken response.

Alvah looked back at the river, watching it flow. If it were dark I might try to kiss her— then again, maybe not yet, he thought.

Belle and Joe rose and walked towards them. Belle said "I'm thinking we should go back to Mrs. Best's house to freshen a bit before this evening."

Alvah and Joe dutifully walked the two women to Mrs. Best's door and said they'd be back to escort them and Marion to the community center at seven o'clock.

The women changed their outfits and exchanged cautious comments about the afternoon. Belle said she was enjoying hearing news from Joe about goings on in Troy, but thought it best to wait until the end of Joe's stay before saying more. She gave a merry laugh at the suggestion he might move north. "I can't imagine him living hereabouts," she said. Myrna knew that eventually her friend would have more to say, and admired Belle's discipline in not proffering premature opinions.

The annual community festival, which took place at the beginning of June, was a popular event. It drew people from nearby towns, as well as the Elizabethtown community. Many people camped on the outskirts of town or stayed in boarding houses. There was a festive air to the downtown street.

Marion was in a cheerful mood, fussing over Myrna and Belle. Myrna wore a new dress with an overall pattern of small blue flowers—forget-me-nots. It had a fitted bodice, rounded neckline and elbow length sleeves. Marion had brushed Myrna's hair and tied it back with a dark-blue velvet ribbon. Belle's dress was of a similar style (Marion had used the same pattern for both), but was peach and cream striped, trimmed with lace at the neckline. Marion had braided Belle's hair and pinned it in a crown. She stepped back and surveyed her efforts, pronouncing both women "lovely". In keeping with her period of mourning, Marion's outfit was a modest, navy-blue chintz. Nonetheless, it was apparent, Myrna thought, that her mother was still a beauty. This led her to thinking of Pa, and how he enjoyed seeing Marion dressed for a party. She sighed.

Alvah and Joe arrived at Mrs. Best's to escort the women. Alvah smiled easily, complimenting all three women, Joe quickly followed suit. Myra returned Alvah's smile. She held back from saying it was a treat to see him in his 'church clothes', too. His pants were fresh and he wore a natty tan paisley vest over a cream shirt. She supposed these were his musician clothes, and wondered where he bought the vest—or could someone have made it for him?

When they arrived at the hall, Harriet Wells waved and gestured to them, so they sat at a table with her. Belle admired Harriet, and even Marion had grown to accept her. Myrna suspected that was because her mother liked people who had good books to borrow, as well as opinions on what they read. The only personal discomfort Myrna found with Harriet was in Harriet's making too much of Myrna's continuing Pa's guiding business. Most people of their acquaintance would think her practical—not revolutionary.

Reverend Horace soon joined them, along with some of Marion's sewing circle. The sewing ladies liked to be in the way of any incipient gossip. Myrna observed that the good reverend was solicitous of Marion. He cast admiring glances her way, too. Belle and Joe were comfortably engrossed in their private conversations. Myrna thought that Belle was a bit flirtatious with Joe. But then, Belle was a natural flirt—or so she said. Since Alvah was busy tuning up his instrument with the other band members, and her table companions were pleasantly occupied; Myrna had ample time to make observations of those around her. She enjoyed noting other's behavior, surreptitiously hearing what was said. She supposed it was similar to her woods activities, being alert to her surroundings. Lyman was across the room with the Johnsons and other North Elba folk. They gave her a friendly wave. Myrna thought she'd visit with them later.

Myrna saw Jesse at the doorway surveying the room. He'd gone to some effort to appear presentable. She studiously avoided eye contact, while keeping him in her peripheral vision. She watched him, obliquely, while engaging Penny, one of the sewing-circle ladies, about sewing quilts. Eventually, Jesse spied the group and headed their way. To Myrna's surprise, he spoke first to Harriet Wells and then to Reverend Horace. Apparently, he'd had an earlier conversation with the reverend, who gestured for him to join the table. Myrna was intrigued by this turn of events. Why had he insinuated himself in their company? Perhaps Jesse was a cleverer fellow than she would have thought.

Jesse's demeanor was certainly subdued compared to his initial behavior. Belle and Marion exchanged glances. Joe looked perplexed, but evidently decided the best course was to ignore Jesse, beyond a pleasant nod. Though it was common practice to add spirits to the punch offered, Myrna saw Jesse wave his hand in dismissal when a bottle of whiskey was passed his way. Myrna continued to remain alert to Jesse's presence, but when the music started she was caught in the sway of it.

The band started with playing group reels that were inclusive and fun. Jesse apparently asked Harriet to join him in a reel. Harriet linked arms with him and walked to the dance floor. It was hard to say if she liked his company, but she was gracious to her egalitarian core. Reverend Horace asked Marion for a reel. She smiled and declined. Myrna then agreed to dance with him. Joe must have given Jesse the word from Belle, because he did not seek her or her friends as dance partners.

Alvah was free to sit at the table with them for the second set, which included waltzes and two-steps played by other musicians. Myrna knew he would ask her to dance, and he did. She was about to tease him about being "surprisingly good as a dancer," but looking into his eyes stopped her. As evening darkened the room, and lanterns were lit—they lightly held each other and moved with the rhythms of the music. "Am I allowed to say you are beautiful?" he said.

"Yes, if it's true," she replied. He laughed and held her closer on the next turn.

The evening was drawing to a close. When the dance ended, Myrna and Alvah looked for Marion. Penny, said that Harriet and Horace were walking her to Mrs. Best's house. Belle and Joe said they'd be along soon, and were visibly surprised when Lyman said he'd like to walk a ways with them. Myrna took note that Jesse was nowhere in sight. She walked with Alvah to where the musicians were putting away their instruments. They said goodbyes and talked about where they might play next. "You play a real nice fiddle, Alvah," someone named Charles said.

Alvah had a small lantern with him, but instead, they decided the moonlight would suffice for their walk back to Mrs. Best's. The main street was broad and the footing was good. They paused by St. Francis' Church and sat on a bench under the large leafy oak. They were talking about the music and people who'd been at the event, when Alvah leaned close and asked if he could kiss her. He saw her hesitate. "No," she said.

"No?" he echoed. "Jesus! Aren't you even curious...to see what it'd be like?" Their faces were so close.

"Truthfully, I'd have to say, Yes," she faltered. "The thing is, we're business partners. In less than two months from now we'll be leading one of the biggest, maybe most important, guiding trips we'll ever do. If we let one thing lead to another...I might, well...look foolish." She crossed her arms on her chest and leaned back on the bench. Alvah sighed and leaned back too. They were quiet.

"You know, I was thinking it might just be a simple kiss, nothing fancy," he said. "But are you saying that once we finish guiding those fellas around Follansbee Pond I'll be rewarded with a proper kiss?" At that, they could not help but laugh. Myrna rose to her feet and Alvah fell into step with her. At Mrs. Best's doorway all was quiet and dark. Alvah wrapped his arms around her. She could feel his beard brush her cheek. "For the record, that was just a hug and a semi-nuzzle," he said.

Myrna opened the door and softly said, "good night". There was a lantern lit at the bottom of the stairs. She took it to the top of the stairway, extinguished it, and made her way to her room. She could hear Marion asleep. Belle was drowsing. Myrna gently pushed her to her side of the bed and climbed in. Belle started to talk, but Myrna shushed her.

Carson rode back with Lyman and Ann to the Duffney homestead the next day. He said he was confident he'd be able to do the chores on his own. Myrna, Marion and Belle stayed on with Mrs. Best, who was pleased to have Marion's company for a few more days. Myrna realized her mother had every intention of maintaining her role as chaperone. Alvah needed to attend to a matter in Wadhams with his mother, but offered to drive them all to a picnic outing on Twin Pond two days hence. Jesse told Joe that Reverend Horace was employing him to do some carpentry at his church and would meet him at the hotel in time to travel back to Troy. Belle confided to Myrna that she was glad they wouldn't have to worry about including Jesse.

The excursion to Twin Pond was as relaxing and carefree as Belle could have hoped. It was the first week in June, and it seemed the weather had tipped to summer. Marion thought to include Mrs. Best, which was a good idea in that she added immensely to the picnic lunch and, of course, was pleasant company for Marion. There was a generous clearing where the carriage was tethered. And there were pine needled rocky knolls at the shoreline for spreading their blankets and picnic hampers. "I declare," Belle said, "this is a festive setting. I'm honored that you all have prepared such a special outing." Joe nodded vigorously, glancing from one to another.

A path circled around the pond. This gave Belle and Joe an opportunity to walk privately, while still benefiting from the decorum of being chaperoned—lightly. Meanwhile, Myrna and Alvah brought fly rods to a secluded cove, ostensibly not in need of a chaperone. Marion and Mrs. Best had brought skeins of yarn with them. Knitting did not require much attention, allowing for some leisurely speculation and gossip. Eventually, they all returned to the blankets spread under the sheltering green leaves of the giant oaks. The ham, cheese and pickled cucumber sandwiches were served with herbal tea. Mrs. Best had made jam tarts. The conversation was piquant and savory, too—or so thought Belle. Mrs. Best spun stories about sailing on the Hudson River as a young woman, prompting Joachim to talk about his life in Troy—and his dad's work on the river boats. Alvah mentioned that he'd been to the town of Glens Falls, but had traveled no further. He said he'd like someday to go by boat as far as New York City, where he'd heard the tides affected the river's flow. The idea of tidal waters fascinated him. Their conversations meandered and drifted in that way, avoiding turbulence, until mid-afternoon.

The next morning, they all met Joachim at the coach to wish him, and, of course, Jesse, a safe trip. Myrna noted that Jesse's eyes shifted restlessly. He seemed anxious to leave. Joachim promised Belle a letter as soon as he reached Troy. He and Belle hugged fondly. Then Alvah drove Myrna, Marion, and Belle back to the Duffney's homestead. Belle's sunbonnet shaded her face—and any expression that it may have worn.

− CHAPTER 18 −

Endings and Beginnings

It wasn't until the following week that Belle and Myrna had a serious talk about Joe's visit in Elizabethtown. And in that short space of time, information galore reached their ears. The innkeeper told Alvah that Jesse had left without paying a substantial bar bill and that Joachim had paid the tariff for their lodgings. Ann Epps had heard from one of the church sewing circle ladies that the cozy relationship Jesse had established with Reverend Horace had come about through Jesse seeking spiritual guidance to mend his ways regarding women and liquor. Jesse took the pledge, and the reverend had even let him stay a few nights at the parsonage. Unfortunately for Jesse, Reverend Horace had found him one time too many with his hand on Harriet's knee. Though Jesse protested his innocence, saying he meant to be brotherly—like a monk. As for Harriet, she was heard to say that she felt sorry for the poor devil and was tutoring him in topics of women's rights and the anti-slavery movement. Supposedly, Jesse was keen on knowing more about the abolitionists, and asked if he might get to meet John Brown.

Ann told Belle that Lyman was suspicious of the Jesse character, and was glad to see him leave town—and said his behavior reflected badly on Joachim.

Ann said kindly to Belle, "Well, you did get to spend nice times with Joachim and the Duffneys. I reckon he won't bring Jesse on his next visit."

Belle wondered how much her Ma and Pa might have conveyed to Ann about Joe's white father and African mother—and if Ann had written to her folks about Jesse's unbecoming behavior.

When the next weekend came, Lyman dropped Belle at the Duffney's for a visit. After Belle helped Myrna with the chicken coop, they excused themselves to take a walk to the stream at the edge of the property. Myrna grabbed a kitchen basket at the doorway. Seeing Marion, she said, "We'll look for wild thyme and mushrooms along the way."

Carson waved when they passed by the barn. They meandered across the field and along a cut trail in the woods until they came to a clearing, the result of bygone logging. "What luck!" said Belle, "wild strawberries. We might as well settle here for a while…to talk and gather."

Myrna agreed. She'd been wondering when, or if, Belle would share her thoughts about Joe's visit. Myrna knew that she, personally, was reluctant to divulge secrets, and assumed as much about Belle. "We always have things to talk about, don't we," she said.

It seemed Belle had given a lot of thought about Joe's visit, and wanted to consider her ideas before having a conversation with her friend.

"You know, I'd anticipated Joe's visit for months and months. His letters were so sweet and full of his feelings about me, praising my fine qualities and so on. He also wrote about happenings in Troy, plus news of my family and people we knew…his letters often made me homesick. But since his visit, my feelings for him have changed—not that I don't feel affection for him; that, I certainly do. I try not to pay mind to Ann and Lyman's talk about his poor judgement in consorting with Jesse, but I confess that it bothers me. And there are other bothers too." She added, "Though I was relieved that Jesse is not really a friend of Joachim's. He hadn't invited Jesse to travel with him, but somehow he insinuated himself because Jesse is an aquaintence of Mr. Gant, Joe's father."

Myrna knew this conclusion must be painful and sensitive for Belle. She didn't want to add more criticism about Joe to the conversation, so she mentioned that there were rumors from the church women concerning Jesse. "Of course, you know how much Penny and the others can make from a tidbit," she said, lightly.

Belle responded, regretfully. "According to Harriet, most of what's said is true. She stopped to visit with Ann past Wednesday, probably hoping to see me, too. I do believe her. Jesse is a rake and a scoundrel. Actually, in some ways he's a comic figure—one can't but help laughing at the incidents involving him duping Harriet and Reverend Horace. But Harriet is an intelligent, worldly, woman who is not naïve—in spite of her silly side. She felt suspicious of Jesse's interest in Mr. Brown—and also Lyman said likewise." Belle grew serious and leaned close to Myrna. "Harriet said that one evening when she'd dropped by the parsonage for tea, Jesse tried to casually pry information about John and the settlement. She said there was something about his intensity that was out of character—unsettling. But I trust you to not tell anyone this, not even Marion."

The conversation was taking a puzzling turn, Myrna thought. Until now, it had seemed Jesse was an annoying rascal who enjoyed tavern life and the company of women, especially women who accepted his advances. But was there something more sinister to his interest in Elizabethtown and North Elba? Why would someone of his sort care about the settlement and meeting John Brown?

"Do you think he might be a troublemaker? Are you going to write to Joachim about your concerns?" Myrna asked.

"I thought about it, surely. But that would make for a ticklish letter, and it would mark our strained friendship more difficult. Also mentioning Jesse's interest in the Brown settlement might raise unwarranted attention to his actions. Besides, Jesse's gone now"

Belle sat silent for a moment, and then continued. "You may gather that Joachim's visit didn't bring us closer. Truthfully, I'd probably expected too much. He may not have changed so much in our nearly a year apart, but I have. I've grown to like a measure of independence. Teaching at the school is rewarding. You, Marion, and Ann have shown strength in adversity. I now also appreciate my mom's accomplishments. Then, there's Harriet, a startling example of women's capabilities!" Myrna nodded at this, along with Belle. "Truly, I've no mind to settle with Joachim at this point. I'd rather be a life-long spinster than have a dreary marriage—And I'm positive about that."

Myrna took a moment to absorb and ponder her friend's revelations. She didn't disagree with Belle's thoughts. Perhaps Harriet was a greater influence on Belle's thinking than she had heretofore acknowledged. Myrna's only objection was that Harriet lived in a rarified atmosphere not available to many women.

"I think you and I have always been in agreement about learning skills and achieving independence," Myrna said. "As for Harriet's independent style, it is attractive, but it's still dependent on the generosity of her husband. I say she's an intriguing woman—she's even won the admiration of the sewing club. You know how Penny used to tattle on her! I don't know how she has managed to fit in, but she has."

Belle nodded. "I also that think Harriet admires you more than you her. But that's no matter. Harriet told Ann that Mr. Wells, her husband, would be visiting this summer. Harriet says she plans to have a small tea at her residence in his honor—and we all will be invited. Ann, the Browns and some church ladies will be included. And, of course, Reverend Horace," Belle paused, "Hope she checks that the Reverend's personal items aren't left under the bed." Myrna and Belle giggled at the thought. Now that she'd said her piece, Belle turned her attention to Myrna.

"You know, you were seen sitting in front of the church with Alvah after the dance. Also when I see you two together I sense a new closeness. And Marion is *very* curious. Is he courting you?"

Myrna could have expected this question. Still, she felt caught off balance. Divulging feelings was not her forte. Holy Mary! She wasn't even sure what her feelings were... exactly. But it seemed fair to try for some level of truth. "My goodness, people do love to gossip," she started, "I don't know what courting entails. I suppose it involves some kind of mutual intent, so no, that has not happened. Remember, first and foremost, Alvah and I are business partners."

"Myrna Duffney, you are obfuscating, not to add, highly exasperating! You could answer simple questions." Belle was scowling at her.

Myrna saw that Belle felt injured by her reticence, so she reluctantly replied. "I suppose I'm not sure of what to say about me and Alvah. I think we have grown closer by planning the Follansbee expedition together—we've always had guiding in common. I think you want to know more about feelings. I can say, I liked dancing with him... his physical presence." Myrna could feel warmth rising to her face. She shrugged.

"So!" Belle exclaimed, "You are beginning to fall in love. I knew it!"

Myrna protested. "I think we know no such thing."

"Really, Myrna, you are far too serious. Being 'in love' is not a contagion. It can come and go. It is hardly ever fatal. It is a pleasurable feeling, yes?"

Myrna gave a quizzical look to her friend, and changed the subject. "Let's see if we can pick enough strawberries for a proper shortcake. Carson works so hard, it will make a nice treat for him."

Myrna enjoyed picking berries and roaming the woods with Belle. She knew Belle found her need for privacy disturbing, but at the same time, her friend was willing to respect her boundaries. Myrna was glad their friendship was back in balance. They were content to walk in silence, finding some chanterelle and trumpet mushrooms, as well as wild thyme along the way, they anticipated Marion's pleasure at seeing what they'd gathered.

CHAPTER 19

Philosophers on the Horizon

The month of July had arrived. Myrna and Bill Stillman corresponded with increasing frequency as the time grew closer. But Myrna was confident that they were well prepared for the August expedition to Follansbee Pond. She and Alvah sat at the Duffney dining table reviewing their planning and supplies list. Myrna said that as far as she was concerned they'd accounted for everything, but asked Marion if she'd mind giving it a final look. Marion had usually done that task for Sam. "I'll make tea for you and Alvah while you double check our lists." Myrna rose from her chair and went to the kitchen.

Marion walked to the corner desk and rummaged for paper to write on. She seemed pleased to have been included.

Gesturing to the sheet of paper before her, she sat across the table from Alvah. "I always like to be prepared to make a few notes, if need be. Though I must say, you and Myrna are ones for detail—Sam loved the particulars of a trip, too." Alvah returned her smile, he saw there was a wistful quality to it. He wanted to talk about Sam, but felt unsure. Marion was scribbling notes, pausing to read. He figured he might as well go to the kitchen with Myrna.

God almighty! Myrna had flour up to her elbows. Apparently, scones were being made. Alvah had the good sense not to mention that he'd thought she didn't cook. She looked up from the pastry board. "I do enjoy baking," she announced. "In fact, I'm pretty good at preparing anything I like to eat."

Alvah nodded wisely. "I can brew tea," he added. "Once I get the kettle on … I'll go find Carson." He was glad that Carson fit so well with the Duffney women.

Marion took her time reviewing and writing. Myrna, Alvah, and Carson looked expectantly at her. When she'd finished, looking pleased, she put the list and her notes aside. "Well, all in all, you've made excellent preparations. Sam would be proud of you. My suggestions are fairly minor…one thing I'd do is get a train timetable for the Boston to Rutland leg of the trip. The Deershead Inn might have one, or the Ausable Hotel in Keeseville. I know you and Bill Stillman have been writing back and forth. Though you may have covered it, I'm thinking you might ask him more about what each of the individuals on the trip expect they'll need. This could be a fussy and demanding bunch of fellows. They're used to traveling in rarified circles—no matter what Stillman says. They might like the idea of 'roughing' it, but some of them spend most of their time in libraries or schools." Marion paused. "Sam and I talked quite a bit about this prospective group, even though we hadn't concluded how to approach their inevitable idiosyncrasies." Marion noticed Alvah's furrowed brow and Myrna's look of dismay. "Now, now, don't be feeling daunted, just recognize there are probably peculiarities about your clients you won't know about until they are at the pond. Don't worry and don't be surprised—that was Sam's philosophy."

Myrna said, "I suppose it's those intangible things that we'll have to be concerned about."

"Really, that is always the case," Alvah added. "I've guided more than one sport who swore he knew the woods and was a good shot, who wasn't remotely able to walk a few miles or shoot straight."

Myrna nodded, then added, "I do have some faith in Bill's judgement about these men, though."

Marion asked whom they'd hired as cook. "You know, having an excellent cook on hand goes a long way to making satisfied sports." Carson chimed that he thought that would be true. He added, "These are the best scones I ever ate."

Marion said they might ask Mr. Bakely, who resided on Moody Pond, if he would be available to cook at Follansbee. It turned out that he was available, and happy to oblige them.

Some days later, a message was delivered to the Duffney's. Marion was pleased to receive a hand written note from Harriet Wells inviting her and Myrna to an afternoon tea to be held in a week. Myrna agreed that it would be an interesting afternoon—meeting Mr. Wells and all.

Within days, it unfolded that Belle, Lyman, Ann, and Alvah had also been included. This led Belle and Myrna to speculate on who else had been invited. "I expect Mary Brown and the Johnsons were invited. Mr. Brown is traveling, and Mary is choosey about these events," Belle said.

"I was somewhat surprised that Alvah and his mother were invited, though Delia is in the sewing circle, and Alvah does have a cordial relationship with Reverend Horace. I suppose we're all considered of a liberal bent."

"You might be surprised at some of Delia's views," Belle added.

Myrna realized that she really knew very little about Alvah's mother. Then again, until recently, she wasn't that curious about Alvah's ideas beyond his woods skills. She would ask more questions, she thought.

- CHAPTER 20 -

Tea Time

The day arrived.

"It's a perfect day for a summer tea," Marion declared to Myrna on their way in the carriage to the Well's cottage.

Neither Marion nor Myrna had been to the cottage, which was set in a secluded grove at the end of a long drive off the main road. Marion was not surprised to see a flower garden, Harriet had mentioned such in their conversations at church socials. There were also rose trellises to one side of the veranda, the red blooms showing nicely against the white clapboards. It was decorated as summer festive. Urns of wildflowers—lilies, daisies and black-eyed Susan's, highlighted by blue dahlias, were set among small, linen covered tables. There was a plentiful supply of white-washed, mismatched chairs with colorful chintz cushions. Marion recognized the fabric from sewing circle and wondered who might have made the cushions, or if they'd been sewn by Harriet herself. Marion noted with satisfaction that the cottage and porch were done up in a lovely way, but not so much as to be beyond the reach of those who had been included in the gathering. It was easy to admire Harriet in this venue—and to anticipate meeting the elusive husband, Milton Wells. She assumed the portly older man talking with Lyman and Belle must be him.

There were a few families from the Brown settlement as well as Reverend Horace and various church members settled on the front porch. Mary Brown was unable to attend, but her daughter and one of the Johnsons soon arrived. Alvah and Delia arrived shortly after Myrna and Marion. After all around introductions to Milton Wells were complete, Delia made a point to speak cordially to Myrna and Marion.

Myrna realized that Harriet had carefully selected a small gathering meant to showcase Milton Wells, and to provide him with an introduction to some homespun liberals—that is to say, people at least acquainted with the political discourse of the day. She'd heard Mr. Wells was a financier and had ties to the import/export business in New York. There were rumors that he was fabulously wealthy, supported suffragists and abolitionists—and that Harriet was his second or third wife. However, since most of these rumors were sown and tended purely in the North Country, it was hard to separate fact from fiction. Obviously, the Wells were educated and well-traveled folk who maintained more than one home, but who knew beyond that? Myrna was amused in thinking of the inevitable after tea discourse she would have with Belle—and Marion, too.

The tea was sumptuous by 'mountain standards'. There were a variety of small sandwiches, including: watercress, cucumber with soft cheese, minced egg with cream and herbs, plum jam and, of course, scones and vanilla pound cake. There were several teas; Earl Grey and raspberry mint. Penny's daughters, Sophia and Maude, had been enlisted to serve, but Harriet cheerfully rose to refresh teapots and platters, too.

Later, as the crowd thinned, some leaving for home or elsewhere, Myrna found herself seated in a wicker settee with Belle, banked by chairs on either side by Harriet and Marion. Harriet sighed, "I'm just so glad Milton and I found time to do this. I suppose he took Alvah and Lyman to the barn out back to show them his new carriage." Seeing Milton with Lyman and Horace at the edge of the garden, Harriet waved, beckoning them to the porch.

Clearly, Milton was used to being at the center of things. He scraped a large rocker to that vantage, while politely asking Penny to bring a tray of small glasses and cherry cordial. Alvah and his mother were about to make their goodbyes, but Milton good-naturedly swayed them to stay a bit longer. He smiled expansively, somehow including everyone. "I've so looked forward to getting to know Harriet's friends. Her letters are full of all the interesting things you've done or said…why I'd be disappointed to not hear more," he said with great charm.

Myrna was fascinated by this jolly, shrewd man. She wondered how he and Harriet came to be matched.

After pleasantries about travel, weather and gardens, Milton directly addressed Myrna. "I believe I may know one of the persons who will be along on the camping expedition you are leading. Harriet told me about the interesting venture in her letters…and coincidently I was having drinks at my club in New York with my good friend Mr. Jim Lowell, when he mentioned that he would be traveling to the Adirondacks on a camping trip with Mr. Stillman and some of the Boston fellows. It won't be his first trip up here, he's quite eager about it. Have you perchance met him?"

"Well, no, I haven't yet had the pleasure, though Bill Stillman has done his best to describe our clients' needs and preferences." Myrna paused. "Before my father died last fall, he, Bill, and I did our rudimentary planning. We spent a week or so camping together on Follansbee Pond. Quite naturally, Mr. Stillman would talk about his friends who might join us…Bill is a fine storyteller and very enthusiastic about this adventure. We correspond regularly. Thanks to Alvah Wood's assistance, we are now well prepared for our Boston guests," Myrna gestured towards Alvah. Myrna wanted to strike the right tone, and not divulge anything that could be construed as gossip. She caught Alvah's eye, hoping he shared her desire for discretion.

Milton nodded vigorously. "From what Harriet says, you've managed to take on your father's business and even establish yourself as a well-regarded guide, quite an accomplishment, I must say." He genuinely beamed his admiration. "I haven't met William Stillman, but Jim Lowell sings his praises. He's had a major hand in publishing that *Crayon* magazine, which I confess is a bit esoteric for me. Have you seen it?"

"No, the *Crayon* is yet to make it this far north," Myrna replied. "I gather you know we are mostly country folk, though that doesn't keep us from reading books or keeping abreast of current events." There were good natured chuckles at Myrna's words. Milton laughed too.

Alvah chimed that Marion and his mother, Delia, managed to find entertaining reading for the church ladies. Reverend Horace added that, thanks to Harriet, the church was accumulating a number of books for a lending library. The assembled reassured Milton that they were well informed, if not exactly learned.

Milton poured another round of cherry cordial. "You know, there is a novel I've read that I'd be most interested in hearing opinions about, especially from a group as diverse as this one. Recently, I met the authoress, Mrs. Harriet Beecher Stowe. Have any of you read *Uncle Tom's Cabin?*"

Of course, many had read it. Marion said, "Oh yes, most of us have read it. In fact, it was one of the novels we selected to read aloud in the ladies' circle."

Delia added, "We like sharing a book that way. It gives us a chance to discuss it after each chapter rather than waiting to borrow, if one doesn't own it." She hesitated to say that a few of the women had poor reading skills.

Milton asked what they thought of the novel and the characters portrayed. This stimulated a lot of discussion about the evils of slavery and the notorious behavior of slave owners like the fictional Simon Legree. Ann Epps said that, to her mind, Uncle Tom was too kind and forgiving, but lauded Mrs. Stowe.

Milton turned to Belle, "And what did you think of the book?"

"I can't disagree with my friends on Mrs. Stowe's sympathies. However, most of us folk living at the settlement were either never enslaved, or are freedmen—I can't speak definitively about Uncle Tom's likely attitudes and behaviors. However, it is just a story, and an author can freely depict her characters." Belle had the floor and Milton's startled attention. Continuing, Belle said. "There is another book written by Mr. Solomon Northrup, a friend of my father's. It's called *Twelve Years a Slave*. It is a true story—one about Mr. Northrup's harrowing experiences as a free Negro captured in the North and sent to enslavement in the South." Belle shook her head side to side. "I found it frightening and mesmerizing…to me it expresses how a person would feel and behave if enslaved." Ann and Lyman nodded in agreement. Most of the others seemed not to have read it.

Milton thought a moment. "You know, I've heard of this book— read a piece about it in the New York Times. But I've been remiss in not having read it."

Ann Epps piped, "It's a personal story; I'd say scary, and not as entertaining as *Uncle Tom's cabin*."

Lyman and Belle nodded their assent.

"Yes, I would suppose that would have to be the case," Milton said, regaining his equilibrium, smiling expansively.

The afternoon relaxed into other topics, light and serious, as the sun lowered in the sky. It was pleasing to get to know more about one's neighbors, Myrna thought, and said as much to Milton and Harriet upon taking her leave.

"Yes, indeed," he replied "that is an excellent thing." Alvah caught Myrna's eye. He walked her and Marion to their carriage, saying he'd stop by during the week.

- CHAPTER 21 -

Snags before Keeseville Arrival

Stillman's letter to Myrna was long and chatty. He was heartened that all of the friends who had signed on for the adventure were enthusiastic about the trip. There'd be ten of them. It was expected most of the men would arrive in Keeseville on August 2nd, where they would stay the night or two at the hotel there before proceeding to Martin's Hotel on Saranac Lake.

Myrna felt excited at the thought…the excursion was to begin in a little over a week. She and Alvah were well ready for their part, as were the rest of the guides. Carson said he and Marion would manage very well during their absence. Myrna and Alvah agreed that it would be fine at the Duffney's homestead without them, though they'd be gone for a number of weeks.

It seemed to be a placid, if anticipatory, week ahead of them. Marion suggested that they invite Delia and Belle for a summer lunch. "I was thinking Alvah might like us getting to know his mother better…and I'm sure Belle would like to spend some time with you, seeing as you'll be away most of August. Oh, and, of course, Alvah is included," she said. Myrna merely nodded. She was trying to finish reading a piece written by Mr. Emerson—Stillman's 'Waldo".

Say what? thought Myrna, when she saw Lyman and Belle arriving together—and too early for lunch. As they walked to the porch, Myrna could see that Belle looked distraught, and Lyman's brow was set in a frown. Marion, who was standing in the doorway, suggested that they sit on the porch. She asked Carson to draw some cold water in a pitcher and bring glasses. Lyman was the first to speak, saying he had information from a reliable source that a known bounty hunter had been asking about some of the tenants at the Brown settlement, and had asked by name about a Miss Wright, Belle's surname. Lyman looked shaken, of course, because he had more or less been charged with protecting Belle.

"The thing is," Lyman said, "We're all used to keeping a close watch on each other, and have had few problems from outsiders. Most strangers who stop by are either lost sportsmen or folks who are curious to meet Mr. Brown and the rest of us." He paused, seeing Alvah and Delia come up the walk, thinking he might as well finish what he had to say in front of them, since some of his worries had to do with the upcoming expedition. Repeating the gist of it with some elaboration, he broached the heart of the matter. Continuing, and looking to Alvah, he said,

"What with you, me, and Myrna traipsing around Follansbee Pond for the next few weeks, I worry for Belle's safety." Adding, "John is in Kansas, and some of his boys aren't around either." He let out a deep breath. "I'm in a quandary. I sure don't want to not meet my commitment to you." He looked with a stricken expression at Myrna. "Actually, I'd be letting Sam down, too."

It seemed that, to a one, they were quiet for more than a few minutes. This was a serious quandary. Myrna was the first to break the silence.

"I have an idea," she paused. "Hear me full out before you state any objections," she said looking at Belle. "We'll bring her along." Without hesitation, and in spite of her request, the men erupted. She let Lyman and Alvah raise and go on about the predictable objections. Belle stayed quiet and alert. The other two women and Carson looked on in fascination.

"I heard everything you fellows have to say, and still say it will work. In the first place, it was never my intention to set my campsite anywhere near our illustrious sports. Alvah and I discussed this in our plans. I've already picked a suitable site for me across the pond—far from the evening campfire chatter of the men. If Belle comes along, it could even be said that she is an assistant and companion for me. Perhaps she might even be called Lyman's niece.

"But won't there be a lot of questions by the men?" Lyman asked.

"No, I don't think that'll be the case. Belle and I will arrive separately in our boat to my site—well after the group has set-up camp across the pond. Alvah and I will make sure your particular client is well cared for, should you wish to check on Belle," she said, addressing Lyman. "In fact, you'll usually be assigned to Bill Stillman, who likes to go it alone anyway. Once these fellas are settled-in, they'll be more interested in their own banter than the peculiarities of the woman guide and her female companion. Believe me, this can work." Myrna leaned back in her chair and delicately sipped some cool water.

Delia opined, "These men are for the most part famous and worldly—excepting they know very little of our woodsy ways. I'll bet they'd hate to ask questions about our rustic woman guide here. And especially after she shoots 'em a deer!"

Lyman shook his head. "Well, I admit I'd rest more easy knowing Belle is protected."

Alvah thought to himself that once again, Myrna showed a remarkable boldness. Jeezsus! You never know what's coming next. He gave Myrna a direct look. "Yes, we can make this work," he said.

Once they all were in agreement, the rest was relatively simple. Belle said she was happy to be part of the adventure. She was fit and had skills in identifying edible plants. She said she'd be sure to not get under foot. Myrna asked Belle that they might have a private conversation the following day, now that it was settled they should proceed this afternoon with Marion's lovely lunch as planned.

Myrna paced the porch next morning after breakfast, waiting for Belle to arrive. She had many questions of Belle that needed answers. She wondered just how much danger Lyman thought could befall Belle. And exactly what made her father such a target of interest to proponents of slavery? It seemed Belle had glossed over the family history—or was she simply naïve?

Belle was her cheerful self, smiling as the porch door shut behind her. "I could do with a cup of tea," she said. "I borrowed Ann's horse, Zeke. He's kinda skittish, but likes to gallop."

They brought a pot of tea and cups to the side porch, where they could see Marion tending the kitchen garden. Myrna called out to her, saying she'd be out to help shortly. Marion waved, saying it wasn't necessary. She was near done, anyway. It wasn't the first time Myrna observed her mother being content there. It was one of the chores Marion and Sam used to share.

Myrna poured two cups from the blue teapot into delft-patterned cups. "I'm hoping you can tell me more...you know, background about what Lyman said, and about your father."

Belle's brows wrinkled briefly. She seemed pensive, and then set back in the cushioned rocker. "You'd think, actually, *I'd* think that I would know more about my family's undertakings. The truth is, they haven't divulged much—ever. They both, Ma and Pa, prefer to keep secrets. What I've said to you earlier is about it. All I do know is my pa's an anti-slavery activist, and I've speculated about some of the folks passing through our house in Troy on business. Also last year there was some ruckus at a plantation in Virginia that he was involved with, but my parents didn't divulge what exactly happened there—though I overheard that one of the plantation overseers died in a skirmish to free a slave. And sometime after that, they told me living here in the North Country was a healthier, safer place. And it is healthier…I can't even express how happy I am that you and your family are so companionable. The Epps' and Browns, too, of course. And then there's Harriet—more forward leaning than most women in either Troy or Albany. So, yes, I've felt pretty safe and happy here, especially now that I've cooled on my friendship with Joachim." Belle leaned forward, taking a gulp of tea. "I have to say, I'm feeling very nervous, and a little concerned about the way Lyman and Ann are treating me these days. Evidently, they've grown anxious about bounty hunters looking for runaways. I really can't say as to whether or not their fears are valid. Lyman is like a second pa to me. He might just be over-reacting to the idea of leaving me alone with Ann at the settlement while he's away. Then there's the fact that Mr. Brown's away in Kansas. He's so fearless…we all feel safer when he's around."

Myrna nodded to the sentiment about John Brown. This all made some kind of sense to her. "What are your honest thoughts about traveling to Follansbee Pond with us? It won't necessarily be easy."

Belle paused. "I can say, I'm actually delighted. You have no idea of how envious I've been listening to you and Alvah talk about it. And Lyman also sounds enthused when he talks to Ann." She grew more serious. "I do think I can be helpful. I'm willing to set a campsite, gather herbs and perform mundane tasks. I'm strong enough not to be a burden—even Lyman agrees about that."

Myrna was relieved by Belle's enthusiasm, though knew she'd be challenged by the inevitable rigors of camp life. She wished Belle could tell her more about the potential threats from outsiders and her family's role in anti-slavery activities.

Marion soon joined them on the porch, pulling a chair to the shade and fanning herself. Belle expanded a bit more on her family, acknowledging that her pa was an activist abolitionist. Marion looked thoughtful and nodded. Once again, Myrna wished for more details, but held her tongue. She guessed Belle had told her all she knew—or at least to a point.

Then they turned to the practical matters of what Belle should carry with her on the Follansbee trip. It was decided that both she and Myrna would need trousers. Myrna said she had one pair for lending.

"We'll outfit ourselves pretty much like the other guides, though a dress would be nice to wear at Martin's. I've already secured a room there. You can bunk with me." It made Myrna uneasy to think the hotel would consider Belle some kind of maid to her, but she didn't voice these thoughts. It was true, as she and Marion sometimes discussed, North Elba, Elizabethtown and the Brown settlement had a strong liberal core, probably borne of proximity and friendship. However, one didn't have to travel far to find prejudice.

– CHAPTER 22 –

Finally Follansbee Pond 1858

> Winding through grassy shallows in and out,
> Two creeping miles of rushes, pads and sponge,
> To Follansbee waters and the Lake of Loons.
>   –*Adirondac* R. Waldo Emerson

Reluctantly, Myrna decided to forgo traveling to Keeseville to meet Stillman and the group of sports. She sent notes to that effect to Stillman in both Boston and Keeseville, just in case, assuring him that all was in order in spite of that change in the plan.

Instead, on August 2nd Alvah went to meet their clients as the Duffney Guide Company's emissary, while Myrna, Belle, and Lyman went ahead to Martin's Hotel. It had been agreed earlier that her brother, George, needn't make the trip to Keeseville. And he was relieved to relinquish that role, saying Myrna and Alvah seemed to have everything well in hand.

Actually, Myrna found not traveling to Keeseville to work very well. They were able to pack the wagon with camping gear, as well as some niceties such as extra woolen blankets, thick boot stockings, sunhats, soap and dried fruits. Once at the hotel, they loaded and prepared their packs; then stashed them safely. Lyman opted to stay in an outdoor encampment on the hotel property with other guides, while Myrna and Belle shared a room at the hotel as planned.

Myrna freshened a bit in the room and then left Belle sitting on one of the narrow beds while she ventured to 'the hole' to talk with her crew of guides. It pleased her that they were respectful to a one, acknowledging how they missed Sam, and assuring her that they were more than ready for the trip. Tim Earhart piped to the group, "Myrna's such a good scout and crack shot, we'll not lack for fresh meat." Some of the men informally thanked her for continuing with Sam's expedition, saying it would guarantee cash for food on their tables come winter. For her part, Myrna said, "My pa picked you to help him and Mr. Stillman because he said you were the best. I appreciate that you are honoring him by putting your faith in me to see you through on his behalf. Honest, it means more than I can say." She smiled "I've already said more than usual."

Tim raised a glass of something and said, "Hear, hear." The men followed suit.

Myrna meandered along the shore before going back to the room she shared with Belle. It was a balmy evening; the sun had not yet set. She bowed along the way to some guides who were not part of the Follansbee party, but nevertheless, familiar to her. She was careful of her comportment, as Pa had advised her. For a moment, it seemed as he were walking beside her. She was grateful to be led by her memories of Sam's teachings.

When she got to their room, Belle had already put on a simple dress for dinner, and Myrna did the same. She'd planned on them dining at the inn, a minor extravagance given they'd be several weeks in the woods subsisting on only nourishing, simple fare. The only other time Myrna had dined at Martin's had been with Pa. Those memories nagged at her, but hardened her resolve to accomplish this task as her father would have seen fit.

Myrna and Belle sat at a small table near the window. Myrna had spoken plainly to the hotel proprietor, Bill Martin, about her expectations regarding equal service for her traveling companion, Belle. She knew he was sympathetic to antislavery causes. Nevertheless, there were glances from other diners as they walked to their table—but this was to be expected, Belle commented, breezily.

Bill Stillman saw them as he walked from the bar to the main dining room. He came to their table in jolly spirits to exchange pleasantries. It seemed his boat was not quite ready to embark on the river, so he'd be getting a delayed start. He had Mr. Lowell in tow, who seemed distant but courteous. When Myrna thought to mention to Lowell that she and Belle had recently had tea with Milton and Harriet Wells—and that Milton had praised his poetry, Lowell became alert and friendly. He then added politely that Bill and the Martin's had spoken highly of her considerable guiding skills.

As Stillman and Lowell bowed slightly before turning to walk to a table, Belle whispered that these intellectuals had high opinions of themselves. Myrna agreed, saying, "I'm happy I remembered to pass along Milton's greetings."

Belle gave a wry look as she sliced into her venison steak. "It does help to have connections with the right sorts of folks, doesn't it," adding, "tenuous as they may be."

"A sobering thought, but true." Myrna was expecting the men from Boston might place them under scrutiny at first. Her usual plan was to over-prepare and stay alert. So far, her feathers hadn't been ruffled. After dinner they walked out on the veranda and then down the stairs and along the path to the shore. They stood and quietly watched the sun alter from gold to crimson before it disappeared.

Once back in their room, Belle hugely sighed as she hung up her dress and slipped into a loose white nightgown. "Whew! What a relief to be away from all the eyes. I was getting tired of sitting straight and acting prim!" she said, flopping on her bed.

"But, you always sit straight."

"Myrna, you very well know what I mean."

"Yep, I do…we're anomalies, and I for one am happy to be that."

Belle tucked both arms around her pillow as she sat at the head of her bed. "I'd say I'm more resigned than happy. And I'm just waiting for one of them to think I'm a serving girl. At least you won't have to endure that."

"No, my dear friend that is the truth." She turned down the lamp. They needed a good sleep before their trip tomorrow.

In the morning, just before dawn, Myrna met with the other guides at 'the hole.' The air was still crisp and dew was on the grass. Lyman offered her a tin cup of coffee from the large pot on the campfire. Most of the men were itching to get to the bountiful breakfast traditionally served to guides in a room off the hotel kitchen. "It's likely to be the best we'll git for weeks," Caleb, an old timer, said.

Alvah and Bill Stillman had been sitting on a bench talking when Myrna arrived. They rose to greet her. "Mornin", Alvah said, "Perfect day for our start. Bill's boat isn't quite ready, but should be later today or early tomorrow."

"It's an annoyance," Bill said, "but these things happen, as you know. At least I know that you, Alvah, and the rest will get the men safely set up on the pond by nightfall."

"Not to worry." Myrna replied, walking from them to the lake. She took her supply list from her shirt pocket, seeing the packed boats ready on the shore. Alvah turned from Bill and walked along side of her. They did their survey and then stood together on the sandy launch area watching the sky lighten over the lake. They were close enough that their forearms briefly touched. Myrna felt Alvah's pleasant warmth, but neither looked at the other or commented. Alvah walked back to the inn's verandah with her. He had a story to tell.

"There was a really funny incident when the fellows arrived in Keeseville. Apparently, some of the townsfolk got wind of the fact that famous Boston people were arriving from across the lake. Well, they were only interested in Professor Agassiz, seeing as he's a famous scientist. It seems that the other men were unknown to them. The thing is, they didn't know what he looked like, and there was a bunch of men standing waiting for the wagons. So Jeb Seltzer takes a newspaper clipping from his pocket and walks around trying to match the drawing of Agassiz to the party that just arrived. Finally, he announces, 'there he is—looks just like his picture!' I'm tellin ya, if you could have seen the expressions on the Boston faces. The rest of us chuckled…or outright laughed. I'm supposing they're thinking we're all kind of backward here in the North Country! But, to his credit, Agassiz did stop to shake everyone's hands. Actually, he is rather nondescript; medium height, brown hair, glasses—looks like a professor and has an Austrian accent."

Myrna smiled. "That's a good one." She walked up the hotel porch stairs and Alvah crossed the lawn to the guide camps.

She heard a female voice with a French accent call her. "Miz Myrna, is zat you?"

"Well, I'll be…Amelie, it's a pleasure to see you! And this gentleman must be your husband."

"Yes … my husband, is here to see a man about logging. And this month is, as you say, our one year marriage anniversary, so he brings me here as a present." Amelie blushed, "I may not fit for travel next year."

Myrna observed that Amelie looked robust and rosy. It was easy to see she might be in the early stages of confinement. Myrna told them about the guiding trip and they, in turn, said they had just completed building a house on Raquette Lake. This time they exchanged directions and mailing addresses. "And now I can read some things in English," Amelie said proudly.

Her accent had somewhat diminished, too. Myrna was pleased that they'd chanced to meet again.

At long last, everyone had been accounted for and had boarded his canoe.

Finally...Myrna thought, as the silky water curled around her paddle. It felt good to be in her canoe with the clear water skimming below her. Belle sat cross-legged in the bow. They both had tied back their hair and wore felt hats to shade their faces. With their trousers and long sleeved shirts, from a distance, they were not distinct from the other guides. Myrna was glad that Marion had insisted, this time, on tailoring the clothes to actually fit a female form. If Pa only knew, he'd have a good laugh at that, she thought.

Myrna was lead guide. When she glanced back at the other guides and their patrons in the boats behind her, she was satisfied with the smooth progress and amiable spirit amongst them.

Belle was enthralled. She was constantly pointing and exclaiming about sights along the shoreline, especially when they left the lake and entered the green, leafy confines of the river. There were abundant songbirds, all manner of colorful finches and chickadees, as well as red- winged blackbirds flitting in the reedy places. They saw and heard plentiful deer, and startled a mother black bear with two cubs. Gliding along created more of a show than trudging through the forest. Although traveling a distance by canoe was a new experience for Belle, she quickly found her balance and soon was not perturbed by the light rapids and rocky places they needed to negotiate. She asked Myrna if she might try paddling for herself once they reached the pond. Myrna said she reckoned they'd have plenty of time for that, once the guides and sports were settled in their respective campsites.

It was Myrna's habit to observe and reflect while on these guiding ventures. She did not require or encourage conversation. Myrna could not help but think about her last time here with Pa. It had been an exciting, good time—memories to hold. She recalled fragments of conversation she and Pa had around the campfire with Stillman—Stillman's curiosity about John Brown and the settlement, and his pleasure in showing them his folio of nature drawings. . She wondered if this time Bill would draw or paint. He was so intent on making this a special time for his friends. She understood that he'd decided to call the primitive open structure he'd built near the shore 'Camp Maple'. It was set near the place of last year's smaller encampment. Myrna would have to build a new shelter across the pond for her and Belle. Fortunately, there would be enough hours of daylight left to make this feasible. And Belle would help. The best luck was that it was a warm, clear day, a hidden factor that counted greatly in creating a satisfying experience for their clientele.

At one point her boat glided alongside Alvah's. They waved to each other. He was acting as guide to Mr. Lowell. Both men instinctively tipped their hats to Belle. She smiled primly, touching the brim of her hat in response. Myrna held her breath to keep from laughing at that awkward scenario. She was also reminded that there were some goings-on she wanted to ask Alvah about Delia and his household. Harriet had recently implied to Belle, that Delia occasionally had guests staying with them. But, she'd said 'shielding guests'. Could Delia's home be a stop on the 'underground railroad'? If so, why hadn't Alvah mentioned it? On the other hand, that would have to be a secret kind of endeavor, she supposed. She was amused to think how once Alvah had accused *her* of being secretive! The truth is, she thought keeping one's inner voice private, was a wholesome virtue.

Paddling into the narrow neck leading to the pond, Myrna spotted the large boulder where she and Belle would make their camp. Pointing ahead, she said, "There's the place! We'll debark to the left of that rock outcrop."

Belle took off her boots and socks and rolled her pants legs. "I can pull our boat a ways up on that sandy crescent." That done, they together unloaded the boat before Myrna began chopping saplings to set the framework of their shelter.

Myrna had scouted the campsite over a year ago, but it had remained fresh in her mind's eye. It was in a small cove obscured from the main pond by a large granite boulder. There was a small clearing and two young maple trees that would serve as handy side poles for their shelter. Myrna neatly lashed the main sapling support horizontal to the two maples, creating the framework for the front, using slimmer limbs for the roof and sides; the back of the roof was angled to meet the ground. The floor was level dirt—delicate pine boughs piled to the back would serve as comfortable mattresses. Belle gathered the best pine and hemlock she could find for bedding and weaving into the roof frets. That finished, she dug a substantial fire pit in front and ringed it with large stones.

Myrna declared their work done. It was a tidy camp in the woods. They were pleased.

"Whew! I believe we deserve a drink of water," Belle said, rummaging in her kitchen pack for two tin cups. They sat, backs to the side of the boulder, surveying their work and sipping from their cups.

"You know, Belle, this went faster than I expected. After all, this camp preparation wasn't something you're used to doing. You fell right to it."

"The truth is I was a bit anxious about it. I made Lyman explain some things about building a camp. We even practiced making balsam bedding," she glanced at Myrna, "Anyway, I think he felt obligated, having stuck you with me."

"So far, so good," Myrna rose to her feet. "I'd best make an appearance at the main camp across the pond, though I believe Steve Martin and some of the other guides came out earlier in the week to build the larger shelters. They had it well in order before the sports arrived. You'll be fine here on your own?" Belle nodded her assent and proceeded to gather kindling.

Myrna's shoulders were tired from the day's paddling and chopping. Still, it was pleasant feeling the now emptied boat glide over the smooth water. She could hear the jocular voices of the men before reaching shore. It was a happy, confident sound, she thought. She docked and quietly approached the perimeter of the clearing. The encampment was fully established. The main, large structure was sturdily built. It was to be home to the ten Boston sports. There were a host of smaller, though neat, camps on the periphery for the ten guides who would be attending to the sports. The cook, Mr. Bakely, had his own set-up with a rustic, wooden table, pots and utensils precisely arrayed to one side. His kitchen, so to speak, was covered with an awning. She quickly surveyed the area where the men would practice shooting. To her thinking, all was completely satisfactory, as it should be. Nevertheless, she was relieved to see it so.

Alvah was first to see her, and then Bill Stillman. They waved to her and approached together. "Is your campsite to your liking?" Bill asked. Myrna nodded. Alvah mentioned they had caught an abundance of trout and offered her one, saying he was lucky to have caught so many in such a short time.

Bill introduced her to Misters Lowell and Agassiz, who had evidently been told about her role in the expedition. They talked a bit about the next day's itinerary. James Lowell politely asked if she and Miss Belle would be joining them at campfire. She replied with good humor, "I think not. We will have our own campfire to tend." Then, with Alvah and Bill, each to a side, she walked back to where her boat was docked. Alvah wrapped the trout in some grasses and set it in the bow of the boat. She assured them that their encampment was mighty impressive. And said she'd be by after breakfast to assist on the shooting range. The men pushed the boat away from shore and tipped their hats as she turned her boat towards the rock in the distance. She knew Pa would approve of the way it was going.

Myrna pulled the boat ashore onto the sand and turned it over, in case of rain. Belle had a fire going and some kind of concoction with mushrooms and cornmeal cooking in a pot. Myrna made quick work of fileting the trout, which they grilled over the hot embers. It was a tasty repast that they ladled onto their tin plates. "This cornmeal mushroom dish is delicious. I didn't realize how hungry I was until I tucked into it. What's the herb flavor?"

"It's an herb mixture I got from Ann—a ground blend of juniper berries, garlic, thyme and Jamaican pepper. The pepper's the only scarce item. It's really good on venison, but there was something about the trumpet mushrooms that induced me to try it in the porridge."

"You had time to forage for mushrooms?"

"This is a lucky spot, plenty of chanterelle back there." Belle gestured towards the dark woods beyond the fire.

Myrna said, "You should see the kitchen set-up Mr. Bakely has at main camp. There's even a work table of sorts. I'm expecting our guides made it weeks ago, before Bill and his friends arrived. For a camp, the whole thing is imposing. Much elaborated on since Pa, Bill and I were here last year. Hope these fellows appreciate it."

"Does it make you feel sad that your pa isn't here with you?" Belle put another log on the fire and poked the embers.

"Of course, but not as much as I expected. Or maybe, yes and no. Though it's not in my nature to be mystical or religious, I feel like he's here with me. Not actually, of course... more like I'm doing my best and I sense his smiling approval. Do you know what I mean?"

"I can't say as I do, but I believe you. You had an especially close relationship with your father. One I envied." Myrna looked at Belle and realized this was true.

They sat quietly and comfortably by the fire. There was a loon calling on the water to entertain them. Myrna said she heard a deer snorting nearby. Once they heard laughter from across the pond and wondered if one of the other guides had told a funny story.

Myrna wanted to ask Belle more about John's trip to Kansas, but it was late. It seemed that she and Belle would have plenty of time to converse over the next few weeks. It was important that they have refreshing sleep before tomorrow.

In the morning, when Myrna arrived at the main camp, breakfast was over. The smell of bacon still wafted on the mild breeze. She knew it was important to establish amiable routines with the sports early on, Pa had always emphasized this. She also knew that today would be the time for her to portray herself as the confident, competent, professional guide that she was. It had been easy when she guided with Pa. Sports and other guides were so deferential to him that their trust had simply spilled over to her. These Boston fellas purported to be more egalitarian than most, at least according to Bill Stillman, but she had no intention of coasting on assumptions. Alvah could be counted on to assume the proper demeanor, but a few of the old-timers had an affectionate view of her as Sam's daughter, the talented anomaly. One thing always in her favor was her slim wiry figure and chiseled face. She reckoned that with her hair tied back and tucked under her broad-brimmed felt hat, she didn't stand out from the rest of the guides. She even walked like a boy.

For the moment, at least, she ambled unobtrusively amongst the others, occasionally stopping to jaw with particular guide friends. Alvah said the sports seemed compliant with the loose itinerary of exploring and rifle practice after breakfast, and hunting, fishing, or relaxing, in the afternoons.

"You know," Alvah said, "Professor Agassiz and Mr. Wyman said they wish to collect plant and insect specimens, and bring them back to Boston. Bill says he'll go out with them today, cause some of the guides are perplexed by the idea of plant gathering." He snorted. "We're all thinkin you might take the sports that's interested to the rifle range. Jeremy, who's never been on a hunt with you, wondered if you mightn't be more patient with novice shooters, being of the gentler gender and all, but old Cal assured him you weren't any kinder than the rest!"

It felt good to have a laugh with Alvah. Myrna felt more relaxed for it. Nonchalantly, she approached Stillman and asked him to assemble those interested in target shooting.

Most of the men were eager to give it a try, whether or not they'd actually practiced much with a rifle. Professor Agassiz politely told her he'd try it another day. He, Mr. Wyman, and Bill wished to assess the pond species.

Myrna set targets at varying distances along the rifle range. She explained they'd each begin with the nearest target. After each shooter, she'd examine and mark for accuracy. She'd also help anyone sight a new rifle, if need be.

"Since I suspect some of you may have had more practice than others, I'll begin by demonstrating. So, bear with me." Myrna assumed the classic pose and snuggly shouldered her Hawkins rifle. She took careful aim and squeezed the trigger. Upon examination, the bullet shaded slightly left of center, a bullseye, nevertheless. The shooters in the group were mightily impressed. Mr. Holmes said, "By Jove, Myron that was a good one!"

Myrna managed to hold a serious expression and nodded. Clearly, Mr. Holmes had thought her a boy! Holmes was all apologies when later, after practice, Jeremy, one of the guides explained she was "Myrna". "No matter, Mr. Holmes, no matter," she said graciously.

By day three, there was an informal ease to the gathering. Most of the men gravitated to join Myrna in rifle practice. Stillman and the other guides must have told the sports about Sam. During breaks in shooting or at lunch, when they asked her to join them, they did not hesitate to ask about her guiding exploits with her father. They were curious about how and why she had become an excellent woodsman. She began to feel as comfortable with the sports as she was with most of the guides. Somehow or other, word got out that she was the local school marm, along with being a hunting guide. No doubt, either Bill Stillman or Alvah had mentioned it. In any case, Waldo Emerson and James Lowell were now both curious *and* respectful. She knew sooner or later she'd get around to telling Mr. Emerson she'd read one of his books.

Professor Agassiz walked over to Myrna the next morning as she sat on a stump cleaning her rifle. She was surprised, as heretofore he'd not shown interest in the shooting range. He looked at her rifle and cleared his throat. "I'm thinking today I should take some time for the rifle practice. Do you suppose you might offer some pointers before I shoot?" His Austrian accent was noticeable, but slight.

He had such a pleasant way about him, Myrna thought. She rose from where she sat and met his jovial smile. "I've just finished cleaning my rifle. Would you care to try it?" Uncertainty, briefly crossed Louis's face. She loaded the gun.

"Come with me," she said, walking the short ways to the range. Myrna drew a line in the dirt. "Stand here like so, and hold the gun to your shoulder," she demonstrated. "It's been sighted and is very accurate. All you have to do is match the sight to the target. Let's try to pop that bottle— the nearest one, bout 200 feet."

As Myrna and Louis were preparing for his shot, Wyman, noticing the scene, walked hurriedly towards them. Perhaps it was his sudden movement. A surge of sports and guides pulled quickly behind him. Myrna was mildly annoyed. She didn't want the professor to lose his concentration. Leaning close she said, "Focus on the bottle and the sighting. Take a deep breath and relax…then shoot." He did.

The bottle exploded, the remnants briefly dancing in the air. The surrounding men whooped and cheered. Someone in the group hollered, "Do it again!"

Louis was very pleased. He grinned at Myrna. "It is better, so I think, to quit while one is ahead. Perhaps I'm best as a naturalist, no?" Once again, the professor had charmed his colleagues, including Myrna. On impulse, she said, "My friend and companion, who stays at my campsite, so enjoys collecting and identifying herbs and plants. Would it be too much of an imposition for her to join you and observe your work? ...perhaps just for a morning jaunt?"

"Of course, of course. I'm always happy to encourage a student. Just let me know which morning."

CHAPTER 23

Belle in the Woods

> Two Doctors in the camp
> Dissected the slain deer, weighed the trout's brain,
> Captured the lizard, salamander, shrew,
> Crab, mice, snail, dragon-fly, minnow and moth;
> Insatiate skill in water or in air.
> –*Adirondac* R. Waldo Emerson

Belle found the novelty of camping in the woods quite enjoyable. Still, she was wary of venturing far from the comfortable clearing that she and Myrna had established on the pond. The lush undergrowth of the brush in August made the perimeter of their site impenetrable in places. But she made a point of extending her explorations every morning. This morning she found what was no doubt a deer path leading in an arc to another small cove, but then, she lost the trail in a clump of raspberry bushes upon her return. She managed to pick nearly a quart of berries in her gathering basket, a pleasant surprise. However, when startled by the sound of crackling branches, she panicked and sustained considerable berry-bush scratches. It sounded like a very large animal…maybe a bear? A large buck? Once back at camp she felt silly for her fright and was determined to clear a trail. She set to the task.

This is hard work, she thought. Even with leather gloves, swinging the hatchet made her hand sting and her arms ache. I'm strong, but not exactly a woods-woman, she observed. Nevertheless, after several hours of swinging the blade, Belle made headway along the trail. She'd continue the next day.

Belle felt spent but satisfied. For the rest of the afternoon she lay back on the balsam bedding and dozed and read. She and Myrna had brought a book by Mr. Emerson and *Dred*, a novel by Mrs. Stowe. I think I deserve to be entertained by a novel, Belle thought, before she napped. She didn't even hear Myrna pull the canoe onto their beach.

Myrna circled the campfire. "What do you think of this splendid fish for our dinner!" she said, holding a trout on her lead line that looked to weigh at least two pounds.

"I thought this might be too much for us in one sitting," Belle said, wiping her plate remains with a biscuit. "The herby potato is nice with it too…don't you think?"

"As we Duffneys say, 'hunger is the best sauce'. "I kind of wish we had some cream for these berries," Myrna sighed.

Belle showed Myrna her progress on clearing the trail. "I may be able to complete it by tomorrow, but it's harder work than I expected."

Myrna nodded, clearly impressed. "Well, I was thinking instead you might like to join Professor Agassiz on one of his botanical jaunts. He says that he and Mr. Wyman plan to explore that inlet across from us, and that you'd be welcome to observe them."

Belle smiled, then looking thoughtful, frowned. "Of course, I don't know them. I hope we can be comfortable with each other."

They walked in silence back to the campfire. Myrna stoked the fire and they both sat cross legged in its warmth. Belle poked at the embers with a stick. They liked to keep the fire crackling.

Then Belle spoke abruptly, "I don't exactly like standing out by my color, you know—especially if they think I'm some kind of uneducated serving girl. I know, I know… we've talked this to death, but still. I can't help but say it."

Myrna responded, sounding exasperated, but then her tone softened. "What in the world am I supposed to do about the realities of our respective lives? That is to say, how should we approach this…I think a ways back we each decided to flout some of the rules and roles expected of us. Look, a few days ago one of the men assumed I was 'Myron'. My hair was tucked under my hat. He simply didn't expect a woman guide in his midst. He got over it. I carried on. I'm not drawing precise parallels here, but you'll have to deal with expectations, too."

"Yeah, and how would you deal with a group of high and mighty white men assuming you are an uneducated serving girl?"

"I, of course, don't have *your* answers. But, I will say, since you are a very attractive, educated, black woman, you may as well act exactly as you are. Dammit all, make them see you for who you are!"

Belle sighed. "I suppose you are getting bored and exasperated about repeatedly going over old ground."

"No, not really. It is good we are friends who don't mind voicing our fears and frustrations. Perhaps it is the same with every generation. But, it does seem we're in a time of change. Many smart people, men and women, are arguing for the end of slavery in this country, and for women's rights, too. Supposedly, our Boston fellows are progressive on these issues. Let's put them to the test."

"Yes, *supposedly*. I still think they are opinioned white men who are full of themselves. The fact that they write words espousing our causes doesn't mean their actions follow their words. I will say, however, the arguments between *us* always give me cheer."

"So, it is a 'yes' to exploring with the Professor?"

"Of course it's a yes! How could I deny myself an opportunity so immense?"

In the morning, after their breakfast, Belle set out in the canoe with Myrna for the men's camp. She was not feeling particularly apprehensive, in spite of her stated misgivings the evening before.

I might as well adopt Myrna's way of dress today, she thought—best I at least blend in camp-style. I'll pack my sketch pad too—might see something interesting. Also should he be amenable, I'd like the Professor to name some of the plants I've drawn.

Belle had with her a small knapsack in which she carried paper, pencils, a small cutting knife and an extra shirt. In her separate gathering basket she'd wrapped the berries from yesterday's undertaking that she would give to the cook.

Mr. Bakely made a fuss over her gift of berries. "The boys'll 'preciate these in my flap-jacks," he said.

Lyman managed to extract himself from his charge, Holmes, long enough to ask Belle how she was faring at camp, and was relieved to hear her enthusiasms for camp life.

Myrna and Stillman introduced Belle to Professor Agassiz and Mr. Wyman. It appeared they had been primed to meet her. The Professor lived up to his reputation for gracious manners, though Belle caught him casting a quizzical look her way

Belle sat quietly on the floor of the canoe. Wyman paddled while the Professor pointed and gave directions. It was still early. Rifle practice was yet to break the peaceful spell of lapping water. The keen naturalists were eager to find interesting plant life today. However, it seemed they were also fascinated by all manner of insects. They had various containers for the day's collection. Belle planned to be as unobtrusive as possible. She watched. She listened. She did not point to possible specimens or offer suggestions. Eventually, she saw they were at ease, barely noticing her. She was in thrall with their erudite comments about pond life.

They decided to debark and stretch their legs before lunch. Both men seemed startled when she took off her boots and nimbly jumped from the boat to tie the line to a nearby sapling. She smiled and said, "That should do nicely. I'll return in a moment." A ways into the woods she found bushes where she made a necessary stop.

They lunched on bread, cheese, wine, and water. Mr. Wyman politely asked if Belle had enjoyed the morning. She nodded 'yes' and rummaged in her pack, finding her sketch book to show them. "I made these drawings on some walks a few weeks ago. I know many of the plant names, but was hoping you might help me with the rest."

The Professor took the notebook she handed to him and began to turn pages. He looked incredulous. "*You* did these drawings?"

Belle was annoyed that her assertion was questioned, but she rallied. "I did the drawings a few weeks back on a walk along a trail near my home in North Elba," she said. "Our settlement is located on a plain surrounded by high mountains. There is a trail through 'Indian Pass' where I like to walk and sketch."

Still looking a bit puzzled, Agassiz said, "Yes, I can help you with a few of the names." After lunch and some initial awkwardness, the Professor and Jeffries Wyman cheerfully added or corrected plant names in Belle's botanical notebook. By this time they insisted she use their given names.

Louis told her the Latin name for milkweed was Asclepius Syriaca, "Not that many would bother knowing that," he commented.

"Still", Belle said with enthusiasm, "It is good to know these things." She carefully scripted the Latin name under her drawing. "I'm hoping to have a booklet of local botanicals to use with our older students. They enjoy foraging for plants, and may as well know the more scientific, as well as common names."

In response to Jeffries query, she replied, "Oh, yes, Myrna and I teach school at the North Elba settlement. Actually, Myrna was the sole school marm before I arrived past fall. She sometimes has classes in Elizabethtown, too. But now that her Pa's passed, she spends more time with the guiding business. She's very adept at that."

Louis nodded vigorously. "I've certainly noted her skills at that…most excellent with a rifle."

Belle was feeling less guarded and more comfortable. "Before lunch, while I was back in the woods, I noticed a veritable flock of beautiful orange and black butterflies lighting on a patch of milkweed plants. Would you care to see them…that is, if they're still there?

Though there were Monarch butterflies aplenty in the fields of Cambridge, Jeffries loved seeing them. He rose eagerly to follow Belle. Louis would have preferred to continue exploring water plants, but he good naturedly joined them. And then, there it was—a vast cloud of orange and black butterflies rose and spun over the succulent milkweed. The three naturalists sat together on a log and gave in to being entertained by the sight.

Eventually, Louis cleared his throat. "Hmm…I hope you'll humor me in returning to our boat." As he stood, the Monarch's flowed away from them in a grand sweep.

Belle followed Louis and Jeffries back to the boat, but not before taking her cutting knife and quickly harvesting some budding pods for her gathering sack. Once more, Belle retreated to silence in the canoe. She wanted to learn new things.

It is no doubt best that I do not make a show of myself, Belle thought. It was enjoyable to hear what Louis and Jeffries said to each other, and what they chose to gather for further examination.

Belle modestly thanked them when they debarked at the main camp, remembering that ladylike manners were in order. Louis gave a slight, courtly bow, saying it was their pleasure.

Belle saw Myrna and Alvah down the shore, and quickly walked to where they stood intent in their conversation. They smiled in greeting her. "Did you have a good day?" Myrna said.

"Yes, "I'll tell all at dinner."

"Me, too?" Alvah asked.

Belle laughed. "Of course...if you come to dinner."

Alvah was itching to see their campsite. He decided he could absent himself from the guides at the main camp for a few hours. Even half an invitation was enough of an excuse.

Good to his word, Alvah docked his canoe at their campsite in about an hour. "I brought along a chunk of venison, just in case," he said. "Actually, I believe you're entitled to it for your part in the afternoon hunt. The cook thinks you gals may be getting shorted on meat by staying across the pond—though, of course it's understandable that you want to be private-like over here."

"Well, I'm glad cook is giving us a thought. It'll be a nice change from our panned trout."

Myrna deftly cut the meat and seasoned it with the package of dried herbs and spices brought along for that purpose. Meanwhile, Belle had a pile of chopped herbs placed on a flat rock near the fire. The meal was to be roasted venison and sautéed milkweed pods. There was also a pan of dried apples simmered in water that would be drained and served with maple syrup.

The three friends fell into easy camaraderie away from the crowd. Alvah had a relaxed look. He sought to make eye contact with Myrna, though he enjoyed the company of both women.

"Hear you made a fine impression on Mr. Agassiz and Mr. Wyman," he said to Belle.

"Oh, I think I might have got under foot. I'm not quite sure what they thought."

"No, really...Jeffries Wyman asked me to tell you that you'd be welcome to go botanizing with them on Wednesday, if you'd like."

Belle gave a carefree sigh. "I'm so relieved they didn't find me trivial. Please tell them I'd like to join them. You know, at first I felt intimidated in their presence—they are both so knowledgeable. Also they tended to politely ignore me. But once we got to talking about my botanical sketches they became friendly like." Alvah nodded, assuring Belle that the Professor had offered a genuine invitation.

"We don't get to see the sports around their campfires after dinner. Would you say they are enjoying themselves?" asked Myrna.

"Oh, they are excellent at that, I'd say." Alvah replied. "Holmes loves to tell a good story. And once Lowell has a drink or two, he becomes very lively and entertaining. Some of the guides tell stories, of course—mostly ones that exaggerate their exploits and such. Well, you know, you've heard em when out with Sam." He saw Myrna's brows furrow. "Don't worry, me and Lyman keep the boys moderately in line. Yes, I'd say everything is going exceptionally well." Alvah stood to leave. "By the way, that milkweed preparation was delicious, Belle." Turning to Myrna, he asked if she would mind lighting the way to his boat.

It really was not that dark, but he wished to have a moment alone with her. Beyond the light of the campfire he boldly reached for her hand. She didn't resist…for a change. This encouraged him to briefly hug her to him. What he meant by this was hard to say, but it did generate a quickening pulse of response in Myrna's body. She pushed his boat from the shore and walked back to the fire, contemplating her feelings. What would it be like to lie naked with him? She wondered.

Myrna put another log on the fire and sat next to Belle. Belle grinned and poked at the fire, "So?" she said.

"I dunno. My body seems to entertain thoughts separate from my mind."

Belle snorted…and then they both fell into inexplicable paroxysms of laughter.

– CHAPTER 24 –

Alvah

Alvah took his time paddling back across the pond. The evening was without a breeze. He lay back on the bottom of the boat and let it drift. The night sky was clear. He became lost in the stars…Big and Little Dipper, Capricorn. Rarely did he take enough time to indulge his interests.

He thought about his mom, Delia, and her recent decision to have their home be a station on the Underground Railroad. Mary Brown and Harriet had said there might be a small family—husband, wife and baby passing through. For all he knew, they might now be at his house. He felt a tinge worried.

Sure, John must have spoken for them. Nevertheless, they'd be strangers. And let's face it, John's a rabid idealist. Alvah was not so taken with John's 'ends justifying the means' actions either.

A few times Alvah almost spilled the beans to Myrna, but he had held back. As Delia had carefully admonished, the whole point of being a refuge for those fleeing oppression was to keep it as secret as possible. He had sworn to his mom that he would do so, and so he had. It felt frustrating. Did Lyman know? Did Belle know? And then, would Myrna and Marion possibly know already? Alvah had some resentment about keeping others in the dark. He really didn't like living with secrets.

Alvah's thoughts turned to Myrna. *If we ever manage to get together, I'm hoping it will lead to something tangible— not some furtive relationship. There's plenty of sneaking around going on. You could even hear it in the sly innuendo* of the stories told by the Bostonians. Of course, then there would be Myrna's reserve to deal with. He knew she seemed to prefer keeping her feelings to herself. For example, when he'd impulsively hugged her, would she have honestly told him her feelings if he had thought to ask? I imagine she'd not clearly say. On the other hand, she didn't pull away. He'd take that for an answer, he guessed. Alvah sat up and paddled towards the fire lights of the men's camp.

At the landing, he pulled his boat to its place. Most of the men, including the guides, were by the campfire in front of the large main shelter. The lively fire leapt and crackled, casting light on the surrounding faces. Later, the assembled would retire to their smaller sleeping shelters, where embers from smaller fires glowed. Alvah thought as he approached the circle of men that the camp showed its best when illumed by moonlight and campfires—magical really.

There was an undercurrent of pipe smoke wafting with the burning pine and maple. The hearty bass tones of Mr. Holmes' laughter underscored the rest. Someone motioned Alvah to sit. Lyman leaned towards him and said, "Billy's about to tell what fool thing he did this morning." Billy Martin was probably the most gregarious of the guides.

Billy starts, "Well, it seems the Professor was very badly wishing he could get an osprey egg to examine and add to his collection," Billy pauses, "He was beyond excited when he realized an osprey had a nest in a tree on the perimeter of the camp. Problem was that the nest sat high in one of the tallest pines. I seen him starin up looking wistful like, shakin his head as if to say 'that's that'. Now I hate to see him so dejected. Also I know I'm an excellent climber. So I decide to give it a go. It's a real tall, tall tree. I climb and I climb." Billy stops to take a swig. One of the rowdies says 'Git on with it!' Billy continues, "That was a dramatic pause... Anyways, I'm beginning to worry 'cause mama osprey could swoop me any moment if she spots me near her nest. But finally I gain purchase above the nest." There is another long pause. "Unfortunately, there wasn't an egg in sight!"

So, Josh says, "What kind of story is that?"

Billy says, "Well, it was pretty thrilling to watch me do the climb, wasn't it."

At that, the Professor chortled mightily. "That it was, Billy that it was."

Alvah laughed with the rest of them. It was quite a feat to scale a tall pine. But he happened to know that when not guiding, Billy was a logger, and no stranger to the danger of logs and trees. After a little more drink and camaraderie, most of the men retired to their shelters. Alvah was one of the first to spread his bed roll. He decided it was a good night to sleep in the open under the myriad stars. He appreciated a deep sleep and hoped that would be the case tonight.

He awoke early and soon felt refreshed. There was nothing like an early morning dip to start the day he thought, as he toweled dry and put on clothes. James Lowell was also on the shore for his morning wash. He liked to engage Alvah as his primary guide. "Alvah," he said, "Would you mind showing me that big tree with the osprey nest?"

"Sure, cook's not even got started yet. We got time for it." He was thinking the tree can't be more'n half a mile from camp. It was a leisurely stroll.

"It's magnificent," Lowell said, looking skyward and rocking back on his heels.

"Yep, it's a beauty. There's the nest, way up." Then, to Alvah's astonishment, Lowell grabs around the tree and starts to shinny up it. Well, he was a limber, fit man and seemed up to it. Dammed if he didn't get right to the crotch with the nest before making his decent. Once back on the ground, breathlessly, he said, "Just wanted to see if I could do it. I'm a little winded, though." He bent forward putting his hands on his knees and taking some long breaths.

Alvah just shook his head. They joked about the foolhardiness of the whole thing all the way back to the breakfast table.

"Where you two been?" cook says, "You almost missed the bacon."

"Oh, I just felt like climbing Billy's tree."

"You must be joshing…right?" said Holmes, looking at Alvah for verification.

"Nope, he did it alright," said Alvah, looking amused. In spite of the tomfoolery on Lowell's part, you couldn't help admiring him. He took risks just for the fun of it.

- CHAPTER 25 -
Pictures and Predicaments

It was something Stillman had wanted to do—a painting of the encampment. It had even once flashed across his mind at Saturday Club. I'm just not sure how to start it, he thought. His idea was to capture this momentous event with his friends at Follansbee Pond in some kind of painting that would include likenesses of this distinguished group of men in their camp setting. Could he perhaps mention the thought, to say, Holmes or Lowell as a spontaneous idea? No, they might quash it before he started. Also he'd have to be careful to not ask anyone to do lengthy sittings.

Finally, he decided to start with a series of quick sketches. There were often occasions during the day when he might sit a ways to the sidelines, barely noticed by the others. And most of them were used to seeing him at work sketching something or other. He thought with satisfaction, no one need be wise to what I'm about. I'll give it a go this afternoon.

Later in the afternoon, Myrna was at loose ends waiting for Belle to return from her trip botanizing with the Professor and Wyman. She saw Stillman sitting at the periphery of camp and started to walk towards him. When she realized he was with pen in hand, probably composing a letter, she hesitated. But he saw her and motioned her over to where he sat on a folding stool.

"My goodness! You're drawing, not writing." She leaned in close. "Is the one in the middle Mr. Emerson?"

"Yep, that it is…or is supposed to be." He lowered his voice. "I've had this idea, but am not sure of it. For the moment I'd like to keep it a secret. I've a notion to do a souvenir painting..." He looked at Myrna and faltered.

"What a wonderful thought! Very original." Seeing he put finger to lips, she hushed her voice. "I like the composition so far. Will all of your friends be included?"

"I think so. Some of the guides, too." He looked at Myrna and smiled. "You have definitely raised my spirits, Miss Myrna. Also, I've been meaning to tell you that this is the best guided camping trip that I've been on. Everything is organized and thought out, no doubt thanks to you. My friends are having a superb time...it's all remarkable. "

"I always say, I can't take credit for good weather and fine cooking."

Bill nodded agreement. "Yes, the cook is exceptional—a rare find."

Myrna saw Belle debarking from Wyman's boat. "I must be going," she said, tipping her hat to Stillman.

As she walked away with a slight saunter, Bill once again thought of the time he saw her dive naked from the rock. Of course, that was a year ago, but that same rock secluded her current shelter. She had a different air about her now. She looked somehow prettier, more confident, too.

Myrna hung back and watched as she was approaching the botanizing party. Belle was at her most charming, thanking the Professor and Wyman.

As they were walking to where Myrna had tied her boat, she asked Belle how the day had gone.

"Ugh, today we mostly caught bugs, all manner of ugly crawly things." She wrinkled her nose..."I told them I'd prefer to gather plants."

"Did you bring them some of that delicious milkweed dish you made?"

"Well, that's another story. The Professor was afraid to sample it, he thought it could be poisonous. Jeffries did try it, and very much liked it. Louis said he would watch him carefully, just in case!"

The day was especially warm and both women had felt the heat during their exertions. Myrna had led Holmes and Lowell on a hike to a rocky overlook. Her knapsack had not been especially heavy, but as was the custom, the guide carried the most weight. In this case, lunch included two liters of ale. It had been a pleasant, jolly time and Myrna kept a fast pace. Now she felt sticky and grimy. Likewise, Belle said jokingly that she had enjoyed a day of catching and then helping to dip worms and bugs in alcohol. They agreed that the first thing they'd do when back at their campsite was swim and rinse their shirts in the pond.

"I don't think we need worry about any of the men noticing us. It's dinner time." Myrna quickly stripped and Belle followed suit. They took a leisurely swim and washed their soiled garments while in the water. They soaped and rinsed, then floated awhile in the secluded cove.

"Cook packed us bread, cheese and cold, roasted venison—says it's in exchange for the berries I brought the other day."

"Good thing. I think neither of us wishes to prepare a hot meal tonight." Myrna did an energetic few laps before exiting the pond. Once toweled and dressed she got to work on building a fire. It would get cooler once the sun set—the smoke chased the bugs, too.

- CHAPTER 26 -

A Visit

Later, as they sat lazily feeding the fire embers, they heard what sounded like dipping oars and voices. The voices came closer. Halooo…a male voice cried. Myrna and Belle looked at each other. It did not sound like Alvah.

A boat scraped on the sand. "It's me, Bill…Bill Stillman and James. We have something for you." It was not yet dark. They were clearly visible to Belle and Myrna. Walking towards the fire, Bill held out a tin box to Myrna. "May we sit for a moment?" Bill sat without waiting for a reply. Myrna scowled, clearly not pleased. Belle nudged her arm, "You may sit for a moment…as long as you don't overstay," she said. Belle thought she best speak first before Myrna raised a fuss. "You know our days are long and we need our rest," she added. She could sense Myrna relax a bit.

Somewhat abashed, Bill fumbled with the lid of the box. Handing the open box to Myrna, he exclaimed, "gingersnaps! Thought you ladies deserved a treat." The gingersnaps had been made by Mrs. Mack in Boston before Stillman left for Follansbee Pond, he said—as a special treat for the encampment. Myrna took one and passed the box. "We're much obliged, Bill. Very thoughtful of you."

"Your campsite looks very nice the way you set it. The large boulder here creates a shelter and reflects the warmth of the fire. Looks like you got the best site on the lake."

"Yep, I had first dibs." Myrna munched another cookie.

"I liked the ridge walk you took me and Holmes on today," piped Lowell.

"You saw all the deer sign back there? I think we'll try an early morning hunt behind the ridge on Wednesday, that is, if you fellows s are willing to rise early," Myrna said.

James pulled a flask out of his jacket and offered it to Belle. She palmed her hand forward in refusal. Myrna said, "No, thanks." She now realized that the men had probably had more than enough to drink. This was mildly discomfiting—not that she couldn't handle the situation.

"You know," James said, "I confess that I'm really fascinated by you women…seriously. Until Bill told me, I had no idea that you both teach at the Brown settlement, and that you actually live there." He said, pointing at Belle. "I met John Brown when he was in Boston past May. He ended up staying overnight at Waldo's house. He has a way with words, such a passionate speaker…Brown I mean, not Waldo. Well they both give excellent speeches, but I'm meaning Brown. I myself have written for an abolitionist journal," James proclaimed. "What's he like when he's at the farm? When he's not, so to speak, in public."

Belle and Myrna looked at each other and shrugged. Finally, Belle said, "Mr. Brown's a very good man. When he comes to our classroom he is kind and patient with the children. He's interested in all aspects of farming, too, though his devotion to his mission doesn't leave him much time for it."

"Well, Waldo has mentioned he's keen on paying Brown a visit, seeing as we're relatively close by. I'd like to see the whole settlement. Are all the women as pretty as Miss Belle?"

Belle frowned. Myrna was tiring of their company. She said, "I don't believe Mr. Brown is home at the moment." Belle added, "He's traveling out West."

Myna stood and gave an elaborate yawn. "It's time for you fellows to find your way back."

Meanwhile, Bill had been steadily drinking. He stood wobbly like, "Myrna, I just… havta say you're… the most by-ootful guide person I ever met." Then he promptly fell over. The drink had overpowered him.

In the commotion, they hadn't heard Alvah arrive. Assessing the scene, he asked James to help him get Bill in his boat. "I trust you feel well enough to handle the other boat on your own?" Myrna could see Alvah's jaw muscle twitch with anger. He and James carried Bill to the boat. Alvah sprinted back to the women. "Are you two alright?"

"Of course...just a little annoyed," Myrna replied. "They did bring us gingersnaps. I doubt they'll let their generosity turn to foolishness again."

Alvah smiled. "I'm your protector whether you need me or not." He nodded to both women and ran back to his boat. He thought... I swear, if Bill heaves in my boat I'll toss him overboard.

Myrna and Belle felt too unsettled for sleep. "Well, that was a surprise. Gingersnaps travel well, don't they. But what do you make of Stillman and Lowell dropping by like that?" Belle asked.

"Clearly inappropriate, though Bill does fancy himself a friend of sorts."

"But the flirting...Have you experienced this behavior from men on other trips?"

Myrna snorted. "Not with Pa around! I guess Alvah's stepping into his place."

"Not hardly! Alvah is just being territorial...like one of those big bucks."

Myrna looked bemused. "Could be. What do you think about Mr. Emerson and James visiting John and the tenants at the settlement?"

"Don't know. Lots of folks are curious to meet Mr. Brown. You should see the pile of correspondence Mary keeps. We were correct in telling Mr. Lowell he's away. I'll tell Lyman about their interest, though he may already know. He worries some about John and all the goings on. What do you think will happen next when we see Bill and James?"

"Nothing much. I'm expecting we'll get an apology. I plan to be nonchalant...courteous, but distant. Maybe thank them again for the cookies. Truthfully, I imagine they'll be feeling plenty embarrassed."

- CHAPTER 27 -

Follansbee Pond Secrets

In the morning Belle declined to row to the main camp. "I think I'll stay at our site today and explore on my own. Besides, sometimes the Professor makes me feel like I'm one of the specimens to be examined. Apparently, I'm an interesting novelty."

"To tell the truth, I wouldn't mind time around here either. I'll try to make it a short day after rifle practice. The men, especially Holmes, seem to favor that activity."

Myrna enjoyed the solitude of the lake in the early morning. It was about a mile from their site to the opposite shore. It was not quite sunrise, so all was quiet on the other side. She decided to cast a line on the water. Really, there was no hurry—and cook would, no doubt, appreciate trout, or pan-fish to add to breakfast. Truthfully, Myrna was hungry. Breakfast with the men seemed a good idea. Besides, seeing the inevitable show of respect the other guides had for her might give a warranted lesson to Stillman and Lowell, should they take note. Enough reverie, Myrna thought, as a lively brookie ran furiously with her line. She reeled and whipped her line, a nice one for her creel. Four more successive tries and the basket was brimming. And the sun was still just poking the horizon. Pleased, she deftly pulled on her paddle for a sprint to shore.

It seems Alvah was of a like mind. Myrna spotted him in a reedy cove, his boat sheltered by a patch of tall grass. She drew close enough to smile and tip her hat while holding her creel aloft, mouthing the word "Full". He in turn looked faux puzzled—joshing, he mouthed the word "Bull?" She knew he'd soon row to shore for breakfast.

Myrna sat at the guide table for coffee and conversation. Apparently the men had fallen into easy fellowship with their Boston clientele. Steve Martin said he didn't think the Professor was a "hunert percent" right about bass fish, but he liked him nonetheless. Charles said they told humorous stories at night around the campfire, especially Mr. Holmes and Mr. Wyman—after a whiskey or two.

Later in the day, two men passing through told Mr. Emerson the big news about the laying of the transatlantic cable. Alvah walked up just then saying it was a feat almost beyond comprehension. The guide, Steve, declared, "To my mind there's just too many new-fangled inventions goin on. I prefer things just as they is." About that there seemed general agreement amongst the other guides.

As Myrna stood to take her leave, walking towards the rifle range, Bill hurried over. He said he was sorry if last night's visit was an inconvenience. "Perhaps I'd lost some manners with the drink," he said.

Myrna gave him a sharp direct look. "If you mean this as an apology, it is accepted…and I will convey it as such to Belle." Then, in a gracious turn she said, "It was thoughtful of you to bring us gingersnaps. We did enjoy them." She saw in her peripheral vision that James Lowell was watching the scenario in the near distance. She added, with her most charming smile, "I'm sure you can appreciate how important private time is to Belle and me after a long day."

"Oh, of course, most certainly." Myrna was about to walk away when Bill added. "Would you mind looking at my latest sketch later today? I believe your opinion is likely the most honest I'll receive."

"Yes, I can do that after lunch."

Yes, thought Myrna, the day was going well. She saw Holmes, and even Emerson, waiting for her on the firing range. She cradled her Hawkins rifle as she walked towards them.

Holmes greeted her warmly. Emerson said, "I fear I'm still something of a novice with this thing." He scowled at his gun. "First thing we'll get it properly sighted." Myrna took the firearm from Waldo and examined it carefully. She fiddled with the top sight. "Mind if I fire it?" she asked. Waldo looked bemused. "Please do."

Myrna noted that unlike some city sports, Waldo gave her his rapt attention—asking questions about the mechanics of the thing, and curious about distance and trajectories. At first, she worried that he was taking too much time from the others. Then, she realized that the group didn't mind deferring to him. Their esteem for him was clearly evident. He was good natured about his lack of experience, too. After Myrna's instruction, his aim improved, but she reckoned that his long-distance eyesight was deficient.

Rifle practice was especially enjoyable today, Myrna said later to Stillman. Of course, they had been at it for several weeks.

Good to her word, Myrna spent some time with Bill looking at his latest efforts to capture the landscape, men, and atmosphere of Camp Maple. Some of the guides had taken to using an alternate name—the "Philosophers Camp"—they'd come to call it.

"Aha! I can recognize the good likenesses you've created," Myrna said. "It is a wonderful depiction of the camp and majestic woods. Why is Mr. Emerson set apart from the others? Or will another figure be added nearer to him?"

"Well, I think in some ways Mr. Emerson is a man apart. He is rare amongst us in intellect and wisdom. That's how I see it, you know. I'm always amazed by what he sees and says when we row out on the water together." Bill continued to dab shades of green from his palette. He had graduated from pencil to paint sketches.

Myrna nodded. "I did read his book that you brought me. I confess, I'd feel intimidated to discuss it with him."

Myrna paused. "No, that's not exactly what I mean. I think what I feel is that I see him without cares here, enjoying himself, and I don't wish to intrude with thoughts of his other life. Does that make sense?"

"Yes, exactly! I'd hoped from the beginning that Waldo would share this experience with me. And I have not been disappointed in his satisfaction with it."

Bill was likeable in these moments. He had a quality of wonderment at his woodsy surroundings.

It was still early afternoon, blue sky and warm. Myrna sought out Alvah to tell him she was making a short day of it to spend time at her campsite with Belle. "Guess you gals deserve to spend some time loafing. Wish I could join you," he said, amiably.

Myrna matched his grin with a mischievous smile. Perhaps neither had forgotten the promised kiss. Yes, it is good to leave the fellows somewhat early. Belle and I will have fun exploring and then take a leisurely swim in the cove, she thought.

Myrna gingerly landed her boat and carried her gear up to their snug shelter. But where was Belle? It was unlike her to wander far, especially knowing they had planned an excursion together. It was then that Myrna noted the water pot was askew on the ground. And there were scuff marks beginning at the trail leading into the woods. Something seemed wrong. A bear? Quite unlikely. Alerted, Myrna concentrated on listening. She thought she heard sounds a ways down the trail. Just to be on the safe side, she quickly loaded her Hawkins and put the sling over her shoulder. She sprinted quickly along the trail for at least a half mile. The sounds became definite and loud. She saw motion in the distance. A man was dragging something through the brush. She saw a patch of blue gingham. Belle! She ran softly, closer to the commotion. She heard Belle's muffled cries. The man was swearing and telling her to be quiet. It appeared that the stranger meant to harm Belle. Clearly there was imminent danger. Her mind raced through the options at hand.

When she was within range, Myrna shouted, "Halt!" The bearded, scruffy man was dressed in worn clothes with a hat pulled down to cover his features. "Stop! Drop that rope!"

He continued to drag Belle towards the inlet stream. Myrna cocked her rifle. "I say, stop or I'll shoot you!" With that the interloper turned and snorted. "Yer just a girl, ain't ya."

Myrna didn't reply. She felt her heart beat quicken. She took two breathes to calm herself and sighted him with her gun. As he reached for his pistol, she fired once, in defense—a lung shot, most likely. He fell instantly. Her rage hardened. She raised her rifle again, but thinking better of it didn't blow out his brains. Moving to where he fell, Myrna took a quick check— no breath or pulse. He was dead. She felt appalled at what she'd done—sickened. There was blood oozing. She needed to leave this gruesome sight—now. Later she could return to assess the incomprehensible situation.

Belle was distraught and trembling. Myrna checked Belle's bruises and asked if she could walk. Belle shook her head in assent. She was too breathless to talk. Once Belle was untethered, Myrna led her with haste into the woods, where they hid out of sight. For all they knew, there could be others lurking. They both felt jittery from the panic and exertion. Belle said that except for bruises and rope burns on her wrists she was unharmed. The intruder had come up behind her, thrown a sack over her head and bound her hands together. Initially, he made her walk on the trail led by a rope. When Belle realized from his words that he was a slave catcher, she quit walking and fell to the ground in order to slow their progress. She knew full well he'd sell her as slave…and she would probably not endure like Mr. Northrup.

"Are you sure he's dead?"

"Quite certain, yes. But we must hide until we know there isn't another one."

They crawled under bushes about a hundred yards off the trail—and waited.

Myrna felt prickly with excitement and strained from exertion. She wouldn't have killed him, if he hadn't drawn his pistol. There was an uneasiness about her. It all seemed wrong, but right.

Once they were quietly hidden from sight, Myrna's mind raced involuntarily. Her ruminations flashed on the scene of killing the man; about shooting game; about her Pa's death.

They lay close enough to feel each other's breath and heartbeats. Myrna was not sure how much time had passed. At some point Belle looked at Myrna. "Thank you. You saved me from certain horror. There's no telling where he planned to take me or to what kind of life." Then to Myrna's surprise, Belle kissed her directly on the lips…and Myrna responded in kind. Myrna felt confused and gently rolled away. She had no idea what Belle might be thinking. It had been a real kiss alright, but then in their heightened state every emotion roiled through them. To her relief, when their eyes again met it was as though nothing happened. Cautiously, they crawled from under the brush, listening and looking as they made their way back towards their campsite. They needed to rest and think. They'd return later to the dead man. There were no sounds of others or sightings on the trail. But then they heard a call, "Myrna? Myrna?" It was Alvah. He was at their campsite and they quickly made their way to him.

Alvah and James Lowell stood together, looking astounded at the sight of the distressed women.

"Whatever has happened?" exclaimed Alvah, rushing towards Myrna. Then, seeing Belle's bruised arm and torn clothes, he gently helped her sit on the balsam mat near the fire pit.

Lowell gathered kindling and made a fire as Belle told her story of her captor throwing a sack over her head and dragging her through the woods. "Terrible, just terrible," James muttered as he worked on building the campfire. "How did you get away from the bastard? Did he try to injure you?"

Alvah said, "We came here because we heard a shot fired and thought Myrna shot a deer,"

Myrna took a deep breath and looked to Belle. "I'm afraid we've omitted some details. I think we have a conundrum on our hands." Both men looked raptly at Myrna. At first Myrna faltered, then gained composure as she spun out the story.

When she had finished, Lowell said, "Are you sure he's dead? Could there be others?"

"Quite so. And, no, I don't believe there are others—at least not in the vicinity. It seemed we'd stayed hidden for a long time. I...I'm not sure what we should do next. I mean he's just lying there out in the open. I checked his pulse and breathing; then untied Belle and we ran. I was worried that others might appear. We didn't dare to linger."

Alvah looked to James and then stood. "Guess we should go take a look. You up for it Belle?" She nodded, yes. She could ignore her bruises for now.

Once at the scene they reluctantly gave the slave-catcher careful scrutiny.

"Oh, my God in heaven! We do know him," wailed Belle. "It's Joachim's acquaintance — Jesse!" Alvah and Myrna exchanged stricken glances.

Indeed it was Jesse—he'd grown a long beard to obscure his face, but it was him. His pack didn't clarify matters. He had papers for a slave named Betty and other bogus personal identification. "What are we going to do now?" Belle said through her tears. Indeed, that was the final question. They sat together on a nearby log and stared at the body.

"We need to tell Stillman and some of the others back at camp, don't we?" Myrna said, uncertainly.

"We'll have to bury him, too." Alvah said. James and Belle were quiet.

"But, Alvah, this isn't usual," Myrna said. "It's not a natural death, or an accident. I shot and killed him, clear and simple. I believe it was justified, but I did pull the trigger—He drew first," she added.

"Yep, it surely qualifies as a conundrum," Lowell paused. "We need to be calm and think things through, so let's consider our options. The body and his meager effects need to be buried. He must have arrived by boat. We need to locate that…"

"And do we have to tell the others?" Alvah stood and paced. "Couldn't we just bury him ourselves? Clearly, he'd planned to sell Belle, probably to a southern plantation or worse. A trial would end in Myrna's favor, but alert a whole bunch of the pro-slavers, which in the end would come to more danger for us here in the North Country."

James nodded. "So the ends justify the means? What do you think?" His words were firm, though his face paled.

"Well, *I am* thinking," Myrna said. "Truthfully, my preference is to dispose of the body and be done with it. And it's more about protecting the camp and our way of life, than fearing going to jail," Myrna blurted.

"I agree," Alvah said, "Jesse deserved what he got."

Belle added, "Truthfully, Jesse didn't show any sterling qualities when he appeared in Elizabethtown this past summer. My guess is that he was, no doubt, plotting then. Yes, I vote for a quiet burial." Belle had a fierce expression, but then broke into tears. Myrna sympathetically held her hand.

For the moment, they left Jesse's body and walked to the inlet stream where they readily found Jesse's boat. They made a plan there on the spot; then walked back to retrieve the body, and dragged it to the stream. There was no denying Jesse had a bullet hole in his right lung. They loaded his pockets with hefty stones, and wedged him under some submerged rocks. Then they capsized his boat and let his pack and basket take on water. Belle insisted they say a prayer for Jesse's soul, so James complied with her request. "After all, he was some mother's son," she offered.

The four complicit comrades checked the area for any tell-tale evidence and then wearily walked back to the campsite. Alvah rekindled the fire.

Myrna thought, Lowell is an admired, respected poet; surely he has something important to say about this. She listened as he grappled with words. When their eyes met, his face said it all. To him my deed was incomprehensible—knowledge neither he, nor I, wanted to carry.

James scowled into the flames. "You realize we've chosen to take a serious action. We will all be endangered should it become known. Do we agree that this incident must forever remain a secret? They held hands together and vowed to never again speak of their dangerous pact.

"I forever promise," Belle uttered, and the rest solemnly followed suit. Belle felt traumatized, yet ebullient to have survived the ordeal.

Myrna observed the others—watching.

James said with a trace of a smile that poets by nature are secretive.

Myrna challenged, "Is that true?"

"Of course, it's true. Veiled hidden messages are a poet's forte. Otherwise we'd write more prose. You know there's nothing quite like taking words and building a structure that's full of clues for the reader to wonder at. Eventually, the hope is that the reader will unwrap a wondrous revelation…or titter and nod at a clever meaning. Truthfully, I sometimes discover new meanings when I reread an older poem."

Alvah said, cautiously, "So I guess even if you ever spilled a secret, no one could be sure what you meant."

"Pretty much, I suppose." Then pausing, Lowell said apologetically, "I guess this is too dark a moment, and too soon to cast lighter thoughts. I believe we are all charged with mourning the loss of our carefree woods idle, if not the loss of Jesse, who did indeed intend harm." He paused, "We can't escape giving a great deal of thought to this day."

They sat in silence for a good while. Each wrapped in cocoons of his or her thoughts.

Finally, Myrna suggested that they think about what to do next. James agreed. That settled, they hatched a plan for the following day. Each were game to do their best.

Myrna would stay at camp with Belle until she recovered from her "supposed" fall down a ravine. That would give them time to think things through further. Alvah and Lowell would explain the sound of gunshot as a missed deer.

Alvah asked Myrna if she'd like him to stay the night for safety's sake. "Goodness no! We don't need to create gossip." James briefly smiled at the two of them. Clearly, they'd like to spend a night together.

The men rose to take their leave. Belle continued to sit by the fire. James walked ahead. Night was falling. When they were out of sight from the others, Alvah stopped, encircled his arms around Myrna, and kissed her deeply. She responded without hesitation. "I reckoned I'd best collect my kiss now while we have the chance," he said. Myrna silently agreed. Unsaid were the likely future repercussions from Belle's ambush and Jesse's death—the secret that four people now shared.

Myrna gave Alvah a parting hug, and then quickly turned on the trail back to the campfire. How extraordinary, she thought...two kisses in one day. And both were good ones! Something to think about...and on a day she'd killed a man. It was a lot to ponder.

Belle looked relieved as Myrna returned to the fire. "I do believe Jesse was acting alone, but I'm feeling spooked now that it's getting dark. I wish it were acceptable for James and Alvah to stay with us, though I know full well it would raise suspicion as well as eyebrows."

"I'm anxious, too. But we'll sleep with my loaded gun next to us. We've got to force this whole incident to the back of our minds."

"I agree, very true. Though I think first we should try to figure out how Jesse came to find me, don't you?"

"Yes, yes, of course. Who do you think might have conveyed knowledge of our whereabouts?"

They were eager to untangle the pieces. This was a portion of the puzzle they could possibly solve. After some thought, Belle realized she'd mentioned the Follansbee trip in letters to both her Ma and Joachim. Myrna said the North Elba community and the guide families had known for months. Belle told Myrna that good hearted Harriet had been fascinated when she heard Belle was going. "She even insisted I carry her special preparation to ward off mosquitos."

Myrna interjected. "Also Marion said there were stories about the famous Bostonians going on this trip in many newspapers—paper's we don't get here in the North. George sent some clippings. So, I'm speculating that it wouldn't be that hard for Jesse to find us—once he knew you were one of the party. He may even have been lurking nearby, waiting for an opportunity."

"But why?" Belle reflected. "He even met me personally and knew that I was close to Joachim. How could he behave so…so despicably?"

"To my thinking, people are willing to perform onerous deeds for two reasons—principles or money. Jesse didn't strike me as full of principles. Then there's the fact that you were sent here in the woods for protection." Myrna saw Belle about to speak. "Wait, let me finish. That is a fact, even if you've been dismissive of it. Remember, the reason you're here at camp is that Lyman was worried about your safety. And, by the way, sooner rather than later we'll have to confide 'something plausible' to him. Truthfully, until this happened I went along with you, thinking Lyman was overly cautious. Now we know there are serious threats. You agree, right?"

"I now do think that, really. Alright, I'll admit that before today I preferred to pretend Ma and Pa were silly to send me so far away. I liked thinking it was mostly about driving a wedge between me and Joachim."

Myrna and Belle sat quietly, each absorbed in her own thoughts. Finally, Myrna asked Belle if she thought she'd be able to handle going out on another expedition with the Professor and Jeffries Wyman two days hence.

"You mean like play acting? Surely…I can lie my behind off if necessary."

Perhaps there was a tinge of bravado, but they allowed a small laugh at that. Their plans might be sketchy, but they had a plan.

That night before sleep Myrna was restless. The deathly nightmare images of the day haunted her at the edge of darkness beyond the fire embers. She'd killed a man. Could she maintain her resolve to continue a façade of normalcy?

In the morning—late morning, the sun was innocently illuminating their tidy campsite. All was calm as they drank their breakfast tea.

Myrna was glad she'd opted to forgo the day's rifle-range session and other guiding duties. Myrna said to Belle, in a tone of bluster, that she thought all the chasing and killing Jesse had exhausted her.

"Well, just try being blindfolded and dragged along most of a mile for making one weary," Belle retorted.

Throughout the day they made a few attempts at dark humor. But in the end, they agreed they were truly overwhelmed by yesterday's events. They weren't exactly sorry about Jesse, they just wished he hadn't found Belle in the first place. "I do have to say, James Lowell has redeemed himself." Belle added, "Well, let's just talk about this thing until we're done with it."

"I guess...one thing's for sure, we need to act like we usually do with the men tomorrow." They puttered around the campsite for the rest of the morning. In the afternoon they foraged for herbs and mushrooms—then they treated themselves to a long luxurious swim. By evening they felt more relaxed. Their moods lifted. Alvah stopped by to check on them and was satisfied that they were coping well. "Would you mind walking me back to my boat?" He said.

Belle laughed. "Oh, go on you two."

This time Myrna was fully ready for him. The kisses felt intense...for both. Eventually, they pulled apart. Alvah walked towards his boat and Myrna turned back to the camp site.

"Wait." Alvah ran to her. "Just one more." They laughed together at the silliness.

- CHAPTER 28 -
Preparations

With her fresh blouse and long skirt, Belle's injuries were well hidden, except for puffiness on her right cheek. "At least I don't go all black-and-blue like you do." She held a small mirror, examining her face.

"Yep, that's an advantage." Myrna was carefully examining Belle's bruises. "Maybe we should have the Professor take a look at the swelling on your upper arm."

"Oh no, I can't. I'd have to get part undressed! I don't think either Louis or I could stand the embarrassment. Besides, it will no doubt be better in a day or two." Myrna's brow furrowed with concern.

"Well, if it stays tender I'll consider it," Belle said reluctantly.

Myrna carefully packed her gear and her rifle. "Guess we should say a Hail Mary and get on with it."

"But, I thought you weren't religious?"

"I save prayers for special situations. A last resort type of thing."

Belle wasn't sure whether Myrna was joshing or not. She gingerly stepped into the boat and sat in the prow, only then realizing the aches in her legs.

Professor Agassiz and Jeffries Wyman stood on the shore awaiting their arrival. As they debarked, Jefferies gallantly took Belle's hand. "Alvah told us all about your nasty fall," he said, looking genuinely concerned.

Tears began to well, but Belle demurely lowered her eyes. "I fear sometimes I'm a bit clumsy."

"There, there," the Professor said in a fatherly tone. "If you feel up for it, Wyman and I will take you botanizing after rifle practice. Would you like that?"

Belle nodded her agreement.

Lowell stood on the periphery of the small group. He saw how vulnerable…and beautiful Belle was. He was glad Louis and Jeffries were gentleman. And he was grateful his own codes weren't being tested.

There was a round of polite concern by cook and some guides. Of course, since no one suspected what had really happened, Myrna's emotional plight was noted only by Alvah and James. Nevertheless, once they all settled into activities, the daily routine went smoothly enough.

However, later in the afternoon Alvah noticed that Lyman was uncharacteristically quiet. He looked troubled. Alvah decided that he would have to talk about this with Myrna before the day was out.

Myrna almost couldn't believe how normal she was feeling. The incident with Jesse seemed a far-away dream, like it happened in another world. Cook asked her if she needed more provisions. He said he'd saved her and Belle some venison back-strap. "I know you refined ladies will enjoy it more than these woodchucks," (his affectionate name for the guides). After shooting practice, Holmes sat with Myrna jawing about the virtues of her Hawkins rifle. Yes, it was a downright enjoyable morning.

Stillman sat to one side, busy with a canvas. "Hey" Stillman waved to Myrna, "come see."

"Bill, I must say this is simply grand—the trees, dappled light, sports and guides. It is perfect."

Indeed, the oil sketch captured the essence of Camp Maple. Stillman was an artist of significant talent.

"Tell me," Myrna asked, "Will the painting go on exhibit?"

"Ah, well, one never knows what will be deemed worthy for a major showing. But if it is bought locally, by that I mean in the Boston area, I think I might feel gratified." He paused. "You know, I do believe our time here has created an historic moment. Do you agree?" Stillman turned to Myrna.

"Yes, I do believe so. Perhaps in ways we can't even imagine." Myna hesitated. Less can be more when it comes to words, she thought. She sincerely hoped the painting would get its due attention.

Most of the men had elected to spend the afternoon fishing or swimming. It was the kind of perfect mid-August day when one realizes summer will soon wane.

As James said, "carpe diem."

Martin, the guide most ready to josh, scratched his head and replied, "carpie de me, there ain't no carp in this here pond!"

Mr. Holmes laughed the hardest, "Really, I must write down some of these bon mots!" Martin rather enjoyed eliciting learned comments from the Boston men. He was the one that had instigated having the guides refer to the men as 'the philosophers'.

Alvah caught Myrna's eye, "Have a moment?" Myrna half expected he might flirt, but he looked serious. They walked to a log away from the group and sat. He voiced thoughts that had already been nagging at Myrna. What should they tell Lyman? When should they tell? It had occurred to both of them that in spite of their solemnly sworn secret, it must be shared with Lyman. They proceeded to go up and down and over what had happened.

Finally, Myrna said, "It's plain that we need to tell him either sooner or later, so it might as well be sooner. If we don't tell him and there's still danger lurking…well, we'd be terribly remiss. Besides, Belle's his charge." Myrna shook her head back and forth. "I can't believe I was so stupid as to think I'd keep it from him—even short term."

"We needn't be so hard on ourselves. It was an extreme, unforeseen moment; now we're having smart second thoughts."

"I sure hope you're right."

They decided to have Belle invite Lyman to their campsite for dinner. Alvah would be there, too. That's when they'd tell him—everything.

"Whew! Hope that's about it for loose ends." Alvah, said it—Myrna had already thought it.

Lyman was pleased at the prospect of dinner with the women and Alvah. He and Alvah rowed across the pond together the next evening. Belle said she felt relieved that they would confide in Lyman.

They took some care to prepare a company-like dinner, even though it was a crossed-legged by the fire kind of affair. Myrna swept the ground and laid down fresh balsam mats. Belle prepared her special potato-mushroom dish and they used a spicy dry-rub on the venison. They'd borrowed a few tin dinner plates from cook, who, hearing they had Lyman coming to dinner, gave them a small pail of blueberry slump.

All went exceedingly well until they unfolded their delicate secret, though they tried their best to make a reasonable, dispassionate account of the incident.

"Jeesus H. Christ!" exploded Lyman, "And two days later you're just gettin to mentionin it!" He shook his head back and forth. "Unh, unh…beyond belief. And to think you all hornswoggled me to thinking this was just a nice dinner. Don't know about the bunch of yez."

With all of Lyman's bellowing, Belle burst into tears, which was a lucky thing, because it immediately softened Lyman's tone. Really, he was near a father to her.

"Now, Belle," he said in a more subdued voice, "It ain't your fault, and furthermore I expect Miss Myrna done right. But, it is one hell of a mess…and I'm plain annoyed at having been kept in the dark for two days."

Alvah spoke up. "I apologize… we all do. It's just that we didn't want to cause a ruckus in camp," he paused, "and wanted to think a bit before telling you."

"Alright, let me cogitate a moment. Now that I'm part of it, I'll help make a plan for what's next."

The three sat silently while Lyman paced the perimeter of the fire. Lyman added one of the larger cut logs to the flame. "First thing is you're goin to show me where this all took place. Then we'll come back here to the fire…I'll have it figured by then."

Belle shook her head and wailed, "I can't!"

Lyman let her go on a bit, and then said mildly, "In my experience, these situations git magnified, grow larger, when you don't face em, so, yes, you should come with us. Nevertheless, someone needs to walk with me and show where it all happened. I want to git it clear in my head," Lyman said.

At the words "growing larger" Myrna's thoughts ran to bloated animal carcasses. Hopefully, Jesse's carcass would not have come loose and floated to the surface. Myrna was sometimes given to graphic images.

Myrna and Alvah rose to their feet. Alvah took the lead with Lyman in tow. Myrna and Belle followed close behind. It was before sunset. The woods were peaceful, and the trail innocent of commotion. They surveyed the areas of conflict, the place where Jesse had died, and then peered into the deep burial stream. Belle found her voice to describe the ordeal. Pointing to a fairly hefty tree limb extending into the water, Alvah said, "Lowell and I dragged that over the um…resting place."

Meanwhile, the yellow finches were flitting overhead, trilling their evensong. All of the natural wood sounds prevailed as there was no conversation amongst the four. When they were once again seated by the fire, Lyman cleared his throat and they all looked expectantly at him.

"I don't think Jesse had a cohort, but I believe it's best we leave the end of this week for Martin's, and then on to North Elba—just in case. As Myna knows, Mr. Holmes and Mr. Hoar have made arrangements to leave camp on Friday. I was to act as escort, in any case. A few of the other gentleman may travel then too. If it's alright with Myrna, she and Belle could break camp and then Myrna act as lead guide for those paddling back to Martin's. Alvah, Steve, Stillman and Bakely, the cook, can stay on and manage the rest of em. What with Belle's recent spill, it would be understandable if she and Myrna leaves a bit early. Well, that's my thoughts," he said, looking to Myrna.

Alvah glanced at Myrna, assessing her reaction.

Myrna hesitated, and then said, "I'm responsible for the group, but under these unusual circumstances that is an acceptable plan. I'll talk with Stillman and the other guides in the morning to make sure this will work. "

They all agreed it made sense.

- CHAPTER 29 -

Leaving Follansbee for North Elba

The final morning Myrna and Belle rowed to the main camp. Myrna pulled steadily on the oars, sprinting across the pond. Belle sat in the prow. Today they were quieter than usual, contemplating their goodbyes to Camp Maple. Together they had picked a pail of blueberries for Mr. Bakely to add to his larder. Myrna planned to spend ample time in rifle practice with the sports in the morning. Perhaps those interested would care to do scouting in the afternoon. Myrna realized she felt reluctant to break camp and leave, but it made sense to do so.

Bakely and Stillman stood at the camp kitchen table, apparently waiting for them. The cook's friendly face lit with glee. "I've prepared a nice spread for our afternoon meal, so don't you gals go runnin off before we serve it."

Belle proffered the pail of berries, smiling at Stillman and cook.

"Wouldn't think to miss it," Myrna added, bowing and walking to the rifle range.

Jeffries caught Belle's eye and motioned for her to join him and Agassiz at their dissecting stump. Belle wrinkled her nose. "Hope slicing up fish innards doesn't ruin my appetite."

After a rather festive late lunch, Stillman cleared his throat and rose to his feet. "Just wanted to say thanks to Miss Myrna for all the help she and the Duffney family provided in inspiring and leading this excursion." He went on a bit more about Sam and Myrna and their early scouts with him. Then he handed Myrna a thick envelope.

"Oh my!" she exclaimed, opening the envelope. "I'll be sure to share this with my guides."

"No need for that, Myrna, we'll be taking good care of the fellow guides separately," boomed Lowell, authoritatively. He raised his glass of cider, "Three cheers for Camp Maple!" Sports and guides alike clinked and whooped in good cheer. James smiled and gave her a wink.

The envelope appeared to be stuffed with a wad of cash. Myrna put it her pack; she'd count it later. For now, she was gratified by the good spirits of those around her. She smiled and wondered what Pa would think. He would love the party aspect of the day. Myrna watched Lowell saunter towards the bench that Belle and Jeffries occupied. Belle had both men under her coquettish spell. Myrna felt amused, but slightly jealous.

They awoke before dawn, ready to begin their journey home. Myrna left the fire ring and lean-to shelter for future campers. They waited by the boat on their beach near the large rock to join the other guides and sports who would be returning with them.

It was a smooth uneventful paddle. Once they arrived at Martin's Hotel, Myrna's guide duties would officially end. She and Belle intended to pitch a tent shelter next to Lyman in an area reserved for guides. They would lie low that night, hoping to see no one. It was unlikely that an accomplice of Jesse's would be there to threaten them. But Myrna and Lyman were well prepared, with rifles ready—just in case. All three would then travel the following day by wagon to North Elba.

Meanwhile, they heard from a friendly guide that John Brown and some of his sons were still somewhere out West—away from the settlement.

- CHAPTER 30 -

Home Again

Myrna was happy to see her homestead. She gave Marion a heartfelt hug at the front door.

"It will feel good to sleep in my own bed."

Marion's eyes welled. "I missed you, too," she said, honking into her apron. "You just never know about these guiding trips. I used to worry about Sam in the same way. After you're washed and settled I want to hear about all your adventures. I'm sure you and Belle must have had a few."

"Yep, guess I'll have that tub-wash first." The thought of a good soak in a tub of warm water sounded mighty appealing. She also needed to consider just how much information she should confide to Marion. She unpeeled her rather ripe smelling outer and underwear, and poured another kettle of boiling water into the tub. Perhaps, for today, she'd start by telling Marion the most attractive highpoints of the Follansbee trip. The dark stain left by Jesse would be avoided. There was plenty of woodland beauty to talk about—and the folksy bonhomie at camp. To tell the truth, Myrna needed to fill her spirit with those images. Certainly, both she and Belle could relate many unforeseen wonderful encounters they'd had with nature at Follansbee. Myrna lowered herself into the steaming water, rolled a towel under her neck, leaned back and closed her eyes. She realized, with a start, it was Alvah who had drifted to the forefront of her thoughts!

Over the next week Myrna fell into a pleasant routine of helping Marion and Carson with household chores. At dinner time, she told them funny stories about the antics of her fellow guides and episodes of daring-do by sports and guides alike. Marion was fascinated to hear that Bill Stillman had taken to painting a picture of the encampment and its inhabitants. Myrna described the oil sketch in as much detail as she could recollect.

"He really is a fine painter," Marion affirmed. "I think it funny that the guides got to calling it the "Philosopher's Camp," too—and that the sports were good natured about it!"

Myrna smiled. She enjoyed sharing these aspects of the trip with her mother.

Days later, Belle confided to Myrna that Lyman had been in contact by letter with her father. And, in a code that the two men had established earlier, Lyman had written about the danger Belle had encountered. He said he presumed that her Ma and Pa were considering relocating her. It seemed the possibilities included either Canada or Boston. Belle thought her mother might favor the idea of Boston, as she had a number of acquaintances in the black community there.

It was no surprise to Myrna when Lyman suggested that she and Marion come to their house for a meeting to talk about events affecting Belle. "Ann will be having dinner set for us, too," he said. "And Alvah and Delia will be joining us."

Myrna and Belle talked some about the prospect of the upcoming dinner meeting while walking on the Epps' trail. Belle said she needed to get out and about, but Ann felt it best she be chaperoned—and best someone with a gun. Myrna was happy to pack a pistol. Belle also had insisted that they convey 'something' to Marion—"just so's she won't be too shocked by Lyman's disclosure at dinner." They knew they could lightly dissemble without revealing the full truth, so that Marion could share something of the ordeal.

As in turned out, Marion was a thoughtful listener. And both Belle and Myrna had felt an immense relief in telling her a modified version of the story.

"Do you think it was too dishonest in saying the man who resembled Jesse got away?" Belle wondered.

"Well, he did get away…to heaven or hell, I guess. Yep, I'm really comfortable with that story. Seriously, I feel much better in telling my ma something about our facing danger and then prevailing in the end…you know?"

"You don't usually call Marion, ma."

"Well, she's definitely my ma, and I'm her daughter, too." Myrna sighed.

Myrna took some time in dressing and brushing her hair that afternoon. She knew it would be a meeting of import—also Alvah would be there. Of one thing she was certain—Lyman would have already considered a number of living arrangements for Belle. But what did Belle want?

Those assembled at the Epps' included the Epps' plus Belle; the Wood's household (Alvah, Delia); and Myrna, Marion, and Carson. It seemed that all those gathered were well aware of Belle's recent frightening encounter, and the possibility of danger to her by slavers—though the cheery room with a lit fire, and spicy aromas of Ann's bean casserole, belied the threat.

"But why would these bounty hunters go to such lengths to seek out Belle?" Delia exclaimed.

"Mr. Wright, Paul—Belle's pa, believes it was an act of retribution on account of his work with the Underground Railroad and his episode down South freeing plantation slaves. It's a way of getting back at Belle's family—plus, a healthy, beautiful young woman like Belle would bring a good price at auction. This kind of thing has happened before, which is how Belle came up here in the first—as some of you already know. Well, it's no secret to any of us that things is getting heated and turbulent about slavery down South. We've all experienced the flood of folks coming through here on their way to Canada." Lyman paused and shook his head. "Ain't got no idea how the future's goin to turn out. Anyway, the situation at hand is how to keep Miss Belle safest."

"But, I'd think she's pretty safe right here with you and Ann, isn't she?" Delia said.

"Well, she is," interjected Ann. "Things might stay good as they is."

Alvah interrupted Ann and his mother. "You know, John and some of the others have taken to doing more traveling for the cause…Lyman's eyes can't be everywhere."

Lyman rose and started pacing the room. "We've ruled out Troy for various reasons." Belle scowled and was about to speak, but Lyman shushed her. "Paul and I—and her ma, Gladys, think Boston might be a good place for Belle to stay—just for a while. The Wrights have good connections there within the black church community. If we move quickly, any up-to-no-good ruffians would lose the scent, so to speak. Of course, Belle has to agree to a Boston visit."

"How would I even get there?" questioned Belle. Her bottom lip quivered. "It's a long trip."

"I agree, I certainly do. But, I've got a thought about it. Now it's kinda tricky, some might not like the idea for a bunch of reasons…"

"This one I gotta hear," Ann said.

"Alright…here it is. Within the next two weeks or so, Belle travels to Boston. And here's the kinda presumptuous part, Myrna goes as her travel companion and to keep her safe. I happen to know the Duffneys have family in Boston—Sam used to talk about it. Now I haven't figured the details and nobody mightn't like the idea, but there's my thoughts."

For a minute or two it seemed no one would speak. Alvah caught Myrna's eye. Neither wanted to jump for this idea. Myrna could see that Belle looked distraught. She had to ask what her friend thought of the Boston visit.

"I think I'm becoming a terrible imposition no matter what I do," Belle replied, looking at Myrna. "I guess it'd be alright to visit Boston if you went with me…but you might not want to visit there. And if you didn't, I'd understand." Her voice wavered.

Marion added. "It is true we have family there, the Peabody's, on my side—and the Duffneys on Sam's side. Actually, Elizabeth Peabody wrote earlier this summer saying among other things how she'd appreciate a visit. It's been awhile since I've seen her. And, of course, there's the Duffney branch, too. Though I've not made their aquaintence. "

Myrna, realizing she wasn't keen on making the trip, said reluctantly, "If Belle decides she wishes to visit Boston, I'll go with her—and bring my pistol." She knew there wasn't another choice to fill the bill for a likely travel companion. "I'd need to return as soon as possible to help Ma with the farm chores."

Carson piped up, "Really, I don't mind doing Myrna's chores while she's away. Of course, I'd still be around to help Delia and Alvah, too." He beamed to think he'd be part of it.

Belle sighed, "If Lyman and my pa think it best—I'll go." Then adding, "If I don't like it, I won't stay."

To Myrna (and Alvah's) dismay it appeared that she, in the company of Belle, would be leaving for Boston shortly. Myrna knew that for all their sakes, she would do her best to accept this turn of events graciously. Glancing at Alvah, she hoped he might initiate a time for them to talk together before she and Belle traveled east, and he did. After dinner, and some more discussion, Lyman rose from the table to bid them goodbye. At the bottom of the Epps' porch steps, Alvah turned to Myrna, "Why don't we try scouting out near Rocky Falls tomorrow, if you've the time." She agreed.

CHAPTER 31

Alvah and Myrna at the Crossroads

Alvah and Myrna got an early start for their morning scout. They'd decided to ride horses to the Brown settlement, and then tether them to trees at the beginning of the trail to Indian Pass. Truthfully, today they were more interested in having a chance to chat, than hunting, although they'd try for some small game before the day was done.

They walked quietly without conversation, carrying their thoughts close until they reached Rocky Falls. There were granite outcrops warmed by the sun at the top of the falls. The trees overhead were turning their burnt golden colors—a summery September day. They sat on a boulder that jutted into the stream. Myrna looked to the sky. "The days are already getting shorter," she said. Alvah nodded at the truth of it.

"I was surprised to hear that my ma and Marion volunteered to take on some of the lessons at the settlement while you are away," Alvah said. "My mind keeps traveling back to all that happened at Follansbee Pond—you know, the good and bad of it. I'm sure glad you and Belle stayed safe. And now, of course, you two will be going to Boston soon." Alvah's expression was perplexed. "Can't say's I'm happy about that."

"Well, it's not like I'm moving there permanently. I figure to get back as soon as we have Belle settled. Her family has close friends there, though I guess we'll initially stay some days with the Peabodys. I remember visiting them once when I was a child, but at that time I was more interested in seeing the ocean than my relatives. Marion has kept up a correspondence with Cousin Elizabeth, who is near her age. She's a well-known writer, who has started several schools for girls…and is reportedly interested in my teaching efforts." Myrna skipped a stone on the water. "I know life is never predictable, but I'd rather be spending the season at home. Though things seem to be changing around here too, especially at the settlement. Do you sense that?"

"Sure, I do. John, Oliver, Watson, and some of the others have been spending most of their time in Kansas, leaving Lyman in charge. Lyman says a few of the tenants feel nervous about John. They're more content when he's at home. Some of them are not exactly comfortable with white abolitionist neighbors either. I judge them to be easy with you, me and our families, because practical friendships have developed. But take, for instance, Harriet Wells, nice as she is; she's considered a foreigner of sorts. Lyman says folks like her and all, but there's lots of head-shakin too—know what I mean?"

"Yep, even took me awhile to take to her. Though I have to tell you, she's gone out of her way to help Belle and me with this Boston trip—even had her husband, who's returning to Boston, carry and deliver letters for us. It should make things smoother when we get there."

They sat silently for a while, the falling water a backdrop. Neither felt at ease saying more. The dramatic events of the summer had tested them and their relationship. There was a lot they might say, but rampant thoughts were dammed behind their tongues. Now, the chain of events that had brought them closer, was promising to pull them apart. And then there was the fact that the possibility of love was a new, untested, concept for each.

Alvah looked at Myrna, searching in his mind for what to say. He took her hand in his. Conversation at this moment wasn't needed. They quickly became entwined in the age-old wordless approach. Inhibitions fled. No thinking was immediately required.

Now these are real kisses, Myrna thought. She guided Alvah's hand beneath her shirt. He pressed his body fully to hers. "Don't stop," she whispered. But words broke the tantalizing spell.

Alvah sat up. "Myrna, I've promised to myself that I'm doing this proper like. I'm thinkin I might want to marry you. At any rate, I don't want one of those compromising situations that fellas snicker about."

Myrna rose and tucked in her shirt. "So, is this a proposal of sorts?"

Alvah hesitated. "Not quite yet, but I'm thinkin on it. I mean I've never considered it before—you know, marriage and all. I reckon it's one of those big steps that take time."

"Umm…I suppose. I think I may not be so conventional about this kind of thing. I met this woman, Amelie, at Martin's Hotel a ways back, before she married." Myrna related the story of the racy letter. "Anyway, she opened my eyes to other ways of thinking. And, by the way, when I saw her at Martin's again, before the Follansbee trip—she's now happily married and in her confinement stage."

"But she's French! They have different ways."

When Myrna and Alvah finished their conversation, they made a pact of sorts. While Myrna was away, they'd give some thought to a future together. For the moment, this would be a secret between them, but they'd not consider other suitors. Though, as Alvah acknowledged, he was unlikely to come across other candidates, whereas, Myrna might have the opportunity to meet Boston menfolk.

That resolved, it should not have been a surprise that they resumed kissing. Myrna interrupted for a moment. "Amelie told me about techniques one can do that allow completion while preserving a woman's virginity." Wordlessly, they continued. It was a warm day. They needn't be encumbered by layers of clothing. They felt satisfied together—twice. They swam in the pool below the falls, sensing a new closeness.

- CHAPTER 32 -
North Elba to Boston

Belle and Myrna were both nervous and excited about the long trip to Boston. They would travel by wagon to Keeseville, cross Lake Champlain by boat, and then journey on to Boston by rail and carriage. Truly, it was a momentous endeavor. Marion and Ann teared up as the women left for Keeseville in the wagon driven by Lyman and Alvah. Belle had a good cry on Myrna's shoulder when they were beyond sight of the elder women. Myrna sniffled into her hankie.

The trip was every bit as arduous as expected. After crossing Lake Champlain, they stayed overnight in Rutland. It would take well over a week before they arrived at their destination. Fortunately, the generous remuneration from the guiding work more than offset the unplanned costs. The part of the journey that Belle and Myrna found of most notable interest was the leg on the Fitchburg Railroad. By the time they reached Cousin Elizabeth Peabody's house in Boston, Myrna and Belle agreed they were happy to have a respite from further travel.

Alvah felt an anxious leap in his chest watching the carriage leave Keeseville for Port Kent. He would miss Myrna, but she'd promised to write. And he was pretty sure they had a commitment of sorts.

Yet now, after two weeks without receiving a letter, his confidence was wavering. But as Lyman said, "two weeks weren't nuthin in the scheme of things"

Lyman was anxious to hear from Belle, too. "Though I expect she's not as eager a correspondent as Miss Myrna."

Lyman peered with sly amusement over his cup. Alvah let the words rest. After all, he'd stopped by Lyman's to talk about guiding a hunting venture. They always enjoyed working together, and were thinking they might handle the Preston party without additional help.

"Bob Preston barely needs a guide, and Charlie and his brother Otis take directions, none of 'ems particularly rowdy around the campfire either. Tell you what … once we're up in the Saranac's we can enlist one of the Moody brothers, if our boys want more attention," Lyman said.

"Fair nuff." There weren't likely to be more guided hunts this far into the season, and the prospect of only a two way split of their earnings was welcome.

In an abrupt change of topic, Lyman asked how Alvah's ma was doing with her charges, the Smith family. Alone together, Lyman and Alvah had begun to speak freely about Delia's Underground Railroad activities. Due to the proximity of their community to Canada, it was becoming frequent for heretofore "paper abolitionists" to become conductors. "She and the wife, Lena, get on particularly well," Alvah replied.

Alvah told Lyman that he couldn't imagine his ma taking this on while his pa was alive. She'd been something of a homebody then. "But, she's always been real sociable, you know."

"An admirable woman for sure," Lyman said. And Ann had been friends of sorts with Delia for years. Yet, Lyman had never suspected the depth of Delia's convictions. Until the past two years, he hadn't known Alvah that well either. The only white guide he ever counted as a genuine friend was Sam Duffney … and Sam had liked Alvah. Of course, he still counted John Brown as his best of friends.

It was getting chilly, so Lyman put more logs on the fire. Neither of them had a particular need to hurry. They relaxed and put up their feet on the bench fronting the fire. Ann bustled in and out, not joining the 'men talk'.

The conversation ambled comfortably. They both had a mutual interest in playing music, Lyman being the more learned. Alvah told him he'd recently written two songs. And then, hesitantly, confessed they'd been written with Myrna in mind. But, Lyman didn't laugh, he just nodded. "Women can often be an inspiration," he offered, "And for good reason," though he didn't say specifics. They agreed they'd probably play together at the next community dance.

Talk turned to other matters. Lyman eventually confided to Alvah that all of John's activities away, at the moment centered in Kansas, were wearing on him. He told Alvah that John was disappointed that he, Lyman, hadn't committed to joining his plans for considered actions.

"But," he said, "I see it this way. There's some apprehension in our settlement right now. I'd say we're all clear on what we think, but maybe not so much on our proper actions. My attitudes are more cautious, but they make for balance. Kinda like a boat in a storm … all the weight can't be to one side. Anyway, that's what I think. I'll tell ya, if John and me weren't such tight friends, I think sometimes I might pop him one." Lyman shook his head. "He's a stubborn, head-strong man."

"The women say he's very calm and kindly in the classroom, when he visits."

"That he is, Alvah. I hope one day he gets to spend more time that way." But, Lyman suspected when he voiced those words, that John probably wouldn't get that opportunity.

- CHAPTER 33 -

Boston Arrivals

Elizabeth Peabody warmly welcomed Myrna and Belle into her home. She had prepared a guest room for them, which was comfortable, even if a little on the threadbare side. It might be said that Elizabeth's interest in books and the world of ideas, had led her to freely neglect housekeeping duties. However, she was most considerate of her guest's creature comforts, insisting that they have a warm bath and rest before teatime. Myrna also noticed that her cousin was not unattractive in person, but nevertheless, was curiously untidy in dress. Belle made the comment, "Miss Peabody seems not the stuffy sort." Myrna agreed, actually relieved by the seeming casual atmosphere. There was an elusive woman named, Emma, who came in to tidy and do errands, but not live-in help.

Tea was served by the cheering hearth in the parlor. Elizabeth plied them equally with questions, and current-laced scones. She was a petite, animated woman who enjoyed recalling incidents from her and Marion's shared childhoods. Myrna enjoyed hearing about the girlish escapades. And then Elizabeth said, "How I prattle on! Really, I'm most interested in hearing about the teaching experiences you and Belle have had. Marion said in her last letter that you have had great accomplishments in the backwoods."

"I suppose it could be called such." Myrna glanced at Belle.

"Truly, our teaching goals at the settlement may be more basic than yours," added Belle. "Nevertheless, very satisfying," continued Myrna. "All of our middle-grade students now read very well, and know their sums. Belle has begun a French class for two of the older students—they've expressed an interest in relocating to Canada." Myrna wavered, remembering that Belle's French lessons might not resume.

Elizabeth nodded vigorously. "How very interesting. I too think it so important to give youngsters, girls and boys, a good, sound education. If it won't bore you, I'll show you a book I've written on what I call kindergarten lessons—not tonight, of course," she declared, "but later, after you get your bearings."

The first thing the next day, Myrna and Belle set about writing to their friends and families. They wanted to tell some about their journey, but mostly that they had arrived safely. After breakfast, Elizabeth supplied them with pen and paper. Myrna wrote to Marion and Alvah, along with a quick note to her brother George. Belle wrote jointly to Lyman and Ann, as well as to her mother. Belle's letters to her ma were somewhat guarded, on the chance they could be intercepted. They felt relieved once their letters were drafted and posted by Emma, at Elizabeth's direction.

The background story, put forth to the Boston community by Belle and Myrna, was that Belle had wanted the opportunity to live and work as an independent woman in Boston. Myrna had offered to travel with her as an escort, and also desired to renew her aquaintence with her mother's side of the Peabody family.

Belle said to Myrna that she surmised Mr. Frederic Douglas might have a fuller version of her situation, as he was in close touch with, Paul, her father. Also, as activists, they kept tabs on incidents involving attempts by pro-slavery types who tried to capture and sell northern blacks. It was likely that John or Lyman may have contacted Mr. Douglas about the incident.

But even the Carteaux family, who would be Belle's Boston hosts and protectors, were not likely to know anything beyond the fact that her parents obsessed over her safety.

Once Myrna and Belle had practiced repeating their story a few times (twice on their train travels, and a bit more elaborately last evening to Cousin Elizabeth), it took shape as a defined reality. Elizabeth had listened intently. She was sympathetic to Belle's plight and Myrna's independent endeavors. She offered to draft an additional letter of introduction to Madam Christina Carteaux, adding... "Though I think she married a business partner last year. I believe she is now called Mrs. Bannister." Elizabeth told them that Madam Carteaux had established two successful beauty businesses in the Beacon Hill section of Boston—adding that she personally hadn't a need for such shops. Elizabeth was a kind and thoughtful host. She offered to assist Belle in making contact with the Bannisters who were a distinguished family of Jamaican and African heritage.

The very next morning, Elizabeth graciously accompanied Belle and Myrna to the Carteaux/Bannister address in the lower Beacon Hill neighborhood. Elizabeth cautioned them that this could be a preliminary visit, as Mrs. Bannister mightn't be home. But at very least, they'd have a chance to leave letters, and Elizabeth's calling card. Elizabeth was in a cheerful mood. "I say we should stop in downtown on our trip back," she said, seeming eager to properly entertain Myrna and Belle.

As luck would have it, after a short wait in the parlor, a rather exotic looking, petite brown-skinned woman entered the room smiling. "Please stay seated—Amanda will bring us tea." She paused, carefully pulling her chair closer to the others. She bowed towards Belle. "You, of course, must be Paul and Gladys' daughter. We know your Papa from his Boston business visits, and I've met your Mama—you've her pretty looks." She looked appreciatively at Belle. "And though you may not remember," she turned to face Elizabeth, "I frequented your wonderful Peabody's bookstore a few times. Ed, my husband, was especially sad to see it close." Mrs. Bannister, after assuring them to call her Christina, spoke with warm enthusiasm.

Elizabeth responded, "When my parents both became ill it was hard to maintain a daily business." She leaned forward. "Truthfully, it is difficult to maintain a steady profit in the business of publishing and selling books— especially when there are other needs to be met. My parents became frail and ill during that period. Also, you'd be surprised at the number of people who browse forever—without making a purchase."

Christina gave a commiserating nod. "My beauty business may be easier in that respect. There are many who enjoy looking well turned out, who don't care about turning a page!"

Myrna worried that they might be drifting, conversationally, into awkward territory. After all, Elizabeth was decidedly unfashionable. Christina seemed aware that a potential faux pas was waiting in the wings, and veered back to Belle, saying brightly, "As soon as it's convenient, Ed and I will be happy to help you get settled. There are many people in our community who can assist you in finding a suitable direction…"

So, it seemed, momentum was beginning for Belle. It was decided that Belle would meet Edgar Bannister and others in the community in a week's time, and then, move into the Bannister residence shortly thereafter.

Belle felt both relieved and anxious at the same time— and voiced as much to Myrna and Elizabeth after their jaunt in downtown Boston.

"My dear, there is no reason to rush," Elizabeth said. "You are welcome to stay with me to sort things out for as long as you wish."

Meanwhile, the attractions of Boston beckoned. Myrna was impressed and drawn to the hustle, bustle, of downtown. She and Belle looked in shop windows displaying clothes, riding tackle, baked goods and all manner of mercantile items. "The buildings are tall and set so close together, just as I remembered," she said with satisfaction. "Perhaps now it's more attractive and interesting, though." It had been over ten years since Myrna, as a child, had visited.

"Troy, New York, where I'm from, has a rather stately downtown, but smaller," Belle explained to Elizabeth, who nodded accordingly.

As they continued their stroll, Myrna observed there were a number of green grocers and food purveyors. She'd be able to buy some treats for Cousin Elizabeth during the week, now that she was familiar with store locations.

That evening, over tea, they talked a good deal about Christina Bannister. "To tell the truth," Elizabeth said, "I didn't want to say much one way or the other before our visit. I may have met her in passing, but had never been in her home. Though I do remember meeting, Edgar, her husband. I understand he's an accomplished painter—Waldo Emerson once mentioned that."

"I did not expect it to be such a grand house," Belle said, "Neither Ma nor Lyman said much beyond that Christina was a good friend who had the resources to help me get settled."

"I should say so!" exclaimed Elizabeth. At the same time, thinking that Belle was so well spoken and attractive, she deserved assistance.

Myrna sat, quietly thinking…It was something of a revelation to see the evident wealth and status of Christina Bannister. Heretofore, all those of African descent that she'd come to know lived in North Elba. And they were farmers like the Duffneys and others in the vicinity. Of course, many, like Lyman, were educated on a level with her own family. She still thought her own house, and the Epps' were well furnished homes to be proud of, but not approaching opulence, like the Bannister's. Even Elizabeth, who was famous in literary circles, had a rather modest home. Though as an unmarried woman, living on her own, her circumstances were admirable. She did have some lovely pieces of furniture, no doubt passed down from the Palmers, her mother's family. And then there were all of the wonderful books! Surely, those were Cousin Elizabeth's prizes. Yes, probably Elizabeth was living just the way she wanted, or so Myrna thought. Myrna was in a reverie—for a moment she lost the thread of her companions' conversation.

Belle was saying in response to something Elizabeth must have said, "I'm sure, knowing Marion, that she must be a wonderful correspondent. We did meet Mr. Emerson and some of the other Boston gentleman, but I was mostly in the background."

"And what was the famous Camp Maple like for you," she asked Myrna.

Myrna was caught off guard. "I'll admit, guiding is an odd occupation for a woman. I suppose I mightn't be a guide if it weren't for my pa. But I like it and am good at it. The Boston men were good clients—easy sorts."

"I say, hooray for you... being willing to forge ahead!" Clearly, Elizabeth approved of Myrna's unconventional independence. "And to think you also teach youngsters—amazing!"

"Yes, teaching is important to Belle and me." On the spot, Myrna decided it would be best to divert Elizabeth away from thoughts about Follansbee Pond. Best she think they were all kindred spirits in the classroom.

- CHAPTER 34 -

Boston Ways

It did not take long for Myrna and Belle to become oriented to Boston proper and its outlying areas. It was readily apparent that there was a fair walking distance between Elizabeth's home, near Cambridge, and that of the Bannister's on Beacon Hill. The women thoroughly explored the Cambridge and Boston Common area within the week. Elizabeth was delighted and appreciative when they brought home buns from the bakery. One day, while Elizabeth was at the Harvard library, Belle and Myrna, with Emma's assistance, prepared an evening meal of herb roasted chicken with carrots. They also bought a bottle of Madeira wine and a pound cake for after dinner.

"Oh, my! I feel guilty leaving you two on your own while I pursue my studies. And to think you did all of this…" Elizabeth said, gesturing towards the table. Belle smiled, looking pleased. It had been her idea to surprise Elizabeth in this way.

Myrna had initially been doubtful about commandeering the kitchen, lest it might be seen as offensive or intrusive, and was pleased by Elizabeth's warm response.

That evening, after a few glasses of Madeira, Belle, impulsively asked Elizabeth if she'd ever considered marriage. Elizabeth was in a mellow mood. She looked reflective, and then recounted a proposal she'd considered as a young woman, from a Mr. Buckminster. "You know, I was very young. He was, I suppose, an appropriate match, but at the time too intense in his pursuit. Anyway, I refused his offer of marriage. I understood he was very distressed by my refusal, quite glum about it. That disturbed me, but I was never sorry about not marrying him. Later, when I heard he took his own life, I felt very sad. Truthfully, I think it is difficult for a woman to have an independent, spirit—and be happily married."

"But, did you never feel that you'd like some kind of deep intimacy with a man?" Belle asked.

"Ah, well, I need to keep some secrets, don't you think?"

Myrna looked intently at her cousin. She was sure there were secrets aplenty.

Once Belle was moved and settled at the Bannisters', Myrna thought to begin making arrangements to travel back to North Elba. She wanted to go home. Unfortunately, before she was far into the process there were a series of snow storms, the most recent of which made maneuvering around Boston impossible, let alone managing the complex configuration of transportation it would take to reach North Elba. She hoped in vain for a small window of opportunity.

But the snow continued, causing her and Elizabeth to be more or less housebound. There wasn't even a chance that she and Belle might arrange to visit in this weather. Myrna sat by the parlor window watching the fresh flakes softly fall on the already high piled banks of snow. She missed Marion and Alvah terribly. She wondered if it was snowing back home, and how they were all faring.

Elizabeth entered the room, observing the morose Myrna seated in the blue over-stuffed, wingback chair, wrapped in a tartan plaid flannel blanket. "Well, at least we have plenty of tea and good books," she said, placing the tray with teapot and cups on a small table nearby.

"I suppose," Myrna replied, with a slight smile. "Thank you for the tea," she added.

"Do you play chess, by chance?" Elizabeth asked brightly.

"Yes, but not very well. Pa and I played some during the winter."

"Perfect. I'm not especially proficient, either," Elizabeth paused, "Perhaps after dinner?"

All in all, chess seemed an amiable distraction for consideration. "I think before dinner I'll try writing in the journal that Marion gave me for recording my experiences during my travels. Up until now I've been too busy to write much."

"Ah, Marion hasn't changed. She is so wise in anticipating your needs. Personally, I find that putting pen to paper can ease any niggling worries that are bothering me. Here, let me light a lamp for you and freshen your cup. And, after dinner we'll commence the challenge of the board!" Then she scurried back to her library.

And so began Myrna's daily writing habit; first sketchy journal notes, and then longer letters to Alvah and Marion. As days went by, Myrna realized that there were things one might write that wouldn't likely be said in a verbal exchange. She liked that.

As for chess, it proved to provide satisfying entertainment for both women. Indeed, neither improved much, and yet they enjoyed the challenge. Sometimes Myrna won, and other times the round went to Elizabeth. They were well matched. Myra began to look forward to playing, and knew Elizabeth did, too.

The weeks passed by. It became clear that winter had arrived and would linger until spring. One day she wrote in her journal:

'Winter is here to stay. I'm not able to leave Boston, probably until spring. I won't see Ma or Alvah or North Elba until then, and I'm sad about it.'

She read it over several times. It was true, and she knew it.

Finally, there was a respite in the frequent flurries. Streets were clear enough for carriages; walkways had been shoveled for foot traffic. It was chilly outside, but visits were again manageable. It was decided that Belle would arrive from Beacon Hill by carriage and stay at the Peabody house for a week or so. Myrna and Elizabeth were both excited by the prospect. When the door knocker sounded, they rushed to warmly greet Belle. Emma took her small valise up the stairs.

    The next morning, Belle and Myrna allowed themselves a shopping excursion in downtown Boston. Myrna had been frugal with the considerable sum of monies from her guiding expeditions, and Belle's parents had sent money to the Bannisters for her needs. They'd already experienced the damp chill of Boston in winter, warm coats were in order. Belle, for her part, wished for something stylish. It was apparent she'd have use for such. Myrna was not opposed to having a pretty garment, but knew she should be practical. Her coat would need to be suitable for back home, too. In the end, she decided on a navy blue worsted, loose fitting jacket, trimmed at the collar, cuffs and hem with navy satin. After being measured, she was assured it would be ready in a week. Myrna liked the style. The color would be fine with the three, rather plain dresses she had with her. Belle ordered a fancier ruffled cloak in a pale mauve color. She whispered to Myrna, after the seamstress went for more goods, "I believe we are receiving best service since mentioning our friends the Bannisters." Myrna nodded in agreement.

    They next stopped in a tearoom and then went on to a shop that sold yarn and needles for knitting. Belle assured Myrna that she could teach her to knit in an hour or so. They would make scarves to wear with their coats, cream for Myrna and very pale pink for Belle. "Let's make one for Elizabeth, too. I think soft blue should do nicely," Belle said with satisfaction. "It will be a Christmas gift from us."

    That evening by the fire they began knitting. "Don't worry, we can unravel the whole piece if there are mistakes," Belle encouraged. Elizabeth, concurred. "When I was a girl, knitting was mandatory for a girl's education," she declared.

Myrna laughed, "It still is, but I've avoided it."

"Yes, Marion says you're rebellious." Elizabeth smiled, warmly.

They sat companionably; the younger women told of their foray downtown. When asked, Elizabeth relayed a bit about her writing that day. "I'm hoping these essays will be a valuable contribution to ideas about education," she said.

Belle looked from the yarn in her lap to Elizabeth. "I've been waiting to tell you…well, to get advice, really, from you and Myrna about an employment prospect that's come my way."

The gist was that a family surnamed Almay wished to have French taught to a child who resided with them. Belle said that Mrs. Bannister, Christina, thought the child might be a cousin or niece of Mrs. Almay's. The family in question was purported to be wealthy and resided in the Beacon Hill area. Apparently, Christina didn't know the family well, saying they were not in the same 'circles'. "I'm, of course, well qualified to teach French, but would like to have more of a sense of the family situation before arriving on their doorstep for an interview." Belle's mother had lived in Paris as a child, and had taken pains to see that Belle become equally fluent in her mother tongue.

"Let me see," began Elizabeth, "I do know that Judge Almay was in the import trades and has built a great fortune. He's also a lawyer by background and his family are not originally New Englanders. So, his entrée to Boston society is that he's fabulously rich, not that he's an old line Bostonian. His current wife's origin is vague. She is very young and her beauty draws comments—his first wife died about five years ago. There have been rumors that his wife's reputation is that of a coquette who graces many parties. On the other hand, I've heard she has attended very well to her step-daughter's education. So, that is what I know—mostly hearsay. But you are an astute woman. I believe you will be able to assess the situation once you meet her. However, I will ask more about the Almays when I have lunch with Doris Cranch next week." Cousin Doris was old-line Boston, and traveled in wide circles of her choosing.

Myrna couldn't help but congratulate Belle on finding such a ready vocational placement. Her feelings about it? Envy was one, closely followed by sensing the certain loss of companionship while Myrna was in Boston. But at the same time, she was happy that Belle was getting a fresh start. She knew that cousin Elizabeth would make good on her word, too.

The looming placement opportunity was put aside for the next few days. Myrna and Belle enjoyed spending time together, often including Elizabeth. They walked to the Commons, stopping to buy treats to bring home, they (mostly Belle) made special dinners for Elizabeth to exclaim over, and they read greedily from Elizabeth's store of books. Belle and Myrna continued their knitting. While pursuing this avocation, Myrna said she actually found knitting to be relaxing.

Finally, the jackets they had ordered were delivered to the house. They modeled them, and the newly knitted scarves, for Elizabeth. "Perfect, just perfect!" Elizabeth exclaimed.

The day came for Belle to return to the Bannister's and begin her tutoring employment at the Almay's. After Belle left, the house felt cold and empty. Myrna was restless. But since her correspondence with Marion and Alvah had lagged, she resolved to spend the morning writing. Actually, she had things to say. She took the green enamelware kettle from the stove and poured the steaming water into the blue teapot. She placed a Wedgewood blue porcelain cup on a tray…hesitated and added another, which she'd bring to Elizabeth's study. Elizabeth thanked her for the tea. That done, Myrna went back to the writing desk in her room.

She shook Alvah's latest letter from its envelope and smoothed the pages on her desk. It had arrived two days ago, while Belle was visiting.

She'd read the news it contained to Belle, but skipped over the more personal passages...mostly. She inadvertently had read, "I keep thinking of our wonderful day at Rocky Falls..." And then stopped.

"It *is* a love letter," Belle had exclaimed.

"I wouldn't say exactly that. You want the rest of the news, or not?" Belle had nodded, yes.

Today, looking back at sharing news with Belle, Myrna wished she had confided more about her feelings. Once again, she was reminded of her own secretive nature. But back to the task at hand, she reviewed Alvah's words, one more time, and then put pen to paper. Dear Alvah, I too miss our times together...

She described the snowy streets that were lit with tall gas lamps at night; the stately jumbled together stores of the crowded downtown area; the magnificent Harvard library; Belle's move to the Bannister's home...The letter continued: She signed it 'Yours in friendship'.

She sighed, re-reading Alvah's correspondence one more time before placing her dated response in an envelope, carefully addressing it, and wondering how long it would be before he received it. She gazed at the grey sky from the small window in her room. Was more snow likely? She quickly donned her new jacket and walked by Elizabeth's study, telling her she was on her way to the post office. As she stepped out, the air was brisk, but she felt all the better for a walk. When she reached her destination, the postmaster was a friendly man of uncertain age. His dark, abundant mustache bobbed when he spoke. She was in luck, he said, as the mail would be leaving by train that afternoon.

That evening after supper, Elizabeth and Myrna resumed their pleasant pastime of a chess game by the hearth. Elizabeth noted that Myrna was a dedicated correspondent. "Perhaps your reports will encourage Marion to visit me. Of course, it's an easier trip in early summer." Myrna agreed. At the moment she was absorbed in the game. She didn't like to be distracted when she was winning. After four more moves, Myrna announced, "checkmate!"

"That was one of our best games yet," Elizabeth enthused, while studying the board. She sat back in her plush, burgundy colored, wingback chair, putting her feet on a leather hassock, which she pulled nearer to the hearth. She encouraged Myrna to do likewise.

"I had an interesting happenstance yesterday," she began. "On my way to Ticknor's, I encountered Mrs. Parker. She's a niece of Ted Parker's. Anyway, Evelyn Parker has established a small school for girls. I believe she has a total of eight young students, including two of her own children. Three of the girls' board with the Parker family, and three others are day students. I have to say, Evelyn strikes me as a delicate young woman. Evidently, she suffered a bout of respiratory illness a few weeks ago. It seems she'd like temporary help with her teaching duties, mentioning she'd pay fairly well. Honestly, I believe she thought I might offer my assistance," Elizabeth confided. "And there are times when I might very well have done that. But I'm so keen on finishing my writing project that I just don't want the distraction of preparing lessons and all," she said, with vigor. Elizabeth took the floral cozy off the pot and refilled their cups. "Tonight I got to wondering if this is a situation that might interest you…now I certainly don't wish to be presumptuous. In fact, I'd prefer you not say yea or nay tonight! You can think about it, and should you find the idea appealing let me know…fairly soon? Oh, and I should add, the school is the next block over…an easy walk."

Myrna was caught by amazement. She surely would not have expected such an offer. Certainly, it would add to her savings, allowing her to contribute more to Elizabeth's household costs. Elizabeth was so unfailingly kind…it was hard to refuse her. She replied, "I will take just overnight to give you a definite answer. It's the suddenness of it, you know. But I'm interested." Myrna hesitated. "Perhaps you could tell Mrs. Parker that I'm willing to meet with her and the students to discuss their lessons before making a final decision. Would you find that an acceptable approach?"

"Oh, yes. Yes, of course. But, please don't rush your decision."

Arrangements were made for Myrna and Elizabeth to visit Mrs. Parker's school. Myrna found Evelyn Parker to be an agreeable woman. The classroom was painted a sunny yellow that reflected light from two floor-to-ceiling windows. There were two long wooden tables in the center of the room. Chairs, in a variety of sizes were set in a semi-circle, facing a large blackboard. One wall had pegs for aprons and coats. The small woodstove near the brick sidewall heated the room nicely. Of course, the classroom was part of the Parker residence, originally a summer parlor.

The girls in the classroom may have been told to mind their manners. They were exceedingly cheerful, even going so far as to entertain Myrna and Elizabeth with a Christmas song—*God Rest Ye Merry Gentlemen*. It was decided that Myrna could, if she so wished, begin her teaching duties right after the Christmas recess. As they'd donned their winter wraps to leave, the girls chimed in unison, "Merry Christmas, Miss Duffney and Miss Peabody." All in all, Myrna found the tableau charming.

Once outside, Elizabeth asked, "What are your thoughts?"

"Oh, I think the school is quite attractive—the yellow color is pleasing. I liked that all of the girls seemed well cared for and alert. Evelyn seems to have given thought to the room arrangement. There are plenty of books on the shelves and paints in the cupboard. I would agree that

Evelyn is thin and a bit peaked. I do have energy and stamina, which will lighten her chores. I believe this will be a good situation for me," Myrna said with approval. Elizabeth clapped her mittend hands together. "I'd so hoped you would like Evelyn. This was the first time I'd seen her classroom—I agree with your assessment of it." She beamed at Myrna. "I do think teaching is in the Peabody blood!" To this, Myna just shook her head in amusement.

Marion's last letter to Myrna had mentioned the Duffney sisters, cousins of Pa's who lived in Boston. Brother George said he thought they were proprietors of an inn of some sort. Marion wondered if Myrna might look in on them. She recollected that Sam may have known them when he was a youngster. She wrote…"it might be interesting to make their acquaintance." Myrna realized she didn't know much about Pa's earlier life. And in rumative moments she thought back to their times together. She would definitely plan to call on the Duffneys.

An opportunity arose. It was mild weather for mid-December, certainly a contrast from the cold, and blowing flurries of last week. Belle was allowed a respite from her tutoring duties at the Almay's, and would be staying with Myrna and Elizabeth for a few days.

Belle was enthused with her tutoring assignment, but said she welcomed spending time at Elizabeth's.

She was intrigued by the idea of finding the Duffney cousins. Elizabeth said their establishment, The Blue Iris, was known to host events for suffragists and the like. Myrna surmised from what Elizabeth said about women's suffrage, that in general she supported it, but didn't have time to attend meetings—"One has to make choices," she said. Apparently, her writing consumed all of her attention.

The Blue Iris was not too far a walk, Elizabeth thought, and drew them a sketchy map with directions. "Anyway, I know you two are used to long treks."

They left the Peabody house after breakfast, wearing their new jackets and scarves over simple dresses. They didn't mind the long walk. Belle noted that the Blue Iris was on a narrow back street, nearer to Beacon Hill and the Bannister's house, than to Elizabeth's Cambridge address. The Blue Iris itself, was a tidy, white clapboard, federal style, building with blue shutters. It was set back from the street, the lawn, now snow covered, was bordered by a wrought iron fence. A bluestone walkway led to the double-doorway entrance, above which set a graceful arched window. A discreet oval sign, with an elegant painting of an iris, hung above the doors. They walked up to the front door and knocked.

The inside vestibule was inviting and tasteful. A reserved woman of middle age greeted them, "May I help you?"

"Yes, I'm looking for Clara and Anna Duffney...I'm Myrna Duffney, Sam Duffney's daughter."

"Sam?" She looked momentarily puzzled, perhaps wary. "Well, now, I'm Clara," her face lit with a smile. "I suppose, I haven't seen Sam in...well, quite a number of years! Actually, since we were youngsters. Please, hang your wraps and come with me to the side parlor. I'll see if Anna is about," she gestured to the parlor. Myrna told Clara that sadly, her father had passed, but her mother, Marion, had suggested that she pay them a visit while she was in Boston.

Belle and Myrna seated themselves on the settee nearest to the hearth, and surveyed the room. The hearth mantle was decked for Christmas with candles and swags of greenery, Belle, in particular, was impressed with the blue and gold patterned Turkish carpet, noting how well it complimented the blue damask upholstery of the various pieces of furniture, and the stately gold colored drapes. "My, my," she said, "I'd like a room like this someday...the colors, I mean."

The Duffney women were gracious and impressive. They were curious about how Myrna and Belle had come to travel to Boston in the first place—and just what their expectations were, now that they'd arrived.

Myrna judged them to be about Marion's age, give or take. Both sisters gave an immediate impression of conservative, understated elegance, having carefully coiffed hair and manicured hands. Anna, appeared the slightly younger, moving quickly and smiling easily. She was slim, dark haired, and showed her navy dress with white lace collar to good advantage. Clara, on initial meeting, appeared severe and aloof, her greying brown hair pulled to a tight bun. She carried her portly, corseted figure with stately dignity, looking stylish in a grey silk dress.

In a short period of time, the four women were relaxed by the fire, freely telling their stories. When it became apparent that Clara and Anna were welcoming and unhurried (explaining they had a cook and staff to assume daily duties)—Myrna did her best to recount Sam's life and accomplishments, and to describe their homestead in the Adirondacks. Clara said she was sad to have lost touch over the years. She truly had fond memories.

After a while, Belle felt comfortable to say she had, in part, sought Boston as a safe haven. "That and the fact that I hope to live independently," she concluded. Clara nodded sagely, saying the position at the Almay's was a fine start. Anna thought that the Bannisters were enterprising and talented. "You are fortunate in having their backing."

After a bit, Myrna felt she had conveyed enough about her immediate family and their Adirondack lifestyle. She liked the Duffney sisters and was intrigued by the Blue Iris establishment. She also was curious about their clientele and ties to the suffragists.

"Oh, in some ways we've been fortunate. I always say, there's a lot of luck in life," Clara confided. "When Harold, my husband, died, I inherited this grand old building that had been in his family. Originally, I'd thought to sell. We'd had no children and it was a large house that would require a great deal of maintenance. Frankly, I wasn't sure what I should do. At the time, I was a young woman who didn't wish to remarry and didn't fancy being idle. One day, when I was about six months into mourning, I was chatting about my dilemma with Anna." She gestured to her sister who sat serenely listening to what may have been an oft told story. "Anna had not yet married, and was not inclined to accept the available suitors. Well, we got to recollecting about the time we'd stayed with Aunt Julia at a lovely small inn on the coast of Maine. And then it occurred to me…to us, that if we dared, we could make this lovely mansion into a modest inn. We decided to call it the Blue Iris, as they bloom in profusion in our front garden." They laughed with delight at the telling. Anna added, "Of course, there's a lot more to the story; family opposition, community hesitancy, recalcitrant workmen, and so on. But once we made the plan, we stuck with it." Clara nodded her assent. "It's perfect for us."

It was a heartening story. Myrna could hardly wait to tell Marion about the Duffney cousins. And she was sure there were other interesting details that hadn't yet been conveyed.

They talked a bit more. Then Belle glanced Myrna's way, signaling it was time to leave. Still, Anna insisted that they see the decorated spruce tree in the dining room. They agreed it was quite a spectacle! As they donned their coats to leave, the hospitable sisters invited them to a lecture on The Plight of Women, presented by a Miss Elking—that would be convened at the Blue Iris two days hence. Myrna told them what a genuine pleasure it was to meet her father's cousins—and that she would send a note if she might accept the invitation.

On their walk back to Elizabeth's, Belle wondered if they should attend the lecture at the Blue Iris. "I don't know,"

Myrna said, "but, it's something to think about. I guess I'd have to say that I would like to visit again."

"Did you notice that your cousin Anna and you have the same cheek bones and nose?" Myrna simply cocked her head and scrunched her eyebrows.

As they sat around the table that evening with Elizabeth, telling about their visit with the Duffneys, Elizabeth said, "No, I'm not inclined to attend that particular lecture, but if you fancy hearing it, you should go."

At the lecture, Myrna sat in a corner spellbound, watching the proceedings. Myrna saw that her cousins, Clara and Anna, were in a subtle way tending to their guests. A nod from Clara sent staff to refurbishing cookie platters or setting out fresh, hot tea. Myrna agreed with most of what Miss Elking had to say about the importance of women rallying to the cause of universal suffrage. But being with the large group of mostly women, along with her cousins and Belle, seemed like watching some kind of theater—and it was a thought-provoking show.

The following afternoon Myrna excused herself from tea with Elizabeth. She simply had to write her burbling thoughts in her journal, and also wanted to respond to Alvah's last letter.

He had written to her about some restlessness at the Brown settlement, and about neighbors in Elizabethtown who were holding abolition meetings. Meanwhile, John's whereabouts was vague, which bothered Lyman some. There was also some pro-slavery talk coming out of Westport, he wrote. On personal topics, he mentioned that he'd taken to writing songs—and one he'd written with her in mind, though she'd have to wait until she got home to hear it. Myrna's heart leapt at the closing 'affectionately'. She liked that, and thought she'd follow suit. Her letter to Alvah completed—she signed... Affectionately, Myrna

Myrna always felt compelled to send off her letters immediately, once they were completed. She quickly donned her outer garments and scurried to the post office. The exertion and chill air left her breathless when she arrived at the postal counter. The dapper, mustachioed postmaster smiled in recognition, by now she was a regular. As there were no other customers about, they made pleasantries. "My name is Bradley," he said. "May I be so bold as to ask yours?" They chatted a bit more. Myrna realized they might even be flirting, not a practiced skill for her. She laughed inwardly, to think the feelings she had for Alvah might be reflected in her face—perhaps enticing Bradley to respond thus. She also thought, if this was flirting, it was quite fun!

Myrna was coming to realize that Boston had its charms. She enjoyed the handiness of stores that carried everyday items for ready purchase, and tearooms that allowed women to gather without being accompanied by men. And here in Boston, she thought with satisfaction, industrious single women, such as, Elizabeth, her Duffney cousins, and Christina Bannister could make a living.

Myrna also thought about Belle, and how well she fell in with Boston ways. It gave her a start to think that Belle wouldn't return to North Elba to reside—perhaps not even to visit. Well, that was a sad fact she had to face. And, of course, there was Cousin Elizabeth—she liked and admired Elizabeth—more than that, she felt a sincere friendship had developed between them. Would they travel to visit each other? It was hard to say. Myrna sighed. Pa always said one shouldn't shy from the truth.

That evening they'd been invited to the Ticknor's annual winter party, by dint of Elizabeth's fame as a writer, and her connections to the publishing community. Myrna was aware that Elizabeth was admired for her considerable talents, but at the same time was thought to be unkempt and dowdy. Christina had conveyed as much to Belle in a conversation. Women, especially, conspired unkindly with superior glances when she entered a room, or so it had been said. Myrna was determined that for this particular evening Elizabeth would look her best. Though Myrna had to smile at herself as she purchased two tortoise shell combs for Elizabeth's unruly hair. How Marion would roar with laughter at the thought of Myrna offering fashion advice! Nevertheless, with the housekeeper's assistance, she'd found a rather lovely lace trimmed, emerald colored, dress in the hall wardrobe; it was found carelessly rumpled, but was now freshened and pressed.

Myrna presented Elizabeth with the combs. There were some initial dismissive grumbles. But Myrna remained firm. Elizabeth acceded to having her hair combed and held attractively by the new combs. She looked pleased at her image reflected in the hand mirror.

The Ticknor party was elegant, even by Boston standards. Myrna was alternately introduced by Evelyn Parker as either, the new teaching assistant or as Elizabeth's cousin. Introductions having been made, Myrna found a vacant side chair and surveyed the room. The Ticknor's ballroom was a step up from their living quarters and the lower level rooms. The ballroom was framed by long windows covered with formal green satin, gold tasseled drapes. Empire style mahogany furniture abounded and Turkish carpets covered the floor. The buffets were strewn with polished silver serving pieces. It was a room meant to impress. Myrna wondered— how often a room of this sort would be used. Some of the women who glided by seemed at home in this setting. She thought, with some satisfaction, that Elizabeth really did look groomed and stately. She also assessed her own image as quite attractive. There were mirrors at every turn. She saw a gentleman staring at her quizzically. As he drew closer, she could see that it was the somewhat near-sighted Waldo Emerson. Finally, he approached her and said, "Have we met?" Myrna smiled.

"Yes, indeed. I'm Myrna Duffney, your guide to Follansbee Pond."

"Ah, yes. Yes, of course, Miss Duffney, I see it now." He looked to ponder and then said, "I think when one sees a person in a wholly different context the mind is easily fooled—don't you?" He cleared his throat. "May I sit here?" he said, gesturing to the chair beside her.

It seemed that Mr. Emerson, or Waldo, in this venue, knew that Cousin Elizabeth had visiting relatives, but hadn't suspected it might be Myrna. He again told her how much he'd enjoyed his Adirondack sojourn. "I would count our trip to Follansbee Pond as a life changing experience," he said. "You know, I've begun writing a poem to commemorate our splendid adventure. When I've completed it, I'll send you a copy. I'm thinking to call the poem Adirondac."

They talked a bit more about the woods. He said he frequently saw some of the chaps from the trip. However, Bill Stillman was off traveling at the moment. She knew Waldo was famous in these circles and that she had probably, in this instance, gained in stature by his attention. When Myrna and Elizabeth were in the entrance hallway putting on their outer wraps and saying goodbyes, Waldo stood by Elizabeth, again, warmly praising the Follansbee Pond adventure—saying he looked forward to future Adirondack expeditions. Myrna could hardly wait to write to Alvah about her chance encounter.

Myrna enjoyed quiet indoor days when it was too chilly or stormy to venture much further than between the classroom and Elizabeth's house. Winter also added to the vagaries of the correspondence between Myrna and Alvah. But the frequency of their writing began to increase the odds of receiving letters. The frequency also led to a relaxed, informal tone. If they thought about it (though they didn't) this led to more intimate, unguarded exchanges. Myrna heard the doorbell. It was a letter from Alvah.

If Elizabeth was in her study, Myrna's letter opening ritual began with a cup of tea by the fire in the parlor, otherwise, she read in the privacy of her room. Alvah's latest letter began...

> Dear Myrna,
> Cause of the snow storms I'm never sure when you might get my letters. On Christmas Day we went to visit Marion and Carson for dinner—me and Ma. Well it snowed something fierce by dinnertime. We ended up having to stay over. I actually slept in your bed. I must say it's very comfortable, even without you in it! ...
> I played them the song that I wrote with you in mind. Marion said it was 'lovely'...
> Your horse Star is getting good care by Carson. Star says she misses you...But we all do.
> Those Duffney women you talk about sound like go-getters alright...In general, Boston sounds lively.
> ...There are two nice women and a baby staying now with Ma and me. I expect they'll be with us until the weather clears...
> I haven't mentioned that we might declare our engagement when you return, tho Carson has begun teasing me about such... Affectionately, Alvah

Myrna responded, then and there. There was no doubt in her mind; she wanted to return home as soon as possible.

Good to her word, Myrna buckled down and assisted Evelyn Parker in teaching her young charges. Several of the girls were eager students, especially Laura and Margaret. They brought to mind her niece Janey. It was a pleasure finding good books for them to read and talk about. Myrna was careful to let her students know that she would be with them for only a matter of months—at most. She knew from experience that young girls had a tendency to become attached to their teacher, as perhaps they would to an older sister—and she wished to avoid too many tearful farewells. But she did tell them stories about the Adirondacks and her students in North Elba. When Laura asked excitedly if she could visit Miss Duffney in the mountains where she lived, Myrna saw no harm in responding that visitors were always welcome. But, she added—it is a very long trip.

Sometimes Evelyn hovered. "I'll miss you terribly, you know," she said. "If you should change your mind..."

And Cousin Elizabeth, of course, was positively delighted at the good reports about Myrna's teaching style, calling her "gifted, in that regard." Myrna told her 'gifted' was too strong a word. In turn, she thoughtfully read Elizabeth's manuscript of essays on educational practices for young children. She found that she could enthusiastically praise it.

One afternoon at tea, after she'd finished reading it and made some notes, she said to Elizabeth.

"You know, this is going to be an important treatise for educators. Some of the ideas you put forth about young children may be unknown to many in the profession..."

Elizabeth nodded. "I certainly hope so," she said, laying the chessboard and pieces between them.

Belle and Myrna were aware that their remaining time together was limited. They resolved to set aside time for each other, when possible, at the end of each teaching week.

Belle had established a pattern of visiting the Peabody home most Fridays after lessons. Often Elizabeth joined them in the parlor, but she also discreetly left them time for private chatter.

"Oh, I'd have to say that the Almays are generous and fair," Belle said, hesitantly. "Mrs. Almay now has me calling her Lily. I think she appreciates that we are near contemporaries. Her husband, who is much older, prefers that I address him formally...probably everyone calls him his honor, or judge. He makes a point of calling me Miss Wright."

Belle leaned forward with a conspiratorial voice. "I've been just dying to tell you...the Almays have two portraits hanging in the dining room, one of Lily and the other of her daughter Jayne." She hesitated to build the suspense. "They are both by W. Stillman!"

"Really?" Myrna was intrigued.

"Yes, at first I was of a mind to tell Lily that I know Mr. Stillman. But then I realized that would raise complicated questions."

"True...very wise. Were the paintings pleasing?"

"Oh, very. Especially the one of Lily. She's a pretty woman." Belle paused, "When she saw me admiring the paintings, Lily mentioned that Mr. Stillman had spent several months the past spring in capturing the likenesses of her and Jayne."

Belle continued, "Of course, there are some usual bothers with working in the household. I've noticed the house staff, especially Miss Conlin, look askance at Lily's informality with me. But then, I'd hardly expect otherwise," Belle sighed resignedly.

Myrna had come to appreciate Belle's deep feelings on the levels of injustice that she endured, though she rarely found words that satisfactorily lightened Belle's moods. "But you do find your milieu with the Bannisters heartening...Yes?"

"Oh, surely, I do. But even there, it can be like living in a bubble. I mean, they are wealthy, well known, and connected to a broad range of entrepreneurs and, of course, abolitionists. I've even been to one of the abolition meetings. But I suspect it's always going to be a fragile coalition...you know? It could melt, burst..." Belle shrugged.

Myrna sighed. As usual, she didn't disagree.

"Just don't you dare say that I should have hope for the future and so on...!" Belle said.

"But, I never...

"No, Ma did."

"I don't mind being your sister, however, I'm not qualified for the 'Ma' role."

At that, they both sighed, feeling perplexed...

Certainly, the very atmosphere of both North Elba and Boston couldn't help but raise these questions about race and prejudice to the surface. There were dreams of freedom. There were nightmares about slavery. But the truth is, it seemed a hopeful time for their Country's future.

Perhaps, Belle and Myrna were just beginning to grasp the forward momentum—and that ideas about the abolition of slavery, women's suffrage, freedom and emancipation, were much larger than just their personal concerns—they were becoming part of a world stage, bit players without rehearsed parts.

Myrna and Belle found themselves reflecting on their respective lives thus far, as they walked the streets of Boston. They were young women who candidly wondered about the future. Of course, they might not yet have the concepts and vocabulary of their transcendentalist acquaintances, but they had the same concerns about freedom and justice that were voiced by Mr. Emerson and Mr. Lowell, for example—And, of course, by their friend and mentor, Mr. Brown.

Myrna and Belle frequently made the Blue Iris a destination on their longer walks. Today they needed a long walk.

They were greeted at the door by Anna, who now seemed more like an auntie, rather than a distant cousin. Once again, Myrna took in the sweep of the curved staircase leading to the upper level and the rounded walls of the reception area. It was an elegant design.

"Sugar and milk with your tea?" Anna said, warmly. After Myrna told them her most recent news from home, Anna replied, "I hope someday that Clara and I might visit your home in the Adirondacks. They say it's a wonderfully scenic place with air that's a healthy tonic."

Belle chimed in. "That it is. The home where I lived was of a rustic rectangular design, but most beautifully decorated with handwoven rugs on polished wooden floors and furnished with well-crafted furniture. And, there is so much land and space…every home is adjoined by a spacious garden." At the thought, Belle grew quiet and looked wistful.

Clara had joined them. She said brightly, "And the train service to Albany and Burlington gets better by the year."

Turning their thoughts back to upcoming activities at the inn, Clara talked about, even shared some gossip about, Miss Anthony and Mrs. Stanton. Both having said they wondered if Mrs. Beecher Stowe mightn't do more for women's suffrage. Walking back to Elizabeth's, Belle said that after an hour with the Duffneys she felt positively enlightened and encouraged!

CHAPTER 35

Back to the Adirondacks

In spite of longing to return to the Adirondacks, Myrna's daily routines in Boston became pleasantly anticipated. The girls at Evelyn's school were eager learners from families of privilege. It was relatively easy to hold their attention. She and Evelyn amicably divided the teaching duties. Myrna was not particularly proficient with sewing skills, such as smocking, but excelled at drawing and water colors. She and Evelyn fluidly gravitated to what they each did best, Evelyn remarking on the ease of it. Occasionally, Elizabeth stopped by during lessons. She was delighted at the students' performance. The youngsters liked reading and reciting for her, treating her like an important dignitary. Myrna and Elizabeth often found themselves in the evenings discussing Parker's classroom, or particular students. Elizabeth said it energized her writing. Myrna had to admit that she'd grown to enjoy her employment. At that confession, Elizabeth raised her eyebrows. "So?" She said.

Myrna laughed. "Checkmate," she said.

One morning, upon awakening, Myrna heard dripping sounds. She realized the ice was melting from the eaves. The side paths were clear of snow that day when she walked to Parker's school. Yes, spring was in the wings. It would not be long before she'd need to inquire into travel arrangements. Her feelings were not exactly mixed about leaving, she thought, but she would miss many aspects of her current experience. That afternoon, after she'd written letters to Marion, George, and Alvah, she took out her journal, deciding to list all the persons she wished to thank for their various kindnesses and assistance during her stay here. Upon reflection, it seemed a rather long list. Time was a fickle friend, moving at its own speed—in this case, too fast. Myrna knew she would greatly miss both Belle and Elizabeth.

After a multitude of heartfelt goodbye's and farewell dinners, including a particularly lovely one at the Blue Iris; Myrna stood on the train platform with Elizabeth and Belle, waiting to board the coach to carry her west to Rutland, Vermont. Eventually, by manner of ferry, steamboat and coach she'd arrive in Keene, NY. It was there she hoped Alvah would be waiting.

In the meantime, the three women hugged and promised to write often. Their eyes may have dampened, but each held any tears for later. And then, finally, it was time to board.

As Myrna sat in the train coach, she, alternately, read her book and watched the scenery through the window. She was restless. The time that sped so fast during her last few weeks in Boston, now creeped like an injured cat. She thought, no wonder people favored carrying watches, otherwise, it was chancy to measure time. She caught the conductor's eye and requested that he alert her before the first stop. "In case I'm dozing," she said.

Well, it was a very long trip on the return, and not much fun without Belle. But once she boarded a steamboat in Essex to Port Kent, she was close to the last leg of the trip. She could see the Adirondacks in her vista and was excitedly anticipating her home. After an overnight at the hotel in Keeseville, a coach carried her to Keene, where she would meet Alvah, and perhaps Marion.

It was mid-day when she alighted with her baggage in Keene. And there they were, sitting on the porch of the Tavern—Alvah and Marion. They waved and ran to greet her. First, Myrna hugged Marion. Then Alvah drew Myrna close in an uninhibited display of affection. Marion looked on and smiled.

At the Duffney homestead it was a happy reunion of family and friends. Lyman, Ann, Delia and Carson were waiting there. They had set the long wooden table with a blue gingham cloth and yellow spring flowers. The best dishes, silver and crockery had been laid. Baked beans, roast chicken and a medley of early sprouts were served. Ann contributed a jar of her spiced peaches. Alvah had brewed some sort of ale that Lyman pronounced as "darned good". There was so much news and so many questions. Myrna was giddy and overwhelmed with an excess of attention. Perhaps travel weary, too. "Please," she said finally, "May I attend to this delicious food for a few moments before answering more questions?"

Lyman and Ann wanted to know every detail she could think of about Belle's living arrangements. Ann teared a bit when she softly asked if Myrna thought Belle was happy at the Bannister's. "Lordy, I do miss her lively ways," she sighed. "Though she could be rebellious and stubborn—especially about that Joachim fella."

Lyman interjected, trying to sound casual. "Has he been in touch with her?" He gave Myrna a meaningful look.

"Oh, I can guarantee that he has not. Besides, she has absolutely no interest in him. Her days are filled with teaching French to the Almays young niece. The Bannisters are very protective of her, especially Mrs. Bannister. Really, you would approve of them." Myrna was cautious in what she said about Belle. Clearly, the Epps' had deep attachments—parental, even. The truth was, Belle as an intelligent, beautiful young woman, was fully engaged in her new Boston environment. The Boston culture, and social events suited her. When they stood together on the train platform that realization had blindingly dawned on Myrna. But she held her thoughts. She said, "Belle has attended several abolitionist meetings with Mr. Bannister." At this, Lyman and Ann looked pleased, and nodded.

Carson was more interested in the trip itself—the train ride, steamboat, and the streets of Boston. Myrna was happy to relate all these details for him. And, at his request, promised to tell him more later.

Myrna sensed that there had been changes at the Brown settlement and in local town politics while she'd been absent, though it was only a matter of months. Delia now openly spoke of the nice family, originally from Virginia, who currently boarded with her. Apparently, the Underground Railroad was fully operational in the North Country.

Myrna dearly wished to know more about all that was news in North Elba, and wanted to tell Alvah and Marion, especially, about her Boston experiences, but suddenly the long days of travel caught up with her. Apologetically, she asked that she might take a nap. There was a rush of, "Oh my goodness...yes, of course...poor dear looks exhausted etc." Before he left, Alvah made a date for a walk in the woods the following afternoon. He smiled, watching her walk upstairs to her bedroom, wondering what she'd make of the note under her pillow. He felt relieved to have her back in North Elba. Myrna found the note just before falling into a deep sleep.

Upon awakening, Myrna was relieved to be in her own bed. She quickly dressed and went downstairs to the kitchen. At breakfast, Marion was full of questions about Boston. She fondly recalled their visit there nine years ago. "Oh, I remember the Athenaeum very well," she said "a very beautiful building. It was new then, and there was a fuss about it. Elizabeth, her sister, Mary, and I were escorted there by Dr. Peabody, her father." She seemed wistful. "I would like to see Elizabeth again. You know, I did receive two letters from her while you were there. You certainly made a fine impression on her."

Seeing that Marion was genuinely interested in the details, Myrna told her more about how she and Elizabeth spent their days. She tried to describe the streets of Boston and Cambridge and the people she met. Marion said she was most fascinated by the Duffneys and the Blue Iris. "I wish I could have met them," she said with regret. "Sam had fond memories from his childhood." Myrna padded barefoot to the stove to bring them fresh coffee and scones. She filled each of their favorite blue cups and again sat across from her ma. Marion smiled at the sound of a door knock. "I'll bet that's Alvah. You'd better set another cup out."

Alvah sat next to Myrna with polite familiarity. They talked a bit about the state of the various barn animals and Carson's plan to expand the garden. After a while, he rose, saying he was going to the barn to speak with Carson. He looked at Myrna. "I was thinking to saddle Star for you, supposing you still would like to venture over by the Ausable trail."

"Surely," she smiled. "I won't need but a few minutes here."

Once he was beyond earshot, Marion said in good humor, "I'd say he's using his courtin manners today." Myrna shrugged, in response. But she didn't deny it.

It was a fine blue sky day for riding and walking. Myrna swiftly forgot about any chores she might have neglected. Besides, Marion had insisted that she take the day for getting reacquainted with the woods... and Alvah.

It felt good to be in her hiking clothes. She carried her smaller twenty-two caliber rifle in her pack and expected to shoot a few rabbits for the evening meal. They rode to the Ausable River and had planned to cross there, but were deterred by the high waters from the spring thaw. Instead, they tethered their horses and walked the trail along the east side of the river. There were welcome signs of spring, though snow was sequestered in the shadows of boulders—trillium leaves and trout lily shoots were evident. Green whorls of tree leaves displayed frills where the sun coaxed. Myrna remarked with satisfaction that in a week there'd be blooms on the trail. It was already the month of May

Billowy clouds tinged lavender-grey began to gather, as almost on cue. Alvah said that they could reach the small St. Bernard's chapel for shelter before the shower, if they hurried. They reckoned the horses would be fine back where they left them. They'd been fed and watered earlier.

The chapel was a wonderfully welcome sanctuary, hidden by deep forest. It had been built maybe twenty years or so past by a semi-retired priest, or that's what he said he was. Father Toby lived in a small room behind the altar— a Spartan space with a narrow cot and woodstove. He came and went as he pleased. Perhaps he no longer resided there, Alvah conjectured. The outside structure was made of neatly fit logs with a cedar shingled peaked roof and a small graceful spire in proportion to the whole. The inside was of polished, peeled, wood— trimmed fancifully with birch bark, as was the raised alter with a hand-carved Christ figure. Light streamed from four thick oval glass windows, two to a side — miraculously unbroken. The whole of it was done by Father Toby, evidently a skilled carpenter.

Thoughtfully, there were two folded green, wool blankets on the bench nearest the altar. There was no sign that the priest, or anyone else, had visited in a while. The stove was cold and the bed stripped. Alvah gestured to the back bench and closed the door. The set of benches were just three rows deep. "This will do until the shower passes. I was kinda hoping Father Toby might be around," Alvah said, "he's a kind, interesting fellow."

They found it was easier having a good talk seated in private, after their sporadic efforts while riding and walking the gnarly trails. The rain on the chapel roof made a steady rhythmic beat. They were full of talk. How did they see the summer? Alvah told her about a guiding trip possibility they might share. "It sounds to me like they're not especially accomplished fishermen, but the pay would be pretty good. What do you think?" He looked at Myrna.

Myrna was pensive. "I'm more comfortable when jobs come directly to Duffney Guides and Outfitters," she said apologetically. "That way, the sports know from the start they'll be dealing with a woman. Marion did tell two of my dad's former folks I'd be taking over the business. Bill Stillman said one of Lowell's friends may want a hunting trip too..." her words trailed. Myrna knew this was getting awkward between them. Like a chess set up—whose move was it? She stared at the graceful Christ figure on the wall, in order to avoid looking at Alvah.

Alvah took her hands in his, causing her to look directly at him. Then his smile turned to laughter. "Guess we might as well get right down to it," he said. "Shoot, I planned I might ask you today, anyway. I was waitin for a sorta romantic moment." He looked into her eyes like he wanted to know the answer before asking the question.

"And?" She said. At that, he embraced and kissed her deeply. "I want us to be able to do that whenever we like and to live in our own house."

Myrna looked at him with her brows slightly furrowed. Alvah had a bewildered expression. "Oh, yes, of course" he said, "can we get married?"

Myrna hugged him back and said, "Absolutely!"

The novel excitement of the momentous agreement left them breathless and overheated. They shed some garments and made good use of the benches and blankets. They felt keenly aware of each other. In a word...happy. Myrna thought, bless Amelie's good advice about pre-marital situations.

Not quite fully dressed, they each wrapped in a blanket and resumed conversation. Myrna told him that on the trip back to North Elba she thought about the Blue Iris Inn and the Duffney sisters. Actually, dreamed about it. It dawned on her that she'd like to do something similar here in the Adirondacks. Continuing, she said, "It would not be as grand as the Blue Iris—perhaps more of an inn for summer tourists. Maybe in the beginning it'd be like a boarding house. Of course, we'd keep up the guiding service."

"Duffney Guiding Service & Outfitters?" Alvah asked.

"Oh, no, it will be Duffney & Woods Guides and Outfitters. What do you think? Is it an appealing idea?"

Alvah considered her wild curls and beautiful flushed face. He was in love. And it really was an appealing idea. "Yes," he said, "I like the idea."

They decided they were officially engaged when Alvah closed the clasp on the amethyst locket he'd placed around her neck. "It belonged to my gramma Woods. Ma thought you'd like it. There's a ring, too. But I figured what with the hunting and fishing that'd just get in your way."

On the spot, they decided to tell Marion that evening and to announce their engagement in the community church on Sunday. They would wait until summer or early fall to have a wedding ceremony. They'd ask Reverend Horace to officiate.

Summer was a speeding season. Time passed in a blur, it seemed.

They decided to honor any of their current guiding commitments separately, but make it known in the guiding community that they were consolidating by October. "Consolidatin!" Bill Martin said. "Yer getting married, aintcha." This came about when Myrna was at Martin's Hotel guiding the Cadbury brothers from Boston, friends of Lowell's. Myrna liked Bill. She replied amiably, "Well, business is business and marriage another matter."

He chuckled, "Ya know, most of the fellas' wuz scared to court ya." She shrugged and walked back to her party. She enjoyed showing favored fishing spots to the Cadburys.

They spent two nights camping on Moody Pond. Myrna was pleased that she could talk about Boston with them in the evenings. They were impressed that Miss Peabody was her cousin. Stephen Cadbury tipped well and said they looked forward to meeting Mr. Woods when they returned next year. She liked the idea that she might build a steady clientele.

Alvah took on a hunting party with Lyman, as planned. They invited Myrna, but she declined, as they had originally agreed. Lyman and Alvah took their sports out Ampersand way, where there were an abundance of deer. Alvah said he was glad she hadn't joined them. Two of the men drank to excess and quarreled every night. They were an uncouth bunch, according to Lyman.

Alvah said that he and Lyman had pitched their shelter a ways from the group, which gave him and Lyman a chance to talk in the evenings. Evidently, John had made a quick visit to Mary and his family the past week. It was supposed to be somewhat a secret. He was there only three days, but by the time he left, the settlement was roiled and moody.

Myrna was concerned. She also wanted to include any important information about the Brown and Epps families in her next letter to Belle. "What do you think is going on?" she asked.

Alvah thought for a moment. He couldn't break confidence with Lyman, future wife or no. He shrugged. "I can't rightly say," he answered.

Myrna gave him a squinty look, but let it go. She had realized changes in the North Elba mood upon her return from Boston. Abolitionists were now highly charged and vocal in some quarters. A small enclave of anti-abolitionists were more entrenched, too. And the words and actions of John Brown and his sons were fueling the swirling conflagration of ideas. It led her to wondering about the settlement school and students. She would have to talk to Marion about the school year.

- CHAPTER 36 -
Summer Readiness

Marion was genuinely happy about the impending marriage. The date was quickly set. Today she had enlisted Myrna to help in the jarring of spiced peaches. Ann Epps was expected to join them.

Marion hummed as she dropped the peaches in boiling water in order to release their delicate fuzzy skins. The procedure, if done properly, allowed for the thin outer layer to slip smoothly from the ripe fruit. Then the attractive whole fruits would be jarred and covered with a boiling solution of spicy cloves and cider vinegar, sweetened with maple syrup. Myrna had brought home from Boston a good variety of spices, including whole nutmegs, cinnamon sticks, and cloves. These were items not readily found in Elizabethtown.

"It's almost like you knew we would have a special use for them," Marion happily declared. She hesitated. "You know, I fretted a bit after you left—thought you might end up staying there. Tell me, did it ever cross your mind to do so?"

Myrna was surprised by the question. When she thought about it, she wondered. Certainly, Boston had its attractive aspects. She wanted to treat Marion's question seriously. "Well, I think circumstances played a large part. I missed you—and home. Then there was Alvah…we'd sort of thought of a commitment. But I did grow to like Boston, although I felt conflicted at first. Cousin Elizabeth and I managed to develop a deep friendship. I really do miss her, especially." She drew a deep breath. "I miss Belle terribly, but Boston suits her perfectly, so I'm pleased that she's settled there. Yes, if it weren't for you and Alvah, I might have considered giving it a try." She added, jokingly, "Shoot, if it wasn't for Alvah we both could have tried it! What do you think of that?" Marion laughed, with a look of relief. "It was a ways back when I last visited Elizabeth. I believe that I secretly wished I could live there, or at least have stayed longer."

"Could you have…stayed longer, I mean?"

"No, I was a married woman. Pa had no interest in either staying or relocating. The mill was going exceedingly well by then," she said softly.

To Marion's surprise, Myrna walked to the other side of the table and gave her a genuine hug. "I'm glad we're here," she said.

Marion wiped her eyes on her apron. "Pa would be very happy about you and Alvah."

Ann Epps gave a light knock on the front door and walked directly to the kitchen. "Whew! It sure is steamy in here…but it smells nice."

Ann was full of good cheer. She'd received a letter from Belle. She read it to Myrna and Marion. It told about spring walks on Boston Common and teaching at the Almays. She'd met men at meetings who greatly admired John. Belle said she wished she could be at the wedding. Ann sighed. "She misses me and Lyman, too."

Ann tied on a red gingham apron she'd brought with her and joined them in their work. The peaches were to be one of the treats offered at the wedding. "Lordy!" Marion exclaimed, wiping her face with her apron. "I can't wait to finish so we can open the windows." They'd kept the windows closed in order to keep out the bees that were lazily drifting by the frames. It did not take them too long to finish ladling the peaches into jars, and scouring the table and sink of any sticky residue.

They rewarded themselves for their work by drawing tall cups of water, which they brought to the comfortable rockers on the front porch.

The discussion of the moment was about Harriet Wells and her well-meant efforts to assist with the wedding. It seemed she was wildly enthusiastic about the event. According to Marion, she was beginning to fancy herself as a kind of adopted aunty. Ann and Marion got to laughing at her antics. "I'm thinking she imagines this is Boston or Philadelphia, and not poor old North Elba," Ann said.

But, when all was said and done, they acknowledged that Harriet was genuinely fond of Myrna and wanted to see that the wedding was a beautiful affair—even if she came too close to stepping on Marion's toes. Surprisingly, Marion was taking little offense. She said she'd come to like Harriet over the past year. "Besides, I'm willing to put her in her place, if necessary."

Personally, Myrna was pleased that the women of the community were so generous in their assistance. She knew she'd spend much less time on wedding rigmarole if left on her own. Her mind was elsewhere, mostly on the practicalities of business. But she appreciated that Marion enjoyed the various women's help with preparations. And most important, she'd learned to be a more considerate daughter. Myna sensed that the wedding part of the marriage was a gift to her Ma. Sometimes she thought the spirit of Sam hovered over her shoulder with suggestions. Not that either she or Pa would ever have taken that literally.

A few days later she received an invitation to tea from Harriet. It appeared to be meant solely for her. Myrna was happy for a day's outing with Harriet.

Stopping at the Wells' gate, Myrna noted, once again, how quaintly elegant was Harriet's cottage. The blooming flower garden was a-buzz with the hum of bees. It was a pity that Harriet and Milton didn't keep bee hives, instead of squandering that winged energy, Myrna thought.

Harriet stood and waved to Myrna from the porch. They exchanged pleasantries as Myrna took a seat opposite on a matching rough-hewn chair heaped with pink flowered cushions. The housekeeper, an unobtrusive young neighbor girl, appeared instantly with tea and small dainty sandwiches. "You are wearing a very pretty dress today," Harriet said with a slight question in her voice.

Myrna smiled with good humor. "I'm hardly opposed to dresses in this warm weather — much cooler than trousers on the legs and ankles. " Myrna sat back and relaxed, though she wasn't used to talking about fashions.

"Are they making a wedding dress for you, may I ask–or is it a secret?"

"It's a secret, certainly. Even I haven't seen it! I'm supposing its crème colored or white ... and simple, I hope." Myrna held her tongue about the foolishness of it all.

"Is this some kind of North Country custom—the secret dress, I mean?" Harriet sipped her tea.

"Nope. They wanted to sew and fuss for this occasion, and I'm not too particular." Seeing Harriet's puzzled expression, she added, "They are very clever. I'm sure it will be beautiful. Myrna saw that Harriet was, apparently, a wedding enthusiast.

Harriet, unexpectedly, laughed uproariously. "Milton's got you figured right! He said you were a most practical, business minded woman. Are we to expect you'll continue the guiding business?"

Myrna replied evenly, "Yes, Duffney and Woods Guides and Outfitters will be our thriving concern."

"Very good. Milton will enjoy sending plenty of business your way. And you already know how much I admire your gumption," she said, energetically. "But that isn't exactly why I invited you. Actually, I am interested in your nuptials." Her eyes twinkled. "I guess at heart I'm a romantic. I'm quite taken with the idea of you two young idealists joining together. Well, I'm not so old, but you know what I mean. Horace, who incidentally, is joyous about performing the ceremony, says you bring hope to the future!"

This was all very well, Myrna thought, but she was hungry and knew it was polite to wait for the hostess to take first bites. "My, these sandwiches look delicious," she said, gazing at the tray.

"Umm, they do, don't they." Harriet popped one in her mouth and Myrna did likewise.

After another two of the dainty sandwiches, Harriet delicately wiped her mouth. "What I'd been meaning to say is that Milton and I would like to offer you this cottage while we're away for a few weeks. Think of it as a honeymoon cottage—our gift to you. I know you and Alvah are planning to live with Marion for a while." At this point, Harriet beamed. "Well, I'll not beat around the bush. When a couple is newly married they appreciate some privacy. Speaking factually, it's more fun being romantic without your ma around. You understand, right?"

For a brief moment, Myrna was speechless. It had occurred to her the awkwardness of her and Alvah feeling restrained around Marion. But there hadn't been another option. "Truthfully, I want to say, yes, to staying here," she said, "but I'll first consult with Alvah."

That part of her business completed, Harriet called at the doorway for sherry and two glasses. She sat down again, arranging her skirts. "You know, I'd like you to think of me as a favored aunt or cousin. Now, about intimate relations between men and women—I consider myself an expert on those topics. I don't believe there's anything you might ask me that I can't answer," she said briskly.

Truthfully, Myrna wasn't quite sure what to say. Finally, she asked Harriet what she thought a novice should know about these things. To her surprise, Harriet had a lot to say about pleasure and avoiding pregnancy. Indeed, she was an expert!

As they parted at the bottom of the veranda steps, Harriet hugged her tightly and told her not to worry. Myrna felt light-hearted at the prospect of a honeymoon cottage.

That evening when she told Alvah about her visit with Harriet he was initially hesitant about her offer. After a while he said, "I'd been thinking of a camping trip near the border lakes, but I can see the good advantages of stayin' at the Wells' place."

"You're sure?" Myrna hugged him and kissed his neck. The marital compromises were already beginning.

"Besides, we can go scouting up there in October," he said.

Myrna received two letters on Thursday—one from Belle, the other from Elizabeth. She was excited to hear from her friends. Belle said she wished she could be at the wedding and asked Myrna to do her best to describe it, right down to what people were wearing and the food and decorations. She said that she'd be thinking about Myrna and Alvah right at two O'clock—the time of the ceremony. She added that there was a gentleman courting her and if the new friendship progressed, she'd tell more…"I'd so love to be with you and Alvah on your wedding day. Please send a sketch of the secret dress!" She wrote.

Elizabeth, in her letter, sent her crisp congratulations and then told her the good news about her book publishing negotiations and the latest going's on in Boston book circles. She wrote…"I do miss our evening chess matches."

Myrna knew there were so many thoughts and feelings left unexpressed in all of their letters to each other. She wished she could tell Belle how perfect it would have been to have her there at the church. Or say to Elizabeth how much she'd prefer to spend some evenings playing chess with her. But though she tried, her attempts sounded like she was either discontent in North Elba or that she hoped to be back in Boston soon. And neither was the case. But it did occur, when she gave it some consideration, that she *could* have made a life there in Boston. Instead, she ignored all of that and told about wedding preparations and the embryonic thoughts of expanding the guiding business. She replied in response to Belle, that their handmade quilt was only on loan—Belle would inherit it as soon as she married.

Meanwhile, Alvah had his hands full trying to subtly persuade Delia that she needed to give more thought to her plan of helping the family she sheltered to cross the border to Canada. The truth was, he'd kept his eye on Reverend Horace for a while, and didn't like his forward manner with women. It was one thing to laugh about Harriet and the Reverend, and quite another to think of his mom alone with him in a carriage for several days on their return trip. He suspected Horace's veneer of respectability wore thin over the miles away from North Elba. Sure, he was a good, steady abolitionist, a kind man, too. Nevertheless…he didn't want his ma hurt or laughed at. The problem was, he didn't know how to broach this without offending Ma. Alvah wondered if he might talk about this with Marion or Myrna. They were pretty astute.

Alvah loved visiting Marion and Myrna at their home, especially now that it had been decided that he and Myrna would reside there after their marriage. But even before that, he'd found the Duffney's a comfortable, tranquil place. He thought it was something about Marion's clear-headed, calm demeanor. That, and the neat but cozy décor. His own ma wasn't given to bothering much about the house since his pa died, though she did fuss a bit with the family staying with them. He probably should have realized how dispirited his ma had become after his pa's sickness and death. Now that he could see it, he felt regret. He saw that his mother had found purpose in helping runaway's and teaching with Marion at the Brown settlement. Alvah was thinking about all this as he watched Marion shell peas for dinner. He dumped half the basket on the table and proceeded to help her. "I've been wanting to ask your advice on something," he started.

"Oh?" Marion raised her brows. "Providing it's something I know about."

"Well, I'm hoping so." He continued shelling.

He explained the situation about Delia and Horace bringing the runaways across the border a few days after the wedding—and his concerns about Horace taking advantage of his ma. Marion slowly nodded and tucked a loosened lock of hair behind her ear. "This isn't exactly my area of expertise...I gather you worry Delia may be susceptible to the reverend's charms," she said.

Alvah smiled, sheepishly. "Something like that. Do women think he's charming?"

Marion was touched by Alvah's protective feelings for his mom. "I can't rightly say. I do believe Horace tries hard at it though. But your mom's a savvy woman. She'll make him mind his manners. And he is a gentleman." Left unsaid, were Marion's thoughts that sometimes a widow yearned for some discreet attention. For his part, Alvah felt better having talked to Marion. Between them they had filled the pot with fresh peas.

- CHAPTER 37 -
New Beginnings

Marion and Ann held the betrothed couple to traditions, or at least Ann's tradition that a couple should not lay eyes on each other for three whole days before the ceremony. And Marion decided that she and Myrna should spend the day before the wedding together, without others.

In the afternoon Myrna and Marion were to picnic in the woods by the stream. "Ma, Are you making this up as we go along?" Not that she minded a bit.

And in due course, finally— the wedding day had arrived. As luck would have it, Myrna woke to blue sky and sun. She tiptoed downstairs to make coffee while the house was still asleep. As she sat in the kitchen sipping her first cup, she realized a keen level of excitement. Was this really happening to her? The feeling was anticipatory...something like waiting with her finger on the trigger for a clear shot at a big buck. She couldn't help but laugh to herself. Was this the best she could do in describing her feelings? Then her mood wavered. She wished Belle was sitting across the table this morning. They would have talked and shared this moment. Belle might have laughed at the comment or admonished her choice of expression.

She was drawn from her reverie by the light pad of Marion's feet on the stairway. Marion came into the kitchen smiling and bent to draw her close in a hug. "You're probably too excited for a proper breakfast. How about sliced apples and soft cheese on bread?"

"Do I seem nervous?"

"Well, I'm sure you are. After all, it is a major event in a woman's life…and for the whole family. Look at me! I'm surely flustered," she said, wiping her spilled coffee from the table.

"Just don't refer to me as your baby daughter today." Myrna's voice was slightly sullen. She caught herself. "I'm sorry, Ma, that came out wrong."

Marion rubbed Myrna's hand. "Just take some deep breaths." Marion thought—and I might very well have called her 'my baby' today. The mind does have a way of reminiscing on days of import. She said, "When Ann arrives, we'll get to put any finishing touches on your dress."

"What if I don't like it?" But Myrna's voice was teasing, not ornery.

Ann entered the kitchen with a bundle under her arm. "Oh, you will like it. Of that we are quite sure." She reached into the cupboard for a cup. "Don't mind?" she said, already pouring.

"You're sure I'm gonna like it."

"Yes, indeed, a mama knows what her daughter likes." She paused. "Besides, we could never get you to any fittings. Shoot, we know your size anyway. By the way, I hear Harriet had a sit down talk with you about the ways of men and women…that true?"

"Yep, you'd hardly believe the things she knows," Myrna joshed. At that, Ann and Marion had a good hoot, and Myrna joined in.

Myrna recalled that years ago, before her menses, Marion had tried to explain procreation. But it seemed so strange and academic at the time, that she had no interest. Truthfully, until Alvah's courtship, she'd not expected to marry.

After their coffee, they went to the living room, where Ann gently unwrapped the bundle containing the dress, and draped the dress over the large rocker. In her mind, Myrna had practiced an appropriate response…just in case she didn't like it. But it was lovely, simple but elegant. The dress was made of white cotton batiste, bordered at the hem and waist with pale blue, grosgrain ribbon. The cap sleeves were trimmed with delicate silk-thread needlepoint.

"Oh! Thank you. It is perfect…and I'll be able to wear it to any future fancy event." Her eyes briefly moistened. "Ma, Ann…I hardly know what to say. It is a special dress," she said. Myrna slipped it on. It was a comfortable fit.

Ann unwrapped pretty, white, kidskin, low heeled shoes—shoes from her own wedding. "These might be a little tight, but they should do. I'm lending them for the day." Myrna slipped them on. "Not too snug," she said.

They spent the rest of the morning bathing and grooming Myrna. As usual, her hair was unruly, a challenge in the August humidity. Ann decreed the best style—a middle part, with small side braids held back by a tortoise shell clip, leaving the rest of her voluminous hair flowing naturally. Ann said Myrna's color was high, what with all the excitement. They agreed that no rouge was needed. Finally, Marion said, smiling. "You really are beautiful!" Pausing, she added, "I wish Sam were here to see you." And then she cried—real nose-blowing, undainty tears, which were contagious. Ann sniffled loudly. Myrna went for additional hankies, and gave them to Ann and Ma. She didn't cry, but she felt overwhelmed by the overflow of emotion. She thought it was just as well that she and Alvah would be living at home—at least for a while.

The wedding ceremony was to be in the small chapel of the church. Ann and Marion had decorated it with bouquets' of daisies and tied white ribbons. Reverend Horace was to perform the ceremony there. Myrna and Alvah had decided only family and closest friends would be at the taking of vows. Later, they'd adjourn to the community church hall where there'd be a proper celebration with food and music. They were a popular couple and family, well known by the surrounding community.

Myrna, Marion and Ann sat with Reverend Horace in a small room adjacent to the altar. Presumably, Alvah, Delia, Carson, Lyman, her brother George and his family, as well as Milton and Harriet were outside, or would soon arrive.

Alvah, who didn't think his wedding outfit was of much concern, good naturedly let his ma and Carson fuss over him. Lyman, who arrived early in his carriage, in order to drive them, pronounced Alvah's hair as a mite scraggly. "Son, you need to trim up for this occasion," he said. "And I told him the very same!" Delia said. Compliantly, he had his beard and wavy blond locks smoothed and shaped. Like most in the back country, he had only one 'good, all purpose' black suit. Delia had brushed it and hung it to freshen on the clothesline. But he wore a new white linen shirt, and Lyman insisted he wear a stylish white, satin, string tie, which he lent for the occasion.

The moment did arrive. The couple stood facing each other, enraptured. It was hard to say whether or not they saw or heard anyone else in the chapel. However, they managed to say the requisite words, and Alvah slipped the ring on her finger, which they'd already agreed might not be practical for hunting and such. Staring at her finger, Myrna said, "Still, it does look pretty."

The wedding feast was a major community event, mostly the work of Harriet and the church ladies sewing group. The makeshift wooden tables were covered with borrowed linen and decorated with vases of wildflowers, including purple hyssop, black-eyed Susan, swamp milkweed, Queen Ann's lace, nodding marigold, and asters. Myrna thought the decorations must be the work of Harriet and Ann. The church ladies and the quilters were carrying bowls and pots filled with homemade specialties. There were cakes and pies and ciders and punches. "Groaning board" was an apt name for the food laden table.

Myrna sighed, "I do wish Belle were here to see this."

"Yep"...Alvah kept looking at her, keeping one arm around her waist. He quickly nuzzled her neck and kissed her.

"Puleez...let's not make a spectacle," she said unlinking from him. They walked together... holding hands, towards her brother George, who was smiling. Her niece, Janie, had woven a bracelet with blue ribbon and white flowers. "Aunt Myrna, you look very pretty. The bracelet goes with your dress," she said, tying it to Myrna's wrist. She touched the dress. "Can I borrow it when I get bigger?"

"Certainly! If I haven't worn it out by then." She turned to her brother to ask about their trip, and news from Vermont.

"I enjoyed getting your letters from Boston. I thought you might end up stayin," he said. "I'm hoping to find time for a family trip to Boston one of these days."

Myrna bobbed her head as she walked towards Harriet, who was beckoning to her. "Sit next to me at table," she called back to George.

There were so many well-wishers and wedding stories as Myrna and Alvah flitted from party to person. As the day ebbed, a coterie of guides and other friends were feeling the effects of the cider. For the most part, they were simply loud and jolly — waiting for the music to start. One noted rascal, Roger—the fella who Myrna had bested on the rifle range a ways back, grew increasingly boisterous. He wove towards George, who had unpleasant memories of him as the classroom bully.

Roger said, "Yer sister looks purty...I wuz surprised she got hitched...didn't think she liked men." He said this in a sneering challenging way. Of course, George didn't know about Roger's embarrassing confrontation with Myrna—or that he'd been teased aplenty since that shooting incident. But George had been enjoying himself up until then. He only vaguely remembered the rowdy, but wasn't about to hear Myrna slighted. Before he thought twice, he popped Roger one on the nose. The fella blinked once, and fell back on his ass, his nose bleeding. "I'd suggest you run out of here fast as you can...or I'll punch you again. You're not going to ruin this family's wedding party!" George said in a lowered, threatening voice.

Fortunately, or not, Myrna and Alvah had been distracted by the music trio that were setting up outside. When she heard tell of it she laughed. "I guess every wedding day needs a few good stories," she said, looking at George's knuckles. George grinned. "Don't get to misbehave very often."

The festive, lively, party was a memorable event. Delia, Marion and Ann enlisted the church ladies to see that plates and glasses were filled. They sat together on the sidelines. The threesome sighed and agreed that Myrna was stunning as a bride. "About a year ago, Miss Myrna told me she didn't favor marriage," Ann shook her head.

"Yep, I wasn't holding my breath about it," Marion declared.

"I don't believe I've ever seen my son this happy," Delia dabbed her eyes, then smiled at Marion. Harriet pulled a chair next to them. "Carson's going to drive them to the cottage and then return with our carriage. This is all so very lovely…" Harriet was a dear character in her own right.

Alvah had put any items he might need for the short trip to the Wells' cottage in his day pack. Marion had insisted that Myrna pack a small valise, such as what one might use for train travel. The couple had decided they might stay at the cottage for four nights. Marion and Delia had insisted they not return sooner.

Family and guests clapped and cheered as they boarded the carriage for the Wells cottage. Myrna and Alvah smiled and waved to the assembled, as Carson cracked the reins on the horses.

"This really is quite grand, isn't it," Myrna said. Alvah nodded.

Carson, gallantly took Myrna's hand as she alighted from the carriage, saying he'd be back to fetch them on Thursday. They watched the horses and carriage recede into the distance.

When they opened the door and entered the cottage hallway, they broke into a fit of giggles. Someone, no doubt Harriet, had indulgently festooned the entryway. Bouquets of summer blooms graced every room, and the pantry had been stocked with fruit jams, cheeses, water-crackers, fresh eggs and bottles of wine. There was a lengthy note on the kitchen table saying that Rose, Harriet's maid, would be stopping by each afternoon to prepare meals and tend to any necessary tasks. Also that they might avail themselves of the copper washtub off of the alcove in the kitchen. "She has very nice handwriting, doesn't she," Myrna said.

The larger of the two bedrooms was at the back of the house. Harriet had taken special care in decorating this room. There were white satin ribbons tied to the bedposts. The sheets and coverlet smelled of lavender. The crystal vases echoed lavender blooms with Queen Anne's lace. And then there was a tissue wrapped package tied with pink grosgrain ribbon, laid on the bed. A simple note card from Harriet read ..."love thee to the level of every day's most quiet need, by sun and candle light" (E. B. Browning). Alvah looked puzzled. "Makes some sense, I guess."

And then, Myrna unwrapped the packaged layers of tissue, to behold a pretty, white, lacy nightgown. She blushed lightly, feeling a mixture of discomfort and passion. "Should I wear it now?" she asked.

Alvah smiled. "Nope, not necessary...maybe later." He began to unbutton her dress— slowly. Myrna liked the unhurried anticipation. When he'd gotten as far as her stockings, she abruptly sat up. "My turn," She said. Alvah looked briefly dazed, but readily complied as her fingers plied his shirt buttons.

Sunset approached. Alvah tried to take his time, as Lyman had suggested in cases such as this. "Oh gosh, didn't mean to be so quick."

It was not so uncomfortable, and she felt deeply stirred. Still, she realized that their former playing and touching activities brought her quicker satisfaction. She kissed him intensely and then pulled away to look sincerely into his eyes. "Dear one, I have a suggestion…"

Alvah and Myrna spent several more days wrapped in the cocoon of their new marriage. Some afternoons they tended to Harriet's gardens, picking and weeding. There were abundant vegetables and a cupboard of spices to experiment with. They roasted, sautéed and baked marvelous dishes from their imaginations. They walked in nearby woods and shot rabbits and birds for meals. Alvah was astounded by how quick and accurate Myrna was with his pistol.

Rose knocked courteously every afternoon to come tidy the cottage, but Mr. and Mrs. Woods were so neat and self-sufficient it was hardly necessary. Rose wasn't needed for cooking. They liked that she usually brought cream and eggs.

The late August weather seemed unseasonably warm. They took to walking in the afternoons to a nearby pond on the property for a luxurious swim. They also talked and talked about ideas for their future together. "I don't see any obstacle for us to begin a new building or add to your homestead, providing Marion likes the idea." Alvah said.

"Once Ma agrees, we can at least draw up a design and figure the costs. You know, Pa once mentioned some kind of boarding house to her."

"Wuz she for it?"

"I can't recollect…don't think he got really serious about it. He loved guiding, that was his main thing. And he retained a share in the mill. George still gives a share of the profits to Ma."

Alvah listened. He sensed that once Myrna became enthusiastic about something, it'd be hard to stop her. He was enthralled hearing her spin words and watching her gesturing. Actually, she now hoisted herself onto a low rocky ledge, apparently not bothered that she was naked. Yep, she was genuinely amusing.

It came time to leave. Carson was due to arrive early afternoon. They sat in the front porch rockers, waiting. They supposed both Marion and Delia might be at the Duffney homestead waiting for them. And they were not wrong. Their happy moms couldn't resist making them a welcoming meal. Since there wasn't anything proper they could ask about the stay at Harriet's, the conversation veered towards crops, animals, the family at Delia's awaiting leaving for Canada, and news from Elizabethtown.

The September harvest kept the Duffney, Woods and Epps families plenty busy. Delia wondered if the family staying with her might remain for the winter.

It had been a good growing year. They along with some of the families at the Brown settlement, worked from dawn to dark; picking crops, turning the soil for next year, baling hay and storing grain to feed animals, carting wheat to be milled, and jarring or drying the perishable fruits and vegetables not destined for the root cellars. It promised to be a bountiful winter. Being strong and young, Alvah, Carson and Myrna were able to assume much of the heavy work on their properties. And they had enough energy to also assist the Epps family with their farm chores.

Alvah was taking a day from the Duffneys homestead to help Lyman. Alvah and Lyman had spent long hours in the Epps' field thrashing wheat. They figured they deserved a longer than usual time sitting in the sun. Lyman had been so quiet and serious the past week that Alvah wondered if he were sick. He asked, apologetically, "Are you feeling somewhat under the weather? You seem a little peaked."

"Nope, sorry if I've been distracted. Sometimes there's too much confusion around here. As you've noted, John and his boys are off gallivantin again…Missouri, Kansas, I dunno. You'd think they might wait 'til after harvest." He stopped... thinking to choose his words. "You know that John makes some of the men jittery with all that's goin on. Jedediah said to me the other day—am I supposed to learn farming or go running around the country? Of course, we were all proud of John this past winter when he helped get those folks out of Missouri and over the border to Canada, but it came as a surprise to some. Well, you and I know that John's a zealot. He can't be bothered about the fine points of the matter. I guess by now I should be used to soothing and placating...but I'm not."

Alvah was taken aback by Lyman's outburst. The whole Epps family were square in John's corner—to a one.

"But, John's acting pretty much like usual, isn't he? Seems like he's getting lots of important abolitionist folks on our side, too. Myrna said he was considered a real hero in Boston."

"True enough. All I can say is, it can be good to bring the kettle to a boil, but if it spills over, there's no telling who might get burned."

"And you worry something's gonna happen?"

"Let's just say, I think John is right-minded and rash. He can't help it. And, yes, sooner or later the flames of passion won't be controlled."

Alvah and Lyman sat a good while in silence. Alvah thought, he'd never waver in his stand against slavery. But he was realizing that, at the moment, the North Country hadn't been tested. It was comfortable to sit here in your rocker and entertain beliefs. Knowing it was a weak unguent, Alvah offered, "We can only accomplish the task before us."

"Yep, and then there's that one about being forewarned." They wearily rose to finish the day's work.

Myrna and Alvah had quickly settled into the Duffney household routines. Marion said one morning at breakfast,

"It's almost like Alvah's been here for years." Alvah smiled, as he usually did, at Marion's compliments. It felt good to hear it, though.

Myrna said now that harvest chores were completed, she wanted to spend some hours responding to her letters. The Boston women were avid correspondents.

Belle's letter was full to the brim of summer soirées that she had attended, and potential beaus who were courting her. She said Mrs. Almay spoke fondly of Bill Stillman. She was very curious to hear about Bill's trek in the Adirondacks, of which Belle said she'd conveyed a little—claiming to have had a distant relationship with him. Belle had been to several abolitionist meetings with the Bannisters. She said many were very excited by Mr. Brown's words and activities. She wrote, "Some of the men with us at Follansbee Pond have been raising money for John's mission. Mr. Emerson, in particular, is quite outspoken." Of course, Belle wanted to know all about the wedding.

In reply, Myrna told her the details about the wedding itself, describing what they wore and the delicious food. She lightly told of Harriet's sisterly talk and the beautifully decorated cottage. She wrote, "I can discreetly say that I enjoyed the days with Alvah at the Wells' cottage." She told Belle how helpful Lyman and Ann had been with the wedding, but she left any news about the Browns to the Epps', since they frequently corresponded with Belle. Myrna also mentioned that she and Alvah were going to do their first guided hunting venture as a married couple in October. And Alvah had painted a new sign over the barn door that said Duffney & Woods, Guides and Outfitters for Hunting and Fishing. They'd all agreed to honor Sam by continuing the Duffney name.

Elizabeth's letter was congratulatory, but brief. She said she'd write more when her house arrangements were settled. Elizabeth went on to say that her sister, Mary Mann, and her children, were now permanently staying with her because, sadly, Mary's husband, Horace, had died. She also enclosed several sweet notes from the students Myrna had taught at Mrs. Parker's. One of her favorite girls had included a small drawing of a bride and groom in the woods.

Myrna didn't dwell on describing the wedding festivities to Elizabeth. Instead, she asked her many questions about the manuscript due to be published. At the end of the letter, she again thanked Cousin Elizabeth. With pen poised in hand, Myrna thought a moment. She then added that she missed her. She decided that was true enough.

The letter from Clara and Anna tickled her. They were full of breezy news about Boston suffragists and abolitionists. They seemed to inflate the romance of her 'woodsy marriage', and were insistent that she provide them with details. They asked, what outfits were popular in Elizabethtown, what kinds of food were served, and about the 'bridal gown', of course. They invited Myrna and Alvah to come stay at the Blue Iris Inn next year—gratis. They said they thought it would make for a lovely first anniversary present. And that they'd provide them with the best suite and all the champagne they could quaff. To demonstrate their seriousness, they asked if Myrna could select a week, so they would hold a room. Myrna was charmed by the Duffney sister's letter. She thought she'd read it to Alvah and Marion, before responding.

Today, Myrna's main destination was the post office, but there were some items she needed at the general store, too. It felt good to be able to trot and gallop at her own pace, without the encumbrance of the carriage.

Riding to town alone gave Myrna time to think and recollect...She was surprised and pleased that Alvah thought visiting Boston next summer was a good idea. Of course, there were the caveats of business and household needs to consider. And, after all, it was hard to predict next year's ventures. But in her response to the Duffney sisters, she'd said that should all go as expected, they'd plan for a mid-summer stay in August. Myrna reasoned that they would travel before sports were likely to hire them for deer hunting, and past the trout season clients. The major harvesting wouldn't be until September.

As she dismounted and tied Star to the hitching post, she saw the wagon carrying the mail was set to leave for Keeseville. The driver waited while she got the letters stamped in the store, which was also the post office. The driver cordially tipped his hat when she handed over the letters. Myrna turned back to the store thinking how she still felt connected to Boston. Luke, the store clerk, addressed her as Mrs. Woods when she paid for the skein of twine and bag of nails. Myrna knew him from elementary school. She smiled broadly and said, "You're the first in town to use my new name." He said they'd all had a good time at the wedding party.

The following week the couple had their first guiding venture as a newly married couple. Alvah liked the way Myrna planned and packed the night before their guiding prospects were to arrive. When he was on his own, he just grabbed what he needed the day of the trip. Mind you, that generally worked, except when it didn't. On the other hand, Myrna made orderly lists and said she thought they should make files on their clients, so's they'd be ready for repeat customers. She added, "This is the way Pa liked to do it—except for the file idea. I just thought of that. Another thing, these fellows know we're just married. But I want them to know we're professional."

Alvah looked quizzical. "Meaning what?"

"You know very well—no touching or leaning me against a tree. We'll act like before we married."

"What about in our tent?" Myrna turned back to packing. She gave him a look…and shook her head. "I'm packing two extra wool shirts. September nights are cold."

The Russell party were longtime clients of Sam's. They were two brothers and two cousins from Charlotte, Vermont, who enjoyed deer hunting. Sam had known Peter Russell back from his days operating the mill. As Peter was quick to remind Myrna, he often spoke with her brother George. He enthused, "We're all glad that you and Alvah decided to carry on with Sam's business. And ain't it something that you took to huntin, too." Myrna put on her professional smile and nodded. "I'm surely aiming to have a productive and enjoyable hunt for you fellows."

Alvah and Myrna had decided to take the men along the Epps trail through Indian Pass. The hunting would be good, and there were some fine spots for making camp. Matthew, one of the cousins, had expressed an interest in seeing the stupendous boulders that lay at the bottom of the pass's deep corridor.

They set camp near Wallface Ponds, behind the cliffs. Myrna was glad to see that the shelter she'd built in July still held…and was unoccupied. They deposited their supplies there. Alvah built a second shelter nearby for him and Myrna. It was a typical crisp October day, sunny midday with a promise of frost at night. The Russell party was used to the camp routines and helped to chop delicate pine boughs for bedding. Then they moved on to the task of gathering kindling for the fires and chopping wood. Myrna worked with Matthew, the youngest member of the party.

"You know, I think this is my favorite part, except for shooting a big buck," she said, referring to the process of making camp.

Matthew asked, "Think we'll be walking in by the boulders today?"

"Depends, let's talk as a group." She knew it wouldn't be wise to try chasing deer in the pass—too hard on both the deer and the hunters, what with the poor footing and ricocheting bullets. But if they wanted a day of interesting exploration, that was another matter.

Peter, the oldest and most experienced hunter, suggested they wait to explore the pass another day. He wondered aloud if it wouldn't be better to do some scouting near to camp. He looked to Alvah, knowing he'd agree.

It was such an amiable bunch of men. They split into two groups, merrily scouting the terrain for a few hours before dinner. The camaraderie was such that they all sat around the main campfire late into the evening reminiscing about previous hunts with Sam, and they told stories of their lives' in Vermont. Myrna was gratified by their warm memories of Pa. At one tender telling of Sam tracking and finding a lost hunter, Alvah reached for and squeezed Myrna's hand.

It was an idyllic week in the forest. The hunting was superb. In fact, the deer were so plentiful that they suspended the hunt one afternoon while Myrna took Matthew on a trek through the boulders. Thanks to Marion's thoughtful addition of dried fruits and pumpkin breads, the meals were a notch above the usual fare, or so the fellows commented. Weather, which could be fickle later in October, held fast. The truth was, they all, to a one, liked spending time together. One evening when Alvah brought out a deck of playing cards they whooped and were as carefree as youngsters. Peter taught them a card game called Kings in the Corner.

At week's end, as they proceeded to pack and decamp, the group asked that they might reserve the very same week for the following year. Alvah told Peter they'd write it on their guide calendar first thing when they got back.

When they came off the trail in North Elba they saw Lyman and his son in the distance. As they grew closer, they saw that Lyman looked distraught. When Myrna veered towards him to ask what the matter was, he waved her away, saying, "I'd best come by tonight to talk."

At the barn, they bid good-bye to the Russells, smiling and waving, and then turned and walked to the back door.

Marion was sitting at the kitchen table looking fretful, hands clasped—seeing Myrna's worried expression, "It's about John," she said.

- CHAPTER 38 -

History in the Making

> The new saint awaiting his martyrdom, and who, if he shall suffer, will make the gallows glorious like the cross.
>
> —R. Waldo Emerson

The news about John Brown's assault on the arsenal at Harper's Ferry on October 16, 1859 reached the North Country piecemeal from visitors and newspaper clippings. It was hard to glean the truth, beyond the fact that John, his sons, and some of his cohorts were being held in the Charlestown jail. Two of his sons and two more comrades were dead. The whole thing was a revelation and surprise to most of the Country.

Lyman and others at the settlement knew John had a long standing plan to raise an insurrection in the South. But the residents of North Elba didn't know, or claimed not to know, the specific target or dates of when or where it was to happen. Lyman claimed that John had been talking and planning for such an event for so many years that many abolitionists weren't paying attention when it did happen.

Those affected most deeply by John's capture at Harpers Ferry and the immediate deaths of Watson and Oliver Brown, and of William and Dauphin Thompson were, of course, the Brown and Thompson families. The residents of the Brown settlement and close friends in North Elba were inconsolable. And the reverberations of the act and its consequences were strongly felt all through the North Country, as well as the whole nation. The dark revelation of the facts at Harpers Ferry stunned like an unexpected sharp, cold hailstorm.

In the aftermath, the families of Lyman, Myrna, and Alvah huddled together most evenings to pour over clippings of the latest newspapers. To their dismay, one week after John's capture, even Northern newspapers disparaged and belittled his efforts.

One evening, as the small group gathered at the Duffney's home, Lyman and Ann admitted to feeling downhearted and dispirited.

Alvah shook open a paper. "I can hardly believe it! Horace Greeley calls John's action deplorable!"

"Yes, and even the *Liberator* is calling the Harpers Ferry raid misguided." Lyman shook his head.

"I see that the *New York Times* decided to publish letters from some of John's financial backers. That should let people know that he had support from credible sources," Myrna added.

"Yes, but I hear most of 'em are denying they knew anything about it. In fact, some have already scooted to Canada," Lyman grumbled.

Marion looked thoughtful and concerned. She went to the kitchen with Delia. They, for their part, were still absorbed in trying to help Mary Brown and the Thompson's. They'd brought some beans and venison to her yesterday and thought she looked thin and peaked; though as they'd talked, she'd rallied and said she was proud of John. Mary said she had been reconciled to losing him, and was praying that she'd continue to stay strong. She said she hoped to visit him in jail before his time…

"It's a hard thing to watch," Delia said. "Same with Ruth and the Thompsons."

When they returned to the living room, Ann Epps was angrily railing against Frederick Douglas. "I think it's despicable that he's seen fit to run off to Canada. He wasn't just an associate; he was a friend...a *friend*. That's like an arrow in John's heart!"

"These things are not that simple," Lyman said. "Frederick's a target, and he knows it. If he's caught...and say, interrogated and killed— will that help John?" Lyman asked.

"But what about deserting John? Shouldn't he have Mr. Douglas' support?" Delia was indignant.

Lyman spoke softly. "Well, it's hard to speak for another man. I believe John knows he has the support of Douglas. He understands the fear in others, and he's not thinking about that. What he cares about are his own words and actions. He's got our attention now and hopes to make good use of it."

Ann wasn't fully buying it, but Lyman's words subdued her. Actually, they all sank somewhat uncomfortably in the conflicting morass of information. Where was the truth?

However, within weeks their spirits lifted. It became clear that there was a great deal of support for John's actions— and, coming from distinguished quarters. The Boston Transcendentalists became increasingly vocal. In one of the newspapers, Thomas Higginson was quoted as saying about John's deniers, "Is there no such thing as honor among confederates?"

Emerson and Thoreau, the most famous speakers of the day, wrote and spoke of John as their hero. They got the attention not only of Boston, but well beyond. They put their intellectual celebrity squarely behind John's abolitionist fervor. Thoreau, who had personally (and heroically) transported Francis Merriam, one of John's accomplices, over the border to Canada, was quoted as saying, "The man this country is about to hang appears the greatest and best in it."

And then there was the comportment and words of John, himself. Even the judge and his jailers grudgingly admired him. He was a decent man—courteous, thoughtful—and firm in his convictions. Slavery was wrong. He was willing to give his heart and soul to right that wrong. Once the tide turned, thanks to the outspoken writers and orators, he was eulogized in the Northeast... even before he was hanged.

Meanwhile, in North Elba, the Woods and Duffney households, along with others, needed to consider some of their guests on the Underground Railroad. The Dalton family who currently resided with Delia had hoped to stay the winter. Abby Dalton and her young daughter, Joy, were congenial tenants for Delia. They worked well together. Under other circumstances, it could have become a permanent arrangement. However, it was decided that for their safety, Delia and Reverend Horace would escort Abby and Joy over the border to Canada. They left hurriedly, early one morning. The Daltons made it safely over the border. Delia and Reverend Horace made it a leisurely trip home.

A pall hung over the North Country in anticipation of the likely hanging. There were hopes in both North Elba and Boston that John might, *somehow*, escape.

Lyman, in his private conversations with Ann and his neighbors, said that would not be John's wish. They eventually came to believe him.

John Brown, in a letter to Mary, said she should spare the expense of traveling to see him. But Mary was adamant in her desire to visit her husband at the Charlestown jail, where he was being held before his imminent death at the gallows. Four of his compatriots were also held there awaiting execution.

The Harper's Ferry insurrection and aftermath was exceedingly difficult for Mary, even though for some time she knew that John would instigate a dramatic event to free slaves in the south—an action that would realistically lead to his capture and death. Still, there was no way to anticipate or calculate heartache and grief from an inevitable act. She took some comfort in the kindness shown to her by her North Country neighbors.

Others, beyond the borders of the Adirondacks, realized Mrs. Brown's plight. Distinguished Boston abolitionists, who had rallied to Brown's cause, wished to personally support Mary Brown on her final journey to be at her husband' side. Wendell Phillips and J. Miller Mckim, accompanied Mary on the long journey to the Charlestown jail, so that she might spend time with John in his last hours. Mary and John were together for over four hours, mostly discussing family matters, and John's last wishes. As Mary later said to Mr. Mckim, it was clear that there was a great deal of sympathy in the jailer's heart.

Wendell Phillips and J. Miller Mckim remained with her at a hotel nearby in town to escort her and the body of John Brown back to North Elba.

John Brown was led to the scaffold and hanged until dead on December 2nd, 1859. Mary opted to not attend the gruesome execution. Instead, she spent the morning sitting at a sunny window in the Wagner House Hotel. At 11:15, Wendell looked at his watch and said, "It is all over!" Mary sobbed greatly, but soon regained her composure. A somber cavalry escorted the body from the execution site to Harpers Ferry, where Mrs. Brown awaited it.

Later, on the return cortege with John's body to North Elba, Mary told Wendell, as they rode in a railroad coach towards New York, that hearing the cell door clank behind her as she left his cell, had all but undone her—and that their parting had wrenched anguished tears from them both when they bid each other good-bye. Wendell silently nodded. "He went firmly and bravely to the very end…and that has been said by friend and foe alike." He gave Mary a handkerchief.

Their trip back to North Elba went smoothly enough.

It was December 6th when they arrived in Elizabethtown. A crowd of friends and neighbors walked behind the wagon as it drove to the Elizabethtown court house, where John's body would lay in state, reverently guarded by several soldiers. The surrounding community came to a solemn ceremony at the court house to show respect for the man—most also for the deed.

The actual funeral and burial spot were according to John's wishes. His opened casket was set out front his house on raised boards for viewing before the December 8th funeral ceremony and burial. Mourners somberly filed by his body to pay their respects. In the afternoon, the Reverend Joshua Young from Burlington gave an impromptu sermon. There also were dignified speeches at the gravesite by J. Mckim and Wendell Phillips, praising the power of Brown's words. Lyman Epps sang John's favorite song, "Blow Ye Trumpets Blow". It was sung clearly and resonantly as Lyman faced the majestic Adirondack Mountains beyond the fields. Most wept openly at the beauty of it.

There were additional memorial services for John Brown in Boston, Concord, and even as far from the nucleus of action as in Providence and Cleveland. African American and white anti-slavery church congregations spoke with reverence about the greatness of Brown's words and deeds. Of course, Brown had his detractors, but the North Elba community were dismissive of those news reports, when they found their way to the North Country.

Mynah and Alvah cut items from papers and saved quotes—from Thoreau about Brown's, "transcendent moral greatness", and the many references to Emerson's speech about John Brown. "The new saint awaiting his martyrdom, and who, if he shall suffer, will make the gallows glorious like the cross." Emerson's words were strong, they were startling to hear or read in print.

Myrna passed a newspaper to Alvah.

"I kind of wish I'd had more conversation with Mr. Emerson at Follansbee Pond, you know? Or even when we met up in Boston."

"Yep, but we do have that book of his...and we did see to it that he had a good time. You even helped him learn to shoot."

"Well, yes…

Some days later, after the initial fanfare, distinguished visitors departed North Elba and ordinary life resumed—or so it seemed.

The Epps and Woods families sat around the Duffney's kitchen table discussing recent news events and the general state of affairs. Marion had brewed a strong pot of elderberry tea and served it along with apple cake to sweeten the prevailing anxious mood. And the friends reminisced.

John had indeed been buried, but shoots of a new strain of active abolitionist sentiments were breaking to the surface. The growing need in the north was to end slavery *now*. Southerners were becoming frightened and more entrenched.

The affable visage of Mr. Brown that North Elba was used to seeing at the farm had been permanently replaced by the bleeding palimpsest of determined bloody revolution.

John himself had passed a note before being led to the gallows. His scribbled note handed to his guard had said… "I'm now quite certain that the crimes of this guilty, land: will never be purged away; but with blood…"

As Marion poured the hot tea into their blue and brown mugs, the conversation heated. The topic was antislavery—war in America. Was it necessary? Would it happen? Who would fight it? …and so on.

"Well," said Lyman, "there's nothing like a home-grown martyr to make you feel guilty as hell for doin nothin'. In my case, I'd like to do somethin more, but I haven't decided what."

He rubbed his forehead distractedly and swigged his tea. "As for war, I hope it doesn't come to that—it seems too fierce an approach—could break everything to pieces. And I'm edging up to getting old. Course I'd defend up here." By that, meaning the Adirondacks.

"I'd sure as blazes fight a war! Those slavers need a good licking. Yes, I'd join up," Alvah was riled.

Myrna shook her head. "Yep, I'd go too."

Alvah seemed confused. "What? As a nurse?"

"Hell, no. I'm a sharpshooter. I'd best fight." She sipped some tea.

They all looked at her…curiously. No one said a word. The moment held. But Marion noted that the clock hands moved.

The End

POSTSCRIPT

There was, of course, a war—a wrenching, horrible ordeal of immense pain and destruction. Lives, loves, lands, were lost to families and institutions. The American world broke to pieces. It never mended and healed to anyone's satisfaction.

But some good came of it. Ralph Waldo Emerson and Wendell Phillips met with President Lincoln. They wanted to ensure his support that the stated mission of the war was to end slavery in America. The *idea* of freedom and anti-slavery triumphed. Today, the spirit of the Transcendentalists lives on. And that is a talisman worth holding on to.

As for Myrna, Alvah, and the rest? After the war, The Woods & Duffney Boarding House eventually took root in the Adirondacks; the Epps family prospered and lived in Lake Placid; Belle became a Boston socialite: And though some friends and neighbors were lost to war, others escaped across the Canadian border, or moved, at least temporarily, to Europe.

The aftermath of the trauma of Civil War gave birth to something new—but perhaps, that belongs to another story.

ACKNOWLEDGEMENTS:

The novel *Follansbee Pond Secrets* could not have been written without the kind encouragement of many voices. I am particularly grateful to: Tom Delaney, Richard Delaney, and Nora Delaney for their editorial input on my early drafts. And thanks to former Assemblyman, and Albany historian, Jack McEneny for his comments on the novel's historical context and his brilliant introductory piece, which captures the essence of the story; And to Times Union columnist, Fred LeBrun for his spot-on remarks on the final draft, which contributed immensely to the novel.

I thank my husband, Russell Dunn, for his unwavering support and editorial advice during the whole book-birthing process.

I thank Jessika Hazelton of Troy Book Makers for her assistance in formatting the text and creating a wonderfully engaging cover.